Bad Medicine

A Novel

R. Barry King

Email: TenEagles999@yahoo.com

Cover Design by Sherri Lynn King
SLiK Designs, Houston, TX sherri@slikdesigns.biz

Printed in the United States of America

ISBN: 0-6154-0263-1
ISBN-13: 9780615402635

Dedication

For Jillian, Chelsey and Chris

And the late

Tony Hillerman, my friend and mentor.

Pronunciation Guide

A-1—A Douglas Skyraider used for close-in support of ground
troops in the Viet Nam era.

Bosque—(bos'- kay) riverside cottonwood grove

Cacique—(kah-see'-kay) Elder and tribal chief

El Jefe—(el hef'-fay) Chief, leader, man-in-charge

El ninos—(el neen'-yoz) the children

H.E.—Stands for High Explosive

IR-fuse—Infra-Red detonator, works as a heat sensor

Jabe—rhymes with Babe

Jeneral—(hen-eh-ral') General, a military rank

Jemez—(hey'-mes) a mountain range and a tribal pueblo in
north-central NM

Jente—(hin'-teh) high office, a moniker

Lancair—A kit plane, pronounced Lance Air for its inventor

Paa Quna—(pah-kyu'nah) Pueblo for deer stew

1

The left engine backfired again and began to stumble as Jabe Rainwater rolled the old Beechcraft left and right in an effort to drain the last of the fuel from his nearly bone-dry wing tanks. Then he made sure his running lights were out for the tenth time in as many minutes and dropped the rickety old plane down just over the wave tops and below radar detection level. If he leaned the fuel mixtures another tad, he might as well get ready for a drink of salt water.

Easy, baby, just another few miles now.

He wondered if the old plane had a spirit that could hear his pleas.

Somewhere out in the gathering twilight the Texas shoreline was still over fifty miles to the north, but he was taking no chances——- the Coast Guard seemed to patrol farther out each night. Flying this low over the Gulf might be merely dangerous in another aircraft, but in this derelict it was sheer insanity. The engines on this tub had a knack for just quitting for no good reason at all—not to mention the bullets the old gal had absorbed from ground fire over the Yucatan.

Relax, he thought as he scanned the ancient instruments. *This old heap'll kill you long before any jungle guerilla or crew-cut sailor does. Way past time you found another job....*

"As if I had a choice," he said out loud.

The fuel gauges had been pegged on EMPTY for the last half hour and he was still miles from a safe touchdown. Here in the middle of nowhere, with the engines already beginning to stumble, he was about to just fall out of the sky. At this rate, he doubted he could even make the coast.

The right engine backfired twice.

Rock the wings again! You gotta stay out of the water, Pal.

When he'd taken off from the hidden airstrip deep in the Yucatan, he had hoped this would turn out to be a great day——- the day he would finally earn his freedom. He thought he'd even settle for just a *good* day. Yesterday had come way too close to being his last. Coming up from Columbia the night before, he'd blown a tire on landing and narrowly escaped a fiery encounter with a fuel truck full of gasoline. How ironic! He'd have survived thirty-nine trips just to die on his final run and never getting his life back.

Just after takeoff on his way to the coast and low over the jungle, he had felt the airplane shudder several times as she took rifle fire from the anti-drug guerrillas hiding below. The damage had been substantial, but if he'd turned around and headed back for a landing, they'd have been laying for him. No way could he break radio silence unless he was actually going down. So, he was committed to limp directly north toward the States and he'd been battling for control for the last 800 miles—across the entire Gulf of Mexico.

His was the last of four flights to head north today and he wondered how the other pilots had fared against the guerrillas. Ground fire had taken a heavy toll over the past few months and some of the dead pilots had been good friends.

Jabe looked down at the whitecaps.

Hard to relax when the dark blue water looks no more than an inch below and you're moving at 200 knots. Contact just one wave-top and….

Lights!

Heading his way. A helicopter maybe a thousand feet up—Coast Guard, no doubt. Would the chopper crew be able to see him this far beneath them in the murk? No way to tell from this distance, but as long as the chopper was showing navigation lights, Jabe was safe. The Coast Guard patrol choppers always went dark whenever they started a pursuit. He glanced west and cursed the dim ribbon of red on the horizon. Still enough light for those flyboys to spot his Twin Beech. Just barely, but enough. Maybe, if he could make the plane freeze in mid-air, they'd pass right over and never see him. But, any movement at all would attract their attention as surely as the deer had attracted his ancestors in the old days........

Focus, dammit!

He had to decide in seconds. Yep—- his current heading made him dead meat. He went to full throttle and pulled up and hard to the right. A plane that was old when he was a youngster groaned and bucked in protest making him believe his earlier assessment of the old heap was right -—she was a deathtrap.

Finally, his teeth fillings almost shaken out, Jabe leveled the cantankerous bird just before it became a boat. At this new heading he had a chance—- sort of.

He yelled, "Koweh hatah nahee, ahyaay, ahyaay......"

He grimaced. War chants weren't likely to help him now. After he'd been framed for pushing dope, the pueblo had thrown him out. Now he was pretty sure the Great Spirit's caller ID was certain to screen out any pleas from the likes of a Jabe Rainwater.

Did the lights change direction? Swing toward his new heading? Eyes played tricks in the twilight. When was the last time he breathed?

He exhaled when the lights passed a mile or so off to his left. It was a good thing the old plane's controls were so insensitive. His hands were trembling enough to send a modern airplane flying this low to a watery grave.

He glanced back over his left shoulder for a final check on the lights and felt his stomach tighten. The intruder started a turn toward him and began to descend. Then he watched as the chopper's lights winked out. Instinctively, his right hand shot to the throttles and pushed them wide open.

Man, are those sailor boys GOOD! Airborne radar never misses a thing. Maybe this load of hash was never meant to see the streets of Houston. Now it's a flat-out run for the roses.

Several deep breaths later, he turned back to his original course. With no gas for maneuvering, but being much faster, he'd just have to beat them to the airstrip and let Papa Bear handle explanations.

He checked his watch. Lia was going to beat him back to the grass strip again. The fact that her plane was much farther removed from the Wright Brothers era than his would make no difference to Papa Bear. The son-of-a-bitch was going to be all over his case. Big deal! He'd finished his forced servitude, so what could the man do? A tongue lashing from that bastard was the least of Jabe's worries; it was what the Bear could do to his family that..........

Low-Fuel light! This time it stayed lit when he tapped it. What little gas he had left would be gone in minutes.

He thought he'd made sure they'd given him enough to get him back home. Of course, every gallon of fuel meant fewer kilos of contraband——- cargo far more precious to the Bear and his bosses than Jabe's worthless hide.

Both engines backfired and stumbled!

Rock the wings, dammit! Climb for altitude, or you'll feed the fish tonight.

Jabe pulled back on the yoke, reached up and wiped the sweat from his brow and climbed the old gal for all she was worth.

No point in worrying about the radar now. You've already been burned!

He wished that just one time he'd be able to land in daylight and Papa Bear would be standing somewhere visible. He'd crash the old heap into the Bear's ass and be free at last from the man's slavery.

No. He wouldn't. The Bear was thorough and never make idle threats. He'd have made arrangements to have the old Cacique killed in case that happened. Jabe needed a decent plan and needed it fast. So far, everything he'd come up with had the Cacique dead as the most likely result. Had the Cacique been anybody else but his own Grandfather, he wouldn't have cared nearly so much. But, the thought of losing his last living relative was..... Well, the Cacique meant more to Jabe than life itself.

Ironic that he was effectively enslaved to a black man. Was it some kind of perverse revenge? Hell, Jabe's ancestors were peacefully hunting buffalo when the Bear's ancestors were being hauled over to America in stinking ships by white slavers. There could be no ancestral vengeance in play here. The Bear's need to control him had nothing to do with revenge and had everything to do with the power he could gain and little pieces of paper with pictures of US presidents on them—lots of paper.

The dark outline of the Texas coast loomed dead ahead.

If your gasoline holds out, you can put this last load down on that poorly lit field in the wilderness and be shed of the Bear for good. If it doesn't hold out....

He tried not to think about that. He'd have to call and report his situation. A forced landing would mean the Bear would need to be plenty fast to beat the arrival of the Coast Guard. Otherwise, he'd blow his cover and probably get a bullet for all his trouble.

Over the beach and several miles short of the clandestine airstrip both engines quit, came back to life and then began a constant stumble. Any remaining fuel was just in his imagination. He was going down.

One thing about a twin-engine airplane—when you lose an engine, you've still got the other one to get you to the scene of the crash. This time the thought brought no chuckles.

The Coast Guard helicopter that had spotted him coming in over the Gulf wouldn't be far behind. Even though he'd been running without lights, he was certain the chopper had been following by radar. They'd be on top of him in minutes and...

Concentrate! You've got a sudden stop looming just ahead.

The left-side engine coughed and went dead.

The big twin immediately began a turn toward the left. He kicked in plenty of right rudder to compensate, then reached for the prop control and feathered it. The right engine might run for another minute or so, but it too would quit in a moment. He had no alternative but to call Papa Bear and give him the bad news.

He reached for the radio microphone and pressed the button, "Papa Bear, this is Taco Two."

"Taco Two, we read you." Jabe recognized the youngster's voice that operated the radio.

Next he heard the growl of the Bear, "Where the hell have you been? You close in for a landing?"

"Yeah, I'm landing all right. I'm out of gas and going down."

"What's your position?"

"Hell if I know. The LORAN just went dead."

Where could he safely land a fully loaded and powerless airplane in mesquite country in the middle of the night? Would there be trees?

High wires? Cattle? Any one of those would prove fatal. He had only seconds to decide. Sweat trickled into his eyes and his mouth felt like it was lined with Velcro.

Headlights! A highway.

The lanes were separated by a wide median. Jabe knew there was grass there. He lowered the flaps and tapped the starter on the dead engine to put its prop horizontal. That would make his impact a little softer.

Better bleed off some speed. No way you'll survive an impact at 150 knots.

U.S. Highway 59 was sliding below and to his left. A turn into the dead engine was risky, but unavoidable. He kept the bank angle shallow and lined up right over the highway. Then his right engine sputtered and died. He'd have to put down in the median between the traffic lanes. He passed over a blinking caution light. Suddenly, he knew the place and reached for the mic again.

"I'm between the lanes on US 59, about even with the Brown Community near the Damon road intersection."

That was all he had time for. He didn't hear the answer, if there was one.

Jabe had come well over a thousand miles only to miss his destination by a mere mile and a half. The Bear would have to handle this one on his own. And if he hurried......

Jabe felt his butt muscles tighten as he lined up for a straight-ahead impact with the ground. He eased back on the yoke to slow down and hoped there were no abandoned cars or Highway Patrol cruisers parked in the median. He couldn't risk using the landing lights. What good would they do anyway? If that chopper crew was anywhere near, they were sure to spot landing lights and he'd need all the head start he could get, if he had any chance at all of escape.

Crank the right prop level! You want to cartwheel this baby right into head-on traffic?

His only chance, if he could survive the imminent crash landing and avoid capture, was to find a hideout and wait until morning. But first he had to get the plane safely on the ground, and from here on the pilot was just a passenger.

2

Shading his eyes from the glare of the early morning sun, tired and sore Jabe Rainwater slipped through a grove of scrub oak and crouched low to the ground. He lay in the prairie grass and watched the activities across the runway of the clandestine airstrip. A late-model Twin Cessna sat parked on the grass—Lia had already arrived.

The night before, he had set his Twin Beech down skillfully avoiding a crash and scampered away into the darkness as the Coast Guard was closing in. But, Papa Bear had cleverly beaten them to the crash site and had recovered the cargo. Now, the Twin Beech sat on the ramp showing grass stains on her belly, but no other visible damage. She must have been flown over early this morning while Jabe was walking in.

Tough old bird! Not likely a newer airplane would've come through as well.

Papa Bear was the Inspector in Charge. He stood in the shade just inside the huge open door of the old military hangar squinting toward the south through a pair of binoculars. His young assistant stood at his side. The Bear's face was shaded by the bill of a dark blue baseball cap with a gold-over-blue insignia.

He was a tall stout black man in his forties and wore a dark blue short-sleeved shirt with the word KODIAK emblazoned in gold across the back. He barked orders like a drill instructor.

Jabe made his way a bit closer and stopped just across from the big hangar door. He had walked and jogged the few miles up from Cottonwood Church where he had spent the night in the belfry fighting mosquitoes and watching the Bear and his men in the distance swoop in to unload the contraband from his crippled plane while keeping the Coast Guard boys and the local law at bay. Now, he dreaded the thought of having to face his old nemesis again. Papa Bear had proven to be far worse than the Fort Worth Federal warden and guards had ever been.

Jabe thought about walking in and taking his medicine. But, then he reconsidered.

Mustn't be too hasty. An Indian never exposes himself unnecessarily. Better move in close and get the lay of the land.

Jabe backtracked, then circled and slipped quietly into the hangar through a back window. He climbed into the roof girders and made his way around the roofline until he lay out of sight directly over the big hangar door. From there, he had a cats-bird view. He could hear the purr of an approaching airplane.

The Bear lowered his binocs, "Looks like Al's finally made it in. Let's unload him and get that airplane out of here as fast as we can. This place is getting too hot for us to hang around any longer. No telling when one of those Fort Bend County deputies will figure all this out. More than likely put some Rangers on us, and those guys can ruin your whole day."

"Can do, Sir," the assistant let out a sharp whistle and ten crew-cut toughs in the same dark blue uniforms rustled out of the office door and lined up on the ramp near the fuel truck.

Jabe heard another door open and a small figure emerged from the hangar office. This time it was someone he was glad to see.

The Bear said, "Lia, my dear. Soon as we've got Al unloaded, we can all go for one of those medium-rare beefsteaks you're so fond of. How does that suit Your Highness?"

Lia McTaggart shoved her chin in the air and cocked her head toward the Bear, "A thick T-bone suits me just fine. But, I can surely do with a lot less of that patronizing 'my dear' stuff. How about that, Your Lowness?"

The Bear chuckled. He always seemed to enjoy getting under Lia's skin.

Out on the runway, Al's black twin bumped down on the bone-dry Texas turf raising a billowing puff of dust, then lumbered toward the hangar ramp. Taxiing up swiftly, Pilot Al Summers braked sharply and swung the nose around to face the runway. That put him in position for a quick departure if something went afoul.

The props had barely swung to a stop when Al popped open the cargo door near the airplane's tail and kicked out the first bundle. The ground crew swarmed over the airplane like worker bees. No less than two hundred of the 10-pound packages followed in rapid succession. Wrapped in brown plastic and about the size of shoeboxes, the contraband was quickly tossed into the open side doors of a waiting van and stacked neatly on the floor. The van had all the markings of a government vehicle and bore the familiar blue-on-white license plate.

Jabe watched all this with a keen eye. Under the Bear's supervision, these guys worked with the flash and intensity of a well-oiled machine as they quickly transferred each bundle.

Al dismounted the aircraft and headed into the hangar, "Hidee Ho, oh big ugly one. I'm way overdue for a pit stop."

The Bear ignored the slur.

Al waved to Lia, "Hey, beautiful."

The last bundle went into the van. Its driver slammed the door shut and hopped into the driver's seat. Part of the ground crew boarded a second van and the pair of trucks roared off toward the highway in a cloud of dust. Several of the men sidled back into the shade of the hangar.

Al returned from the restroom and faced a glare from the Bear.

"You're late again as usual, Doofus."

"Hell, it's a wonder I got up here at all. I took gunfire out over the jungle again. Look at those holes in my wings."

Lia walked over, examined the bullet holes and motioned toward the west, "Rainwater wasn't quite so lucky, Al. He bellied in last night out on Highway 59. He oughta be walking up any minute."

The Bear was still glaring at Al, "Well, Al my boy, I'm just real glad you could drop in and see us again. Always good to see you down safe and sound. Your attitude improved any since last week?"

Al shot an irritated look toward the Bear, "Not likely."

He moved past the powerful black man toward the shade of the hangar, and then called back over his shoulder, "Working for you assholes is the closest a person can get to being a full-fledged prostitute. And don't give me any of that trumped-up 'concerned' feeling for the safety and welfare of your pilots. You couldn't give a damn about any of us."

The Bear followed him into the shade. "Well, it's not that I'm *that* concerned about your personal welfare, Al. After all, there's a lot more flying talent right where I found you and Lia. She beat your time up here from the Yucatan by almost an hour, old son. At this rate, she'll have her duty completed in half the time it'll take you. What's all the foot-dragging about, anyway?"

"Well, Hell's bells. She's got a faster airplane. And she's using some of that high-octane Government Issue gasoline you guys only give your pretty boys—and girls. And what the hell did I get? Gomez and his men filled my airplane with *tractor* gas! You bastards are absolutely trying to kill me, aren't you?"

"Who, me?" said the Bear. "What would I want to do that for, Doofus? I'd only have to break in another one of you low-life convict ingrates." He chuckled.

"Al my boy, I just can't understand why you're always complaining. Rainwater didn't even make it all the way to the airstrip last night—came down in the median out on the Highway. It took all I could do to get his cargo unloaded and into a safe place without the help of the Coast Guard and the local sheriff. And I've been here all morning swatting mosquitoes and chasing off duster pilots who landed at the wrong strip, just so you and Lia here would have a safe place to land. Seems like you'd appreciate that. Sure am glad that tractor gas got you up here in one piece."

"Yeah, uh-huh. Only thing you're glad to see is all that stash! Anyway, Rainwater is undoubtedly elated that he made his last run and finished up his obligation in one piece. He'll have a new lease on life with that official pardon in his hand."

The Bear shifted his weight and averted his gaze, but he made no reply.

Al stopped beside Lia and winked at her. "Hello, Gorgeous. You have a smooth flight up?"

She smiled for the first time this morning, "Yeah, I had a nice enough flight and no rifle fire this time. Nothing but blue water and high cumulus to look at for eight hundred miles. It's always a comfort to see that Flower Garden Reef finally slide by under the wing about a hundred miles off the coast. But, I'll be thankful enough just to go back to my uneventful life. If and when this turkey ever lets us go, that is." She nodded toward the Bear, "How about it, Blackie?"

"Oh, you two will get what's coming to you, alright. Old Papa Bear can promise you that."

Lia's eyes widened, "I didn't like the sound of that AT ALL."

Al scowled at the Bear, "All I know is whenever I've delivered my last load for you Shylocks, all I want to see is Texas in my rearview mirror. You turkey dip-shits are really going to miss me then."

Bear rubbed his chin for a moment, "Funny you should mention that."

Al winked at Lia, "Funny I should mention what? Funny you never considered yourself a turkey dip-shit?"

The Bear's tone was serious now, "Funny you should mention our missing someone. We haven't seen or heard from Taco One. He started out ahead of you this morning with his largest load yet and radioed just after takeoff. Then he went silent and that was that. We haven't heard a peep out of him. Nothing. Had some cash and weapons on board, too."

"Afraid you might have lost another shipment, aren't you?" Al sounded pleased that something might have slowed the flow of drugs into the U.S.

Jabe worried that yet another fellow pilot had met with an untimely end.

Bear said, "If we've lost another load, it'll just mean extra trips for you pilots who are still in the saddle. If he didn't go down, he's probably taking life easy in Bermuda or Saint Kitts about now. But, that's okay. We'll find him and clip his wings—and maybe a few other body parts as well."

Al said, "Not the kind of thing old Skeeter would do, I'd say. He'd have too hard a time fencing the stash and hiding the airplane, or trying to sell it without a title and logbooks. With the limited range of these little twins you've got us flying, we've had to stay on a straight course out over the jungle. I'd say he was shot down like the others and hasn't had time to walk out yet. That's what I'd say."

"You'd say? Hell, you'd say anything at all to cover for that ratfink convict friend of yours. But, I'm not going to worry about it too much. He's expendable just like you are."

The Bear was temporarily interrupted as his assistant handed him a clipboard for his signature on the tally sheet.

"I just hate giving this kind of news to the Boss, that's all. Fact is, I won't have to be bothered with you jailbirds for more than about another month or so. With all these losses with the little twins, we're moving up to bigger payloads. Soon as the big birds have a landing strip that's safe and secure, we're going to make you two a deal you can't refuse. For a shortened sentence, Al, you might just get the chance at flying one of the big multi-engine transports."

"What would we want to do that for? I'd just like to get back to doing easy time at Fort Worth Federal and have you out of my hair for good."

Two relay pilots climbed aboard the parked twins, started the engines, taxied back down the sod strip and lined up for takeoff.

The Bear shrugged, "Well, any way it turns out will be okay with me. I'm taking a big promotion down south at the end of the month. I'm bound for bigger and better things. Anyhow, when we shift to the New Mexico operation, Texas will be a whole lot better off without you ex-cons fouling up the air around here."

"When you sons-a-bitches gonna cut me loose, anyhow?"

"When you've paid your debt to society, son. You signed on the 40 loads, Sonnyboy."

The twins roared overhead and began a turn toward the south.

"Pay my debt? Any debt I owe is just in your dreams. You bastards framed every one of us, just so you could get your flying done." Al just shook his head and clinched his fists. "Polite society would string you up to the nearest light pole, if it knew what you were up to."

"Well, it's not likely they'll ever know anything. I'm operating inside the system, son. And you and your convict friends are well outside of the establishment. Don't ever make the mistake of forgetting that."

Al let it go.

"Now get in the car and I'll treat you two to a steak dinner. Think you can behave that long? After all, flying for us isn't half as bad as lying around in that pen up north now is it?" The Bear motioned them toward a dark blue sedan parked just outside the hangar. When Al and Lia were safely out of earshot, he called for his assistant who came over on the double.

"I'm not waiting around any longer for that Indian to show up. Take your men and go find him. Chances are he'll be on the road somewhere between the Brown Community and Damon."

The kid said, "Just bring him back here, or what?"

"No, don't do that."

"What'll I do with him?"

"You know what to do with him. He just made his last run, right? So we'll give him that early retirement we promised him. Just do him. And make sure he has no ID on him. He'll go down as just another John Doe."

"Well, maybe Chief John Doe, huh?"

The Bear didn't laugh, "And make damn sure the remains can't be identified. Got it?"

"No head, no hands."

"That's my boy. Stick with me son, and you'll go far. But, don't ever cross me. You got that?"

Jabe felt a shiver go up his spine. Now he was on the run. *Good thing I didn't just walk in and report as usual.*

Bear waved to the kid who had taken his men and boarded a van. He watched as they cranked up and headed out toward the highway. Then he slammed the hangar door shut, locked it, climbed into the sedan and followed them out.

The car's front doors bore the peculiar gold-over-blue insignia. The bold print circling the crest read "United States Customs Service."

3

In the gray early morning light, a solitary man carefully picked his way through the underbrush in a steaming jungle cauldron deep in the heart of the Yucatan peninsula. Juan Goyona, a Mexican man of middling age, wiry and athletic, wore a close-trimmed moustache and the jungle fatigues and armament of a military guerrilla. He was a man on a mission.

He'd gotten an early start with his little band of jungle fighters and had deployed them widely along the trail. They had fired at two drug planes last evening and he was sure his men had brought down another quarry. He'd given each of them an individual hill to search.

Out of earshot of the others now, he made his way carefully along the overgrown trail. He hoped they would be unmolested in their business. This part of the coffee country was fairly deserted during the months after harvest and he expected to see no one else this far up the hillside trail. But, still he feared they might run into some competition in their search. They could do without a brush with the local Federales. He figured he had no more than an hour or so before running into them.

In the dim gray light he could just make out a tear in the fabric of the jungle ahead as he hacked his way through the damp tropical vegetation overhanging the pathway. The first rays of sunlight filtered through the forest canopy close overhead as he came upon a torn piece of shiny metal half-hidden under a mango tree. He picked it up and made a closer examination—clearly a fragment of aircraft aluminum. He was getting close.

Looking ahead several yards, he could make out the edge of a small island of open space that verified there had been a very recent catastrophe that had flattened the normally impenetrable mass of jungle vegetation. Then he saw what he'd come for.

He moved forward and pushed the fern fronds back away from his face to reveal the unmistakable form of a wing and engine nacelle with the extended landing gear pointed upward. His heart beat faster. The steady flow of sweat running down his face tasted salty-sweet on his parched tongue.

He thought it strange that the aircraft hadn't burned on impact. They usually did. Strange to be sure, but fortunate. Today, he and his men would have some booty when they returned to camp.

His eyes followed the wing toward the fuselage now hidden from the sunlight under a pile of ragged vegetation. It was a miracle that fire had not consumed the cargo—along with any cash and weapons he might find.

The cockpit of the black, twin-engine aircraft had been completely crushed on impact. No one sitting up forward in the cockpit could have survived a crash like this and he hesitated at the thought of what he might find. What remained of the fuselage had come to rest on its back, angling up a steep incline with its rear door cracked open.

He could see nothing inside but darkness as he moved still closer, perching himself just below the wreck and looking upward into the cabin. Then on closer inspection, he could just barely make out a stack of brown plastic packages the size of shoeboxes just inside the door.

Seeing no one around, he laid his automatic rifle aside and standing tiptoe, he reached for one of the packages. Barely able to grab one end, he tugged at the parcel without effect. He needed more room to work. So he scrambled a little higher, put his strength to the test and jerked open the door.

At the same instant, something fell toward him from out of the dark cabin. He tried to duck, but the object struck him square in the forehead. Out of pure reflex, he caught it with both hands. Knocked temporarily off-balance, he staggered backward.

He steadied himself and held the thing up for a closer examination. It was the cleanly severed head of a human....

When he came to, Juan found himself lying on his back. He sat up and blinked, trying to rid his mind of the sight of the dead pilot's eyes staring sightlessly out from beneath the brim of a blue flight cap still held in place by a set of pilot's headphones.

He looked down the trail and saw the grotesque thing lying where he'd apparently thrown it. Nauseating though it was, Juan thought he'd really like to have the baseball cap. It would make quite the trophy, so he retrieved the cap and kicked the remains away down the slope of the hill. The blue cap bore a peculiar gold-over-blue insignia he found very official looking.

He grinned briefly and then threw up the remainder of his breakfast.

He caught his breath and started back down the trail to look for his men. He'd gone no more than a couple hundred yards when he heard the sound of trucks in the distance. Over across the valley he could see them. Six military troop trucks in convoy heading straight towards him.

No doubt about it. Federales!

4

A well-dressed man in his late thirties strode down a hallway on the second floor of the Old Executive Office Building in Washington, D.C. He turned and passed through a huge archway that led into an outer office. Winking at the receptionist he walked on through the door into the next room. He waved a greeting to the smartly dressed executive secretary who said, "Good morning, Sir. He's expecting you."

Moving past her and entering the inner office, a darkly lit room of mammoth proportions, Special Assistant Wade Breggard closed the door behind himself. He walked over and stood directly in front of the big burly man who sat behind the desk.

He glanced around to make sure they were alone, "I'd say good morning, Sir. But, I don't think you'd agree."

The man behind the desk, known as El Jefe by his partners south of the border, raised his eyes from his pile of papers and pulled hard on a freshly lit cigar. He was the image of a brooding executive in his mid-fifties. He let his words slip out past the stogie clinched in his teeth, "What is it, Wade? Bad news?"

"Another one down in the Yucatan, Sir."

Jefe slowly removed the cigar from his lips and looked directly at his assistant.

"Dammit all to hell! That's all I need."

"I'm sorry, Sir. I just got the word a few minutes ago. Went down yesterday shortly after takeoff. We were expecting our usual shipment of four loads. The other three flights got up here more or less on schedule, but the first one didn't make it."

"Yeah, just like how many others didn't make it. What's that put our losses at so far? Seven?"

"No, Sir. Only six."

He swiveled in his chair and looked out at the Capitol Complex through the giant floor-to-ceiling window directly behind his desk. Sunlight filtered through what was left of the usual morning rain clouds.

"Well, it *would've* been seven. We came damn near to losing that one last night down in Texas—to the *Coast Guard*, no less. That's more than a loss a month since we started and it's got to stop!"

Breggard shifted his weight and muttered, "Yessir."

"This nonsense is costing me something like ten million a pop. They can get off the ground in Columbia with no problems at all. Then, when they get to the Yucatan, those Mexicans cut us to pieces. Hell, with these kinds of losses our pilots will stop flying altogether. With things getting this deadly, they'll just flat refuse to take off. That'll shut us down right now!" He turned back to face his assistant.

"Not to mention the cost of the aircraft losses and the cash." He drew a big puff, inhaled and blew out a great cloud of smoke, then bit down hard on the cigar. "Sit down, son. Any word on the salvage efforts down there?"

Wade took a seat, "No Sir, too early to tell anything just yet. Our contractor, General Mendoza, has sent in an armed Federale rescue detail. But, they'll have to move fast to beat those guerrillas. They can strip a plane bare in twenty minutes. Should hear something more definite later this morning."

Jefe stood up and placed a fist on his desk. He leaned forward and jerked the cigar out of his mouth.

"Wade, we've got to re-think our whole strategy here. Are you confident in our lackeys down there? What the hell has that Mendoza been doing for us since we contracted him? Isn't he able to provide the protection we need? Are they able to deliver on their end?"

"Well Sir, we don't have any further information from him yet. But, I'd bet he'll find this aircraft in the same condition as the others."

"Looted and burned!"

"Yes sir."

"Damn." He jerked his glasses off. "At this rate, I'll be out of business by about this time next week. This is getting way too expensive,

Wade. It gets harder every day just to keep all the balls in the air. Now our brainless First Executive is out on another of his idiot crusades and wants to legalize drugs. Hell that would destroy all our profits in one fell swoop. It takes all my time just to run around Congress behind him and try to undo the damage he causes. He entered office on the promise he'd fight the drug problem. I thought we could count on that stance. You can't trust a damn thing he says."

He turned and walked slowly toward the window, "I'm having to call in all my chits from the House AND the Senate, and at this rate I won't have much of a campaign arsenal when the election comes up. Looks like I'm going to need a whole new strategy for dealing with that buffoon in the White House."

He replaced his glasses and resumed puffing on his stogie. Then he moved slowly toward his desk shaking his head in the affirmative. He grinned.

"And I think I know just how to fix his squeaky tin wheels."

Wade nodded, "Well sir, I understand he's got close to a sure vote on his legalization bill, and if it passes…."

"Then we can kiss off this whole business."

"Is there anything I can do to help, sir?"

"Well, let's start by bringing in Mendoza. So far, he hasn't lived up to his agreement, and I'm damned tired of it. We pay him for safety, but I think he's playing me for a fool. Those people work both ends against the middle. Hell, you can't trust them. We'll see just who the fool really is. You bring him up here. I want to talk to him up close and personal."

Jefe sat down and took another long pull on his cigar. He leaned back in his huge leather chair and began to blow smoke-rings in rapid succession.

"Yes sir, I'll get him up here right away. But, he's trying to work in a country where we simply can't and don't own everyone who is connected. Those small twins are vulnerable out over the jungle. But, as soon as we can move up to the big transports, I don't think we'll have any more losses."

"Are you sure they can make the entire trip up here with only one re-fueling stop?"

"Oh, I believe the Bear is right about that, Sir. On the hop from Mexico, they can stay mostly over water where it's much safer. Only thing is, we may eventually have to cut the pilots in on the profit structure."

Jefe watched his column of smoke-rings float toward the ceiling, and then he shifted his gaze back to his assistant.

"That makes good sense, Wade. We'll proceed on that course. But, we have to get the New Mexico Project completed. Have the Bear come up here and report. Maybe a little push from me will do the trick. You think so?"

"Everything is ready to go, sir, except for the landing strip. Our man out west is having some trouble with the locals up there in the high country. They resist every little change that comes along, and the Bureau of Indian Affairs has been of very little help to us on this. Those Indians have lived in primitive conditions for centuries. I don't think there is any hope they'll ever come into the American system. Not even the BIA has been able to accomplish very much over the past century or so. The pueblos suspect everything we try to do for them. It's just unbelievable."

"Aw hell, Wade. All they need is some type of new government program. The public always loves a new program. Call it health or education and they'll go for it. That'll get the BIA Commissioner out there on board. Use my name, or whatever it takes. I need that new airstrip and I need it *NOW*!"

5

Steam rose from thick vegetation crowding a jungle trail as men dressed in battle fatigues and bearing machetes cut away at the bright green growth impeding the progress of their small company of guerrillas.

The point men blazed the trail through the undergrowth. Next in line were two forward armed guards carrying their weapons at the ready. Several dozen guards and bearers followed and the trim figure bringing up the rear of the column as "tail-end Charlie" was the brains of the whole outfit.

Juan Goyona was well known to the inhabitants of the entire Yucatan. He was proud of the men under his command and he kept a watchful eye on them from under the brim of his newfound headgear—a dark blue baseball cap with an impressive gold-over-blue insignia.

They'd had a close call with the Federales earlier that morning when one of Juan's confederates had accosted the commander of the troop trucks and led him off in another direction long enough for the guerrillas to unload and burn the downed aircraft. Now they were near exhaustion and ready for a rest.

The men leading the column didn't carry the familiar AK-47 submachinegun so common to the Latin American military. Those were the weapons carried by the men farther back on the trail. Instead, these two carried long-barreled Browning automatic shotguns. The 12-gauge Browning had proven to be far more effective here in the jungle at close range than an automatic rifle. Triple-ought buckshot delivered a deadly blow close in. Any target within 40 yards would simply evaporate. After all, in this thick tropical growth a man could see barely ten yards in any direction. So the weapon of choice was the shotgun.

The bearers wore heavy backpacks loaded with camp gear and food rations. And they each hefted the additional burden of a bagful of narcotics.

They came to a clearing that marked the edge of a tented guerrilla camp and the bearers lowered their packs and weapons to the ground. Then they threw their booty in a pile and stood at ease to drink from canteens. Some squatted on their heels to cool off in the shade.

Juan remained standing and eyed an approaching group of military-clad figures, the leader of which was a slight figure compared with the rest of the company and wore a brown fedora.

Juan grinned and asked, "Que pasa?"

The leader stopped in front of him and gave up a brief smile, "Nada." The voice was soft, but firm.

Juan reached up and removed the fedora that had concealed the face of a woman and a fine head of long jet-black hair. It tumbled over her shoulders and down her back well past her waist.

Juan grinned like a baboon, "Mi amor." He was glad to see his Juanita.

"Y usted?" she half whispered as she threw her arms around Juan's neck and gently kissed his cheek.

Juan was thrilled to see her again. Anyone could tell that he idolized her. Her unflawed use of the Castillian dialect was a direct indication that she possessed much more than the poor education common to the natives in this part of the world.

Juanita was a pleasant apparition compared to the grizzled company of jungle fighters who made up the remainder of the group. She was only a head shorter and was as slim and trim as Juan. Her sleeveless shirt revealed the biceps of a bantamweight boxer—she was as physically fit as any of the whole crew. Her complexion was a medium chestnut brown and her gray-green eyes flashed with a brilliance that betrayed her inherent inquisitiveness and intelligence.

Juan held her at arm's length and considered her beauty, "Wait 'til you see what we bring."

Other men arriving from the camp hefted the booty off to a stone circle in the center of the clearing, piled them high, then doused the whole lot with gasoline from red Jerry cans and set them ablaze.

Juan held his weapon high over his head and addressed his resting comrades, "Amigos!"

"Si, Capitan." They held high the weapons they had liberated from the downed airplane.

"Muy bueno, no?" he said to Juanita.

"Tu hayaste dinero?" she asked.

Juan unshouldered his loaded pack, unzipped it and held it open. The familiar green of stacked and banded currency bundles peeked through the open zipper.

Juanita smiled her approval, "Cuanto dinero, Juan?"

"Enough to last us a long while." He handed her a stack of the bills.

Juan held his weapon and ammo belt high again, "With these, we can carry on our fight against the drug traders with their own guns. Es muy bueno, no?"

Juanita wasn't impressed by the fire-power, "Y el ninos, Juan?"

Juan understood her perfectly, "Si, Juanita. El ninos. With the money, we can buy food and clothing for our children and build them a schoolhouse."

Juanita was staring at Juan's cap, "Donde agarraste eso?" she wanted to know.

Juan touched its brim, "It looks good on me, no?" He was sure she would approve.

"No!" was her immediate reply. "Tu te miras como Gringo ahora! Quitala!"

Juan complied and snatched it off his head with a chuckle. He didn't like the idea of looking like a Gringo to Juanita. He would don it again later, when he was out of her sight.

"Juanita, with this we can help the people of this village and the children. It is the only consolation I have with this dirty jungle fighting. One day we will put an end to the drugs and the killing, Juanita. One day."

Juan looked around at his loyal band of followers. "One day we will all return to our homes, our wives, our children and our lives. But not until the drug traffic, the death and the killing, and that man Gomez are all gone. Not until we can live in peace once more."

His small band stood up and one of the older of the fellows came forward and lifted the cry, "Viva Juan! Viva Juanita!" The men repeated the salutation and cheered.

"Ah Domingo, mi amigo," Juan grinned in recognition of his friend. He lifted an arm and placed it around the smiling Domingo's shoulder, "My lifelong amigo. What would I do without you and these compadres by my side?"

Out in the firepit the dwindling pile of drugs was going up in a cloud of smoke. It had been a profitable day. This pile of hash and cocaine would never hit the streets to poison and kill their own children nor those of the Norte Americanos in the U.S. Juan and company were making quite sure it would never reach its destination. But, after several hard years they were beginning to run out of encouragement.

"Ah, Domingo, the money and guns will be put to good use fighting these evil people, God willing."

Domingo sighed, "Si, vaya con Dios."

Juan hated the powers that were responsible for this reckless drug business that had spoiled the peace and safety of these gentle agrarian folk. He longed for the solitude and freedom he'd once had as a child in these tropical hills. He could only hope that someday the peaceful times would return. But, first the drug-runners had to go.

Practical man that he was, he knew that peace would be some time yet in coming. He also knew that he would need a great deal of help to re-establish that peace, if it was to come again. And where that help would come from, he had no idea at all.

6

Jabe sat on an empty vegetable crate and braced himself against the constant swaying of the trailer van as it rolled down Highway 6 toward Galveston. He had made his way through the cactus and mesquite brush to the truck stop on U.S. 59 and watched for a southbound van with a Galveston address painted on the tractor cab. He'd lucked out and found a semi pulling an empty trailer deadheading back with no return cargo.

Better lay low for a few days at Dudley's place and plan your next move. How would the Cacique advise you now? No matter. Not much I can do to regain the acceptance of the tribe, unless..."

He tried to imagine what lay ahead of him. Back on the reservation, he'd always been taught to rely on the advice of his elders. But, this time he'd have to trust his own wits. The Bear would launch a manhunt, and would pull out all the stops to capture him.

No way can they know about Dudley unless they nose around the pueblo, and that might take a few days.

An hour later the truck slowed in town traffic and finally bumped to a halt. Jabe slid out the back and dropped to the ground as the driver cut the switch.

He made his way out of the terminal and toward the street. He found himself on Harborside Drive, just a two-mile hike to Dudley's hotel. He'd have to be cautious going in there.

Some minutes later he climbed over the rear wall of the hotel parking garage and moved quietly through the ground level. He kept a keen eye out for strangers as he sought the bright red 1959 Austin-Healey 3000-6. He found it right where Dudley always parked—smack up front facing the lobby. Dudley liked to keep a keen eye on his Sweetheart from his perch at the front desk. Jabe was grateful to see Dudley was on duty.

He backtracked, circled around back of the hotel and took the fire escape up to the second floor. He found a window ajar in Dudley's room, climbed in and picked up the telephone. He dialed O and Dudley answered.

"Dudley, it's me, Rainwater."

"Man, I haven't heard from you in forever. You get telephone privileges, or what?"

"Anybody there with you?"

"The lobby's empty. Where are you, J.B.?" Dudley always called him J.B.

"I'm here in Galveston."

"You rascal! You get out early and don't even let your Pal know ahead of time? Hey, that's not an outside line. You in the hotel?"

"Don't move. I'll be right there."

"What?"

Jabe crept down the stairs to the lobby and slipped into one of the over-stuffed chairs facing the desk where Dudley sat.

He put a finger to his lip, "Just stay where you are, Pal. I'm sure the place is under surveillance, or soon will be."

Dudley sat straight up in his chair, "Who's looking for what?"

"Not what, *who*."

"What's the matter? You didn't get out early, did you? You break out? What's happening, Man?"

A stranger walked in off the street and plunked down a suitcase. He made for the desk and asked for a room.

Jabe looked at the floor and pulled his cap lower over his eyes. The man paid him no attention.

"That'll be fifteen bucks for a single. We've got fresh coffee around the clock and the Waffle House is just down the block." Dudley handed the man a sign-in card and took the cash. Then he offered to assist with the suitcase, but the man declined and went straight up the stairs.

Dudley came out from behind the counter and shook hands with Jabe, "Man, the last time I saw you was months ago before you were sent up."

"Yeah, the only chances I had to call you were few and far between. Sorry about that. You still got my things?"

"Of course, I do."

A taxicab screeched to a stop outside and three men got out. Jabe stiffened while he watched their movements. The men retrieved their suitcases from the trunk.

Relax! Not likely to be any of the Bears goons—yet. Moving way too slow for that.

Dudley said, "Go on up to my room and wait for me. My relief is due in about a half hour. Your sea bag is in the hall closet."

Jabe called back over his shoulder as he ascended the stairs, "Watch yourself, Pardner."

He locked the door behind him and made for the shower. Toweling off, he rifled the refrigerator in hopes of a meal of sorts. And that's sort of what he got—just a lone dill pickle and half a can of stale beer. He was ravenous, but it would have to do for now.

He picked up the TV remote and scanned through the channels with the sound on mute, then settled into the recliner. He paused on the World News Network. A WNN reporter was standing near a Twin Beech sitting low on the grass while emergency vehicles and a crew of firefighters could be seen moving in the background. Jabe turned up the sound.

".....and the gas tanks are all bone dry. As far as we can tell, the pilot was uninjured, although he or she is nowhere to be found at the present time. The local Sheriff's officers on the scene tell us they think the plane was heading inbound for a landing at a small airstrip near here. But they have not been able to locate the pilot. The nighttime Gulf Coast fog apparently hampered the landing attempt and the airplane simply ran out of gas short of the airfield. The pilot was forced to put the plane down here on the grass median between the traffic lanes of U.S. Highway 59.

"Fort Bend County deputies tell us that they found U.S. Customs officials on the scene when they arrived about ten o'clock last night. Any cargo that may have been on board had already been removed and transported. The only things left at the site were this empty twin-engine airplane that landed wheels-up, and the scar left in the wet grass between the highway lanes. It's simply mystifying.

"Customs officials are saying nothing about the incident, or giving any other reason for their prompt appearance at this crash site. But, as I reported earlier this year, I think they know a lot more than they admit.

"No flight plan was filed and the FAA in Houston and the NTSB office in Dallas say they will be launching a routine inquiry, but the results of that effort will not be made public for at least six months.

"For World News Network, this is Don Samuelson reporting live from the crash site near Damon, Texas."

Yeah, so what else is new?

He switched channels and scanned through half a dozen soap operas. Then he landed on another newsman reading the copy on his teleprompter.

".......our information and the available statistics show that all the efforts exerted by our own government and the international anti-drug agencies are simply unable to slow the tide of drugs entering the United States.

"Conservative estimates indicate that the total revenue drain on the American economy is 400 billion dollars a year and climbing. But in spite of all the negatives, our sources tell us that many politicians high up in the Administration want to legalize the use of hard narcotics in an attempt to empty more of our prisons and to generate revenue from drug taxes. At any rate, as every school child knows, that is just the kind of Forward Initiative favored by the New World Order and the World Parliament.

The newsman turned to a guest he was interviewing.

"Well Bob, we have no official confirmation yet, but some congressional aides are predicting the President will soon reveal a radical plan to fall in line with those NWO Initiatives. And he's not likely to ask for a general referendum, is he?"

"No, that's not the President's style, Tom. He's pretty much a one-man show. I understand he doesn't even consult with the Vice President on many of his decisions. And actually, I and many of my colleagues in the congress think the NWO Initiatives are a pretty good idea. The legalization program just makes good sense for America. Drugs are so pervasive in the prevailing American lifestyle that they've become a mainstay of the economy. That's why those in the Attorney General's office are in complete agreement with the Surgeon General that all narcotics should be legalized in America.

"Do you think that is a wise thing to do, Bob?"

"Oh, of course it is, Tom. Why, all the great nations of Europe have legalized them in recent years; Holland, France, even the UK and some of the other Com…., uh, socialist countries in our own hemisphere—Canada, as well as the South and Central Americans. They realize you can't fight the cartels that are now a powerful voting block in the Global Economy and the New World Order. So, we believe it is best for all Americans, in order to have any say at all in the World Parliament and in framing the new Global Constitution…"

Jabe turned the TV off. That old dirty feeling came back.

What the public doesn't know……. And I've been helping with the deliveries!

He tried to think of other things—his home on the pueblo, his Grandfather and his adobe home out in New Mexico. He listened deep within himself and tried to hear again the sound of his Grandfather's voice. But, the mournful call of a distant foghorn broke the spell.

He raised his eyes to the ceiling in time to watch a cockroach scurry into a far corner and hide there away from the light. Jabe eyed it carefully and slowly rose from the chair, flexing his fingers for action.

He crept toward the insect and followed its movements with keen reflexes. He had made quite a game of stalking these elusive creatures since he disliked the pest control services and their noxious chemicals. He knew Dudley refused the monthly dousing with insecticides. So, Jabe stalked and eliminated them one by one and he rarely ever missed.

The wary arthropod made a sudden dash for the floor at Jabe's approach. Just as it did, his hand shot out and forced the roach to take to its wings. Jabe's timing was perfect and he caught the little vagrant in mid-flight then quickly closed his fingers over his captive, but held a loose grip.

He could feel the tiny creature moving about and pushing in every direction for an exit from the temporary cell formed by his fist. He'd teach this interloper a lesson. He let the pitiful insect search in vain for an escape and after a minute or two it ceased to move about. Jabe smiled in satisfaction.

Trapped aren't you? Yeah, I know the feeling little guy.

He moved to the open window and unlatched the screen then reached out and flipped the critter into thin air and watched it fly away.

"Go pester somebody else for a change, and don't come back."

He latched the screen, pulled the shades closed and let his eyes adjust to the dim interior, lit now by the late afternoon sun filtering down through a solid overcast. He had never quite grown accustomed to apartment living and much preferred the soft, earthy feel and smell of his Grandfather's adobe kiva.

Leaning back in the recliner and closing his eyes, he tried to take his own advice and let his body slowly relax. The months of dawn-to-dusk flying and the unrelenting tension had tightened his muscles like piano strings. It gave new meaning to the words "high-strung." He hurt like hell.

The fatigue and the thoughts of all his dead pilot friends came in like a flood. They unleashed themselves without warning and sent his mind into a whirl. He tried to remember his Grandfather's face and drew nothing but a hazy blank. In times of trouble, Jabe could usually conjure up the Cacique's voice and sometimes even talked with him. But, now it wasn't working.

He let himself sink deeper toward the dim world of slumber. But, an Indian warrior never really sleeps. He can hear everything around himself. And if someone unsheathed an arrow or cocked a firearm, or as much as dropped even the proverbial pin, he'd be up and on his feet in an instant. He consciously halted his drift and listened for the Cacique's voice again.

Grandfather, is something wrong? It's me, Jabe, but I cannot hear you.

Longrifle's voice was usually at Jabe's beck and call. The old Cacique had been the Chief of his native pueblo ever since long before he was born. Jabe's parents had died in an auto crash when he was only a year old and the old chief had raised Jabe alone. Dudley's folks, who had been missionaries at the pueblo, had been riding in the same car and were also killed. The drunk who hit them head-on didn't even get a scratch. Jabe and Dudley had been inseparable in childhood and were roommates still.

So, the Cacique was the only family Jabe had left in this living world.

"……my Son, my Son…….." Jabe could hear the voice coming through faintly. "Jabe is not your name. My Grandson's name is Joe Bob. Listen to the…. medicine man…..medicine man….medicine man…."

What could old Ten Eagles do for me now? And when will Grandfather ever get over my nickname!

Then the voice was gone…..

Jabe settled back and considered his surroundings. Dudley's hotel digs reminded him of his old dorm room back at the Indian School.

Jabe had been christened Joe Bob Rainwater by his parents. The names on his birth certificate were Joe and Bob, sure enough, and his driver's license as well. Not Joseph and Robert, as anyone would expect. As the passing years found him living part of the time with an uncle in the city, he would attend an occasional public school. His teachers would invariably call the roll with "Joseph?" which would be followed by silence from young Joe Bob. Then "Robert?" followed by, "Joseph Robert?" When no one else spoke up to claim those names, he would simply say, "My name is Joe Bob." Then would come the slow and deliberate explanation from the teacher as to how his real Christian names were Joseph and Robert, not Joe and Bob, as his parents just didn't know any better. It was that way all through his public education. Funny, but the Native American teachers at the Pueblo Indian School had never seemed to have any problem with his name—only the European teachers at the American public school. It was as if their credo was that they would Anglicize this heathen child in the face of all obstacles. He began to prefer just J.B. Then, during one of his visits home, his childhood chum who was slightly tongue-tied came out with "Jabe," which was as close as he could get to J.B., and it stuck. Unconventional perhaps, but that's just what Jabe had liked about it. Anyway, it did rhyme with Babe, didn't it?

"Your name is Joe Bob, Joe Bob, Joe Bob."

"Hey, J.B." Dudley came through the door and spoiled it all. "My relief showed up and I don't have to be back here for three days. What say we get something to eat? You've got a lot to catch me up on. Are you awake? What's shaking, anyway? Huh?"

Jabe sat up and stretched. He was sore all over.

"Well, it's a lead-pipe cinch you got nothing to eat in that useless fridge of yours over there. Why don't you unplug it?"

At the diner a few blocks away, Dudley started for the door and Jabe waved him away, "I'd feel a lot better if we chose a spot a lot farther away from the hotel, Pardner."

"Okay, suits me. You think we can expect visitors sometime soon?"

"Sometime soon. I'm sure of it."

Over dinner Jabe caught Dudley up on the events of the past six months.

Dudley chuckled. "Well, I always knew you were an outlaw."

"Yeah, and now it's finally official. I can't stay around here very long and get you involved, Pard. I'll be finding another place to hole up."

Dudley sat back and looked at his friend, "Like hell, you will. I'm the only place you've got. You just stay out of sight for a few weeks and all this will blow over, J.B."

Jabe only shook his head. He was looking at the best friend any human ever had. But, he was never going to endanger Dudley.

"We'll see, Old Pard. We'll see."

Dudley had been the hotel night clerk ever since he and Jabe had moved to Galveston. Jabe had worked as a longshoreman at the Port of Galveston while Dudley's daytime activities were a varied mix of hotel clerk, college courses, kung fu, creative writing classes and strenuous physical workouts. He spent a considerable amount of time crafting a home-built two-seater airplane in an isolated hangar out at nearby Scholes Field. His Dad had bought the kit-plane and all the components, but died before he could fly her. The project was finished now and the little bird was airworthy. Dudley expected her FAA flight certificate to arrive by mail any day now.

Jabe reckoned Dudley was in perhaps as good a physical shape as he was himself. Before Jabe had been shipped up the creek, they had often raced each other down the beach. Sometimes Jabe would let Dudley win. But when it came to running an obstacle course, like hopping over the riprap boulders along the jetties, Dudley had a very fine edge over Jabe, having been trained in high school to run the high hurdles at blinding speed. Dudley had quite an impressive collection of sports medals, letters, jackets and trophies from his four years on the track team at Wharton High School. So Jabe tried to keep the competition out on the flats where he had the advantage. Just an old Indian trick to retain control over the situation—always make the competition follow you!

"Tell me, J.B. Do you ever miss the times you spent as a police officer out on the rez?"

Jabe didn't even hesitate, "Yep, sometimes I do."

"You know, there's a story circulated among the waterfront bandits and drug dealers that you'll scalp anybody who makes trouble or disturbs the peace around here?"

"Is that what they say?"

"So I hear tell."

Jabe laughed out loud. His tribe represented peaceable First Americans. He was a little surprised at the rumor. Still, before he went to prison, he'd been quite keen on keeping the peace in his little section of the world.

"Well, that rumor is just their guilty consciences giving them a witness. Let's not disturb conventional wisdom, Old Pard."

Jabe ordered another dessert and gazed out across Seawall Boulevard at the offshore rigs that lit the horizon out on the Gulf. He wondered how many loads of cocaine and heroin had come into the country during the day and flown just over the tops of those same rigs.

The two old friends passed the evening right up until they started serving breakfast. Finally, in the pre-dawn, Jabe needed to be outside moving around. Maybe that would burn the extra energy he was feeling and bring some much-needed shuteye.

Out on the street, the two old friends made their way toward the docks. The night people were slipping through the inky stretches of Post Office Street and the back alleys of the harbor on their way to nowhere. Those folks involved in legitimate business were either asleep at home now or were already at work on the docks. But, here was a seedier side to society lurking about in the shadows. Only a few late-night truck deliveries broke a pattern of sinister activity down on the streets.

Jabe knew this scene by heart. The local drunks and winos lay passed out on the sidewalks. The few still wobbling around were weaving up and down the street panhandling everyone visible. They knew Dudley and Jabe and gave them a wide berth.

Jabe surveyed the scene and mumbled, "This place is turning into a sewer. These dealers are barking their wares right out in the open. Look, there's a buy right over there. Is all this invisible to the cops?"

"No, the cops are doing their jobs, J.B. But, even when they bust these characters, liberal judges often wink at the dealers and look the other way. Galveston's finally made it up a few notches in the world. Now, it's just like Houston and Dallas."

"And any other of the white man's cities I've seen."

"This area used to be a friendly, peaceful place until things went to pot. Doesn't even look like I remember it, J.B. My uncle used to bring us down here to the beach in the summertime. Things sure were a lot different then."

Jabe stopped and bought a newspaper from a vending machine. "Used to be, the citizens who lived here in Galveston worked day jobs in the city and lived in the suburbs, paid their taxes, went to church, and were fast asleep this time of night. Now look at the place."

The front page stories were so revolting he walked back and paid the fare again just to return the paper to its holder.

A shit-faced drunk walking across the street toward them circled around and began an approach. But, he must have recognized them just in time. He turned and ducked off down the street on the double.

"J.B., those same fine folks you mention don't vote the same way they used to. Now they expect the government to provide all their wants and needs as well as protection from this sort of thing. After all, don't the politicians promise to improve society and provide safety?"

"Boy, that'll get a vote anytime."

"But, what's amazing is how things have gotten so bad in just these few short years. Are things this bad out on the reservations?"

Jabe thought on that. He recalled how, back in the 1960s, anyone was safe on the streets of just about any of the cities. It was a rare occasion to find a family who locked their back doors at night. Back then, some folks never even locked up their cars or took the keys out of the ignition when parking downtown. Imagine that! You could actually trust others to respect private property. But, since the late '70s, folks were no longer able to safely walk the streets or enjoy a night out, so they just stayed home.

"If the pueblos ever get this bad, I'll quit being an Indian."

"Yeah, right! With that look, you'd just blend right in, wouldn't you?"

In a dark side street, Jabe could see the shadows of the strolling dealers. He knew them on sight—the Tambourine Man working the north side and Guitar George under the streetlight over on the south. They moved on when they saw the big Indian and his muscular hippie friend approaching.

Rounding a corner, Jabe and Dudley disturbed a drug buy in progress. The customer bolted at their appearance. Annoyed at the disturbance and the loss of a sale, Waterfront Willie wheeled around and froze instantaneously at the sight of the Indian.

Before Willie could move, Jabe reached out and seized a dirty collar, "How's business, Willie?"

"Aw, Maaannn! You are *BAD* for my business! Why don't you honkies leave us alone, here?" Willie was being as loud as possible. That would benefit his dealer buddies who might not have seen Jabe's approach, and his signal had cleared the street.

Dudley kept a watch for trouble as Jabe's hands went swiftly through Willie's pockets and he let the contraband fall into the grate that was the drop inlet to the storm sewer. Willie had lost lots of smack this way, but Jabe never took his money.

"I'm telling you for the last time, Willie. Stay off my street, you and your low-life dealer friends. If I catch you down here again..." He shoved Willie towards the lighted end of the street and followed him out. Willie would have to carry on somewhere else tonight.

Jabe felt himself relax some and thought he'd be able to sleep now. "Hey, Pal. What say we get some of that coffee and chicory you're so famous for?"

A pale full moon was setting as they turned the corner and headed back toward the hotel. The dim blue dawn outlined the ship's masts in the harbor as they turned the last corner.

Jabe and Dudley approached the front door cautiously. When they were sure things were quiet, they entered. The night man waved Dudley over and handed him a letter.

"Oh, right. Thanks, Sam." He tossed it to Jabe. "Looks like a letter from your folks out in the pueblo country. It's the only real mail you've gotten lately. Weeks on end go by around here without so much as a high-interest-rate credit card offer."

The envelope was addressed in the graceful hand of his Grandfather Longrifle. He opened the letter and unfolded a small note. The tone of his Grandfather's single line gave him cause for concern.

"Come home my son, so that I may see you once more again."

7

Colonel Lucifanio Gomez turned to the driver of his Army Jeep and shouted, "Vamanos! Andele pronto!"

Then he ducked to avoid the bouncing barrel of the .30 caliber Browning machinegun mounted on a tripod just behind the front seats, grabbed the handrail on the dashboard and held on for dear life.

The corporal at the wheel steered from side to side avoiding the deepest of the potholes in the dusty road and finally arrived at the edge of a town. They flew down the dusty main street and into the plaza, made a grand swing around the stone fountain standing in the center of the square and came to a screeching halt at the front of a moldering old adobe building.

Above the open double-doors hung a sign that read "FEDERA-LES." Gomez stepped out on the gravel and hesitated just a moment. The General was not a man he liked facing on a good day, and the news he had to deliver now was less than good—much less. He braced himself for the storm just ahead.

Two white-helmeted guards standing outside the door briskly drew to attention and saluted the trim immaculately uniformed officer as he gave a return salute, then bounded through the doorway, down the hall and up the stairs. Rounding a corner and striding into an outer office, the Colonel returned the salute of the duty orderly and entered the inner office. He came to a stop before an immense oak desk and popped a stiff salute to the older and much heavier officer seated behind it. The man in the high-backed leather chair wore a star on his uniform shirt-collar and epaulets.

He looked up at the Colonel, "So......, Gomez. You have not been in to see me for so long." The general gazed upon his harried friend for a long moment and waited while the Colonel caught his breath.

Then, he slowly returned the salute. "What is it that you have come so far to see me about? Come, speak up Mi Amigo."

"Mi Jeneral, por favor. I am sorry to be the bearer of bad news on such a beautiful day. I am afraid that one of the Gringo aeroplanes may have fallen into the jungle and we are looking for it even as I speak with you. I fear it may have met with an unfortunate accident and the cargo may be lost." Gomez stared straight ahead and readied himself for the tirade he knew was coming.

The General stood up slowly and fixed the colonel's eyes with his own.

"What do you mean? Have we lost yet another shipment? Have we no control at all over these mad jungle guerrillas?"

The colonel stiffened his stance and stammered, "Si, Jeneral......, I mean......, no Jeneral......, I mean I hope I am wrong and the Gringo has only lost the use of his radio again. We have not heard him confirm reaching the Gulf waters on his way to the Norte."

The general was silent, and turning slowly he looked at the floor as he paced toward the open window. Silhouetted against the brightly lit sky outside, his huge frame appeared ominous. "Gomez, the guerrillas are bad enough, but those Gringos will be the death of me. They demand much more than we originally agreed to deliver. There are many more of their aeroplanes coming up from the south and needing gasolina. I have trouble enough getting them the fuel they demand."

"Si, Jeneral."

"They take, and take, and take from us. And every time they lose another shipment they refuse to pay us for our labor. They are just about to break us down and steal us blind. These are the swine of the earth, these Gringos."

The General gazed down into the yard below and tapped the windowsill, "Gomez, you will find this lost shipment. And when you recover the goods, take all that is left back to the airfield. Comprende?"

"Si, si, Jeneral. Con permiso, Jeneral. I would like to take personal charge of the search, por favor, and find this shipment. With any luck at all, I believe we can....."

The desk phone rang, and the general quickly answered, "Hola, Jeneral Mendoza aqui. El Jefe? Si, si. I will wait."

Then a long silence as he listened quietly while staring at Gomez. And finally, "Jefe, it is so nice to......Si, Excellency."

Gomez could hear the voice on the receiver clear across the huge desk. Jefe was shouting at the Jeneral.

"Si, si...Oh...si, si. Muchas gracias. It will be done, Excellency. Adios."

The general hung up the phone and it rang immediately again. He answered, "Si......, Gracias." Replacing the receiver, he slowly walked back to the window and looked out upon the lawn and gardens two stories below.

After a long sigh, the General said slowly, "Well, well, Colonel Gomez." The General's voice rose and quivered in a shrill crescendo. "It seems that we have indeed lost.... another.... shipment."

"It was reported to me that the product was captured by those rebels and...., and....," then he shouted in a rage, "ALL BURNED UP!"

Then wheeling around, his face reddened and his eyes wide, the general growled through clinched teeth, "I want you to find the culprits responsible for this and bring them to ME."

Then his voice rose even louder, "No, wait. If you find it is that rebel Juan Goyona, kill him on sight. I want him and his entire band of thieves annihilated. Wipe them out. Kill them all. Comprende usted?"

Louder still, "I want them shot and quartered and hung out in the sun for the crows to eat. KILL THEM ALL!"

Now the General was screaming, "Gomez, what are you waiting for? Go and get him now! Don't come back until you have killed him. Madre de Dios! Go and find him now. Vamos!"

Gomez snapped a salute, "Si Jeneral, you can depend on me." Then he whirled and ran out of the room, shot down the stairs and out into the street.

Climbing aboard the waiting jeep, he shouted to the heavens and nobody in particular, "Goyona is a dead man! And all who are with him! Driver, to the campo."

The corporal whirled the jeep around the fountain and flew back down the streets. They disappeared into the jungle and the village quiet returned with the settling dust.

Gomez mumbled to himself mentally planning his actions as the jeep took him swiftly toward his armed camp. He could see in his mind's eye the ultimate destruction he would unleash on the rebel guerillas in their jungle hideout. He would claim the respect he richly deserved from General Mendoza. His only problem was that he had no clue how to go about it.

His driver said, "Colonel. The Jeneral, he is very lucky to have you as his soldier in the field, no? The men in the campo say that you are the Jeneral's Bulldog."

Gomez smiled, but made no reply. He was delighted to have the opportunity to annihilate the jungle rebels. He had elevated himself to quite a height in the operation that had been built by General Mendoza and the mysterious El Jefe, the Norte Americano. Now he commanded an entire battalion of trained Federale troops. He roamed and terrorized the entire countryside at will in support of the General's illicit narcotics trade. But now, he was in sore need of some luck.

"That is the truth, amigo. I have been entrusted with the safety of the drug shipments, but so far, even though we have an informant keeping tabs on the guerrillas, I have not been able to keep them from shooting down six of them. It is as if the Bulldog has no teeth. Carrumba!"

He knew he would have to round up Goyona and his men very soon, if he were to escape the wrath of the General. He would arm his men to the teeth and go after Goyona in his own back yard. He had a column of heavy trucks and enough men and firepower to wipe out hundreds of these rebels, if he could only discover their hideout.

"When we find them, we will make an example of these renegades and strike fear into the hearts of any other jungle fighters. If any of them should escape the slaughter, we will burn their villages and destroy their will to go on fighting."

In the eyes of the rebels, he would become invincible and make his position the image of a veritable fortress. But first, he would have to find and attack their hideout and kill that rebel Goyona. The General would settle for nothing less.

8

Late in the afternoon, A Southwest Airlines 737 landed at the Albuquerque SunPort and taxied to the terminal.

Jabe deplaned, collected his sea bag and made for the rental car counter. He had paid his airfare in cash but he knew that Customs would be checking the flight manifests. No way could he be traveling incognito. The desk attendant would not take cash for the rental car, so he presented the required credit card and hoped for the best.

He found his car on the lot, dropped his bag in the trunk and came face to face with a young Indian fellow about his same age. Jabe recognized him.

"Hello Charlie. What are you doing at the airport?"

"Hi, J.B. I expected you'd come back for a visit some day. The Cacique thinks he is sick. Did he send for you?"

"I got a note in the mail. Have you seen him?"

"He goes to the council office every day and then he goes home and sits in his kiva. My Grandfather Hahtahway goes to see him, but all they do is fight. It is the same as when you and I were growing up, only worse."

"Yeah, they sure do a lot of arguing alright, for a couple of lifelong chums. Longrifle always talked a lot about Hahtahway. How is your Granddad?"

"Oh, he's as good as ever. Hahtahway always has a lot of advice for Longrifle that he does not want to hear—about how he should run the pueblo and all that. But, the Cacique goes ahead and does as he pleases. He will try out his own ideas and then, in the end, comes around to doing it the way Hahtahway told him in the first place. They were born on the same day, you know."

"Yeah, so I've heard. And I think they will die on the same day as well. I think they've bonded too closely to go on living without each other. And it isn't so easy to get a man like Hahtahway off the tribal council, even if my Granddad wanted to. Hahtahway was elected by the people, and I think they all know how valuable he really is to the welfare of the pueblo."

Charlie nodded. "Hahtahway tells Longrifle to take an aspirin for his headaches, but the Cacique will not listen. He thinks he is dying. Will you see him soon?"

"I'm going up there right away. Where are you headed?"

"Back to Tucson. Been ranching over there trying to carve out a living in the wool market. I've got a couple of Navajos for partners and I'm learning to ride like one."

"You've got to keep your eyes on a Navajo, Charlie."

"Not this time, J.B. They're my partners. It's the white competition that better keep their eyes open. We've already got 40 percent of the market over there, and those high-technology ranch operators don't even know what hit 'em. They can't compete with low cost and hard work. We make a mean combination. Navajo tenacity and Pueblo ingenuity." Charlie let out with a chuckle as he turned to leave.

"Okay, Charlie. Sounds like you've found pay dirt, alright. Take care of yourself and good luck with those foreigners you've got for partners."

Jabe boarded his rental convertible, let the top down and drove out the gate toward the setting sun.

An hour later, driving along the riverside bosque toward his home, Jabe Rainwater was lost in thought. The half-filled afternoon flight up from Houston had been as smooth as silk and he had been able to relax on the plane.

Now as he drove along at a leisurely pace with the air in his face, the soft summer breeze smelled of jasmine and of tamarisk and the syrupy fragrance of rabbit broom. The slight hint of pinon smoke from a bread oven tickled his nose and lint from the riverside cottonwoods in bloom was thick in the air. He had almost forgotten how blue the sky was here in the high desert. He had never grown accustomed to the continual gray-brown hue of the air pollution that accompanied "progress" back in the sea-level cities.

How utterly different were the waters of the Rio Grande here in the pueblo country and those of the Houston Ship Channel. The rainbow trout in this river, and the San Juan upstream, were still wonderfully edible, and ever had been.

Pushing his sunglasses up over his brow, he winced at the bright sky overhead. In fact, the deep blue reached all the way to the distant horizon and gave contrast to the purple hillsides that were steadily darkening with the gathering dusk.

He had seen that color of blue only one other place in his life, and he would never forget where. It was the color of the surf along the coral reefs offshore of the islands in the Caribbean. He had trained there as a Navy Seal and the sight of the water always reminded him of the sky-color he had seen every day as a youth in his mountain home. That cobalt blue brought a stirring in his chest that put a momentary catch in his breath and a definite wetness to his eyes. He was home again.

In an earlier part of his life, those feelings would have been second-nature, but life in the big-city culture had made him feel almost embarrassed to experience such an emotion. He was glad that no one was around to notice and he remembered a time long ago when it wouldn't have mattered to him.

All this sensory perception transported him back to a simpler time he knew only too well. He pulled off the gravel road, cut the ignition and coasted to a stop in the sand. The only sound was that of the water gurgling around the rocks at the river's edge.

His earliest memories were of this place. Here he had learned to swim and fish the river, hunt deer and antelope in the nearby hills rolling away to the West. It was here that he learned the joy of living in an unspoiled part of Creation.

And it was there, just below the roadway at the river's edge, that he had learned the skills of a young warrior. He had been instructed in all the ancient tribal ways by the War Chiefs and by the Cacique and by the elders who had so learned them before and were then passing this vital information on to the young men of the tribe. It had ever been and would ever be so.

As a youngster he had been so light on his feet that he had earned the tribal name Tsoomn Pa'a—"the dear who runs swift and sure." Then later as a young adult, he had served as a tribal War Captain and was destined for further promotional honors and duties when he felt the call of his country and went into the armed services. He had a choice of the branches and chose the Navy just because he thought they had the sharpest and most colorful uniforms. It was after his hitch in the Navy that he and Dudley had thrown in together.

He had learned to fly and had worked his way up to Captain for a regional airline operating throughout the Gulf Coast and the Caribbean. He had felt leery of some of the flights and characters he had transported. He should have known more about what was going on. Then from out of the blue, he had been arrested and convicted of drug trafficking and had been recruited to fly for U.S. Customs in return for a pardon.

Some pardon! I was going to end up fish food in Galveston Bay.

It was after dark when he pulled into the town plaza. Jabe's home was the tribal Pueblo of his birth. This village of 600 souls or so was nestled in the mountain foothills not far from the Rio Grande. The lights were still aglow in the tribal offices, so he headed there.

Finding the door half-open and hearing muffled voices, he slipped inside and stole quietly into the sacred hall of the tribal council. He arrived in a darkened end of the room unnoticed by several men who were crouched at a table in a lighted corner conversing in low tones so as not to be overheard.

One was an older man in a tan uniform and the younger three were an odd mix. The obvious leader, and Indian wearing a business suit that marked him as a legal type, sat opposite the older man. A young brave on the far side looked like a regular village tough wearing his hair braided and held down by a beaded headband. He had his chair tipped backward leaning against the wall. The nearer gent with his back toward

Jabe wore his black hair long, straight and free. His leathers suggested he'd been on a hunt and he wore a Bowie knife on his belt.

Jabe stopped and fell back against the wall in the dark to listen. The young lawyer fellow at the table raised his voice.

"I don't give a damn what that old man says! It's going to take new blood to lead this tribe into the next century, and I'm just the one who's going to do it."

The older gentleman leaned forward and placed both hands on the table, "Well we have rules here. Not just anyone who wants to be Chief is going to lead this pueblo anywhere! I'm going on record here as having to say I won't be involved in any move to oust that old man who has served this pueblo for forty years with no other thought than to make this a good place to live and raise our children. If you want to make trouble for him in this council, you'll do it without me. And if you want to make trouble for him outside of this council, you'll have to walk over me to do it."

Jabe recognized in that voice an older warrior whom he'd known since childhood. A warrior yes, for this man was Indian Joe, the village Chief of Police and a tougher job than his was nowhere to be found. Any tribal coup d'tat would need this man's support to have any chance of success.

The stout-bodied six-foot policeman, skin tanned almost black from a lifetime of working out in the open, stood up and leaned over the table to address the young lawyer sitting opposite him.

"This so-called council meeting is over. It was improper to call such a meeting in the absence of the Cacique, the War Chiefs, and the full council in the first place. Now I'm going back to work as if this meeting never took place and you three better forget this business. Cause if you don't, I'll run you out of town for making trouble. And if you think I'm kidding, you can hide in the bushes and watch."

The three youngsters around the table flushed crimson. Even with their Indian skin, Jabe could see them blush and sensed the trouble ahead.

Indian Joe continued, "You guys made a big mistake telling me all of this. I'm not having anything to do with it."

Wall Sitter looked up and snarled, "What the hell do you know, old man? We didn't tell you nothing. At least nothing you're gunna be talking about."

He straightened as if to stand, but not nearly fast enough. Indian Joe's foot shot out and kicked the chair leg. It went airborne leaving Wall Sitter crashing to the floor as the other two stood in defense. Hunter's hand went toward his knife just as Joe's fist struck his jaw sending him over backwards.

Legal Eagle stood up and just drifted in reverse. He backed into the wall with the big policeman right in his face. With nowhere to go, he let out a squeal, "Hey man, just cool down. We're not so far apart, you and me."

"Like Hell we're not," snarled the big cop as he grabbed the youngster's lapels. "You'd better give up this plan of yours, or it'll bury you. Too many people know the kind of society you have in mind for this place."

Stopping just short of punching the kid, Indian Joe reached out with his free hand and frisked the young lawyer. All he found was a cell-phone. The two on the floor were slowly regaining their feet.

"Now I suggest you fellows go on home and forget about all this. You savvy that?"

Seeing that his friend needed no help, Jabe slipped outside the way he had come and waited in the front seat of Indian Joe's Bronco. He slouched down so as not to be easily seen.

Indian Joe came outside and headed for his truck as the three troublemakers came out behind him.

"We'll talk with you again, Old Man," Jabe heard them retort as they climbed into a late model Mercedes and roared out onto the road and headed west.

Joe opened the truck door and climbed halfway inside. Then he reached for his sidearm and began backing out.

"Hold on, Joe. It's just me, J.B." Jabe hadn't meant to startle the officer, knowing what he'd just been through.

"Damn. You really know how to scare somebody! I'da blown you apart if you'd waited another second to ID yourself. What the hell are you doing in my truck, anyway?"

"I just saw what happened in there."

"You just stood there in the dark and didn't lift a finger to help me out?"

"Oh, you were doing alright the best I could tell. Anyway, I made sure you were all together before I came outside. You handled that little shivaree okay and I'd have only been in your way."

"Well, dang me for sure, you rascal." Joe climbed inside and took the wheel.

"Yeah, I know. I'm a rascal. But you didn't think I was such a no-account when we busted them rustlers back in the canyon over there one rainy night. No sir, you didn't. Did you now?"

"Hey, we did a number on those thugs, didn't we?" The moonlight coming through the cottonwoods framed Joe's face and Jabe could see the concern fall away.

"Yeah, did we ever! And that was the end of the cattle trouble for years, as I remember." Jabe was relieved to hear that old familiar jocularity return to Joe's voice and demeanor.

"I haven't seen your ugly face around the rez since you got out of the service. Where'd you go after that big shindig they put on for you here at the Pueblo?" Joe was obviously glad to see Jabe again.

"Oh, I haven't been around much since then. Been working for the government."

"I know about the time you were doing up there in Fort Worth, J.B. What the hell was that all about, anyhow?"

"Well, Joe. You've heard it from a hundred other cons, but I would never lie to you. I was framed on a drug charge. I just got a release. Thought I'd come by and check up on old Grandpa. I don't think anybody else on the rez will want to see me."

"Well, that's nothing a cleansing ceremony won't cure."

"I sure hope you're right about that. Have you seen him?"

"I sure have. He's doing just fine. He thinks he's getting old and he's got this feeling he won't be long for this world. It'll do him a heap of good to see you're back again. Are you, J.B.? Back again, I mean?"

"Well, I'm back for a while, as long as the rez'll have me anyway. I got a note from him in the mail saying he needed to see me again right away. I never got a letter like that from him before and it kind of worried me. So here I am."

"And it's good to see you again." Joe extended a hand and the two shook on it. "I'll come by and check up on you two in the morning."

BAM! The left front tire blew out. Joe and Jabe jumped back against their headrests. A small beam of red light crossed in front of their faces and they ducked.

POW! A shower of glass flew from the driver's side window.

"Damn!" was all Indian Joe could manage. Another round ripped through the Bronco and took a chunk out of the steering wheel.

Jabe jumped out the passenger side door and pulled the big cop along with him. The two of them landed on the ground as more bullets riddled the cab and blew out the windshield.

A Jeep roared out of the trees some distance away and headed toward the open canyon country to the West.

"Those sonsabithes are getting downright pesky," Indian Joe was holding his left arm and there was blood on his shirt.

Jabe made sure the firing was over and then helped Indian Joe back inside the office and reached for the first aid kit on the wall. The wound was superficial and Jabe had it cleaned and bandaged in a jiffy.

Several men came running in to see what the trouble was. One of Indian Joe's deputies was among them.

He took a look at Joe's arm and his eyes opened wide, "What the hell's going on here. You guys start a war or something?"

"Or something...." Indian Joe answered. "We couldn't see who was doing the shooting, but they were driving a Jeep."

The deputy said, "Oh that really narrows it down. Couldn't be more than a couple hundred Jeeps around here. Anyway, I saw it leaving and radioed for a cruiser to check the canyon roads until I can get down there and help out. Wanted to see if you were okay first."

"Well, they won't be back tonight. Not after all that excitement," Jabe allowed. "You going to be okay now, Joe?"

"Yeah, my deputies can take care of anything I need."

Jabe started toward the door and then hesitated, "Anything I can do to help where those three are concerned?"

"Well, I don't know yet. It depends on them. I think they're just trying to frighten us. I'll tell you about it in the morning. Get some rest and we'll go for a ride along the river tomorrow."

The big tribal cop didn't seem to be unduly concerned, so Jabe let it go. "See you tomorrow, then, and watch your backside."

Jabe walked outside, scanned the area for trouble and headed back toward his rental car. Soon now, he would see his Grandfather Longrifle and find out what was troubling the old man. He had an itch on the back of his neck that told him those two toughs and their lawyer-friend had ordered the shooting, but who were the people in the Jeep and just what was the Pueblo up against? He hoped Longrifle could provide some answers.

9

Jabe arrived at Longrifle's adobe home in the dark. An early evening chill was in the air. Autumn was arriving a little sooner than usual at this mile-high altitude and the night-time temperature in the high chaparral of Northern New Mexico would get even colder toward dawn. Jabe drew his collar tighter and headed for the house.

He knocked on the door and listened, but he heard nothing. It was too early for the Cacique to have turned in for the night. No light visible and not a sound.

Looking around the place, he could make out a column of smoke coming from the chimney of the ceremonial kiva that Longrifle had constructed out back of the house. It sat in a small apple orchard that had come near to the end of its useful life. The gnarled old trees didn't make many apples anymore, but they had great round trunks thick with bark and they'd put on plenty of summer foliage that kept the kiva cool in the daytime. With the late evening chill, Jabe was sure Longrifle would be sitting close by the fire.

A wool rug covered the entrance to the kiva.

Navajo, no less. Imagine that!

Jabe pushed the rug aside, looked in and whispered, "Grandfather?"

The dim light from the fire pit outlined the old man sitting near the center of the small round room he had dug into the ground. He sat cross-legged and was wrapped in his brightly colored robe. He looked straight ahead and rocked back and forth. He didn't seem to hear Jabe.

"Grandfather?" Jabe said a little louder.

Slowly and quietly, without turning his head the old man said, "You don't have to yell at an old man! I heard you drive up on the lawn. Do you think I cannot hear any more?" His gaze was fixed upon some point in space above the fire.

Jabe felt his face flush even redder than it normally was. He was a bit amused at his Grandfather, "Well, you never know. I haven't seen you for a while, and...."

"Come inside before you let all the heat out. An old man could freeze to death with you standing out there holding the door open. Did you come to see an old man die?"

"Door? This old thing is hardly a door. What in blazes are you doing with a Navajo rug around this place, anyway?"

"It was cheap enough. I traded for it and I got the better of that old Navajo."

Jabe let the rug close behind him and sat down across from his Grandfather Longrifle.

"Now what is all this talk of dying? Your letter sounded like there might be trouble and so I...."

"Too much talk," Longrifle said. "Talk is what the trouble is. Too much talk and not enough action."

Jabe knew when to keep quiet around his Granddad.

"I have been the Cacique of this pueblo ever since your mother was a young girl. I was Cacique when she was growing up. I was Cacique when you were born and I watched you grow up and become a man. I am still the Cacique of this place. The Great Spirit has told me that I will be the Cacique until I die." Longrifle was silent for a moment. "You got here just in time, my son. I think it might be time for a new Cacique."

"Grandfather, you are too young to die. You are still full of life."

"Today, I am full of life," Longrifle's gaze shifted to the fire and he ceased rocking. "But tomorrow I think I will die. I have called for the medicine man, Ten Eagles, to come and see me tomorrow. He will know if he can do anything for me, or if I should just go ahead and die."

"Ten Eagles, that old scamp? Is he still around here? I can't believe that old man is still alive. He must be over a hundred years old now!"

"He is a hundred and five. He will know the right medicine for me. He will be here at sunup and then I will have my medicine." Longrifle looked at Jabe, "I am glad to see you again, my son. Have you come to stay or will you be leaving again soon?"

"I'll stay as long as you need me, Grandfather. How can I help you and what would you have me do for you?"

"I think you will know what you can do for me soon enough. I am glad you are here with me once more again. You can wait with me until the medicine man arrives. Do you know how Ten Eagles got his name?" Longrifle began rocking again as he looked up toward the log roof.

"Yes, Grandfather, you've told me that story many times before. I think I remember it all."

"Well, he was just a little baby then," the Cacique ignored Jabe's complaint.

"One day his mother could not find him anywhere. He must have crawled out the door and off into the woods. The people searched the pueblo and the countryside for days, but they could not find him. Then there came a great thunderstorm that washed out the canyons and made the river swell out of its banks. The lightning was terrible and the people stayed inside for cover. The lightening and thunder rolled for an entire day and a night."

Longrifle was silent for a moment as he mentally pictured the scene.

"At the end of a week, they gave up hope of finding the little one alive after so long without food or water. The medicine man at that time was the father of my friend Hahtahway. His name was Pa'apeh, the 'deer that runs through the woods.' And one day he walked down by the river to do some of his medicine. He looked and saw a great cloud of vultures circling in the sky not far away upriver. His heart sank and he was afraid that the child was surely dead. Do you know what happened next?"

"Yes, Grandfather, I remember this part, too." Jabe resigned himself to hear the whole story yet again.

"Well, he went upriver to have a look. And when he got there, he saw that those vultures could not land on the ground. The baby was sitting on a rock at the edge of the river in the shade of a giant cottonwood. And perched in that tree were ten eagles that swooped down one at a time and caught fish from the river. Then they would bring the fish to the baby and feed him just like he was one of their own. The eagles flew up and challenged the vultures and scattered their number, so they could not attack the child."

"When Pah'apeh approached the child, he had to do some strong medicine to protect himself from those eagles. One of the eagles swooped in to grab Pah'apeh, but he ducked and reached up and snatched at the eagle. A wing feather from the eagle floated down through the air and settled beside the child who then picked it up and laughed. Then Pah'apeh saw the mark on the child's forearm. It was a black burn mark that was similar to the one on his own shoulder where he had been struck by lightening when he was a young man."

Jabe picked up the story, "So the people were glad to get the child back and his mother called his name Ten Eagles," he concluded.

"Yes, that is right. Ten Eagles was destined to become the greatest medicine man in any of the pueblos. He will be here soon enough."

Longrifle talked and reminisced until the early morning hours. Jabe mostly listened. He was glad to be back home again. He leaned back against the smooth adobe wall and positioned his woolen coat as his pillow. It was good to hear his Grandfather's voice again. It brought back many wonderful memories of his life in the pueblo society he had left behind when he decided to become "civilized" by joining the Navy. Now he realized how much he had missed the pueblo life and the fraternity of his Indian heritage.

Longrifle was still talking when the sun came up. Jabe awoke peacefully to the sound of his Grandfather's soft voice. The old man didn't seem to detect that Jabe had even been asleep. He was retelling an episode when Ten Eagles had run the Federal authorities off the pueblo for challenging his right to practice medicine.

".......and when they saw the medicine man put on his buffalo robe and headdress they said, 'Are you going to shake a rattle at us and chant some hoodoo in all your fancy getup?'

"Well, Ten Eagles just danced a circle around them. And when he had them in a tight bunch, he threw snake oil on them and had a good laugh as they all ran off toward the rio to jump in and try to wash it all off." For the first time, Longrifle broke a faint smile at the remembrance of the event and Jabe laughed aloud.

"Grandfather, did that really happen the way you tell it? That was a long time ago."

A strange low voice came through the doorway, "Oh yes, that is exactly the way it happened."

Ten Eagles pushed through the doorway and entered the kiva. He stood straight and tall despite his many years and Jabe knew he was in the presence of an important man in the pueblo.

"Except that it wasn't snake oil. Longrifle has that part wrong."

Longrifle looked up, "Well, I remember it was some kind of strong Indian medicine that got rid of those Federal men in a hurry."

"Indian medicine, my foot! It was skunk juice. And that was strong enough to do the trick. After that, they wouldn't come within a hundred feet of me."

They all had a good laugh again at the expense of the Federal men.

Longrifle let out a gasp and fell backward flat on his back. Jabe rose and moved toward his Grandfather, but Ten Eagles got there first.

"He is out cold again. He has a bad headache that does this to him. Now leave me alone with the Cacique and I will make medicine for him. It's good that you have come back to us again."

So Jabe left the Cacique in capable hands. He sensed somehow that this day would bring him closer to his roots than he had ever been before. But, he still did not know the reason he had been summoned home so suddenly. He wondered about that.

Perhaps the big Indian policeman might have the answer.

10

The sun had still not cleared the Eastern foothills as Jabe left the kiva in the dawn shadows and donned his jacket. The bright blue sky signaled he would need eye and head protection as the sun gained altitude on a perfectly typical, crystal clear day in northern New Mexico.

He started for his car to retrieve his hat and sunglasses. Then, feeling hunger pangs, he diverted toward the house for a bite to eat when he heard hoof beats and looked around toward the bosque.

Indian Joe was mounted on the biggest black stallion Jabe had ever seen and was holding a pair of reins leading a beautiful bay mare already saddled. As Joe rode up, he tossed Jabe a chunk of bread that was still warm from the outdoor oven where it had been baked only minutes before.

"Have a bite of the best bread this side of the Rio,"

Joe turned the big stallion and slung a canteen around the mare's saddle horn. "Filled it at the spring on the way over. You'll need a draw on this before too long. Mount up and we'll take a ride."

Jabe grinned, "Don't mind if I do."

Taking another bite and holding the chunk of bread in his teeth, Jabe mounted the mare from the right side, Indian style. He took the reins in both hands and urged the mare into a trot in order to catch up with Joe who was already at full gallop toward the river.

Jabe knew better than to run a cold horse. She handled superbly though, and soon enough he was in hot pursuit.

Riding this old river again, Jabe was lost in a world of sensory perception. The familiar scent of piñon and tamarisk in bloom took him far away in thought. He had ridden these hills and valleys many years ago as a child, and still they were the same. They represented the few things in this world that don't change—things of great value to him. He had been away from home far too long.

He remembered the serenity he had found here all those years ago with someone else—a pueblo girl who was very dear to him. They had watched the mountain, as it turned pink, then red and finally purple in the changing colors of a southwestern sunset. The mountains stood still in mute testimony to all the things that never change. An Indian knows that nature was designed for giving man happiness and Jabe had found an abundance of that gift in this river and canyon country. His ancestors had chosen their home well.

He turned and looked over his shoulder at the majestic snow-covered summit of Mount Taylor shining brightly in the morning sun some eighty miles away to the West -—a brilliant carpet of white against the dark blue sky.

She had been his constant companion then. Glancing toward the river, Jabe thought he caught a glimpse of her walking beside the water. But suddenly, his vision blurred and he reached up to wipe the haze from his eyes. He looked again and saw nothing but the moving shadows of the cottonwoods swaying in the breeze.

Joe whistled for him to hurry and catch up.

They wandered the bluffs above the bosque and rode atop a high mesa overlooking the river and the valley. Smoke from the cooking fires in the pueblo curled skyward and the sun felt warm against Jabe's back. Toward the northwest, the pine forested Jemez Mountains stood starkly green against the dark blue cloudless sky. They walked the horses to cool them down, then stopped and dismounted.

"I brought you some breakfast." Indian Joe sat down on the grass and opened a sack he had brought along. Together they relaxed and shared the meal. Jabe had almost forgotten the taste. It was Paa Quna— deer stew, and a dish only prepared to celebrate a special occasion. There was a bowl of fresh steamed squash and plenty of warm bread.

"My wife cooked this up when I told her you were back again. But, I told her you weren't worth the trouble." Joe grinned.

Jabe was hungry after his night with his Granddad. He sat back and savored the moment. Here he was in an unspoiled part of the world enjoying the fruit of the land and clear cold spring water fresh from the ground.

"I'd like to pay her a visit and tell her what a big liar you are. Maybe I can bring her a deer while I'm here."

"Don't bother. Freezer's full. I had a good hunt last spring."

What a concept. One hundred percent natural food! No man-made chemicals to be found in any of this chow.

Jabe leaned back and gazed straight up at the deep blue heavens. He knew this place only too well, and he wondered if anyone raised in a city could even conceive of such a place; clean food, clean water, and clean air.

Living in an environment such as this and consuming a wholesome diet accounted for the ripe old ages his elders had lived to attain. Old Ten Eagles was just a youngster compared to some of the other tribal elders. The Cacique just prior to Longrifle had lived to the age of a hundred nineteen, and the previous medicine man had served the Pueblo in that office for over nine decades and finally dropped dead while chopping firewood when he was a hundred and eleven.

Good genes and clean living.

The horses were grazing on the prairie grass and strayed only a short distance. Well-trained horses will stay close to their riders and look in their direction often, just to make sure the men don't leave them. Jabe noticed their occasional glance in his direction and marveled at their faithfulness.

Joe said, "Aren't they something?" He had been watching them too.

Jabe nodded in agreement.

"A horse is the mount of the gods. They're in a class all by themselves, J.B. You take a young horse and break it to a saddle and he's a faithful servant until he dies. They'll carry whatever you pack on them and go at any speed you want. If you want them to run, they'll run for you all day long. A horse will run at a rider's command until it drops dead."

Jabe agreed, "What more could you ask of them?"

Joe's expression took a serious turn, "I once saw a drunken Indian do that to his favorite mount. He ran that horse all day long, alright. He was having so much fun he never stopped to consider what he was doing. Well, that horse just ran his heart out. Finally collapsed and fell dead right out from under that Indian at full gallop."

"What'd the Indian do then?"

"That Indian cried something terrible. Cried for days and days. The way he carried on was a caution."

"That's a terrible thing to have to see, Joe."

"Aw, I was only about eleven then. But, I never forgot it. And I've never ever just stood by and watched anyone treat an animal that way since. I get so damned mad if I see anyone take advantage of an animal like that."

"I know what you mean, Joe. A horse or a dog has got a heart as big as all outdoors, don't they? You gotta love 'em. And an animal that's lost or abandoned is a pitiful sight."

"You know, I feel that same way. I used to take in stray dogs. People in the countryside got to bringing me every stray that wandered up. I assembled quite a collection over the years. I don't think I ever met a horse or a dog that I didn't like."

Jabe had watched the familiar face of his friend go quite serious and knew something was on his mind. The horses circled slowly and started back toward their riders while grazing contentedly.

Joe continued, "They're just like children..... Innocent. Some folks call them dirty and the like. But I think they are clean and pure at heart. They have faith you're going to treat them right, even when you don't. And they always forgive being mistreated. They don't even seem to keep a memory of it. That is a very rare trait in a man though."

"What's the trouble in the pueblo, Joe? Granddad hasn't said much, but something's afoot."

Indian Joe was silent for a moment. Then he looked at Jabe. "J.B., the life of the Pueblo we have known for so many years is in great trouble. There is an element in town that is poisoning our home. There is a new breed of Indian in the society that I do not recognize. Those three young bucks you overheard in the council office show no respect at all for the tribal authorities. They think they can live outside the traditional laws and deviate any way they want to—all at the expense of everyone else."

"Yeah, I noticed that." It was the same kind of disrespect Jabe was so accustomed to in the white man's society. This was the kind of behavior he had seen in the likes of Guitar George, the Tambourine Man and Waterfront Willie. And as far as he could tell, their particular kind of deviant behavior was getting to be more the norm of the society rather than the exception.

Jabe had not been raised to disrespect authority. He had been trained in the pueblo to respect his elders and to foster the time-honored traditions of his culture. He had experienced the same kind of training in his country's military. But, these young toughs had no concept of any responsibility for maintaining order and fostering the good in society. They made fun of tribal tradition and disrespected their elders. Where would that leave them in times of trouble?

Indian Joe continued, "They only want one thing, J.B.—power. The power over others to live above the law and to escape any responsibility at all. I've seen it in white society; self-assumed privilege. They have the attitude that they are somehow better than all the others and not subject to the same laws and conventions. That is an attitude that will lead them to destruction. And if it is not checked at the start, right here, it will take us along with them and wreck our entire society."

"What was that all about in the council chambers, anyway?"

The big Indian didn't seem to hear the question. "Our Pueblo culture has been in these hills and valleys for ten thousand years. Our traditional law and order is the only means we have ever had to preserve our way of life. It's not just a good idea—it means survival!"

He paused for a long moment. "You've heard the elders say it many times before.......'For when the enemy sees your depraved condition and the fact that your discipline is wanting, it gives him great courage—and then he will strike you a death blow......'

Jabe finished the thought, "...and you may never see it coming."

He had seldom heard Indian Joe wax philosophical like this, but he knew when to keep quiet and listen. Joe looked sadder than Jabe had ever seen him as he continued.

"The lives of our children are our most precious asset. You and I were taught here in the ancient ways as children and we had a good life. The children who are young today are not in as good hands as we were. All who live here are not watching out for the good of the children. There are some who bring drugs and narcotics to the pueblo and sell to our children. Drugs and killing is all on the TV sets in their homes."

Indian Joe looked into Jabe's eyes. "Our children are rebelling against the rule of their parents and their elders. We try to catch the drug dealers in the pueblo, but there are too many and we cannot post a policeman on every corner. The conversation you overheard in the council had to do with an attempt to force Longrifle to give up his office and appoint one of those young toughs as Cacique."

Jabe sat bolt upright, "The hell you say."

Joe nodded, "That's what they're going to try to accomplish. They want to have control over the business of all the pueblos. They want us to stay out of their way so they can make much money selling drugs to our children. And they wanted my help! I guess you understood my answer to them."

Jabe was incredulous at the news. Suddenly the peace and tranquility of the morning was shattered. "What in hell is going on these days? Have you asked the authorities for help?"

"Who, them? Yeah, sure I asked them. And what do you think they told me? They claimed it was pueblo business and it was out of their hands......just like always. They are going to support anything that seems to have any power to destroy us."

"Assimilation, right?" Jabe had heard those words all his life. Not often mentioned in polite society, it had been the goal of some national authorities for two centuries. The goal was to assimilate the Indian into mainstream American society by any means—any means whatsoever.

The Indians understood it only too well. The system of Indian Schools had been devised to keep children away from their parents while the government educated them. The absence from the tribe and their traditional ways was seen as a benefit in bringing the Indian into "modern-day society."

"Some things never change." Indian Joe got to his feet and started for the horses. "I'm meeting some of their number in about an hour from now. Want to come along?"

Jabe was quick to follow Joe toward their waiting mounts. "I wouldn't miss this for the world."

Just as they mounted up, they heard the sound of distant gunfire coming from the direction of the pueblo—two shots in quick succession, then another two shots. It was the familiar crack of a Winchester 30-30.

11

Indian Joe galloped into the pueblo at a full run just ahead of Jabe. Gunsmoke was wafting from behind the corrals near the village compound.

Ten Eagles glanced up at Joe and went back to firing his Winchester, "You heard the sound of my rifle. Perhaps some other Indians will hear it as well."

Indian Joe walked his horse around to cool him down.

Jabe rode up and dismounted, "You just practicing, or getting ready for something?"

"Oh, I just want to be ready when the trouble starts."

Ten Eagles directed a steady fire at a row of pinecones he had set up along a fence rail behind the council offices. As he pulled the trigger, one pinecone after another sailed into the air. As each one slowed near the top of its arc, Ten Eagles shattered them with a quick second shot. A small crowd of laughing women and children had gathered and seemed to be highly entertained by the spectacle.

"Expecting some excitement, are you?" Jabe knew the old man's walk might have slowed some, but he still had a keen eye and his marksmanship was unmatched in the pueblos.

"It doesn't hurt to let them hear you practicing. Hand me that box of ammo, son." Ten Eagles indicated a box of shells sitting on a fence post just where Indian Joe was tying up the stallion.

Joe pitched the box of ammo to Ten Eagles who caught it with one hand and stuffed it inside his shirt. If it ever came to a fight, you wanted to be sure you had that old medicine man on your side. Ten Eagles finished off his last pinecone, blew the smoke from the breach and calmly began to reload.

"I'm finished practicing and the people are all armed. My rifle is ready and so am I."

Jabe looked around. "What people? All the men are out on round-up, and there are only the women now."

"Just the same, they will be here soon to talk with you. And I don't trust them for a white man's minute."

"Who's they?" Indian Joe said.

"Those Indians who sell our children bad medicine. The ones who want to take over this pueblo."

"How did you know I was meeting with them today?"

"How do I know anything? I have a little medicine of my own. What will you tell them when they demand control over this pueblo?"

"I don't think they're stupid enough to want to fight us out in the open. Anyway, I've already stirred the pot a mite. I met with them last night in the council room and we had a little altercation."

"Is that how you hurt your arm?" Ten Eagles patted his own arm in reference to the bandage on Joe's.

"No, somebody else did that for me. Don't know who yet, but I'm gunna find out."

Jabe said, "Well, I think they will fight anyone who gets in their way, Joe. The only thing they understand is what Ten Eagles is holding in his hands. What the hell is so important about this place that they have to take it by force, anyway?"

Ten Eagles continued, "It's that lawyer-politician kid and his big-city bosses who are stirring up the others. They want power over us and the money from selling their bad medicine. They want the Cacique out of the way so they can carry on their business. I've heard about how it is in the white man's cities. That is what they want to do here as well."

Indian Joe said, "I think there is more at stake here than just the pueblo drug trade, maybe much more."

Just then a black Mercedes sedan drove into the parking lot out front. Three Indians emerged from the back seat and started for the building.

"It's those same three toughs I met last night."

Ten Eagles shouldered his Winchester, "That is what I figured. But, I think the people are ready."

Some of the windows and doors of the houses were swinging open to allow the inhabitants a better view.

The three stopped in their tracks when Indian Joe came from behind the building, "You boys come back for some more council talk?"

The lawyer answered, "Don't get in our way, old man. You were just lucky last time, that's all. We've come to see the Cacique, so go away and leave us to our business."

Jabe had circled the building and come up from behind,

"If you came here to see Longrifle, you'll be talking to me. He's not available just now."

Legal Eagle turned to face Jabe. His buddies half-turned so as to keep one eye on the big cop and the medicine man. At Jabe's appearance, three big fellows wearing black suits got out of the Mercedes and stood at the ready. At the same time, several women came out of their houses and stood under the cottonwoods with their hands out of sight at their sides.

The lawyer held up a hand to halt the three goons. Then he said to Jabe, "Who in the hell are you?"

"Oh, I just came over to help an old medicine man and that cop over there. They have to deal with a lot of riff-raff who come around here looking for trouble, and sometimes they get plumb tired out dealing with the trash that blows in. What is your business with the Cacique?"

The Hunter raised his voice and addressed the pueblo in general, "That old Indian Longrifle is too weak and feeble to lead this reservation anymore. The people need him to step down and make room for a young warrior to lead this pueblo in these modern times."

Then turning to face Jabe again, "Anyway, that's something we'll talk over with him."

The three started toward the door to the office and Jabe blocked their path. "Not today you won't. You boys can talk with the three of us. And if you don't like that, you can take your trouble somewhere else."

Ten Eagles levered a round into his Winchester to help make the point.

Seven of the pueblo women had taken up positions behind cottonwood trees in their yards. They had a commanding view of the whole

R. Barry King

scene and taking Ten Eagle's lead, they produced seven more Winchesters and levered in rounds of their own. All this had a definite calming effect on the three toughs.

Legal Eagle went perfectly still. He stood there looking down the barrel of a .30-30 held by an old medicine man with a reputation as a sure shot. Even if the women's fire was ineffective, Ten Eagles would make damn sure this Indian would never see the light of another day. Even an old man couldn't possibly miss from this close.

"Okay. Now you just cool it, old man. We'll come back another time."

The three toughs drifted backwards toward the Mercedes. "I'm not going to fight with an old man and a bunch of women. Did you hurt yourself, big man?" the Lawyer prodded Indian Joe.

Joe started toward him, "You won't face us out here in the open, but you'll sure as hell ambush us under the cover of darkness!"

The three toughs were slowly backing towards their car.

The Hunter yelled, "Watch out that old medicine man doesn't hurt himself with that Winchester."

Ten Eagles retorted, "Oh, I can hit where I aim, young man."

They reached their Mercedes and dove into the back seat just as one of the goons, who had been retrieving something out of the trunk, stood upright and shouldered a rocket launcher. Before anyone could do anything to stop him, he let go a round at the council office and Indian Joe and Jabe hit the deck for cover. Only Ten Eagles was left standing.

WHAM! The entire building went up in a cloud of fire and smoke. Flaming debris rained on the women taking cover under the cottonwoods. The torpedo with the rocket launcher jumped for the open car door as the big Mercedes lurched backward. The crack of Winchesters rang out and mingled with the echoes of the explosion now returning from the distant hills.

Jabe watched as Ten Eagles took careful aim. Before the Mercedes could turn around, he put a group of three shots into the driver's side of the windshield. The big sedan was in full reverse and taking rounds from eight .30-30s. The bark of the rifles was punctuated by shots from In-

72

dian Joe's .357 service revolver booming in quick succession. Black paint and glass shards flew off the Mercedes in every direction. The driver whipped it around, cleared the parking lot and accelerated down the blacktop. Ten Eagle's aim was dead accurate, but the bullets were not penetrating into the car's interior.

Joe and Jabe got to their feet and moved away from what was left of the council office now burning out of control. The dust was settling as the Mercedes started up a rise in the road a half mile away.

Ten Eagles raised the barrel of his rifle allowing for the distance and nudged the barrel over a half-inch for windage. Then he let go a final round. A moment later, they saw a red taillight lens leave the Mercedes and sail through the air like a Frisbee.

Indian Joe said, "Damn! That car's a half mile out going away and you still hit it."

"Well, that wasn't so good," Ten Eagles seemed dissatisfied. "I was aiming for the trunk lock and I missed it by more than a foot."

Jabe was staring at the inferno left where the office had been, "Nobody was in there were they?"

Ten Eagles shook his head, "I should have unlocked it an hour ago, but I was practicing my marksmanship."

"Well, they sure as hell want Longrifle out of the picture," said Indian Joe. "So let's just say he was in there and they got him. We'll have to keep him out of the way for a while."

Jabe saw the strategy of it, "Well, if I know my Granddad, he won't like it any. He's not one to hide from trouble. Let's just make sure we keep him out of sight until this thing is over."

Joe said, "Maybe Hahtahway could hide out the Cacique for a while. That way he'll have a chance to give Longrifle a crash course in pueblo leadership." He winked at Jabe.

"Well, I don't see we have much of a choice. Old Hahtahway will sure have a captive audience and I'll never hear the end of it."

12

Papa Bear had his nose pressed to the cabin window as the government Gulfstream III executive jet broke out of the low overcast and landed on runway 33 at Reagan National Airport. They had been stuck in a holding pattern over eastern Virginia and he was still slightly dizzy from the constant circling. A warm front was pushing through the Washington area and the fog had been late in lifting. A steady drizzling rain began to fall.

The pilot taxied toward the private terminal at the far end of the field, well away from any inquisitive public citizens or news cameras. The cabin door swung down and the Bear and his companion hurried to a waiting limousine. It departed through a remote gate and headed toward the Capital complex.

Minutes later, it halted at a curbside. The two men made a hasty dash for the cover of the Old Executive Office Building. They entered the high-security lobby, quickly cleared the checkpoint and took the elevator up. Outside an office on the second floor, a Marine guard snapped a smart salute, and then opened the door for them.

Papa Bear and General Mendoza shed their hats and raincoats into the waiting arms of a receptionist and entered the inner office.

The Bear said, "Good morning, sir. I apologize for the delay. Couldn't get a landing clearance."

The General's salutation was barely audible, "El Jefe."

The boss was sitting behind a perfectly clean oak desk. He was smoking a cigar and casually looking up at the column of smoke as it rose toward the ceiling. His face was dark and indistinguishable, being backlit by the brightening sunlight coming in through the huge window directly behind him. He leaned forward slowly and looked squarely at the Bear.

"Gentlemen, I'm glad you could come up here." He seemed relaxed enough.

"I don't like being surprised. So, I was in contact with the airport approach controllers and followed your progress all the way to touch-down. Nasty weather out there. Please take a seat."

The two men sat down on the leather sofa.

"Now, what have you got for me, gentlemen?"

The Bear said, "I'm afraid the reports you received yesterday have now been confirmed. Another shipment is down, sir." Then he waited for a response.

Hearing none, "We lost the cargo and I believe we can expect..."

"*We*, hell! *We* didn't lose anything, Mister. You did. Now I'll tell you what *I* expect, by God. I expect you gentlemen to do what I'm paying you to do. I'm losing too damn many shipments and I'm tired of the losses."

The Bear looked at the floor and clinched his fists, but the General didn't move a muscle.

"How much did it cost me this time?"

The Bear leaned back slowly. "Well sir, according to your orders and expectations, it was a rather large shipment—14,000 pounds of product. And a sizable quantity of cash en route to our bank in the States."

"Dammit! If this keeps up I'll be ruined in short order. I need that cash flow so I can keep you gentlemen in the gravy and continue fighting the majority party. I've got little enough as it is and they've got purse strings that reach half way around the world."

"We'll be in far better shape when we can get the big birds flying, sir." The Bear knew that if he and Mendoza failed at working out the boss's master plan to build a sizeable war chest for the upcoming election, the boss might as well retire to his cabin in the country and give up his ambition of the White House.

"What's your plan for making up the losses?"

"The bigger payloads will do it in short order, sir. But, those inmate pilots are getting harder to find and train. Then we have to convince them we can shorten their sentences. And the risk of one of them talking is beginning to worry me."

"You've already had to send some of them back to the pen for refusing to work. You handled that, didn't you? Have you got a replacement pilot and aircraft ready to go yet?"

"We're working on it, sir."

"Well, just make damn sure you stay on schedule. Or, I believe I might have to make some other arrangements." The boss leaned forward and took the cigar out of his mouth.

"General Mendoza, it was your part of the bargain to warranty safe passage for our shipments, was it not?"

The general uncrossed his legs and began patting his knee, "Si, si, Jefe. It was another unfortunate episode with that guerrilla jungle fighter and his band of thieves. It will not happen again, Jefe, I assure you of that."

"Don't call me that."

The Bear said, "I'm sure he didn't mean anything by it, sir. In his culture, there are many terms for The Boss, and......"

"I know that! I just don't like the term. General, what are you doing about this jungle guerilla of yours? The pesky bastard seems to be operating at will."

Mendoza raised his head high and said, "At this very moment my men are taking him out, Excellency. We have informants in the jungle and we know where his camp is located. I believe we will not be troubled by him again."

"Seems I've heard that promise before. Just see that it happens this time. I'm damn tired of his interference."

The boss picked up a newspaper and tapped the front page, "And that, Mr. Papa Bear, was a damn close call down in Texas the day before yesterday. You barely got in there ahead of the local cavalry or I'd have lost two loads in the same day. That belly-up landing came damn close to wrecking this whole project."

"Won't the Drug Czar be all over this, sir?"

"That clown? He can't hurt us a bit. I control his budget and he can't even spit without my permission. That's the way I set it up, so we won't be having any trouble out of that office." He stopped to rub his eyes. "Oh, he'll promise to look into the matter, appoint a special commission and all that. I'll see he makes all the right motions."

The Bear said, "Can you fix that news network so this goes away, sir?"

"Oh, I don't think we'll have to worry too much about that news story. Nobody will do one damn thing about that report."

"Are you sure about that, sir?"

"I'm sure. The public in this country went to sleep years ago. At least we got the load in safe. And your pilot is apparently okay as well. So what happened down there in the jungle this time, Mister Papa Bear?"

"I think you know exactly, sir. That government-issue equipment you give me is second-hand junk. Like I said from the beginning, we'd need self-sealing fuel tanks. And we got no armor at all. What more can you expect of us? What I need is that remote strip you promised us, and….."

"Okay, Okay. Point made." He swiveled his chair back to the desk and picked up the phone. "Mr. Breggard, come in here for a minute, will you?"

When Wade came through the door, the boss said, "I want you to go over to that WNN network office as soon as they open the doors this morning. Have the editor over there muzzle that sonofabitch Samuelson before he begins to really hurt us. Tell the general manager I gave the order. And I don't want to see any more news clips of that story. Make damn sure he understands what I'll do if he doesn't comply."

"Yessir." Wade went out and closed the door.

"We'll continue as if nothing has happened, gentlemen. I'll keep those Texas law dogs off your backs and you two will deliver everything I order. I'm paying you both well enough for that, eh?"

The Bear nodded, "Yessir, you are."

"And General, I expect you to take care of that guerrilla problem of yours down there in the jungle. The foreign aid your country gets is ample payment for the protection I need for this operation. And I think you can expect to do very well in your bid for the President's mansion down there. Comprende usted?"

The general was grinning now and appeared much more relaxed at the sound of money, "Si, Excellency, you are very kind. My people have benefited from your gracious and generous policy toward my country and the funding you have provided."

Jefe grunted.

"Much of which has found its way into your own personal bank account, I'm sure. General, spare me. I understand you'll be running your own campaign for office soon enough. Then you will have plenty of opportunity to repay all my favors."

"Now, Mister Papa Bear. There are some things I want you to do to help step up that landing strip project over in New Mexico. We'll need it pronto now that we've lost the use of our base down in Texas. I've included here the items I want attended to." He handed the Bear a fat brown envelope marked, "TOP SECRET."

"Right away, sir. I'm flying out there on our return south."

"Don't open that envelope until you're airborne and then burn it. And make sure the General isn't seen by anyone while you're out there. I don't want any more surprise news reports out of that renegade WNN bunch. They just haven't learned how to play the game yet."

Jefe leaned back, and shoved the stogie back in his mouth. "Good luck, gentlemen," and the meeting was at an end.

The Bear and the general rose and started for the door. Jefe looked squarely at Mendoza, "And general, how soon did you say you would be taking care of that little problem down there in your back yard?"

The General glanced at his wristwatch in mid-stride and grinned, "This very minute, Excellency. Just this very minute. Adios." And the two of them walked out the door.

A Mexican Federale Army Jeep raised an enormous dust cloud as it sped along a dirt road that led deep into the jungle. Colonel Gomez kept muttering over and over again, "Today is the day that you will die, Juan Goyona. Today is the day."

His driver responded, "Do you think that we will have the good fortune to find him today, Colonel?"

"Oh, I believe that we can get a little help in finding him. Pull up to that trail-head."

At a wave of the Colonel's hand, the driver slowed the Jeep and coasted to a stop near the entrance to a jungle trail. A horse and rider emerged. Diego Garcia was a handsome figure of a jungle fighter clad in the familiar fatigues as he sat his sturdy black Mustang pony, Cimarron. Gomez could make out several more armed men who waited in the shadows along either side of the road.

The Colonel stepped out of the Jeep and greeted the horseman who dismounted, squatted with the Colonel beside the Jeep and began drawing figures in the dirt.

"They are camped here by the rio, Colonel. Their tents are not well hidden, but the compound is heavily guarded. The rio is not wide along here and you have an easy approach from the norte."

"How many are they, amigo?"

"Maybe a dozen or so? Sometimes we see a few more than this. Sometimes not so many. But they are very busy, all day, all night. They are coming and going all the time. This Goyona and his men, they never seem to sleep, señor!"

"Never sleep, Diego? Surely they are not super-human! You only have to stay awake yourself and you will see them sleep. Maybe this is a lesson that I will teach you and your men before this is over."

"Perdona mi?"

"I will go in when they least expect it, Diego."

"I am not sure you can trap them so easily. We have killed a few of them, but they always get more help."

"Killed a few of them? You? I hear a lot from you about all the guerrillas you have killed, but I never see the bodies or the graves. Diego, are you sure you did not dream this while you slept?"

"Nooooo, señor! We catch them one or two at a time when they wander away into the jungle. We cannot leave the bodies to be found. You never see them because we have to bury them quickly in this heat, so they do not begin to stink and we are discovered. Better they just disappear into the jungle, no?"

"Si, Diego. They just disappear. Like magic, eh?" Diego's face went sullen, "Perhaps you can find them all by yourself without my help, no?"

"I believe I pay you very well for your help, amigo. But, sometimes I expect to profit from my investment. You are getting very expensive and it seems to me that your information is only useful on occasion. I'm not so sure it has ever done me much good."

The Colonel got to his feet and boarded his Jeep. His driver started the vehicle.

"But, why am I complaining, amigo? You and your men have done more than I could expect. This time I will find that Goyona and destroy him for good." The Colonel waved his hand and immediately the column began to move out.

"Adios amigos," the Colonel said and tossed a bag of coins to Diego.

Behind the lead Jeep were two more with .30 caliber machine-gun mounts and then a column of three canvas-covered trucks carrying infantry.

Diego smiled, "Ahhh! It is just as I thought mi paisano. Hasta luego y muchas gracias." Diego handed the loot to his companions, mounted up and disappeared into the jungle.

13

Darkness was falling when Jabe entered his Grandfather's kiva. He found Ten Eagles making medicine with a bird feather, muttering and adding a grunt now and then for emphasis as he waved the sacred device over the old Cacique.

Longrifle asked, "What was all that racket out there? I was asleep and the earth shook me awake."

Jabe wondered how much the medicine man had told him.

"The people thought they'd build you a new office so they started on it today. They were just clearing off the old foundation."

"What's wrong with the one we had?"

Ten Eagles said, "You're getting a new one, so just hush up and be still."

Longrifle insisted, "Will somebody tell an old man what the hell is going on?"

"Grandfather, there is some trouble in the pueblo and you cannot go to your office for a while. Ten Eagles will explain it to you."

"Was it those young fellows you and Indian Joe had trouble with?"

Ten Eagles said, "Hush and be still." Then he went back to his muttering, only louder this time.

"I'll hush up when my medicine man gets me my health back. Until then, my son, you can tell me what I want to know."

The medicine man stopped his hand in mid-wave and held the feather still, as if wanting to preserve the power.

Jabe knew when to be straight with Longrifle.

"Yes, Grandfather, it was the same ones. They have their own plans for this pueblo. They think you are out of their way and that they can do as they please now. But, I think I know what I can do that will persuade them differently."

"Too much talk!" Ten Eagles was impatient with all the noise. "How can the medicine work with all this commotion? Now, I will have to start all over again."

The Cacique ignored him, "I know you will do what needs to be done, my son. I will take my coffee now."

"And some food, please," added Ten Eagles.

Jabe ducked out of the kiva and found Isabel preparing dinner in the kitchen. She was very handsome for a Hispanic woman of sixty. She had served the Cacique since she was a teenager.

"Hi Isabel. He's asking...."

"For his coffee? I know his routine by heart, young man. Here is his dinner and there is enough for his doctor and his Grandson. Will you take it out to them for me? It's good to see you home again."

Jabe was glad for the chance to carry his Grandfather's meal and took the covered tray. On his way to the kiva, he stopped long enough to set the tray down on a tree stump and drop an aspirin in his Grandfather's favorite coffee cup. Jabe had been keeping the tablet handy since he'd talked with Charlie at the airport and was looking for the chance to administer it. Old Hahtahway knew Longrifle even better than the medicine man did.

Jabe delivered the tray without disturbing the machinations going on inside the kiva, but he poured the coffee himself before leaving.

He had an idea where he might find the troublemakers, but he wanted to complete his reconnaissance in private. He hiked out toward the West in the gathering dusk taking only a canteen of water, his binoculars and the service revolver he'd borrowed from Indian Joe. In order to avoid detection, he stayed off the Jeep road and the more heavily traveled hunting and cattle trails. Instead, he took the old brush-covered deer trail that wound its way up to the edge of the high mesa.

It was practically dark when he arrived on the mesa. Overlooking the flat terrain, Jabe had an unobstructed view all the way across the grassy meadow to the far side of the mesa. He peered through his binoculars and searched in the dim twilight for his target. He could barely make his way in the gathering darkness, but he could move without making a sound. Then he saw what he had come for. The glow of a wood fire at ground level was only a pinpoint of orange amidst the darkness.

He took the light of the distant campfire as his guide and made his way swiftly and surely. Getting closer, he could see movement around the area and kept a close lookout for sentries that might be posted.

Not close enough yet to hear conversation, he could only guess what these men were up to. They had a field communications van, an equipment truck and a camp kitchen. They were billeted in tents, probably six men in all. He could make out a single piece of equipment in the distance—close to the campfire was a tripod mounting a small telescope. Not believing these men were out for astronomical observations, he reckoned it was rather a surveyor's transit. This was a survey party, but surveying what?

Then he saw someone he recognized. A familiar Indian came out of a tent, walked over to put some wood on the fire, then turned and looked Jabe full in the face. Jabe raised his binoculars slightly to avoid detection by any chance of reflected light from the campfire. This Indian looked close enough to touch in the 12-power optics of the Navy binoculars.

It was the Wall Sitter who had just left the pueblo council office in ruins. Farther beyond the campsite, Jabe could just make out the lines of the big Mercedes as the firelight reflected off chrome plating.

These guys are camped right on pueblo land!

He started toward the camp, not fully knowing what he'd do once he got there.

Nearly tripping over a survey line marked with heavy construction twine, Jabe lifted a 30-foot length of it, shoved it in his pocket and circled the camp so he could get in close and check out the vehicles.

No sentry. Imagine that.

These guys were overconfident—just the kind of amateur competition Jabe liked the best.

Sliding under the rear axle of the Mercedes, he cut a short length of twine and tied the revolver to a frame member, then fixed its aim squarely on the gas tank. With the free end of the twine tied to the trigger, he carefully cocked the hammer and slid back out. Crawling quietly, Jabe took cover behind a boulder and yanked the twine tight.

Instantly a fireball erupted where the Mercedes had stood. The night was split with a roar and it was all over but the shouting. The explosion rained the entire campsite with burning gasoline.

As the fireball climbed toward the heavens, Jabe bolted for the trail he had used coming up. The burning camp made a brilliant orange light that provided good visibility on his return trip toward the edge of the mesa.

The confusion in the camp was complete, but he knew they'd have no difficulty figuring out who was responsible. They'd be coming for him alright.

Back at Longrifle's kiva, Jabe entered quietly in case the old man was sleeping. Longrifle was lying down, but he sat upright when Jabe entered.

"Ten Eagles did the work of a good medicine man. I can finally lie down and sleep without the pain in my head. Did you have a nice walk out on the mesa?"

"How did you know I went out there, Grandfather?"

"Ten Eagles told me about the visit you had from those people. I figured you would want to see for yourself if they had gone or not. He said they had traveled West on leaving, so that's where I figured you went—up on the mesa to look for them."

"You're too much for me, Grandfather. That's where I went, alright. I think they're going to be more trouble than I thought. I have to clear out, just for a day or two to let things cool down a bit. While I'm gone, I want you to……"

"Stay out of sight?" Longrifle was way ahead of his Grandson. "Ten Eagles thinks they will assume you are the new Cacique, being my nearest relative. Maybe you would be safer away from here right now. Where will you go, my son?"

"There are some people I need to see, Grandfather. They are friends of the pueblos. I'll find help and then return, but I need to leave right away."

Longrifle removed a silver chain and amulet from around his neck and handed it to Jabe. "I have worn this eagle ever since I was just a boy. It has kept me safe and out of harm's way for many years. Now you need it more than I do."

Jabe looked at the exquisite artwork of the cast silver bird, "Thank you very much, Grandfather."

The Cacique leaned back and adjusted his bedclothes, "They think we are savages, you know." Longrifle was staring into the fire again.

"Who does?"

"The white man's society." Longrifle could change subjects in mid-stream with ease.

"Oh, them."

"They make fun of our way of life and our religion. They think their way is better than ours. They think they are more civilized than we are."

"I've run into plenty with that attitude, for sure."

"They even think they can teach our children better then we can. And they make fun of our medicine, too. They think their medicine is better than ours."

"Well, some of it seems to work."

"Don't ever take me to one of their hospitals, my son. People die in those places."

"I know that for a fact, Grandfather. Don't worry. Ten Eagles and I would never let anyone take you there."

"Is it true, my son, when I hear that one of the white medicine men is going around killing the old people?"

"Yes, Grandfather, it is true."

"Why do they let him do that?"

"Some of the people hire him to kill them when they are sick. He thinks the old and the sick are better off dead. So, he helps them die."

"He thinks he has the right to kill them and rob them of their dignity?"

"Yes, if they want him to."

"He thinks they should not live out the days given to them by the Great Spirit?"

"That's right."

"He thinks he knows better than the Creator?"

"I guess so."

"And the white man's society blesses this medicine man?"

A long silence. Then, "Yes, many of them do."

Longrifle lay back on the pillows and closed his eyes. After a moment he said, "And the white man calls _us_ savages."

"Grandfather, you are old and wise. I don't think the world understands the wisdom of what you have just said. There certainly is a contrast between their world and ours. You have served this pueblo for many years as a wise Cacique, and you will remain to serve many more. But first, something must be done about these trouble-makers. I will come back as soon as I can. And when the pueblo is free of these people, we can walk the river and the prairie and you will have a new office.... Grandfather?"

The Cacique was fast asleep.

Jabe donned the silver eagle and slipped quietly away. He lost no time getting out of the village. He packed his bedroll with a few clean clothes and some traveling food and left his rental car keys in the kitchen for Indian Joe with a message that read:

> Please turn in the car for me, Joe. I'll be gone a few days trying to get us
> some help. Something came up and I had to leave in a hurry.
> Jabe
> PS: I left a smoke signal for you up on the mesa. Go check it out—but
> take along some help and watch your backside.

Jabe moved out under cover of darkness. He had another long hike ahead of him and he was thankful the night was cool. He knew they'd be watching the roads for his departure and attempt an ambush, so he shouldered his sea bag and made a beeline through the woods for the old Santa Fe rail siding. He didn't have to wait long for a slow freight pulling toward the North. He'd be rolling up through Raton Pass and heading down over the plains toward Dodge City before sunup.

With any luck at all, he could be in D.C. in about three days. He only hoped he could find his old chum Franklin Gilmer and that, somehow, Franklin could provide help for the pueblo. But, this would all have to happen fast, if it was to be of much help to the Cacique.

14

The government Gulfstream III jet made an easy touchdown at the Albuquerque SunPort and taxied to the general aviation terminal at the west end. The Bear, General Mendoza and another Customs man deplaned and immediately boarded a waiting Bell JetRanger helicopter. It departed toward the north along the Rio Grande.

Twenty minutes later crossing over a familiar bend in the river the Bear motioned to the pilot who turned toward the west and began a descent. A large mesa loomed in the distance as the Bear searched the landscape. Near the center of the table-top flat mesa he saw a black scar and several burned-out vehicles. The chopper landed close by the camp and the Bear and the Customs man exited as its pilot shut down the engines. General Mendoza kept his seat aboard the aircraft as instructed.

Standing beside the burned out hulks was the Lawyer, the Hunter and one of the black-suited muscle-men. The Lawyer sported the same smart business suit, but beside him stood the Hunter smudged and blackened by being just a little too close when the place had gone up in flames.

The Bear was not amused at the Hunter's appearance, "Well, look at you." Then to the Lawyer, "Is this how you plan to uphold your end of our deal?"

The Lawyer began to protest, but the Bear cut him short, "You were going to deliver this piece of real estate intact and I even gave you some help here. But, it seems to be more of a job than you can handle."

"Oh, we can deliver it okay. We just had a temporary setback, but that little problem will be soon rectified. The pueblo is ours and we can do as we please. The former management will give us no more problems. I believe the Cacique is in his happy hunting ground now."

The Bear made a sweep of his hand, "No more problems, huh? I guess I'm just imagining all this. From the looks of it, this carnage is retribution for something you did down there in the pueblo. Have you idiots started a war, or what?"

The Hunter said, "What does it matter to you? We will deliver on what we bargained for and you can be safe in your office while the real work is being done out here."

The Bear ignored the invitation to an argument, "Who drew first blood, you guys or the 'former management'?"

"What does that matter now?" asked the Hunter, starting toward the Bear with a glint in his eye.

The Bear shot out a sure hand and grabbed the Hunter by the jaw, "You get cute, and you'll be pushing up sunflowers, Junior."

Lawyer stepped between them and restrained the Hunter. The Bear held his grip for a moment, then removed his hand and the Hunter stepped backward rubbing his chin.

Lawyer said to the Bear, "He'll be alright, just give him some room, okay? He's been through enough for one night and we're all a little edgy."

Bear glared at the Hunter and then turned to the goon, "You boys been any help to these fellows like I asked you?"

"Oh, we provided some ordinance delivery and took care of that old man down there in the pueblo."

Bear was not impressed, "Uh-huh. I can see what that got you just looking around here."

A tall fellow dressed in khaki walked over from the burned out supply truck. He looked at the Lawyer and shook his head. "Not much left I can use. Everything's burned the hell up. My help has run off and I'm on foot now. I've got a survey to run here with nothing left but a transit. And I'm supposed to be finished with this survey by tomorrow. How the hell am I gunna do that? Any ideas, Sherlock?"

"Don't sweat it," the Lawyer replied. "We'll get you some new equipment and I can round up some Indian help."

The Hunter spoke up, "Fat chance of that, now. Word of this kind of attack travels fast and you won't find any of the locals willing to take this kind of risk."

The Bear was thinking fast, "Well, then why don't you go over to Gallup and hire some help off the street? A hundred dollars a day will fetch a whole bunch of hungry Indians."

Hunter objected, "What the hell would you know about Indians?"

The Bear was confident, "Oh, I've just about got you Indian fellows figured out, all right. It's a deal they can't refuse. A hundred a day and they don't even have to leave Indian country. There's not another job this side of the Mississippi that pays an Indian that good."

Hunter seemed insulted, "You think Indian people can't figure out what's going on here? You think they won't ask questions. Perhaps they'll think high wages came to New Mexico overnight by magic? You think we are stupid?"

Bear's volume increased, "They'd damn well jump at the chance to make some good money. So go and get 'em. I need this landing strip graded smooth and operational before next week. The earth movers and heavy equipment will arrive out here in two days. So you redskins better get it in high gear, or there'll be hell to pay."

"Okay, okay." the Lawyer waved his hands to calm the Bear. "But, we've got a serious problem right now. We can't risk bringing in the heavy equipment with all this interference we're getting from that Rainwater fellow. He's the one who did this to us. All we need is a little protection from that guy." He seemed downright paranoid.

Bear glanced back at his ordinance man, "Well, I don't know who this Rainwater fellow is, but…."

"We'll take care of him right away, sir. Color him gone."

Bear motioned toward the Customs official, "You just give this man here a list of what you'll need. He'll have some replacement vehicles sent out from town in about an hour. My guys here'll take care of that Rainwater fellow so he doesn't get in your way again. But, you're going to have to stay out of the pueblo so as not to provoke this kind of retaliation again. Ya hear? Now, I'll be back up here again to check on you, so don't screw things up for me."

The Bear took the Customs man aside, "I believe we need some political help with this project, so I'm going over to BIA to make sure we get it. We'll tell them that if our people can't get this airstrip into operation, the DOE lab at Los Alamos will be delayed in their defense work. We'll tell them the project is crucial to national security and we can't let anyone stop us, no matter what their objections. Now, find out what these men need and get it up here pronto." The man nodded.

Bear started for the helicopter, then spoke over his shoulder, "You guys are getting well paid and I expect a little more performance. Find that Rainwater trash and silence him once and for all. I didn't come down here to do all your work for you." He hauled out a cell phone and began dialing.

The pilot started the turbine as Bear headed back and got aboard the chopper. It took off and headed north.

At the Santa Fe airport the Bear left the General to himself inside a secure maintenance hangar and boarded a black government sedan that was waiting there. It headed into Santa Fe and stopped at the Federal Building.

The sign over the office door read, CHIEF, Bureau of Indian Affairs.

The Bureau Chief opened the door to his inner office, welcomed the Bear and invited him to take a seat. "Now what can I do for you, Inspector?"

The Bear began his sale, "Well, sir, you may know that Customs is involved in a survey to locate a landing strip on a pueblo down south of here at a place called West Mesa. Frankly, I'm having some problems and I'm afraid we're going to need a little help from you in securing full cooperation from the Indians down there."

The Chief frowned, "I'm only aware of a preliminary survey to determine the suitability for a training compound that will be attached to the BIA school down there. Nobody said anything to me about any *landing strip*. What's going on here, anyway?"

"Oh. Well, Customs is being asked by the Executive Branch to expedite construction of a landing strip to provide secure transit of equipment and personnel to and from the weapons lab at Los Alamos as part of the New World Order deal with our allies and they need a site that is positively remote and secure."

"Say what?" The Chief seemed stunned.

Bear quickly continued, "Transfer of the shipments from the landing strip to the lab will be by truck or helicopter. They just want the final air hop or road trip as short as possible. The transfer of the facility to the BIA school for aviation training will take place as soon as the strip is decommissioned. That's all there is to it."

The Chief caught his breath, "Well, that's the first I've heard of any intended air traffic into my pueblos. And it's a training facility, you say?"

"Yessir, a training facility. It goes to the Indians when its mission is over."

The Chief was nodding his head, "Yeah, that's what they always tell me. And what's the time frame for that, Inspector?"

"Indefinite, sir, but we don't think any more than two years or so."

"Yeah, I've heard that before. I don't trust anyone in the executive branch any farther than the DC city limits. And I've heard all their promises about how they're going to help the Indians and all the swell things they're going to do to make this a better world. Now they need *my* help for one of their international deals, is that it?"

"National security, Sir," Bear could feel the whole project begin to slip away if he could not convince this man.

"Oh, I'm sure. National security at stake and all. Where have I heard that one before?" The Chief looked up at the ceiling for a moment, then continued, "Well, I can put the word out down there, just like you told it to me, and see if we can get their cooperation. But don't expect the Indians to believe any of this crapola, 'cause *I* sure as hell don't. And I'm going to need everything you've just told me in writing. In *writing*, Mister."

"Sir, we've already had some violence toward our survey crews down there and...."

"So, you're getting the feeling that maybe you're not wanted down there on those pueblos? My, my. I wonder why?"

The Bear protested, "I've been assured this will only benefit the pueblos, sir."

The Chief leaned back in his chair, "Yeah, that's what they always say when they need something from those Indians. Do you know that those folks, and some of us, couldn't care less about any New World Order? They'd already been here forever when European travelers found them and told them that the land of the Indians was a New World. Boy, that was big news to those Indians!"

"Look sir, I only have my job to do, and....."

"And so do I, Inspector." The Chief stood up and appeared to be fighting to control his temper. "But my control over those Indians is in name only. I can't stop any of the residents down there from reacting to what they perceive is a threat to their existence. So you'd better stay out of their way the best you can and I'll make a plea for peace through official channels, and we'll just have to wait and see. That's the best I can do for you. After I've done that, you're on your own from here on." The Chief moved to the door and opened it.

The Bear got up and shook hands with the Chief, "Well, we certainly appreciate anything you can do, Sir"

Driving back to the airport, the Bear reflected on the candid attitude of support the BIA Chief had shown toward his charges. He was a guy who would not compromise his position to the whims of Washington. Here was a fellow to be watched and considered dangerous.

15

Juan Goyona was weary from the day's forced march toward the Pacific shore. He called a halt for his men at one of the many small springs that dotted the jungle and let his heavy backpack fall to the ground. Diego moved to his side.

"My little beachside comida is just an hour's march to the west of here, my cousin. You will not be safe as long as that Gomez is around here. You can make camp a little way into the jungle from the hacienda. Then, he will not even know that you are there, no?"

Juan drew a long drink from his canteen and mopped his brow, "Si, Diego, you can believe we will not let ourselves be seen around the compound. That Gomez has the eyes of a cat. I had a running in with him a few months ago. He took a shot at me and he almost missed."

Juan pulled his collar open to reveal the scar where a bullet had creased his neck.

"If it had not been for my friend Domingo, I might have died. Gomez was so intent on killing me he did not see it coming. Domingo rushed him like the toro and knocked him down so that he lost his weapon and we barely had time to escape from there. His comrades, they were nearly on top of us. Do you remember that little party we had with Gomez, Domingo?"

"Remember? I'm having mucho trouble forgetting about that. We almost got killed, all of us. But we needed some ammunition and Gomez was running the only store in town. So we helped ourselves to some of his supplies. He only got there a little too late to stop us."

"He got there early enough to give me this little reminder of his hospitality." Juan indicated his scar again.

"Even so, we got the supplies we needed," said Domingo. "And ever since then, when we are running low, all we have to do is find Gomez and there are his supplies waiting for us."

Diego was getting his gear together and preparing to move out, "Domingo makes it sound so easy."

Juan was jovial in his rebuke, "But he is not the one who took the bullet, eh Diego?"

Domingo was quick to retort, "Why should I take the bullets when I have such a nice friend as you to take them for me, eh Capitan?" Then the comrades in arms had a good laugh together.

Diego shouldered his pack and motioned for his men to follow him, "I hate to leave such a touching scene as this, but I am afraid I must go back to work taking Gomez's money. I will see you in a day or so at the hacienda, amigos. Adios." Diego shook the hands of Juan and Domingo.

Domingo rose to his feet and stretched the kinks out of his back, "Diego, you had better keep a close watch on that diablo Gomez. He has a nasty habit of coming out of nowhere when you do not expect he even knows where you are. Do not give him an inch, compadre. Even a burro will begin to suspect a trick if he does not get his carrot, no?"

Diego waved in agreement and disappeared into the jungle. Juan and his men struck the trail for the beach. Domingo fell in at the rear.

An hour later, they rounded a curve in the path and Juan saw smoke rising ahead in the distance. He signaled a faster pace and soon they arrived on a palm-covered hill overlooking the beach. Below them was a scene of carnage. The hacienda was ablaze and the compound was in ruins. All their supplies had been destroyed.

"Madre de Dios!" Domingo gasped in disbelief.

Juan said, "That Gomez has been here ahead of us. That diablo has burned down Diego's little house. I wonder did he give Diego enough dinero to build a new one?"

A bullet pierced the foliage close beside Juan. The entire column of men hit the ground. The first rounds cut the jungle vegetation into shreds on both sides. Fire was coming from their entire front quarter and they had to scramble back along the trail they had just come down to find cover. The ambush had worked perfectly, and this time it was Gomez who was laughing.

Getting to his feet, Juan ordered a retreat and his band took to their heels. Now, cut off from their refuge and running low on supplies, Juan wondered when he and his men had ever been in this bad a shape. They would have to fend for themselves again with only the jungle for cover.

"I'm getting too old for this……," he cried aloud and resigned himself to the guerilla life he had grown to loathe.

Another bullet cut the branch just over his head. Juan ducked on pure reflex, as if it would do any good.

"OKAY, we are leaving!" He picked up the pace and hurried his men along. His legs seemed to weigh a ton apiece and he was facing a forced march of many miles yet. It would prove to be yet another sleepless night.

16

Jabe lay curled comfortably atop his sea bag dozing in and out of a comfortable slumber. The events of the past few months had left him numb from lack of rest. The sway of the boxcar and the rhythm of the wheels over the rails had been more than an adequate inducement to sleep.

For the first half of the trip, he had been all alone in his own private boxcar. But, he had shared it with another hobo on pulling out of Memphis and had the company of a talkative companion as far as Charleston. Now he was alone again and glad for the solitude.

His refuge on wheels was a bit slower perhaps, but a freight train was the travel mode he much preferred over the noisy, crowded and boisterous mayhem of air travel. No jet engine noise to destroy your hearing, none of the ever-present clear-air turbulence, and no pushing, jabbing mob to deal with. Just the comforting click of steel-on-steel. *Yessir,* Jabe thought, *this was just ideal.* And besides, they would be looking for him in all the airports and bus stations, so he'd taken the last mode of travel they would ever suspect.

Nowadays, the railroads were keen on keeping the freeloading hobos off the cars. The railroad bulls had checked the cars at every stop along the way, so that a Bo had to leave the train on approach to the yards and walk around to pick up an outbound. But, Jabe had perfected a much easier method. He could swing his sea bag up out of sight over the header of the doorway for a cushion, then climb up and lie against the rail of the sliding door. Somehow the bulls never thought to look directly overhead for a freeloader. An old Bo had taught him the trick. The bulls would just cast the flashlight beam over into all four corners and go on to the next car, and they never checked the cars twice on a stop. Very predictable folks, those yard inspectors.

Jabe hadn't realized the extent to which some portions of the population still relied on freight trains as a means of reliable and fast transportation, not to mention that the price was right. He had seen no less than sixty riders going in both directions since leaving New Mexico. The hobo subculture was born of the Depression Era and had remained an active part of American life even after all these years.

He thought about the simpler times he had experienced and, all told, he thought he preferred the freights to airplanes; if he had the time for leisure, that is. How many other people felt as he did?

Jabe moved to the doorway and watched the country roll by as if it were attached to a moving curtain. This train had taken him through most of the mid-continent and he had seen the picture-perfect farms and small towns that most folks only see on the pages of a calendar. He had been three days on the road now and the scenery had changed dramatically in that short time. In stark contrast to the earth-tone colors of the arid dry-farming agriculture of the Southwest, the Virginia countryside was a patchwork quilt of small farms and pastures that glistened green, yellow and gold in the morning sun. It looked the same as when he had first come here during his basic training. Now, all that seemed an eternity ago.

The freight was slowing now for its entrance into the Washington Metro Area. As the train made the last turn for the yard, Jabe waited for a secluded spot for his departure and let himself down to the ground in a trot alongside a hedgerow. It would be an easy walk into the city.

Close by the railyard and well away from the city-center, he rented a cheap hotel room and paid in cash. Renting a car was another matter entirely and he had to use his credit card. "Absolutely no other way," said the rental agent.

Damn. This modern society'll be the death of me yet.

No way could he remain undetected at this rate. Their computers would spot the transaction in a heartbeat. He shuddered to think what it would be like when the government ordered all the cash to be turned in and all you had was plastic! Then there would be instantaneous recording of all your activities and no way to even know who all had access to the information. Yet another freedom gone and no one would complain—or no one would dare to.

Jabe left his seabag in his room and walked to a telephone booth at the end of the block. He dialed a number and waited for an answer.

"Dudley, it's me."

"Well, how are things up there in Billings, anyhow?" Dudley sounded tight and distraught. He spoke in a sarcastic high sing-song that told Jabe all was not right. "Did you see my brother when you went through Laramie?"

"Yeah, and he wanted to know when you were going to pay him back that loan you owe him. Wants to know if you've changed very much since he saw you last. Are you okay?"

"Aw hell, he knows I'm good for that little loan he made me. Yeah, I'm fine. When you coming back home, Pardner? There's been a couple of guys asking for you. They come around pretty often and really want to talk with you. They're strangers to me, but they said it was very important they found out where you are right now. What'll I tell 'em?"

"Oh, they're probably just some old Navy buds of mine and I'd sure hate to miss seeing them. Tell them I'll be home in about a week or so. Bye, Dudley, see you then." Jabe got off the phone as quickly as possible. He hoped the call hadn't been traced and that Dudley had been successful in making any listeners think he'd gone north. He dialed another number.

"Franklin? It's me, your old pueblo buddy. Remember the old buddy you had out on the pueblo? It's me, J.B. Who'd you think it was? No, I'm here in town. I didn't want to call you at your office and I damn sure didn't want to come down there. I've got to see you today.......
Alright, this evening then....... No, I can't come near your digs and I'm kinda hiding out in the boonies. What about the Jefferson Memorial at noon....... Then how about noon tomorrow? Okay then. And you can come alone? Fine. Roger that and I'll see you there."

Jabe had known this man since their childhood days on the reservation. If he could trust anyone, it was Franklin Gilmer.

Jabe drove back to the hotel and spent the night lying on his bed staring up at the ceiling.

Toward noon the next day, he drove over to the mall, parked and walked to the Memorial. He waited for Franklin to arrive and stayed well away from the milling crowd. He wanted to make sure his friend had not been followed. Finally Jabe saw him arrive.

Franklin milled about with the sparse crowd and maneuvered in a circuitous route to the center of the Memorial. He stood and waited for Jabe to appear. He didn't have long to wait.

Jabe wandered slowly over and stood some distance away against the wall and opposite the man he'd known practically all his life. Franklin looked about the same as he always had. He and Jabe had grown up on the pueblo as close friends and both had gone into the Navy the same summer. While Jabe was going through the Seals' underwater demolition school, Franklin was training in military intelligence at the Naval War College. Upon his graduation, Franklin had been assigned to the Office of Naval Intelligence at the Pentagon. He had enjoyed a long and rewarding career and was nearing retirement. Jabe was hoping to get some help from his long-time friend.

After a moment, Franklin moved around closer to Jabe and took a seat on one of the marble benches along the outer wall. Jabe waited a moment, and surveyed his surroundings to see if anyone else moved for position. Seeing nothing suspicious, he sat down at the other end of the bench.

Franklin began, "I'd shake your hand, Joe Bob, but I don't want to call attention to you. If you'd wanted any attention, you'd have let me know you were coming. You're a rascal, you know that?"

"Yeah, so I've been told."

"It's been a long time, Jabe. What brings you to D.C.?" Franklin seemed just a little on edge and Jabe hated to bother his friend, but he needed help.

"Oh, I just got to missing your beautiful face, Franklin. That's all."

"Yeah, I'll just bet you did. I haven't seen you since your Seal training. How long have you been out of the service and what are you up to these days?"

"I've been out for a while now, but I could never settle too far from the water. Been living on the Gulf Coast and working the waterfront. I was just out to the home place and I found it a bit inhospitable. Some strange things are going on out there, Franklin, and I need some help."

"What sort of strange things, Jabe?"

"Some thugs have come in and they're making a move for control over the whole pueblo. They blew up the council office in hopes of killing my Granddad and if he'd been at work in his office as he usually is, they would have surely succeeded. I left him at home with the medicine man and told him to stay in the kiva until I can guarantee their safety. Trouble is I've already confronted the hoodlums. Blew some holes in their plans and they've got my number now. I hopped a freight to get here, Franklin, and I'm out of options. I thought maybe you could give me some help with all of this."

Franklin had listened quietly, "I've never seen you when you were out of cards like this, J.B. What's the game out there and who are those people?"

"Well, you'd think they'd be outsiders as usual, but these guys are Indians. Oh, they have their outside help okay. But, these guys are Indians, Franklin. They're trying to get the Cacique out of the picture, and I think they mean to kill him yet. I don't know exactly what's up—seems to be related to drugs. They came damn near to killing Indian Joe. He's my witness in all of this. He has caught some of the local dealers selling to the children and seen them prosecuted for it. They do some time and get out again. Then they're back to it again. The Cacique warns the people, so the dealers want him out of their way. But, that is a business that will continue whether there is a Cacique or not. He can't be everywhere at once. Neither can the police. I'm afraid it involves much more than just selling drugs to a few Indians."

"That guy Indian Joe. He still the local lawman?"

"Nobody else. And he's doing what he can, but they almost killed him a few days ago. I don't think the pueblo is safe anymore, Franklin. They are too powerful and they have completely upset the peace of the reservation. I wouldn't be here asking for help if I could handle this thing by myself."

"What has the BIA said about all this?"

"Joe called the BIA chief and apprised him of the trouble, but he played dumb. I know that guy, and he's normally of great help to us. I think they're holding something over his head."

"Oh, it's over his head alright."

Jabe turned and looked directly at his friend, "You know something about this, Franklin?" Jabe knew that tone of voice and sensed a certain recognition on Franklin's part.

"Not everything, Jabe. Not just yet, anyway. But what you've told me sure fills in a lot of holes in what little I did know. I heard you were back on the pueblo, but I was also told you had a hand in the drug trade down there. Thank God you contacted me. I was afraid it might be true."

"You thought *what?*"

"Well, when you haven't seen your old buddies for a while……"

"I haven't changed any, Franklin, and I hope to heaven you haven't either. I would hate to have wasted this trip and come all this way just to…"

"Okay, Jabe. You can relax. I know you'd never have come to town at personal risk if you had anything to hide. And you can be sure that I won't let anyone know that you're here. I'm glad you came to see me. Now, how is your Grandfather?"

"Just as well as ever, but I'm going to need some outside help to keep him that way."

Franklin got to his feet, "Let's get something to eat and you can tell me all about the old home place."

The two old friends strolled over to a vendor, bought sandwiches and walked together along the Tidal Basin.

Franklin began, "When I first got to ONI, it was a real revelation, Jabe. I knew there was some funny stuff going on in government, but I had never realized the extent of it. I always thought those alleged under-world connections with the sitting Administration might be just a pack of ultra-conservative hallucinations. Then we had some real unsavory happenings like some mysterious 'suicides' and the White House being visited by a continuous flow of known felons. You remember the Chinese connection?"

"Campaign contributions for atomic and defense secrets and the like?"

"And the like. How do you think they keep Most Favored Nation trade status in light of their human rights record? Well, I never believed all this could ever be true, Jabe.

Franklin paused for a moment, "But sadly, it's even worse. It's no secret around D.C. that the Customs Department has been running a supposed 'sting' operation in the drug trade. The story for public con-sumption is that the brains at the top in Customs expect to bring down the South American drug lords in one fell swoop. Trouble is, no one at Justice seems to be taking the credit for this and Customs says they can't talk about it. And while they constantly maneuver, reposition, and make conflicting public comments, one of their drug planes goes down short of the runway in South Texas and it's clear to anyone taking notice that they're operating a humongous drug trade into the States. Any idea where all the money's going?"

"That'll go to anyone who happens to be in power. And I was the pilot of that plane that didn't make the runway, pal."

"The hell you say!"

"Lots to tell you, Franklin."

"Well, bingo again. The money goes right to the top. But, ev-erything is on hold just now. I've looked into this on my own, Jabe, and from the bits of information I've been able to piece together, Customs has temporarily suspended their shipments. They're apparently trying to find a safer landing site so they can get their drugs into the States unno-ticed. That Samuelson report really put the public on notice and things are just too hot down in Texas right now. They can't risk carrying on as they have been."

"Yeah, I heard that WNN report. And that's where the pueblos come in?"

"They're looking for an isolated location where they can land and unload without any threat of detection. The Southwest is perfect for that kind of operation. Low population density and cooperative environment from the locals in control. Some of the state governors even support wholesale drug legalization."

"Yeah, so we hear on the local TV news. And that isolated location you mentioned just happens to be the high mesa out west of the pueblo. That's where I had a run-in with them a few nights ago."

Franklin nodded, "It figures. Officially, the project is a defense initiative to support the national labs in New Mexico. A perfect plan, if they can get the landing strip built. And they're planning on upgrading their fleet of aircraft to the C-130 Hercules."

"A fleet of Herkybirds?"

"You got it."

"These guys have got a lotta huevos!"

"Well, the public is so fast asleep depending on the government to save them from all their social ills, they'll just go on about their business confident they voted right and it's all just an illusion. The Establishment goes on about their dirty business as they always have. Nobody ever does anything to stop this kind of thing. The media isn't going to cause them too much trouble. Every time some loose cannon like that Samuelson fellow comes up with some hard evidence, they shut him up in a hurry."

"Funny how we never heard another peep connected with that news report. What did the so-called 'Drug Czar' have to say about it?"

"Well, he's a good man. But, he gets absolutely no help at all from the power block. Every time he proposes a real program of interdiction, the people at the top all go on TV to brag about how much good it's going to do for the country, they make a bust or two, and then.......nothing. The power brokers go in and dismantle every effective program he has in place and substitute some gutless fraud."

Franklin seemed too frustrated for words. His voice trailed off, "Nothing ever happens that really hurts the drug trade. It only escalates." He looked down at the ground and just shook his head.

Jabe was silent for a moment, "Franklin, the health and well-being of the pueblo is at stake here. If the white man's society is going to stand by and let their world disintegrate, then they get what they deserve. But I'm not willing they should use the Indian nations to facilitate their own destruction. And I'll be damned if I'll let those Indian toughs they've recruited help them out."

Franklin agreed, "I feel the same way too, Jabe. Now what can I do to help?"

They talked a few minutes more and Franklin agreed to be Jabe's ear-to-the-ground in official circles. Mainly, Jabe needed a strategic source of advance information on the government's agenda for the pueblo. He bid his friend farewell and spent the remainder of the afternoon walking along the mall. He mulled over the information he'd gotten and determined that his only hope was to stay in close touch with Franklin. Then, just at dusk, he drove back toward his hotel.

He parked on a side street a few blocks away and went in on foot. By natural instinct, Jabe hesitated to walk straight in, so he watched the hotel from down the block. His suspicions were confirmed when he saw shadowy figures moving in the dark doorways along the street. He figured he'd been found and was now under surveillance. He waited for a change in the guard, then took advantage of the momentary distraction.

He made his way up a fire-escape ladder and along the rooftops to his hotel room. Entering silently through a window, he gathered his seabag and climbed back up to the roof. He crept silently across the rooftops and then descended to the sidewalk across the street from his car. He approached it with caution and went to his knees to inspect the underside.

Sure enough, there was a loop of wire hanging down where no wire should have been and his eye followed it to a bundle wrapped in black electrical tape—the car was rigged with a bomb.

Boy, these guys are dangerous! Now he was on foot again. Several blocks away he called the local bomb squad and hitch-hiked out of town. He'd let the police sort it all out.

Back along the hedgerow, Jabe hopped aboard a south-bound freight. This trip would take him toward the Gulf Coast of Texas and he knew full-well they would be expecting him to go there.

17

Dusk had turned to darkness two days later coming into Houston's Settegast Yard when Jabe left the freight and hiked out to the freeway. He was lucky enough to hitch a ride with a friendly motorist down the Gulf Freeway toward Galveston.

As it turned out, the man had seen his sea bag and recognized him as a fellow Navy man. Jabe got a lift right near to his hotel, but had the man drop him a few blocks away. He was getting downright edgy now, since that scrape out on the pueblo. So, out of caution he called Dudley from a phone booth.

Dudley reached for the phone and a black-gloved hand covered his. A stern look from its owner told Dudley just what to say. Even so, he'd have to warn Jabe somehow.

"Hello."

"Dudley, you okay?"

"Yeah, I'm fine. I didn't know you were coming in so soon, so I sent your cleaning out and Healey has it now."

"Healey? The guy from Austin?"

"Yeah, you know that Healey. Always ready to oblige when you need him the most. Well, I've gotta go now. Got some business to take care of somewhere else. You plan to come by?"

"You have company. So I guess we're planning on leaving soon?"

"Roger that. I'll see you in a jiffy, and don't be late."

Jabe left the phone booth, circled the block and crept into the parking garage across the street from the hotel. There on the ground floor was Dudley's vintage Austin Healey. "Mr. Healey from Austin, I presume," Jabe chuckled.

The rakish two-seater was backed into its parking slot all ready for a fast get-away. Jabe found his things stuffed in the back under the tonneau along with Dudley's sea bag. He threw in his own bag and zipped the cover closed again.

The Healey 3000-Six was one of the prettiest sports cars ever built and always caught an eye and turned heads when Dudley drove it along Seawall Boulevard. Tonight, Jabe wished it wasn't painted red.

Looking across the street directly into the hotel lobby, Jabe could see Dudley standing behind the clerk's counter facing two trench-coated types who were seated along the far wall in dim light. 'Why did they always have to wear those silly trench coats?' he mused. There was another man standing outside near the doorway.

Jabe needed to distract them long enough for Dudley to get a good run for the door, so he carefully made a loop down the block, up the alley and around to the side window of the janitor's closet on the ground floor. He found a loose brick and made good use of it. Jabe tossed it through the window and made a leap toward the street in the very same move.

The crash drew the two lobby goons toward the back room and Dudley bolted straight for the open front door. Jabe came running out of the alley toward the street. He had made a precise estimate of the time it would take the outside man to intersect his path. His calculation had been dead reckoned and he caught the poor guy completely off balance.

BOOM! The goon and his pistol went sprawling as Jabe hit him at full speed. His Browning automatic went sliding across the street and was free for the taking. Jabe scooped up the 9mm with one hand and took cover behind the low garage wall as Dudley vaulted over his head and made for the Healey.

"Thought you'd *never* get here," Dudley yelled.

Gunfire erupted from the hotel lobby. A bullet zipped past his head and Jabe returned the fire.

"Those damn fools are trying to kill somebody, J.B. What the hell did you do to get their dander up?"

"I'll tell you all about it, Pardner. Later." He pumped a few rounds into the lobby windows to give Dudley enough time to get to the Healey.

Dudley landed in the driver's seat and inserted the ignition key, "Praise the Lord and pass the ammunition." He lit the fires in the Healey's big six, shoved her in gear and sped for the garage entrance as Jabe placed some accurate fire into the lobby. The bullets sent the goons to the floor just long enough for Jabe to leave his post and make a dive for the speeding Healey. He plopped into the front seat just as Dudley sped past him.

Once on a straight track they looked back to see the goons running into the street. At the same instant, they instinctively ducked and the windscreen blew into pieces in a shower of glass shards.

"These guys are playing for keeps, Jabe. Want to tell me about it, now?"

"Drive, man. Just drive."

Jabe turned back and fired until the breach locked open. Dudley made a turn toward the beach and the safety of high speed along Seawall Boulevard. He mashed hard on the accelerator and let out a whoop, "HoooooooBoy! Them guys don't fool around much, do they? What'd you ever do to get them all that upset, anyhow? I was sweating blood in there 'til you showed up."

"Oh, I've got plenty to tell you about, Old Pard. Sorry about your windscreen, Dudley."

"Don't worry about it. It's only flat glass and cheap at any rate. I haven't had this good an adrenaline rush since our service days."

Dudley shifted into high gear and the Healey was near full speed within six blocks. At more than 130, the wind coming over the bonnet and through the Healey's smashed windscreen made Jabe's eyes burn. Luckily, Dudley's eyeglasses served as a handy pair of driver's goggles and he seemed to be in full control at this speed, although he was running without lights. Seawall Boulevard was deserted at this time of night. All the hotels were serviced from back streets, so no service trucks drove the boulevard and bathers were not allowed on the beach during curfew hours.

Jabe thought he could make out a dark sedan passing under the streetlights along the boulevard well behind them. It too was traveling without lights.

"You often drive this fast around town?" Jabe asked as he studied the sedan, decided it was traveling fast, but not gaining any ground on them. It looked like a Mercedes.

"Only when I'm in a hurry," was Dudley's matter of fact answer. "After those hoods started coming around looking for you, I packed all your things back there under the tonneau and put most of my gear in the trunk. Figured you'd have to make a run for it and I didn't want to hang around this town and night-clerk that flop-house hotel the rest of my life. So I thought I'd just invite myself along and help you out."

"That's my Bud." Jabe was glad for Dudley's help. They had been together in many a tight spot before and Jabe knew he could depend on Dudley. "Any idea where we're headed?"

"Oh, yeah." Dudley grinned and pointed toward the rotating beacon at Scholes Field flashing its green-and-white greeting. He was watching an oncoming vehicle. This one had its headlights turned on.

"Oh boy, just what we needed."

The oncoming car slowed down as the Healey sped past. Then it made a turn for the far curb. A State Trooper was making a speed-turn as he switched on his light bar and siren. The patrol car came around in a wide swing across the traffic lanes just in time to smack the invisible Mercedes fender to fender.

BOOM! Jabe watched in fascination as the two cars went airborne in a cloud of sparks. They sailed Frisbee-style, side-by-side, landed right side up and sat there smoking.

Dudley let out another whoop, "Wow! Now there's a good cop. Right on time and right where we needed him. They ought to give that guy a medal. Whew!" Dudley let out a breath he seemed to have been holding ever since they left the hotel.

Then Jabe saw a second Mercedes rocket past the wreck and head straight after the Healey. These guys had covered all the bases.

"He had a backup, Dudley. There's another Mercedes." Dudley let up on the gas and let the Healey coast, "Not to worry, Pardner. We're almost there." He used the hand brake to slow the car so the brake lights would not function and made a right-hand turn into airport.

Jabe knew the place. Scholes Field had been a bomber training base during WWII. The government had given it to Galveston County after the conflict. It was serving as the regional general aviation airport and housed an FAA Flight Service Station. The FSS was closed during the night and the place was deserted. Having no control tower, it had radio-controlled runway lights that only turned on when a pilot summoned them for arrival or departure. In the hours before sunup, the whole field was dark except for the lone rotating beacon flashing green and white.

Dudley drove straight toward the hangars.

Jabe wondered why Dudley had taken a dead-end road into the airport. "What're we doing here? You still building that airplane you always dreamed about?" Was this the precise moment Dudley had chosen to unveil his pet project?

The Healey came to a stop at the doorway of Hangar 13. Only the skyglow of the city lights reflecting off the low overcast lit the scene.

"Finished her several weeks ago and she's been thoroughly flight tested."

They hopped out of the Healey. Dudley unlocked the hangar door and rolled it open.

"Don't have her licensed yet, but she flies like a dream. I didn't want to tell you until I could take you up. I never expected to need her this badly or this soon."

Dudley parked the Healey inside the hangar as Jabe viewed a truly awesome creation. She was a gleaming Lancair 235 with the same red paint job the Healey sported. She was a low-wing, two-seater with re-tractable landing gear and Dudley had modified the canopy to roll back fighter style. Jabe knew this baby could out-fly and out-run practically anything else in the sky. Now, she would get the chance to prove it.

There on the cowling in white script lettering was her name—*Dances with Clouds*. Jabe thought the name was fitting. And the idea of making for the clouds just now made good sense indeed.

Jabe could hear the Mercedes making the rounds of nearby hangars as he retrieved their bags and placed them behind the seats while Dudley grabbed the towbar and latched it to the nosewheel, then nimbly pulled the little sportplane out onto the paving and swung her around. Jabe pushed the hangar doors closed and snapped the lock in place.

Dudley mounted the left wing root and lowered himself into the pilot's seat as Jabe climbed in on his right. The engine caught on the first couple of turns and ticked over at a rough idle, then smoothed out. Being in sort of a hurry, Dudley left the engine warm-up and pre-flight check to be completed during their taxi and eased the throttle forward. The Lancair moved swiftly down the concrete as Dudley steered for the runway.

Jabe caught sight of the slow-moving Mercedes coming around the back row of hangars, "Hey, Pard. You'd better turn on the 'invisible' switch, 'cause we've got company."

"Invisible switch is ON. We'll leave the runway lights off and get out of here in the dark." Dudley knew this airport well enough for that. He checked the magnetos, set the altimeter and ran the preflight checklist while moving at fast taxi. If he hurried, maybe they could still get out of Texas alive!

They reached the far end of the field and Dudley made his turn onto the runway. He rolled the canopy closed, then pushed the throttle to the firewall and 235 ponies came to life under the cowling. Just then, the Mercedes came thundering out onto the runway at midfield with headlights blaring. It headed straight for them in a head-on rush.

Gunmen hung out of every window firing at the accelerating airplane. The Lancair rocketed down the runway and into the air just over the oncoming Mercedes. Bullets flashed past on both sides of the airplane and Jabe thought he could feel hot lead piercing his bottom-side. Dudley jerked the landing gear handle and the wheels clunked up into their wells. They were safely up and away......just barely.

Jabe quickly felt his underside for bullet holes, but found his clothing intact. He checked the airspeed indicator and saw the needle swinging past 100 knots as the ground fell away and they sped swiftly out of pistol range. Dudley kept the nose low to build up speed, departed straight out on the runway heading, crossed low over the seawall and dropped to about a dozen feet above the waves.

The swift little two-seater quickly accelerated and in a few seconds the airspeed indicator was tickling the 200-knot mark.

Jabe yelled out loud, "Wow! This little baby can lift up her skirts and fairly tiptoed through the dew!" Dudley smiled and nodded in agreement.

But, Jabe was still hopping mad.

"Dammit all to hell. Don't those sonsabitches have anything better to do than go around shooting at us?"

Dudley was too busy to respond. He was navigating in complete darkness and had to turn on the landing light to illuminate the wave-tops so he could see well enough to keep the airplane out of the water.

When they were well away from the coast, Dudley turned on his navigation and anti-collision lights, just in case they met a low-flying crew chopper coming in from the offshore rigs. You never knew what to expect out over the Gulf and Dudley was taking no chances. He settled into a fast cruise and took a course toward the south and down the coast.

Dudley took a Houston Sectional Navigation Chart out of the cockpit side pocket and handed it to Jabe. He tapped a finger to indicate a location for Jabe's benefit, "We'll land at Lake Jackson. I've got a good friend down there we can stay with. We'll stash the plane and stay out of sight for a few days. Maybe take in some great saltwater fishing." Dudley climbed for altitude and took up a heading that paralleled the beach.

Fifteen minutes later and well out over the Gulf, Dudley pulled around and headed back in for a night landing at the Brazoria County airport. He had no more than straightened her out on course when an airborne searchlight suddenly caught them square in the eyes. Without hesitation, Dudley killed his navigation lights, pulled the wings vertical in a hard turn and dived for the wave-tops. Reversing course, he called on all the horses again and they were on the run.

He looked at Jabe, "Man, this is really getting tiresome. Look over there."

Two more airborne searchlights ignited in the darkness off to their left. There was nothing to do but turn out over the Gulf again.

They watched as several more of the airborne lights appeared all along the coast. They were being pursued by a dozen aircraft.

So, Dudley did the only sensible thing a man in distress could ever do. He ran like hell and headed straight for Mexico.

Jabe said, "Well, don't that beat all. Looks like we ain't welcome back home anymore. Imagine that!"

Dudley took one last look back over his shoulder, "I think I know what's in store for us if we try and land in Texas tonight. So how's your TexMex, J.B.? Looks like you'll be needing it later today."

"Are you serious?" Jabe couldn't believe they could make it all the way to Mexico over the Gulf.

"Well, if the sun comes up and we're still dry, we just might have a chance. You got any other suggestions?"

He didn't. He was stumped. Things had gone from bad to worse in a hurry and it was getting mighty clear that his pursuers had a network of resources that was just uncanny. How had they gotten airborne assistance so fast? And so much of it! Those guys had to have the cooperation of the country's top intelligence networks. Well, they were U.S. Customs, after all. But, more importantly, who was behind it all?

Dudley was staying near the wave-tops in order to avoid radar detection. Better nobody knew where they were headed.

Jabe settled back in his seat to think things over. His mind was plumb tired out and before long he began to doze into half-consciousness. He fought the on-coming sleep and tried going over everything that had happened these past few days. But, he couldn't uncover any clue as to just WHO might be behind all his troubles. The steady purr of the engine lulled him into a slumber.

Dudley rolled the canopy back an inch or two for ventilation. Jabe sat up and realized he had been asleep. They had been airborne nearly three hours now. Jabe was dog tired after the night's excitement and he marveled at how Dudley could maintain enough concentration to fly a demanding high-performance airplane.

There had been a strong norther blowing at takeoff and Jabe was glad for the tailwind. He could make out a hint of blue off toward the eastern horizon and the night was one of those rare crystal-clear marvels that graced the Gulf only occasionally. It would be a fine day for flying. But flying where?

"Got any idea where we're headed, Captain Pilot Sir?" Jabe knew Dudley well enough to know he had a plan in mind, but couldn't resist asking him.

"Well, señor. How about we take that long vacation down south you've been talking about for years now, huh? I don't know when we'll get a better chance than this. Do you?"

"Nope, sure don't."

The sun came up bright and clear just forward of the left wing—a huge orange ball that appeared to just sit there on the horizon. The surface of the Gulf had hardly a whitecap and the wave troughs indicated the wind was still dead on their tail.

Jabe asked in a mariner's tone of voice, "What do you make the wind, Cap'n?"

"I make her about 15 knots to the good. How about you?"

Jabe was about to agree when his gaze fell on the twin fuel gauges. He couldn't believe his eyes. Both of them were pegged on EMPTY— and no land in sight.

18

Dudley leaned back against the headrest and grinned, "Yep, about fifteen knots I'd say, and a good norther at that. At this rate, we'll make the coast of Yucatan in short order." He reached up over his hairline to make sure his sunglasses were in place. Then he yelled, "Hoooooo Boy! Mexico, here we come!"

Jabe tapped Dudley on the arm and pointed to the fuel gauges, "How we gonna get there, Cap'n? The fuel gauges say we're *empty*!"

Dudley looked at the gauges and then rocked the wings trying to make them move. "Well, I thought I might've missed something during construction and you just found it for me. I forgot to wire up the fuel gauges. What do you know! There's always a detail or two that goes undone when you put together one of these homebuilt bad boys. But, I think we'll be alright. I remember filling the tanks when I put her in the hangar last......At least I think I did."

"Oh, that's rich." Jabe folded his arms and stared straight ahead looking for some sign of land while Dudley fiddled with the circuit breaker buttons and tapped on the fuel gauges shaking his head in disbelief and wearing a concerned look.

Dudley insisted, "I'm sure I filled both tanks, J.B. I do it automatically when I'm done flying. It's a habit that's hard to break." He let out a nervous chuckle.

Jabe was not amused, "You *think*? Well, that doesn't help us much if the engine quits. At this altitude we'll be in the water, but quick."

Dudley tapped on the gauges again. The needle on the left wing tank gauge swung slowly up a fraction of an inch and then settled back to the empty mark.

Dudley put on his most convincing voice, "Aw, we'll be okay, J.B. Trust me. Those gauges just aren't working, that's all. The chart for

Mexico is right here and we don't have far to go now. So just hang on and we'll be just fine."

Jabe knew that Dudley had been navigating by satellite signals since leaving the Texas coast. His Global Positioning System receiver had kept him dead on course for the Yucatan.

Dudley handed Jabe the air navigation chart and tapped the Yucatan with his finger, "We should cross the coast about here."

Jabe wasn't relaxing a bit. "First rule of aviation is to always take enough fuel to make your destination, Cap'n."

Dudley let the jab pass, "Now that the sun's up, why don't you take the controls awhile and get the feel of this baby?"

Jabe flew the little bird like he'd built her himself. "I'm still worried about the gas situation."

"Aw, we've got plenty. So just relax, will ya?"

Jabe tried to get his mind off the gauges, "Well, I was just wondering who taught you to fly, anyhow. Seems they skipped the lesson on fuel management." He pulled up and made some lazy turns, then settled back on course.

"Who taught me? Well, I guess I was taught by about the best instructor that ever lived. Anyway, she was the best I ever saw."

"You were taught by a lady? An Aviatrix?" Jabe somehow found that a little odd.

"Oh, yeah. And what a lady she is. She's been a certified FAA Check Pilot from the tender age of twenty-five. Gave flight instruction at Scholes Field. Had a list of clients as long as your arm. She sure had a reputation in aviation circles."

Jabe rocked the wings and tapped the gauges again for good measure.

"Sounds like you knew her well. Funny, you never mentioned her before."

"Well, to tell you the truth, I was sweet on her. We went out for lunch several times and we hit it off nicely. We dated for about a year. We were getting really close for a while there."

"And then?"

"I don't know, J.B. She just disappeared one day. I couldn't find her anywhere. Her flight schedule had been cancelled and her boss was no help at all. She didn't have any family that I knew about. All of a sudden she was just gone."

"And you never found her?"

"I never saw her again. Don't know if I ever will. I don't know why she'd up and leave like that. It just wasn't like her."

Dudley was silent. He steered the Lancair out of pure reflex. Then, "Her name was Lia. Blue eyes, red hair. And, I'll tell you for certain, she was some kind of a knockout babe. That's for sure."

Jabe reflected on that. No way could this be Lia MacTaggart.

The navigation display on the instrument panel was already showing the irregular curve of the Mexican coast. They had been in the air for close to four hours and had crossed the entire Gulf of Mexico. Just at dawn now, the line of palms along the beachhead was beginning to show in the distance. But, the fuel gauges still showed empty.

Jabe handed the controls back to Dudley, "Are you sure we have enough gas to make the coast?" He still was not completely convinced.

"Sure, we'll be fine. Don't worry about it. I got you this far didn't I? When have I ever let you down? Just relax and....."

POW! The engine backfired once, popped again, and then ran smooth once more.

Dudley looked at Jabe wide-eyed, "Uh-oh."

He rocked the wings to slosh the remaining fuel around to completely scavenge the tanks. Then he shoved the throttle full open, hauled back on the stick and continued rocking the wings in a power climb for altitude. The engine ran strongly for another couple of minutes as they climbed past 4000 feet. Then it sputtered and went silent.

Dudley explained, "Okay. Now *that's* empty, J.B." He pushed the nose over level and established a shallow glide toward the beach. Jabe, who had been perfectly silent since the first backfire, was clinging to his seat cushion with one hand and holding onto the instrument panel with the other. He was getting ready for an impact with the ocean that he felt was unavoidable. Every few seconds he would unconsciously decide the grip he had was insufficient and would move his hands to other grappling points.

He continued this fidgeting until he earned Dudley's stern rebuke, "Would you cut that out? I'm trying to concentrate here!"

"Sorry, Cap'n. I only do this whenever I'm really WORRIED!"

The line of palms was getting closer and a narrow strip of white sand was visible—the beach. Even though Cloud Dancer's airframe was aerodynamically clean as a pin, Dudley was maintaining the best angle of attack in an attempt to stretch the glide distance. The Lancair was now approaching the coast at a speed of about a hundred and thirty knots, but she was getting down closer to the waves. At sixty-five knots, the wing would stall and she'd hit the water. Dudley skillfully bled off the remaining airspeed at just the rate that kept them ten feet above the breakers.

If they hit the water before they reached the beach, Jabe wondered if they'd survive the impact.

Down to ninety-five knots now, and the spray from the breakers was spattering the windshield. Jabe didn't see how they could possibly make the beach. Dudley rolled the canopy open a few more inches and gulped the fresh air in deeply.

The airspeed needle dropped to eighty knots and Dudley brought the nose up and slightly left. Seventy-five knots and the wings shuddered their warning of the approaching stall. That could be fatal. And they would quickly lose speed in the turn down the beach. Jabe resigned himself to the inevitable.

Dudley had been concentrating on the approach and was doing a fine job. He lowered the left wing a little too much and caught the very tip-top of a wave. Cloud Dancer pivoted slightly, but Dudley's hard punch on the rudder corrected the yaw just in time. Completing the turn, the last of the breakers whipped past under the wing and Jabe could see the sand beach coming up fast. Just as Dudley brought her around for landing, the airspeed indicator fluttered just above sixty-five knots and the wings were about to quit flying. Dudley was completing his turn and rolling out level as the plane mushed downward just above the sand. He was sweating bullets about now.

Jabe shouted, "Are the wheels down?"

"Dammit!" Dudley's hand shot to the gear lever as if laser guided and tripped the handle down. "I had the feeling I was forgetting something."

The wheels whipped down and locked into landing position a split second before touchdown. Just a slight bump and they were rolling smoothly along the beach.

Neither of them said a word.

Dudley steered toward a slight clearing in the palms and they rolled to a stop in the shade. They just sat there breathing heavily and staring straight ahead.

Jabe slowly and cautiously let go of his iron grip on the instrument panel and managed a whimpering giggle as Dudley slowly slid the canopy all the way open. Then they unbuckled their safety belts, rose slowly, climbed out of their seats and dropped to the sand. When they tried to stand, their legs gave way and they sat right back down in the sand again. Dudley looked over at Jabe and grinned—and that's all it took.

Jabe threw his head back and shrieked in unbridled laughter. Dudley had no choice but to join him. They just lay back in the sand and yelled, kicked and beat the sand with their arms until all their pent-up tensions were exhausted.

When they had regained their breath, Jabe slowly got to his feet, "That scared the poop plumb out of me, Cap'n."

"How do you think *I* felt about it? I nearly ruined my brand-new beautiful airplane!" Dudley gazed at Cloud Dancer with obvious affection.

Jabe set about clearing a path in the driftwood and beach litter ahead of the plane. "We better get her hidden in a hurry. We don't want to be discovered by any of those Mexican banditos I've heard so much about."

They pushed the little bird farther up under the palms, unloaded their bags and set to work building a breastwork of palm fronds around and over her that would keep her hidden at least until they could get her to a safer harbor.

Dudley was getting his strength back now and thinking clearly. "I'm sure I graced someone's radar scope when I went for altitude on that roller-coaster approach we made. I bet they'll send someone to search the beach along here."

"Well, she ought to be safe here for a few days. We can stay out of sight up in those dunes. Damn, but I'm hungry." Jabe calculated it'd been better than sixteen hours since he'd eaten anything. "Maybe we can find some fruit in the jungle to go with these coconuts." He threw one to Dudley as they moved out and started up the beach.

"Suits me fine. We don't want to be too close by, if the airplane gets discovered. Nothing but beach for a hundred miles up north of here."

Dudley was studying the aeronautical chart, "Let's move south and see what we can find."

They moved cautiously down the beach staying well under the cover of the palms and found some mangoes to compliment the coconuts. A hilltop overlooking the beach made a convenient lookout while they munched the wild food nature had provided. The view up and down the beach was unrestricted and they could see the little cove where the Lancair was concealed. They had the perfect vantage point for a campsite.

After their meal, they lay under the shade of some mango trees to relax, breathe easy and let the tensions of the day melt away.

Dudley remarked, "This is one hell of a situation. What in blazes are we doing here anyway?"

Jabe took stock of the situation and began a ritual recounting of their adventure blow by blow, "Now let me see if I can catch you up on some things. A few days ago we were minding our own business and then this letter came along from my granddad. So, I went to see him and he was having trouble out of some young toughs on the pueblo, see. So I tried to help him out with them, but they weren't listening. In fact they tried to kill him, so I went up and burned them out."

"That why you went up to D.C.?"

"Well, I was outgunned and had to leave there in a hurry. I had some questions that needed some answers, so I went to see Franklin Gilmer."

"He your old Navy buddy?"

"That's him. When I left the service, he stayed on and got some pretty impressive advancement at ONI—that's Naval Intel. He knew just what I needed to know. Keeps his ear to the ground like a good Indian."

"He was some help to you then?"

"Franklin told me a lot of things. Granddad is having trouble from some government people out there in the pueblo."

"The ones you said you burned out?"

"The same, together with some of their Indian hirelings. They are heavily invested in the drug traffic coming into the Southwest."

"The hell you say. Government people?"

"U.S. Customs Service, partner. Best he could tell me."

"You mean those sonsabitches we were running from back there are from the U.S. government?"

"I'm sure they are only hired help. I was as surprised as you are about it."

"Damn. This thing is really big. That means it goes all the way to the top."

"How else do you think it could be that good people's efforts to stem the drug supply into the U.S. always come to nothing? The White House appoints one Drug Czar after another, but they can't get anything done that's very effective. Last statistics I saw indicated a steady increase in drug sales, ODs, deaths, and you name it. The revenue from it must be unbelievably enormous. And who's to stop 'em?"

"Well, for all the smoke and rhetoric........."

"Nothing. That's what. Absolutely nothing's going to really put a dent in this business. There's just too much money changing hands, and those in control of it are going to do whatever they think they need to do to keep the supply moving. And that's what I ran into at the pueblo."

"Why the pueblo?"

R. Barry King

"Franklin says they want a secluded port-of-entry for landing big transports in secrecy. BIA is being duped into supporting a 'training project' that will result in construction of an airfield and a bunch of their henchmen have descended on the pueblo to force the Cacique to bless the project."

"So, that's what you ran into."

"Those bastards tried to kill my Grandpa. So, I paid them a visit. We made it look like they had killed the Cacique and he's in hiding until this thing is over. I think he'll be safe until I get back there."

"Well, how are we going to get back there, now?"

"I'm thinking, I'm thinking."

"Ooooooookay fine, old Pard. You go ahead and think. I believe I'll just ease down the beach and see what I can find. We can't stay camped here. Maybe there are some friendly folks around that we can stay with. Maybe buy some food and some gasoline for the Lancair. Looks like that might be a campfire or a cook stove under that column of smoke over there. I'll go have a look-see."

Dudley got up and started down the slope for the beach.

Jabe offered his companion a belated compliment, "By the way. My compliments to you, Cap'n. I thought you did a superb job of getting us down safely. But, next time I go flying with you, remind me to check those damn gas tanks myself."

"Yeah, yeah. The passengers are never satisfied, are they?"

Dudley made his way cautiously down the beach keeping to the cover of the tree line. Ahead of Dudley in the distance, Jabe could see a faint column of smoke rising above the treetops. That's where Dudley would head. Maybe the source of that smoke was a bread oven. Maybe even a barbecue. A settlement perhaps. And if so, who'd be there? Jabe wondered if they'd be friend or foe.

19

Jabe laid back and watched the clouds forming and evaporating overhead. He had been lost in thought for a while when he raised his head to survey the beach below. This was no time to be caught napping and all alone. He studied the shadows along the treeline in both directions, but nothing moved.

His mind traveled back to another time in Texas on a similar stretch of deserted beach on Padre Island. He remembered the woman he had shared a part of his life with.

They were both very young then. She had been fond of swimming in the surf and they had walked together barefoot along the water's edge. Time seemed to stand still when Jabe was with her and they had ventured several miles that day before they realized it. She had run up into the dunes to pick a cactus flower and had weaved it into her hair.

He felt his heart beat faster in remembrance of that scene long passed.

She had looked at him in that deep and penetrating way she had, seeming to stare right through him. She giggled at his obviously puzzled expression and ran past him round to the backside of the dune—a challenge he couldn't pass up. Jabe took the more direct route and climbed for the high ground up on top. When he looked over to find her, there was her bikini lying in the sand. All he saw was her backside. She was running toward the surf and turned to yell, "Bet you can't catch me."

Jabe was sure that he could, but he wasn't quite sure what to do when he caught her. His heart had gone to his throat and it had pounded his brain into numbness. He had never been in this kind of a situation before, and frankly he didn't have any idea what to do next.

She sent the water flying as she ran into the breakers and dived under the waves. She swam underwater and came to the surface beyond the breakers still wearing the flower in her hair.

Her face was that of an angel. Her black locks framed her face and seemed to enlarge her dark eyes. She was beautiful to him—more beautiful than any woman he had ever known.

"Come on in Jabe, the water's great. Afraid to get your hair wet?" She laughed and kicked water in his direction.

He was afraid okay, but not of wetting his hair. "Come on. You're tearing my heart out. Get your clothes on before the Beach Patrol comes along and hauls us in."

She was laughing so hard she took water and came up coughing. "Boy, are you a killjoy!" she choked.

She swam back through the breakers and then stood up and walked straight toward him. Jabe tried to look away, but it was hopeless.

Her bronzed body glistened in the sun and her black hair fell over her shoulders and framed her breasts. She was taught and trim and she had the chassis of a Vegas showgirl. Nothing to hide here. Everything was right out in the open—and for his eyes only. When they were alone together, she was completely uninhibited. He had loved that about her.

Jabe glanced back toward the breakers with his heart and his head full of that day long ago. He thought he glimpsed a movement in the sun-drenched surf, just under the water. Then it disappeared. He was sure it was his imagination. No, there it was again, something the color of shining bronze. Something very familiar.

It was her!

Suddenly he felt dizzy and very far away on that Gulf Coast beach again. He felt that familiar wetness in his eyes and that light-headed woozy sensation he'd never known what to do about. His breath came in deep gulps and his heart beat fast. Could it really be her?

Jabe stood gingerly to his feet and made his way along the line of dunes. He kept the low hills between himself and the surf. Climbing up for a better view, he peered down in anticipation. But, he had lost sight of her. Then something dark floated to the surface and he could see her clearly. The blackness of her hair framed her face again and she stood straight up in the surf—that familiar bronzed body shimmering in the sun.

Jabe's hands began to tremble and his heart went into his throat. He lifted his binoculars and frantically tried to focus. He took a step forward, but his foot sank in the soft sand. He felt his weight shift, but it was too late. He tumbled face-forward down the dune and everything went black.

The color of blue slowly filled his vision. Then puffy white clouds came clear and a shadow moved across his face. A girl was looking down at him. It was the bronze face and the black hair of the girl he had known so long ago. Tears flooded his eyes and he asked in his native tongue, "*Is it you?*"

The girl only frowned and said, "Perdona mi, Señor?"

Jabe wasn't sure where that voice had come from. It didn't match the face he was looking at. The girl he had known spoke only the native language of the pueblo. But here she was again, and only the bikini was different. This didn't feel like a dream. His head was hurting too badly for that.

Jabe held up a hand to test this apparition for reality. She took it and helped him slowly to his feet. If this was a dream, it was in full color and slow-motion!

Even though his head was throbbing and his vision was still clouded, he could see a group of men approaching from the beach. He took her hand and pulled her toward the cover of a dune, "Hit the deck before they see us." In his haste, Jabe tripped over his own feet and went face-first into the sand again.

"No, Señor. Esta mi compadres." Then she addressed the approaching group of men in Spanish.

Jabe crawled to his feet again, just in time to face the grinning Dudley, "Hey, pardner, seems I can't leave you on your own for even an hour. Did you hurt yourself?"

Jabe looked up sheepishly and sat back down to let the stars set in his head, "Well, I just didn't expect to see anything like her on this disserted beach."

Dudley laughed and introduced himself. "I hope he didn't frighten you, Señora. Jabe, this is Juan Goyona and Domingo. And I can see you've already met Juanita."

She grinned at Jabe.

He looked into her eyes and still thought he saw someone who was very familiar to him, "Yep, we've met, alright. Maybe more than once."

"Juan and his crew were camped under the jungle cover just down the beach there, but the Federales paid them a visit. That's what's left of their camp and supplies." Dudley pointed toward the column of smoke.

Juan Goyona stepped forward, "Señor, your amigo tells me that you are in need of some assistance in returning to your home. We have no gasolina for your airplane, but I think I know where we can find some." His English was not perfect, but he had the image of a fighter. He extended his hand and Jabe felt a kindred sprit in Juan's firm grip.

Juan and Juanita took the lead as the group started up the beach toward the cove where the Lancair was hidden. Jabe brushed away the sand from his shirt and navigated cautiously, with Dudley close at his side.

Dudley said, "You're not walking very straight. Did you take a tumble back there?"

"Nothing I can't handle, thank you. Are you sure you can trust these yayhoos?" Jabe straightened his sore back and tried to ignore the throb in his head.

"Just checking. After all, she told her brother you had fallen down the dune. Did she just make it all up?"

Jabe snapped, "I don't remember. I might have tripped, or something. Just knock it off, will ya? I swear you could talk a man's ears off, Cap'n."

"Yeah, yeah. The customers are never satisfied."

"What about these folks you've run into?"

"Well, I guess we'll have to trust them. They're on the run, just like we are. They're targets of the local regime. And they know their way around here, which we don't. So, what's your preference, Professor? Do we stick with them, or do we go it alone?"

Jabe thought for a moment. He had a good impression of Juan as a fighter, and he liked the firm handshake. Domingo looked like a natural guerrilla and his men seemed to be well armed. And, what Jabe liked the most, they didn't appear to be a part of the local establishment.

All told, he and Dudley seemed to be in good hands. And that Juanita! She was something else again. She was unbelievably beautiful, and she aroused feelings in Jabe that had long been asleep. Jabe wasn't quite sure what was happening to him, but he was sure he wanted to be around her. There was someone she reminded him of, and he liked being reminded.

Jabe kept his voice down, "Well, let's see where this takes us, old pal. But keep an eye out for a chance to get us out of here. You can't trust anybody in this part of the world."

They reached the Lancair and the men unshouldered their weapons to rest under the palms. Juan walked over and surveyed their hiding place and the Lancair all covered in palm fronds. "I cannot see an airplane in there, Señor. You have hidden it well. I think it will be safe here for a little while. But we must get you some gasolina, so you can be on your way. It would not do to have that Colonel Gomez come along and find you here."

Juan turned toward his men, "That Gomez is a little slow in the cabeza, even for a Federale, eh Domingo?"

But, it was Diego who emerged from the jungle trail directly behind Juan, "Si Amigo, but he can be very destructive. Just look at what he has done to my little cabana." He managed a wry grin as he nodded toward the smoke rising from his burned out hacienda. His small company of guerrillas joined the other men under the palms and set down their backpacks and weapons.

Juan turned and threw up his arms to welcome Diego, "I am surprised to see you, my cousin. I thought you would be captured by now."

"Oh, I think I can keep out of trouble with that Gomez. Can the chicken outsmart the fox? He is a slow fellow, that Gomez."

"Oh, he is a slow fellow, is he?"

"Oh, si. Even now, he is out looking for you in the jungle. And here you are on the beach. I see you have some company, Juan."

Juan turned to Jabe and Dudley, "Let me introduce my cousin Diego. He is the fox who outsmarts the chicken." Diego shook hands with Jabe and Dudley.

"The fox who takes the chicken's money as well." Diego produced a new bag of gold and tossed it to Juan.

"Well, come and join us for a little siesta, Diego, and tell me how the fox is getting along these days and how he comes by his money so easily. What did you tell the Colonel that was worth this kind of dinero?" Juan dumped a pile of the gold 50-peso coins into his hand and showed them around.

"Just that I had seen you moving inland and that you were locating a new camp over that ridge," Diego was pointing toward the green hills in the distance. "He pays very well for bad information." He laughed at his own brilliance.

"And how long will it be until he discovers I am not there and comes looking for me again, Diego?"

"Oh, he will find you alright. I have provided a little surprise for him in the hills over there. When my men start shooting at him, he will think it is you and the price on your head will go up again. Then the bad information I give him will be worth even more." Diego seemed confident in his scheme.

Juan just shook his head and laughed, "Diego. You will be the death of me some day."

The group of comrades sat down for a chat and shared a military ration. Juan told Jabe and Dudley about his campaign to drive out the drug traders, thugs and bandits who controlled his jungle home. He told about how they occasionally downed a drug plane with rifle fire.

"So you were the ones who shot up my Twin Beech?

"Que? You were a pilot for these outlaws?"

Jabe laid out the facts for Juan and he seemed satisfied. Under the shade of the palms, Juan laid out their strategy.

"I have a brother who works for the drug traders and services their fleet of airplanes. When they ship drugs to the Norte, he has a bad habit of rigging the fuel pumps to a timer. It shuts off the flow of gasolina to the engines just as they fly over our part of the jungle. The crew never lives through the crash. Then we have another load of drugs to burn and maybe some new weapons and bullets."

Jabe felt a shiver go up his spine and felt quite the lucky one indeed to have escaped such a fate. That was probably what had happened to his friend Skeeter.

"Sometimes the airplanes carry American dollars as well. Then our people can buy a few comforts and put some clothes on their children and the old ones. So, that is why Gomez is after us."

Jabe was listening intently and trying to avoid the distraction of looking in Juanita's direction. She was taking a snooze in the shade and was still wearing that skimpy bikini. It was all he could do to keep from staring at her, so he kept both eyes on the beach toward the South.

Then he saw something catching the glint of the midday sun. Jabe thought it was the sheen of the rollers crashing on the beach maybe a mile or so away. He studied the motion and noted the rhythm of the flashes. He figured it had to be the reflection of the sun bouncing off the windshield of a vehicle coming towards them. The image grew steadily in size and several distinct forms became evident. It was a column of trucks.

"Is that your friend Gomez?" Jabe motioned toward the south.

Juan took one look, "I think the chicken has found the fox, Diego."

He motioned toward the south as he stood up, then grabbed Juanita by the hand and helped her to her feet. "I do not believe we will be staying for siesta."

20

Jabe watched the column of trucks coming steadily toward them. Juan and his men quickly hefted their equipment and swept the sand clean of any evidence that they had been there.

Diego gave orders to his men, then turned to Juan. "I think you will be safe in those caves up on the ridge. If you hurry and get up there, I can send this chicken off to chase the wild gooses. Then I will join you there."

Juan was obviously worried that Diego might get caught, "What makes you think Gomez will believe you again, amigo?"

"Well, you see, he is not dead and he still has all his trucks. That can only mean he did not go where I sent him, or that my men did not get there in time. They were ready to blow him apart. Or, perhaps he did not believe me. I will find out. Now, go quickly. I will see that the Colonel does not get close to your airplane, Señores."

Juan started everyone for the caves. They kept low and made for the high ground up on the ridge. Diego and some of his men stayed behind on the beach to meet Gomez, stopping him short of the hidden Lancair.

When Jabe and the others were well along their way up the trail he stopped and looked back toward the beach through his binoculars. He could see Diego in conversation with the Federale Colonel. Diego was waving his arms and gesturing wildly, but the Colonel only shook his head. This time Diego would get no gold.

Jabe turned to follow the rest of the company up the hill and was startled to find Juanita waiting for him.

"Vamos a la caverna, Señor Jabe."

She half-grinned every time she spoke to him and it made him jealous of that lucky Juan to have such a fine-looking wife. Jabe happily followed the curvy Juanita up the hill. He was wearing a half-grin of his own.

As they approached the caves, they were met by some of Diego's men coming down from another trail. They engaged Juan in conversation. Juan translated for Jabe and Dudley, "They have missed the Colonel up in the hills, so Diego has some explaining to do. Gomez has been here and searched the caves already, so he thinks we are somewhere else. Very good, no?"

"Very good, yes," Dudley said. "He thinks the place is deserted, right?"

Juan replied, "Oh, si. We can camp here in peace for a while. Diego will send Gomez to another part of the country for now. And these fellows will go and wait for him and this time they will arrive in plenty of time to give Gomez a proper welcome. Gomez will think he has found me there. Then the price of Diego's bad information will go up again."

They made camp in the shelter of the caves. Then Jabe and Dudley moved out to the cliffs to see how Diego was getting along with the Colonel.

The column of trucks was moving back up the beach and Jabe could see Diego and his men coming up the trail toward the caves. Jabe felt a hand squeeze his arm and turned to find Juanita close beside him.

"Diego comes aqui, no?" She was staring at him with a peculiar look in her eyes. Jabe's heart started pounding and he went light-headed. He liked being close to her, but he sure wished she wouldn't do this kind of thing in broad daylight.

Dudley was peering through his binocs, "Yep, here comes Diego." Then he turned and saw the look on Juanita's face and realized she was not really interested in what Diego was doing at all. Jabe's gaze was fixed on hers and Dudley could only make a whistling sound at what he saw.

"I think she really likes you, J.B."

Jabe was frozen. He wished he could say something. But, what? She tightened her grip on his arm and his blood ran way too hot. What was this woman trying to do to him? She was obviously with Juan. So why was she behaving like this? Maybe she just enjoyed teasing. Well, he would have nothing to do with this kind of situation. Right now he and Dudley needed the friendship and good will of their benefactor. Juan was their only meal ticket and they needed the safety he could afford them until they could strike out for home. Jabe needed some excuse to look away, but he was definitely enjoying the emotions he was feeling. Damn, but she was captivating!

Juanita heard it first. She broke eye contact and looked out to sea. Then Jabe came to his senses and recognized the familiar drone of a Lockheed Hercules in the distance. By the time Jabe got his bearings, Dudley was already on target with his powerful binoculars. The C-130 was about three miles out and headed straight for them.

Dudley studied the oncoming transport, "She's awfully low over the water, J.B. Obviously ducking radar. I wonder where she's headed."

At that moment, they were startled by a black cabin twin that came from behind them, roared over their heads and down over the beach on a course opposite to the inbound Lockheed. The sound of its approach had been masked by the drone of the Hercules. The twin was on a course toward the States—the precise direction from which the Herkybird had come.

Juan came up quickly from behind them with an AK-47, dropped to one knee and began shooting at the twin as it departed the coast. He fired without any obvious effect until he emptied the clip. "That is one of their airplanes taking drugs to the norte, señor. We have shot down six or seven of them already. And there is one of the big ones. They know we can shoot down the little ones over the jungle, so they will be flying the big ones over the water now. Then our rifles are useless."

The Lockheed flew past the twin about a mile offshore and the two pilots rocked their wings in salute. The twin continued out to sea and the big transport turned toward the south just above the waves about a half mile offshore.

Jabe was still trying to ignore the attentions of Juanita. Dudley surmised, "Well, the pilots sure knew each other. Did you see all that wing-waggling going on?"

Jabe had seen it alright, but he didn't answer. At Juan's approach, he had expected Juanita to react by releasing his arm, but she only held on. This was more than he could stand. But, he didn't want to cause an incident here in front of his host, even though Juan seemed to ignore the attention she was paying him.

A grinning Diego approached them from along the ridge, "Ah, mi amigo. I heard you shooting. But, you only give the gringo plane a little kiss goodbye."

At the mention of a kiss, Juanita tightened her grip again.

Jabe needed to get out of this box she had him in. In a moment he said, "Con permiso," and knelt down to tie his shoe, gently breaking her hold on his arm. He went to his knees and sat there on the ground Indian-style. Juanita only frowned at him.

Juan greeted Diego, "Como se va, amigo? And what kind of a story did you have for the Colonel this time?"

"Oh, he was very sorry to have missed running into you. He even wanted his money back. But, I sent him to search another trail. You were seen there only an hour ago. This time my men will be there on time to give him a proper reception and he will think it is you. He will find his wild gooses this time and they will give him his money's worth. But, I do not think he will be back for a while. He say that Juan Goyona cannot cause him any more trouble. He say they will be flying far out to sea from now on."

"Si amigo, and there goes a shipment even now." Juan indicated the departing twin. I am afraid when they begin to use the big ones, we will not be able to stop them anymore." Juan shaded his eyes and watched the low-flying C-130 continue south along the beach in the distance. "Now you can relax and enjoy the peace and quiet, Diego. I think we will be of little bother to them now."

Diego considered the situation, then he said sadly, "Si, now I will have peace and quiet. But, what will I do for an income?"

Juan thought for a moment in silence as they headed back to the caves. "Well my friend, the drugs will pass us by on their way to the norte and perhaps the violence will go with them. We can return to our homes once more and live a good life without all of this trouble."

Diego summoned his men and prepared them to move out. "Come, mi amigos. The Colonel is waiting to chase us again. And this time he will have to go home on his foots. Adios, my cousin. Hasta luego." He took his column of men down the trail to meet Gomez at the appointed rendezvous. His men were heavily loaded with ordinance.

Moving inside the cave, Juan looked at Jabe and Dudley and began to sound a little more hopeful, "And now maybe we can be rid of that Gomez for good. Amigos, we will make camp and rest here for a while. Then we will see if we can help the two of you get back to your home. Juanita will prepare a good meal for us in the morning. I believe you will enjoy her cooking."

Juan gathered his weapon and a fresh canteen of water from the supplies, then headed outside again, "Domingo, por favor, have one of your men assist me. We will take the first turn at night guard. You will relieve us at midnight, no?"

Juan apparently saw some satisfaction in this turn of events. Jabe saw something different. He had no way of knowing what was going on back home on the pueblo, but his Grandfather was still at risk and he needed to get back there.

On the other hand, here he was in the middle of the drug superhighway and he wondered if this might not be the better place for him right now. There weren't any airports within 200 miles of here. So, where had that cabin twin come from and where was the

C-130 heading? Some clandestine strip in the interior, no doubt. The twins were a liability to them now, so the long-legged C-130s were being brought in to increase the payloads and they had the ability to penetrate into the U.S. interior. The smugglers had shifted into overdrive now and it was clear from what Franklin had said that they were planning a new destination for their shipments—the pueblo.

Settling into the cave for some much-needed rest, Jabe and Dudley chose a distant corner away from the others. Juanita lay close to the fire and slept. Jabe could not get over how she reminded him of his sweetheart of long ago. He watched her lying there in the dim light and his thoughts drifted far away to that other time and place.

"What ya thinking, Pardner?" Dudley was watching the face of a man he knew very well.

"Who, me?" Jabe was straight-faced even for an Indian, but he knew his friend could sometimes see right into his mind. "I was wondering where we go from here, Cap'n."

"Well, that's not really what you were thinking about, but we do have some options." Dudley had been thinking as well.

"And they would be?"

"Well, for one, we could take that vacation and stay here all season." Dudley knew that choice had its own set of problems.

"And what would we use for money?"

"Good point. Or we could get some gas and go back home, right?"

Jabe was less than enthusiastic, "Back to Galveston and a royal reception by those goons at Scholes Field, eh?"

"Well, I don't think I want to go back there. A hotel clerk can find work anywhere and there are other ports besides Galveston for your kind of work."

Jabe could see problems with all the options. "With things the way they are back home, we might be better off staying down here for a while. The Cacique will be safe with Hahtahway."

Dudley was losing confidence in his own suggestions, "Well, what in hell are we going to do down here if we stay? We've got no money, no food, and no way to get any, right?"

Jabe considered the thought, "I don't really know that, yet. Maybe we can get some help from Juan on that account. I only know that I'm not going back until I can figure out how to fix a bad situation out there on the pueblo. If I go back without a trump card to play, they'll damn sure build and operate that landing strip at their leisure and have those big birds dropping huge loads of dope right in my backyard. And they'll like as not try to kill me again. No peace in that."

Dudley was a man in search of a plan. "Well then, let's see what our Mexican friends can do for us. Maybe we can stay until the heat's off, then get some Avgas and head back north. We can figure out what to do about your problem back home on our own soil where we at least know the language. Then we can leave this jungle behind for good."

"Cap'n, you can read my mind like a book. I can't see much use in staying here any longer than we have to." The two comrades settled back for some R&R and they'd wait for a chance to break out on their own.

Jabe tried to relax and actually napped a little here and there, but something kept gnawing at his insides. The feeling lingered there just like it used to while he waited for the order to jump off on a Seal mission. It was something ominous.

He knew the feeling well enough to keep his reflexes sharp. He remembered the first time he had ever felt it. He was only a lad then, but he had sensed the eerie quiet and listened to the faint rustle of the prairie. He was experiencing that same old strange sensation again. He had lain awake deep into the night and listened while the others had slept. He had heard the birds moving in the dead of night, restless when they should have been roosting quietly.

It had been silent at first. Then the sound had come all of a sudden. He had been the first in his family to hear the rocks rumble and to feel the earth move. It had frightened everyone in the pueblo. That had been his first time to experience an earthquake.

Now, remembering the terror of that night long ago, although he felt quite drowsy he tried to keep alert even though Dudley and the others were fast asleep by now. Just as he began to feel a little more at ease, he felt that familiar tremble in the ground.

Then all hell broke loose outside.

21

The first explosion jolted Jabe wide awake and he was on his feet in an instant. From somewhere down the coast came a rumble familiar to any military man. It was the sound of a raging battle. The thunder started in the distance and then moved closer until it rolled past with ear-splitting intensity. Everyone in the cave came alive and sat straight up.

The whump of mortar rounds falling into the ground punctuated the thunder. Now and again Jabe could hear the sharp twang of steel against steel as a round found its target. First came the sound of the detonation, then the tremble in the ground and the puff of wind as the shockwave passed.

The staccato chatter of small arms provided the treble notes in this symphony of destruction. The hellish racket went on for several more minutes. And suddenly it was over. Then came the silence—the terrible silence. Only Death makes such a sound.

Domingo, who was lying nearby, spoke first, "That will be the welcome that Diego arranged for Gomez. The Colonel pays very well to get beat up so badly. He is one of those hombres who pays someone else to hurt them. He es muy loco, I think. Do you have these kooky ones in your own country, Señor Dudley?"

"I hear tell," Dudley replied. "But our kooks only go in for whips and chains, usually."

"Whips and chains? Aye, yi-yi!" Domingo couldn't believe his ears. "I think I would rather face the mortars and the bullets, señor."

Dudley saw Juanita turn away and giggle. He thought he'd have to agree with Domingo's analysis.

Domingo continued, "But, maybe that will be the last of the Colonel for a while. Diego will take his time getting back here, so the Colonel cannot follow. I think he will not trouble us any longer. He always gets, how you say, the small end of the bargain. But we are very low on weapons and bullets. That was the last of the mortar rounds. They found a good use while we had them. I will not miss seeing the Colonel again. He was a lot of trouble to us."

Jabe thought Domingo was just the kind of help he liked having around. He and Diego and their men were all in their middle years and physically fit.

Jabe asked, "Where did your men learn to fight as they do, Domingo, and how do you get your weapons and supplies?"

"Me and my men? We were all in the war against the Sandinistas. We went down to Nicaragua to fight along with the, how you say..... the Contras. Many of us still have familia in Nicaragua. We went there to fight the Communists, the Sandinistas, when we were young men and we got our training from the Gringos who were sent to help. Juan was our Capitan then. And so he remains."

"And how do you get your munitions? Your bullets?"

Oh, the Gringos, they gave us mucho supplies when they left us to fend for ourselves. Until recently, we had no use for it. And then the drug dealers and outlaws came into our country. So, we began to fight them. And then came this Colonel Gomez. He has kept us very busy and now we are short of bullets. We will have to go into the jungle and get some more."

"Where do you find bullets in the jungle, Domingo?"

"There was a little place that I had. I called it my little rancho. Under the floor in the basement, we kept a little room full of guns and bullets and a field mortar left over from the old days when we were at war. But it is all gone now, as you saw. We have been very busy, señor."

Dudley settled back to relax again. "Yeah, we can see that you have, Domingo."

A voice came from the entrance, "Si, very busy indeed. Domingo, did you hear the welcome that Diego gave to the Colonel?" It was Juan returning from his turn at night watch.

Domingo turned to wink at Jabe, "Aye, Caramba. Si, Capitan. That Diego makes enough rackets to wake up the dead ones. It is enough to keep a man from his sleep."

"Si, he is a very noisy fellow. But, that will be the last of the noise from Diego for a while. We are getting very low on bullets." Juan took a place on the floor near the entrance to rest. "In the morning, Domingo, you will take a little walk into the jungle. And I will wait here for Diego."

"Si, si, Capitan," Domingo replied, heading out for his turn at night watch. "We will go in the mañana."

The small group of weary comrades fell back to rest. The day had taken its toll on all of them and Jabe slipped into a deep slumber that was a rare thing for him. He dreamed of Juanita. And then the vision shifted to another beautiful woman he had known so long ago. He was on the beach again. He was smiling at her as she approached him. She reached out to touch him and he felt....... someone gently shaking his shoulder.

He looked up sleepily and saw Juan leaning over him. The dim light of dawn filtered through the cave opening. Had he been so sound asleep that he hadn't even heard the approach of another human? 'Wow,' he thought, 'I must really be exhausted.'

"Señor, would you like something to eat?" Juan handed him a tortilla filled with roast pork. "I have some of Juanita's carne adovada for you. I will meet you outside when you are ready to go."

"Go? Where are we going, Juan?" Jabe was still not awake enough to remember the previous night's conversation.

"Domingo will take you to the bunker, señor. You will enjoy a little walk in the jungle. With any luck, you may even find that Gomez. We can never tell where he will show up again."

Domingo was standing ready to depart, "And I suppose we could throw some rocks at him, no?"

Jabe wondered if these guys ever slept. He got himself together and shook Dudley awake. They wolfed down their pork burritos and grabbed spare canteens for the journey. Jabe savored the spicy breakfast and looked at Dudley who seemed to be breathing heavily and had sort of a tear in his eye.

"Man, this stuff is hot, hot, hot!" Dudley pulled hard on his canteen. "But good, good, good." He grinned, now fully awake and ready for an adventure.

Domingo and several of his men moved out down the hill into the jungle. They formed the head of the column as Jabe and Dudley fell in behind. Not far inland, they came upon what looked like an old helicopter landing zone. The clearing was fairly overgrown now. Small saplings lined the perimeter and prairie grass covered the ground. Domingo led the column toward the far side of the clearing and up a small rise.

Jabe sensed they were walking on the roof of an underground bunker. Domingo stopped and motioned for Jabe to come up. He pointed down the far slope to a dip in the earth that was barely visible.

"Here it is, señor. And we hope Gomez never finds this place."

Jabe could see that they were standing on the mounded earthen roof of a military ammo vault. He followed Domingo down as they made their way around to the bottom of the dip. Domingo pulled away the undergrowth enough to reveal a rusted steel door. Sure enough, it was the familiar double-door of an ammo dump. The door was unlocked and it swung easily on its stainless steel hinges. 'Remarkable,' Jabe thought. After all these years, it wasn't even rusted shut. Amazing thing, that good old Yankee ingenuity!

Dudley joined Jabe and Domingo inside the bunker. The floor was strewn with ammo boxes and gun cases. Domingo's men went through them and selected the items they needed, loaded their packs and headed outside again.

Domingo said, "Diego will need some more of these mortar rounds." Then to one of his men, "Pepe, por favor. Toma usted una pocos de estos, tambien."

Pepe, Jabe and Dudley each hefted a box of the mortar rounds and headed out the door.

Once outside, the men took the cover of the jungle to rest up for the trip back. The sun was getting high and the heat and humidity was stifling. Domingo lay down for a smoke on his pipe and launched into a jovial conversation as Jabe and Dudley sat on their ammo boxes and mopped their faces.

"We have been here three times now and we always take away all we can carry. There is a lot more here than we will ever need. And the bullets, they always work just fine. We never find any deads." Domingo drew a long pull at his pipe and blew three perfect smoke rings.

"You mean duds?" Dudley suggested.

"Si, señor. The bullets are always alive, never dead." Domingo lifted his arms as if aiming an imaginary rifle into the branches overhead and squeezed the invisible trigger, "You always know that when you pull the trigger they will always shoot. And they are getting very old now."

Then he lowered his arms and looked at Dudley, "But, they look just like new. I remember one time when we were fighting the Sandinistas. It was back in the Civil War. We were given some weapons that my countrymen had bought from some Asian supplier. And many times when you pulled the trigger, they did not shoot. You never knew if they were going to work or not. I prefer to stake my life on the Americano goods. And especially when they are free."

Dudley agreed, "And myself, señor."

Jabe was listening to a low-pitched drone that was approaching from somewhere.

Dudley continued, "When I was a kid, I had one of those cheap rifles from China, and...."

"Knock it off, Dudley, and listen. Do you hear that?" Jabe was straining to catch the sound again.

The drone grew louder and the men tightened up against the tree trunks for cover. The jungle canopy vibrated and leaves fell as a C-130 flew past low overhead. It was traveling at top speed just over the treetops and there wasn't time to get its bearing before it thundered past and disappeared toward the north. It was undoubtedly headed for the U.S.

Domingo never moved a muscle as he lay up against his tree trunk. Puffing on his pipe again, he said, "There they go again, señor. They are not afraid of flying over the jungle in those big planes. They know they are safe from our rifles. You can never get off a shot when they are so fast. They do not go by the roads any more. We stop them too easily on the roads. And they cannot carry as much in a truck. So, now they go in the air. They are more visible out to sea, but our rifles cannot reach them when they fly over the water."

Jabe was thinking again, "Domingo, are there any big machine guns in the bunker?" That remark got Dudley's attention and he sat up to take notice.

"No, señor. Only the weapons my men are using and they cannot help against an airplane as fast as that."

Dudley was quick to inquire, "Are there any more ammo dumps around here, Domingo?"

"Only one other that I have seen. It is in the jungle, not far from here. But it has no bullets or guns. Only bombas. And they are no good to us."

"Bombs?" Jabe thought for a minute, then turned to look at Dudley.

Dudley had a peculiar look on his face, "Bombs? Here in the jungle? There ain't any airports around here that can support jets. And helicopters don't carry bombs."

"Exactamundo, Cap'n. What say we go have a look-see? Domingo, do you think you can find this place again?"

"Si. It is very near to here."

It was a short two mile hike up the coast. They found the earthen bunker and forced the door open. There on the floor were neatly stacked rows of metal tubes about eight feet long and twelve inches or so in diameter. They were painted the familiar military olive drab. Jabe could read the MilSpec numbers stenciled in black, but he couldn't remember what they meant.

Dudley started prying an end off one of the metal cylinders and Jabe issued a caution, "Better be ginger with that thing, old Pard. The H.E. is old enough to be unstable."

"Well, looky here." A surprised Dudley was peering into one of the cylinders and Jabe joined him. There in the half-light was the red head of an IR-fuse. These were not bombs. They were looking at the business end of a heat-seeking air-to-air missile. And the bunker contained several dozens of them.

Jabe couldn't believe their luck, "Imagine that, old Pard. Missiles! And they didn't store these things very far away from their active air operations. Must have had an airstrip close by. Domingo, is there an old airstrip near here?"

"Si señor, on the other side of the trees." Domingo pointed over his shoulder.

Jabe and Dudley followed Domingo out of the bunker and through a line of trees that bordered a clearing in the jungle. The old gravel airstrip angled slightly downhill toward the beach. It measured 200 feet wide and about a thousand yards in length. Patches of brush grew here and there on the hard-packed surface. There were several Quonset huts still standing near the trees.

Dudley surveyed the strip with the keen eye of a pilot, "These old strips weren't much to look at, but they'd handle a whole squadron of A-1s, J.B. Those were the types sent down here to train and equip the Contras. When the training was completed and they transferred the aircraft, they were nice enough to leave some ordinance behind when they pulled out. Probably thought they'd have to come back here again someday."

Dudley and Jabe quickly inspected the huts. The faded sign over one of the doors optimistically read "BASE OPS". Inside were a few metal tables and chairs that were solid rust from the jungle humidity, but the floors were dry. A look inside the larger building proved it had been an engine shop. Jabe studied the place carefully—the doors were wide enough to accept a small homebuilt aircraft.

Dudley glanced quickly around, "Nothing we can use in here."

Jabe was thinking ahead of his friend, "Hold on, Cap'n. That palm-thatch cover we left over your Lancair will be turning brown by now, and that's certain to attract attention. Soon as we can find some gas, we could move it up here and store it out of the rain. Let's get some of the brush cleared off the runway and look for some gasoline."

"Not a bad idea at all, I'd wager." Dudley was in full agreement and spoke briefly with Domingo.

Domingo's men used their machetes to clear away some of the taller brush to allow Cloud Dancer enough clearance to land, but they left enough undergrowth so as not to make the old strip look freshly cleared.

They moved out for the trip back. Between them, Jabe and Dudley carried one of the missile tubes. Jabe knew that Dudley had excelled in his military ordinance training. Maybe these missiles would come in handy against Gomez, if he dared to come back again. And somewhere in this backwater jungle, Jabe hoped they'd find a few gallons of gasoline. The Lancair was their only hope of avoiding a very long walk back to Texas.

22

Back at the camp again, Jabe and Dudley arrived with their newly-acquired ordinance and found the dank cave air alive with the aroma of Juanita's cooking. She was preparing masa and baking tortillas on a flat skillet. Jabe resisted the temptation to approach her. She glanced at Jabe and threw him a smile.

Juan was in conversation with Diego who was relating his most recent success against Gomez. Diego was enjoying the first hot meal he'd had in quite a while.

Juan asked, "And I have been wondering, Diego. How did I do in my battle against the Colonel this time?"

"Oh, mi Capitan, you did very well at first. The Colonel took a beating and then he chased you away toward the western beaches before losing you in the jungle as always. But, now he has no more trucks. So, he must go home. And, since he believes he has chased you away, I do not believe he will return again soon. Perhaps he will fly over once in a while. But his trucks and Jeeps are blown all to hell."

Jabe and Dudley set the canister down in a far corner of the cave and made for the chow.

Juan saw the burden they carried and asked, "Por favor, what have you there? One of the Gringo bombas? It is enough to blow us all to hell and save Gomez the trouble."

Dudley was quick to reassure, "Oh, it won't hurt anybody Juan. It's safe enough without this. The fuses have to be armed before the thing will detonate." Dudley held the explosive initiator in his hand and tossed it over to Juan, who eyed the odd-looking thing suspiciously.

Juan did not seem convinced, "Just the same, I will be much more comfortable if you will set that thing outside of here."

Jabe answered, "Okay, Juan. Come give me a hand and we'll move it right now." By now, Jabe had a plate of chow in one hand and held one end of the canister in the other. Juan gave assistance and they carried the missile outside again.

They set the canister down and Juan took a seat on a rock ledge while Jabe dug into the chow. "Domingo tells me you saw the old airstrip."

"Yep, he took us up there and showed us around."

"And what is this that you have found in that old bunker, señor? Is it something we can use, no?"

"Well, I don't know yet, Juan. The bunker is full of airborne ordinance. No machine guns or the like. But, if we can figure a way to use these missiles, they might come in handy." Jabe patted the canister.

"So, they may be useful against the Federales?"

"And maybe against the drug shipments as well."

Juan threw out his chest and smiled his biggest grin, "Aye, caramba. You can always count on Juan Goyona. He can find you anything you need. Even in the jungle." Then his face wrinkled into a frown, "What are they, señor Jabe?"

"Juan, they are rockets that can be fired from airplanes. They can hit another airplane from very far away."

"Ah, muy bueno. And you can carry them in your little aeroplane, no?"

"Well, no. I don't think so, Juan. It takes a much bigger airplane than we've got. The best we could ever hope to do is to figure out some way to fire them from the ground."

Jabe moved back toward the cover of the cave with food on his mind and Juan followed.

"And you could hit the big airplanes they are sending over the water?" Juan was very astute for a jungle guerrilla and never missed a beat.

"I think not. That would take a lot more equipment than we have to work with here in the jungle, Juan." Jabe held out little hope that the missiles could be used against the C-130s.

Juanita met them with steaming plates of her best enchiladas.

Juan said, "Gracias, Juanita. Muchisa mas gracias."

She smiled and winked at Jabe, then turned and went back to her work. Jabe wished she wouldn't do that. She seemed to be paying very little attention to her husband.

"That is too bad, señor Jabe," Juan was disappointed.

Then he announced, "But, I almost forget. Señores, Diego has brought you a little surprise. Diego, por favor. Show us the gasolina."

A smiling Diego produced two red Jerry cans whose paint was slightly scorched. "We took these from the trucks that Gomez will no longer need for they are blown all to hell, señores. And Gomez has now taken to traveling on his foots."

Dudley came over, grabbed the cans and opened one. He sniffed the contents and then smiled at Jabe. "It's gasoline, alright. Truck fuel, but they're both full."

"How far will this much get us, Cap'n?"

Ten gallons? It's only a fraction of what we'll need to make the hop north over the Gulf, but we'll take whatever we can get." He took Diego's hand and shook it. "Gracias, Diego. Muchas gracias. Are there any more?"

Diego shrugged his shoulders and grinned, "Not today. Maybe mañana."

Jabe spoke up, "Well then, ten gallons is all we've got for now. Thanks, Diego. It'll just have to do. Now, the sooner we can get the airplane moved, the better."

Dudley agreed, "Let's get cracking."

Jabe saw that Juanita had taken an interest as she whispered something to Juan who spoke up, "Juanita would like to see the little airplane. Por favor, can she come along too?"

Before Jabe could object, Dudley answered, "Sure she can."

But, Juanita was looking at Jabe. "Gracias, señor." Then to Dudley, "Muchesa mas gracias."

Out on the beach, they found the airplane wet from an early morning shower. The little bird was quite dirty under its wilting canopy of palm fronds, but unmolested. With help from their friends, Dudley and Jabe managed to push Cloud Dancer back out onto the hard sand near water's edge. Then they emptied the Jerry cans into the right wing tank.

Jabe replaced to fuel cap and said, "Well, ten gallons might be all we have, Cap'n. But it's enough to get her to safe harbor. Best I can recall, those tanks were empty for sure when we landed. One day you'll ding her pretty airframe, if you're not careful."

"You ever gunna let me forget that episode, J.B.?"

"Not before I have my fun with you."

"Okay, J.B. old pardner. I guess I'll just have to put up with that for awhile longer. So why don't you take this bird up to the strip for me? Think you can do that? You didn't seem to like my flying coming in here."

"Oh, your flying was terrific. Absolutely perfect. It was your fuel management that needed some tweaking. But, I can fly her up there, if you wish." Jabe was looking at Juanita and saw her anticipation. Her cutoff shorts and halter top showed off the absolute legal limit of her own pretty airframe.

Dudley retorted, "I wish you would. I brought her in here on pure adrenaline and I don't think I could stand putting any dings in that air-frame, after all my hard work at building her from the ground up. I know every rivet, every bulkhead, and every inch of her skin. And she ain't got any flaws."

Jabe was studying another flawless frame—Juanita's. "No flaws at all, I'd say."

Dudley asked Juan to send two of his men upwind to survey the beach for any trash or debris that might make for a hazardous takeoff. Then he personally checked the wheels for clinging brush while Jabe performed the customary preflight walk-around.

Dudley signaled the wheels were clear and Jabe climbed into the left seat and tried the master switch. The gyros came to life and the fuel pump pressure climbed into the green. He switched on the magnetos.

"CLEAR PROP," he yelled.

Juan and Juanita stepped back a few paces. Dudley glanced around and held a thumb's up. Jabe cranked the engine and applied two shots of the fuel primer, coaxing the Lycoming to life. It caught and ran slightly rough at first, just as usual. Then it settled into its regular smooth idle and Jabe motioned for Juanita to board from behind the wing.

With Dudley's help, she gracefully ascended the wing and settled into the right seat giggling and wearing the biggest grin Jabe had ever seen. He seemed more comfortable with her, now that she was on his turf. She still had a faintly familiar look, but Jabe was sure he'd never seen a woman quite like Juanita before—ever.

Jabe nudged the throttle up to taxi revs and turned her down the beach and into the wind. He checked the oil temperature and saw it was in the green. Then, switching through both mags and noticing no drop in the RPMs, he pulled the canopy closed and gunned it. The little plane lunged forward and Jabe rotated the nose-wheel off the sand and let her build airspeed. In barely more than a hundred yards Cloud Dancer was off the deck and headed for the big blue. Jabe tucked up the wheels and turned out over the water, climbing for altitude.

He was careful to keep the Lancair low enough to ensure they wouldn't show up on any radar screens. He stole a glance at Juanita who had been giggling and grinning since climbing aboard. She was aghast at the view from their altitude of a hundred feet. "Ay-ay-ay!..... Caramba!..... Aye, Chihuahua!"..... All of which meant "_WOW_" in any language.

Jabe turned inland for the airstrip. Even though he knew he had to conserve the precious little fuel they had, he couldn't resist making a dive for the low ridge of hills behind the beach. He arced Cloud Dancer around, then he split the valley between two of the highest dunes and blew past a tall palm tree. He played in and out of the dunes while Juanita shrieked with laughter. Climbing toward the airstrip, Jabe spotted a rain shower not far away. He made for it and gave the little bird a quick dowsing. The dirt and dust came away quickly. Dudley would appreciate the wash job.

Turning for the strip, Jabe powered back and set up a shallow glide that put them over the runway about fifty feet high. He flew the length of the clearing and found it free of obstacles, so he climbed out and circled back for a landing.

Cloud Dancer touched down and Jabe brought her to a stop in front of the old abandoned engine shop. He cut the switch and rolled the canopy back, unbuckled Juanita's seat belt first and then his own and climbed out. When he came around the tail, she was standing on the wing root waiting for him to assist her. His heart took that old familiar leap into his throat as he realized he would actually have to put his arms around this beautiful woman in order to help her down off the wing.

He stopped in his tracks and approached slowly, offering his hand only. He still considered her off limits.

She just put her hands on her gorgeous hips and frowned at him, "Señor Jabe, por favor." She held out both arms and beckoned to him, then tipped forward and lost her balance.

Before he knew it, he quickly moved to catch the giggling Juanita. She caught and held him tightly and made sure there was plenty of body contact as she slid down into his waiting arms.

Jabe let her down easily and then looked around to check the treeline for the imminent approach of Juan and the others.

"Okay!" Jabe managed to let out some of the air he had been holding and noticed she wasn't letting go right away. Her eyes came up to his and froze his attention. Jabe was lost in those dark, flashing, mesmerizing eyes.

"Okay," she repeated and pulled herself up to kiss him smack on the mouth.

Jabe felt what seemed like a sledge hammer pounding his brain. He also felt a shiver of anticipation running the length of his spine. He felt a lot of things all at once. But, one thing he didn't feel..... was the need to let go. He found himself kissing back and although he couldn't condone the feelings he was having, he knew he wanted her.

All he could hear was the quick rhythm of her breathing and his own pulse pounding in his head. Then slowly, the sounds of the jungle returned and he could hear the call of birds and the whisper of the wind in the trees—and the sounds of the men approaching from the beach. He let her go and tried to look cool.

"Well, praise the Lord, Pardner. You got her here in one piece," Dudley sounded genuinely glad Cloud Dancer had survived the transit from the beach. Or was he referring to Juanita? Jabe hoped he hadn't seen the kiss.

Juan was not far behind, "Now my little Juanita has become a little bird that flies in the sky. Por favor, Juanita. To tu gozar de volar in la fermamento?"

Juanita was quiet and subdued and still looking at Jabe when she replied, "Oh, mucho gusto, Juan. Mucho gusto." Jabe thought she sounded less than convincing.

But Juan did not seem to notice. "Bueno, bueno. Now we can move the little bird into this fine garaje those Gringos built for us."

Dudley orchestrated the placement of the Lancair inside the maintenance shed with the help of Juan's men. Jabe followed them inside, and in the dim light of the interior he noticed a row of dust-covered equipment boxes along the back wall. He unlatched one and raised the lid. Inside he saw what looked like radio equipment.

"What have we over here, Cap'n?"

Dudley came over and peered inside, "Well, dang me for sure! It's their base communications gear and I haven't seen any of these relics since the late '60s."

"You know what they are, Pard?" Jabe wasn't sure they were anything very useful.

"Just a bunch of communications gear from the last war. They use vacuum tubes and they've been obsolete for decades. Looks like a base transmitter and a receiver. Built to run on 12 volts DC. Those smaller units are spares for the fighter planes."

Dudley was fingering a smaller black box with several short wires attached, and mumbling, "I don't have a clue as to what this thing is.

Whatever it is, it belongs in an airplane. Uses 24 volts, has an output terminal, uses a connector that looks like....," he went searching in the boxes, "that one."

Jabe watched Dudley lift a braided cable and shove its connector into the box. Dudley looked up and grinned, "Know what we've got here, Old Pard?"

"Yeah, according to you, just a bunch of old dusty junk."

Dudley laughed, "Yeah, that's true enough. But this junk might be useful. These are the launch mechanisms for those missiles over there in the bunker. So what do you think of that?"

"You mean they can be used to fire those missiles?"

"Yepper."

"And we could actually launch one of them….."

"Uh-huh." This time, Dudley was way ahead of Jabe.

"And just maybe we could get set up to knock down one of those…"

"Absolutely. All we need is a couple batteries out of those trucks and Jeeps Gomez so kindly provided."

Now Jabe was grinning as well, "And you know how to wire them up, I'll wager." Dudley's grin only widened as he nodded in the affirmative.

Jabe straightened his frame and took on his ecumenical look, "Well, bless you my son. You have done well. Yessir, very well indeed."

Domingo came in and beckoned to Juan, "Por favor, mi amigo. Un avion."

Stepping outside with his friend and cocking his head toward the west, Juan heard something that concerned him. In an instant, Jabe and the others were at his side. The sound coming from the west was all it took to confirm the approach of a helicopter.

23

The sound of a rotary wing is unique and there is no mistaking it for anything else. Jabe tried to get a bearing on the helicopters' direction of approach. Then he saw them. The two choppers were the old Sikorsky H-34s with radial engines. They were old alright, but they could carry their weight in troops and ordinance. They passed by well to the north and appeared to be following the coastline. Obviously a routine beach patrol. They had moved the Lancair just in the nick of time. Cloud Dancer would have been clearly visible from the air.

Jabe had always marveled at the sight of an aircraft that had no conventional fixed wing, but could actually fly by rotating its wing overhead—egg-beater style. Some said that helicopters don't really fly at all—they just beat the air into submission. Strange way to fly, he thought. And yet it had become a highly refined means of conveyance. Trouble was, these two machines were out conveying men and ordinance meant for a kill—and the target was J.B. & Company.

Suddenly the choppers banked left and disappeared below the treeline. Jabe's heart skipped a beat as he realized they were landing on the beach. What had they seen to make them do that?

Juan was the first to move and then everyone followed as they all struck for the beach. Juan gave an order to Domingo, "Por favor, mi amigo. Stay here with Juanita and we will be back shortly. The little airplane must be kept safe from Gomez, so that our friends can return home." Several of the men stayed behind and the remainder of the force went with their commander.

In only a matter of minutes they had gained a brushy hilltop above the beach and could see the choppers sitting on the sand close to the water's edge, their rotor blades quite still and their crews out combing the beach. Then Jabe saw what had attracted them.

There at the water's edge where the waves of the approaching high tide were lapping, he could make out the reflection of a silvery line; a narrow stripe in the sand running parallel to the beach. His throat tightened as he realized these men were looking at a tire track—the track that Cloud Dancer had left in the sand during takeoff only a short time before.

Juan addressed him in low tones, "Senor Jabe. I believe your little airplane has left a calling card in the sand. Do you think they will read the signs and know what made the track?"

"Well, if there is any Indian blood down there at all, you can expect they will." Jabe was less than hopeful these fellows could possibly miss the plain writing that Cloud Dancer had left for them to find.

The incoming tide had already obliterated the seaward track so that only one imprint remained. He watched the men as they walked along the beach and motioned to each other. The track was too narrow for a Jeep or a truck tire, more the size of a wheelbarrow—or a light airplane. He wondered if they would make that connection.

Directly, they climbed back aboard their choppers and departed toward the east staying low over the beach. Had they missed the meaning of that lone track in the sand? Jabe hoped so. Any self-respecting soldier would have understood it immediately, and the thought did not leave Jabe feeling very confident.

Dudley said, "They'll damn sure be back up here, if they made any sense of that tire track. They'll head straight for the airstrip and we have no other place at all to hide the Lancair. We damn sure can't take her back to the beach."

"And we don't dare leave her up there either," Jabe was in full agreement. "We'd better get back up there and see about moving her somewhere else."

They moved out as Jabe continued, "I'm just a mite curious about where those choppers are based. Do you have any idea where they might have come from, Juan?"

"Si, I believe they come from a military camp they have built in the norte of Quintana Roo near the border with Yucatan. It is only about 50 miles, an hour or so. But señor, there is no road. Only the jungle."

"That's east of here?"

"Oh si, señor Jabe. It is toward the Caribbean, but it lies not far from the beach near the hills. It has a nice little harbor for supply. I have seen it only once when we blew up an airplane there. That was before Gomez was sent here to kill us. Now it is very difficult to get close to it. They guard it very well. So we have not been back there. That was a year or so ago."

"Gomez, eh?" Dudley still seemed apprehensive about the safety of his airplane. "I'll bet we haven't seen the last of that fellow, have we Juan?"

"Oh, I do not think he will be so quick to come looking for us soon. At least not on the ground again. It cost him quite dearly the last time he came." Juan seemed confident.

After the sight of the helicopter, Jabe was feeling vulnerable. "Well, I'm not one to just wait and see. If the tide had been just a few minutes later, then both tracks would have been visible and we could have been dead meat. We can't get that careless again about leaving signs for Gomez. It's just a wide open door for him."

On the walk back, Jabe placed an arm around Dudley's shoulder, "I've been thinking, Cap'n. You remember that fight Diego had with Gomez? Well, I think we ought to ask Diego if he can go back up there and get some truck batteries. Then you and I should fetch that missile over here from the cave. If we can figure out a way to fire the thing off, it could come in handy against those choppers if they have a mind to meddle with us."

It was mid-afternoon before Jabe and Dudley got back from the cave with the missile canister. They could smell another delicious meal cooking and Juanita was busy at an old wood stove the gringos had left in the Ops hut. They unloaded their burden and joined the other men outside. Jabe had grown quite accustomed to Juanita's cooking and allowed as how he hadn't ever tasted any better.

Dudley responded to the savory smells, "If I'm ever caught up in another war like this, Juanita gets my vote for camp cook. Juan, you are a lucky man indeed."

Dinner finished, Dudley and Juan took the KP duty and cleaned up the utensils. Juanita needed the relief. The rest of the men busied themselves with their own chores and Jabe went outside to enjoy the fresh afternoon breeze. He made for the shade of a palm tree and lay down, just glad to be alone for the moment.

Juanita wandered outside the hut, paused in the afternoon sunlight, raised her arms high over her head and yawned and stretched like a pussycat. Then, Jabe saw her start down the beach trail. He felt that was a foolish thing for her to do, going off all alone. So, he followed a short distance behind. Better he kept an eye on her. What if something happened to her? Didn't she have sense enough to play it safe and remain around the compound?

Down on the beach a stiff breeze was blowing and the surf was up. Jabe chose a high dune for his lookout position and lay on his belly in the soft sand. He could see in both directions up and down the beach. Nothing was stirring but the wind and the waves. She ran out onto the sand and began taking things off. First her halter top came away. Then off came her shorts. She dug into a pocket, retrieved a bar of soap, waded into the water and began washing out her togs.

There she was, down to nothing but her red neckerchief again. She seemed to never take that off. Jabe had seen this once before, but it got better every time. Juanita brought her duds back to the treeline and hung them out to dry, then made a headlong dash for the breakers. Jabe was again caught with his heart in his throat and hardly able to breathe.

What if Juan notices the both of us are gone and comes looking?

Now wouldn't that be just peachy? No, that would never do. He had to get her back to the compound before they were missed and someone came looking. He jumped up and started down the dune, and this time he was careful to keep his footing. Getting to the beach on a dead run, he stopped short as she came out of the water and headed right for him wearing a huge grin. She offered her hand and Jabe's heart took off like a trip-hammer.

Then he saw what she offered. It was the bar of soap.

Juanita tossed him the soap, laughed out loud and made for the tree where she had hung up her togs. Jabe got the message—he needed a bath something terrible.

Well, if it didn't bother her, it didn't bother him. So, what if they got caught? Now it didn't seem to matter anymore. Off came his togs and he made for the surf to follow her example. She watched from the treeline and laughed as he enjoyed a good sudsing. He was careful to stay in long enough for her togs to dry. He watched as she dressed herself again.

He washed out his own clothes and donned them before coming out of the water. They would just have to dry while he wore them. No way was he going to be caught with his pants down!

She met him with a fresh coconut, already pierced. They shared the cool coconut milk and lay against a log under the shade of the palms. He was comfortable with Juanita and it felt so complete he no longer worried about Juan finding them. Somehow he just didn't care any more.

The sun was dipping into the trees to the west making a display of yellow and gold, orange and crimson. The two of them lay back against the log and silently watched as the hues went to magenta, then blue, then purple. They watched the light fade and disappear. Words were not necessary or even wanted. Jabe liked a woman who appreciated that.

He built a fire and was content to watch Juanita relax in the sand. She leaned back against his chest and looked up at him with those deep, dark eyes of hers and he wondered what she was thinking. Still silent, they were content to just relax and watch the stars come out.

It was an hour or more before the full moon rose over the breakers down the beach toward Cozumel. She had been perfectly quiet and seemed content to just watch the night sky with her new-found companion.

R. Barry King

"Juanita…..," he ventured. These were the first words he had ever said directly to her on purpose.

"Que, señor Jabe?"

"Did you know that you are a very beautiful woman?"

"Si, señor Jabe."

That startled him. He wasn't sure she really understood English, so he tried again.

"And that I feel very comfortable whenever I'm around you?"

"Si, señor Jabe." Her smile was ever-present.

"I wonder if Juan will be worried about where we are and why we've been gone so long."

"Si, señor Jabe."

"Does that mean you are worried that he might be worried?"

"Si, señor Jabe."

"You can quit that "señor" business and just call me Jabe, or J.B., you know?"

"Si, señor Jabe."

"You know, you look like a teenager, Juanita. Just how old are you, anyway?"

"Si, señor Jabe." Juanita was starting to grin with all this banter. She seemed to enjoy it.

"That Juan fellow acts like he doesn't even know you exist. So why do you stay with him?"

"Si."

Jabe was getting bolder, "You think I'm good looking?"

"Si, señor Jabe."

He thought he'd give her a test, "Maybe we could just lie back here in the sand and have a little roll in the hay. What do you say?"

"Si, señor Jabe."

"I can say just about anything I want, can't I?"

"Si."

"And you don't understand a damn thing I'm saying, do you?"

"Si."

Jabe began to feel some of the pressure of the past several days come away being here with Juanita. He looked directly into her eyes. He thought about another woman he had loved so long ago.

Then he continued, "You look very much like a girl I loved many years ago. I can't believe how much you do." He studied her every reaction. He was feeling things he hadn't felt in years.

"When I first saw you, I couldn't tell that it wasn't her. You've got the same color, same skin, same hair, same gorgeous shape." Jabe drew a deep breath. He hadn't talked of this with anyone in years. That was before his time in the service. It was before anything else he could remember. He put another piece of driftwood on the fire.

"She was a girl from my pueblo and we grew up together. I fell in love with her and when we were old enough, she became my wife." Jabe looked for any sign of comprehension in Juanita's eyes.

Then he continued, "We had a wonderful life for a few years. We wandered the woods together and swam in the surf along the Gulf beaches. We had the world at our feet. And then she began to grow weak and couldn't keep up with me."

Jabe could feel the warm wetness of his tears on his cheeks, but he didn't care. "I came home from the hunt one night to find her....... cold and still. I ran for the doctor, old Ten Eagles. Well, he's not a real medical doctor. He is the medicine man in our pueblo. But, I'd rather take his medicine over anything else I've seen. And he came right away. He said some things I didn't understand. And my wife opened her eyes. I just knew she'd be okay after all, but she only told me in a whisper that she was going away." Jabe's voice had fallen to a whisper as well. "She said she'd known for quite a while that she was going to that other world, but for me not to worry. I'd get to see her there again, when I came there myself. She was too weak to say any more, so I just lay down beside her and held her close to my heart until she breathed no more."

Juanita looked into the fire, but said nothing. There was only the sound of the surf and the trembling whisper of his voice.

"When the sun came up, Ten Eagles and I wrapped her in the blanket the pueblo had given us for our wedding gift. We saddled our horses and he came with me and together we carried her up on the high mountain at the edge of Indian country over to the west and buried her there where the snow never melts. I can see her resting place from any point on the pueblo, the snowfield near the summit of that old white mountain. Every morning the sun causes the snow there to shine pure white. And every evening the blue western sky outlines the whiteness of that place. All pure, all clean and white."

Jabe stroked Juanita's hair. "There is a place beside her that will be my grave when I leave this world. Only Ten Eagles and I know the place. Some day when I am very old I will go there and wrap myself in my blanket and lie down in the snow beside her and breathe my last. Then I will see her again. Did you know that we will see our dead loved ones again some day?"

Juanita didn't answer right away. She only looked at him.

Directly she said, "Si, señor Jabe." Then she slid her arms around him and laid her head gently on his chest for a moment.

Jabe hadn't felt the warmth of a woman for way too long. His head felt lighter than a hot air balloon and he was suddenly quite dizzy. He tried to sit up, but could only relax and let himself sink back into the sand. He lifted Juanita's chin and looked into her eyes. Then he untied the red scarf from around her neck and let it fall to the sand as her lips came up to meet his.

The pounding in Jabe's head was deafening again. Then the world went spinning like a top and the starry sky seemed to rise and fall with the rhythm of the breakers. It was several hours before it slowed down enough for Jabe to regain his senses and catch his breath.

A meteor shot clear across the night sky and went from yellow to white and then green and red as it spent itself in the outer reaches of the atmosphere.

"Ooooooooohhh!" was the moaning response from Juanita.

Jabe removed the silver eagle and chain from around his neck and slipped it over her head. It looked much better on her than it did on him. And he thought Longrifle would surely approve.

24

The fire had died down to embers and Juanita was asleep with her head on Jabe's chest. He could feel the warmth of his own passion ebbing with the dying coals in the fire pit. The moon was high overhead and he had no idea how long they'd been away from the camp. They would have to be discrete on their return. He gently stroked Juanita awake and kissed her again.

She looked up with half-closed eyes and sighed, "Oh, mi Corazon."

He lifted himself to his knees and she clung tightly. Just like him, she wanted to stay. But, even she must have known better than to push their luck any further.

He pulled Juanita to her feet, smothered the still-warm coals with sand and filled in the fire pit. She slipped her hand in his and they walked in silence toward the compound.

Back at camp, they found everything quiet. Jabe saw Juanita safely back to her quarters. They said nothing, but he squeezed her hand, stroked the amulet around her neck and kissed her cheek. Then he quietly turned in without even looking for Dudley. He could do without any questions tonight.

He lay awake far into the night with only a single thought on his mind. There hadn't been many times in his life when he'd felt this helpless. Although Juanita had rekindled a fire in him that he thought was dead forever, here he was in this isolated foreign jungle all alone except for his pal and countryman Dudley. Not that he didn't appreciate the help they had received from Juan and his men. But, Juan and Juanita were in their own country and Jabe was way outside of his. He felt stuck.

What and who was there to help the pueblo out of its problems back home? How was his grandfather getting along? He felt quite anxious and needed to get back there. But, how? They had a perfectly good

R. Barry King

airplane that could carry them home in a few hours, if only they could find the gasoline they needed. All it would take was another fifty gallons. But it needed to be high-test aviation fuel, not auto gas. This little bird required the correct fuel for a long flight. Oh, it could burn a gallon or two of Gomez' cheap truck gas without any major engine problems. But, several hours of operation on that stuff at cruise speed would trash the engine and they'd be forced down at sea. Where in the world would they be able to get 50 gallons of 100-octane avgas?

And, the military airfield that Juan had told him about? That had to be a new installation of some sort, because it surely wasn't the fuel stop he and the other Club Fed pilots had been using. He needed to see it.

Jabe had slept hard and awakened late. He went outside to find Dudley enjoying a plate of huevos rancheros, "Mighty good vittles, my friend. Want some?" Dudley nodded toward the approaching Juanita. She grinned a greeting as she met Jabe with a steaming plate of this dish fit for the gods.

Jabe accepted it with a broad smile and said, "Gracias, señora." His use of the formal salutation was meant to remind her that she was a married woman.

Juanita cocked her head to the side and her grin faded a bit as she handed him his breakfast.

"Que?" she asked.

Just then, Juan came up with Domingo at his heels, "Señor Jabe, I trust you slept well. Did you see the fire in the sky last night?"

"Huh?" Jabe was caught at a disadvantage. He looked to Juanita for help. She waved a pointed finger across the heavens, "Ffffssssssssst."

"Oh, the meteor? Yeah. We, uh...I did. I saw that. Wasn't that something?" Now he was really confused. Juan had obviously seen the meteor. And if Juan had been up and about that late into the night, that would mean Juanita and he had certainly been missed. But, Juan was not complaining.

Juanita only laughed and went back to her cooking. If Juan didn't want to pursue it, neither would Jabe.

170

Dudley laid his plate aside and motioned for Jabe to follow him. "Come along with me, old Pard. There's something I want to show you." Jabe was happy to follow his partner out of a tight situation. He ate his fresh-cooked breakfast as they walked and hummed his approval, "Umm, but this is good!"

"Yeah, you bet it is, J.B. But, I've got something here that's even better. Diego went for those batteries early this morning. You had the right idea about that, J.B."

Inside the old operations hut, Dudley had laid out a makeshift workbench. There on the bench sat two of the truck batteries that he had wired together in series. They fed through an old knife switch to the braided cable on the launch mechanism.

Dudley began, "I was awake way into the night trying to think of a way out of here for us."

"Yeah, myself as well," Jabe confessed. "Did you come up with a way to get us back home?"

"Well, no. Not yet, anyway. We sure as hell can't go anywhere in the LancAir without avgas. So, having nothing better to do, I wandered in here and began playing with these electronics. That's what I used to do when I was a kid and couldn't sleep. I'd go to putzing around with my ham radio stuff and build something. And, like as not, it would actually work. So, I says to myself, I says, 'self, what if you could wire up one of the launchers to these here truck batteries and get 24 volts on the pigtail to the igniters?'"

"And self had an answer for that?" Jabe wanted to know.

"Oh, did he ever, J.B. Your hunch was right-on. The electronics in these babies is fed from a NiCad storage cell that is charged from the launch platform—that's the aircraft that carries them. So, with these here truck batteries, I charged them up last night and got the targeting and guidance systems to work just fine. But, the critical thing is these igniters are all shot from the humidity and the heat. No way to start the rocket motors."

Jabe nodded, sort of confused, "So?"

"Well, there's where I had to improvise. See this tin foil? Well, it's actually aluminum. I've wrapped it across these two terminals? That's where the igniters used to be wired in. If current flows through there, it will flash-burn the foil and that functions as an igniter and lights off the solid fuel in the rocket motors." Dudley pointed to the spot as he pushed the button on the launcher. ZAP! The tin foil went up in a bright flash and Dudley chuckled at his own genius, "And we have ignition. Lift off. And, etcetera."

"And that means....?"

"It means we can launch one of these little birds. All we needed was these here two truck batteries, and—voila! Now we can light off these Bad Boys. I can wire them up in a jiffy."

Jabe was thinking as he muttered, "Wow, I figure it would be quite a surprise for those dope runners to loose a whole C-130 shipment, wouldn't it?"

Jabe was determined to make the most of a bad situation. If they couldn't get back to the pueblo just yet to try and stop things on that end, he would just as soon do what damage he could on this end.

"How soon can we try this thing out?" Jabe asked. "I remember something about that warhead. It's a heat-seeker. It locks onto a moving infra-red source, right?"

"Yepper," Dudley grinned. "You're right as Rainwater."

Ignoring the pun, Jabe continued, "Well, what all do we need for a trial run at those Herkybirds, Cap'n?"

"All we need is a high vantage point like a hilltop for a launch site. Somewhere near the beach would be best. There's less chance for confusion if we fire it over water. The target acquisition is random, and the electronics will lock onto the first heat impulse the antenna receives and that might take a few seconds. So, all we have to do is just wait until they fly past. Then we put it in the air as they're going away. It'll hit anything that's flying. Run right up the exhaust pipe."

Jabe said, "My, my. It all sounds so simple."

Dudley frowned, "But, I don't know if it'll work, J.B.? It'd be a miracle."

Jabe was quick to reassure him, "I'd wager on it, old Pard. Anyway, what've we got to lose?"

Dudley grinned and that old self-confidence returned. He was always game for a thrill, "Ooooookay, fine! But, just don't feel too bad if it doesn't work. I don't have any of the tools I really need here and........."

"That's okay. We'll just try her out and take what we can get. Just like at the carnival—Ya pays your money and ya takes your chances."

Jabe felt it was worth a try. He conferred with Juan on a likely location and they settled on the same nearby hilltop just a mile or so down the beach west of the caves where they'd seen the outbound Herkybird before.

Jabe turned to Dudley, "Juan and his men can give us a hand. Let's go and give her a try, Cap'n. What do you say?"

"Okay. Let's DO IT!" was Dudley's reply. Quietly, Jabe would have preferred Dudley had used another term.

Dudley loaded the missile into its tubular canister and put the batteries into old ammo boxes for the trip upcountry. Diego loaded the whole affair aboard his trusty Mustang. When the men were ready, Juan gave the signal to move out. Domingo would remain in camp as a rear guard and relief cook to give Juanita a day to rest.

Juan held his weapon at the ready and buckled an extra ammo belt around his waist, "Adios, Domingo."

Domingo replied, "Adios, Capitan. You will return in the shutting of an eye."

Dudley gritted his teeth. "In a wink, Domingo. We'll be back in a wink. And if you hear a big bang, don't come running, okay?"

Jabe hurriedly finished another plate of Juanita's breakfast, collected his gear and ran to catch up. Dudley and Juan were already at the trailhead along with several of the men. Domingo and Juanita waved their goodbye.

The men covered the distance rapidly over the fairly flat coastal terrain. The trail began an upward slope as Juan signaled a halt. The hilltop they sought was just ahead of them. They rested a few minutes and then continued their climb. At the summit, they had a commanding view out over the Gulf to the north and over the jungle for quite a ways inland to the south as well.

Diego unloaded his pony and Dudley set to unpacking the gear. Jabe had Juan's men fashion a launch rack out of saplings and bamboo. Following Dudley's instructions and a pattern of lines drawn in the dirt, they quickly constructed a passable cradle for the rocket that pointed it skyward at a low angle out to sea. They dug a pit behind the missile and threw up a dirt bank to absorb the fiery blast that would send the rocket into the air. Jabe helped Dudley wire up his batteries and then they took a seat on a log a few yards away to wait.

Jabe surveyed the launch pad and observed, "No need to set the jungle on fire if she works like I think she will. That earthwork should contain the flames from the blast-off, alright. You ever work with one of these missiles Cap'n, or is this a first for you?" Jabe was as curious as he was hopeful.

Dudley was catching his breath, "I was an ordinance chief when you were in Seal School. We had a lot of these to play with. Of course, we were working with airborne launch platforms, uh, airplanes you know. But, voltage is voltage, no matter what the power source. So, in theory, these truck batteries should work just fine. Why are you bugging me, anyway?"

"Oh, I was just thinking," Jabe said in his casual way.

"Thinking what?"

"Oh, just that maybe the thing will explode right here on the ground when you give it the juice, that's all. You know, it might just decide to blow up in our faces. Mayhaps we ought to string up a long wire for the switch and launch it from way over there," Jabe pointed to a grove of brush thirty yards away.

"Think it might be safer for us over there, do you?"

"Exactamundo. At least it's a bit shadier."

Dudley ran the extra length of wire and everybody took the cover of the brush grove and dug in. They lay back in the late morning warmth and waited. Noon came and went. They broke out some rations and the men had a smoke. Mid afternoon and still no airplanes. Dudley and Jabe had been on edge all day.

"How long will those batteries last, Cap'n? They haven't had a good charge in days," Jabe was looking to break the tension.

Dudley had reclined on a log in the shade and was adopting a matter-of-fact attitude, "A wet-cell battery is fine for quite a while if the load isn't great. And these little birds don't use much current. They should be fine for weeks."

"What's that?" Jabe jumped to his feet and was straining to catch the sound again. Way up the beach and out toward the west over the jungle, Jabe could here the drone of turboprops. Dudley saw it about the same time Jabe did. Sure enough, it was a low-flying Hercules crossing the beach and heading out over the Gulf several miles away.

Jabe was standing with his fists clinched, "There goes another shipment, for sure." He stared after the big C-130 in obvious disgust.

Dudley propped himself up on an elbow for a better look, "Too far away for a shot. Damn!"

At the same instant the jungle shook and there came a deafening roar from just overhead. Then the whoosh and passing shadow of another Herkybird as it passed directly over them only a few dozen feet off the ground and headed out over the water. Everyone instinctively hit the ground.

The startled Jabe picked himself up, "You sneaky sonofabitch!" He grabbed the launch button and held it high above his head and clamped his thumb down hard.

But, nothing happened. Again, he pressed the button. Still nothing. He glanced toward the missile, then shook a fist at the departing C-130. "Dammit Cap'n, she's getting away!"

Dudley only cocked his head, "Maybe not, J.B. Sometimes you've gotta be patient. Give it a chance to lock-on."

Jabe continued, "Come on, baby. Wake up and GO!"

Juan sprang to Jabe's side, "Señor, does it not work? Does the little bird not want to fly today? While the big one is getting away, the little one has decided to stay in the nest?"

Dudley waited patiently, knowing the missile's sensors took a while to lock-on, and it wouldn't fly until it had a target. But, he secretly wondered if the electronics had deteriorated beyond hope over the years of damp storage in that old bunker.

Jabe was shouting now, "Come on, Baby! Lock-on and go for it." He was pointing toward the big transport now fast departing toward the north. He turned and looked at Dudley, "He's right there all by himself, Cap'n. What's the problem?"

Dudley glanced at the missile and still hoped for a miracle. The missile sat there, just a pile of cold steel. Why wouldn't the damn thing work? Was it just too old and moldy by now? Dudley shook his head and watched it all in fascinated frustration. His heart sank for Jabe's sake. And Juan had expected so much from his gringo friends.

Jabe was still talking, "Come on, Sugar, talk to Papa. Lock-on and Go.... Go! Go!" Tears flowed down his cheeks as the disappointment overwhelmed him.

He turned to Dudley with a quizzical look and asked, "Is she just too old to fly, Cap'n?"

This was too sickening to watch. Dudley could only glance out to sea and shrug his shoulders.

Juan put a hand to Jabe's shoulder, "Señor, you did your best. The little bird is too tired to fly. Let's go back to camp and get some rest."

Jabe could feel that old familiar tightness in his stomach. The C-130 grew smaller and smaller as it pulled away toward the north at better than 300 knots. It undoubtedly carried many tons of drugs that were destined for the bloodveins of thousands of Americans—many of them just children. He could only guess at how many of them would die.

Already three miles away, four pale smoke trails left behind each of the C-130's turbines marked its path out to sea. In a moment, it would disappear—out of reach.

Jabe watched the big transport grow smaller in the distance and felt it slipping away. His pleas subsided to a trembling whimper, "Come on. Wake up and go for it, Baby. Come to Papa. Come to Papa."

Then, without any warning at all—WHAM! A fiery blast and a deafening roar blew everyone down to the ground and a sharp concussion took the wind right out of their lungs. Without so much as a burp or a fizzle, the missile leapt into the air just ahead of a blinding point of light and roared off the hillside on a trail of white smoke. It rocketed out over the Gulf and made a series of zigzags in the general direction of the big transport.

Jabe came to his feet first, caught his breath and began to shout at the top of his lungs, "ATTABABY! ATTAWAY to GO!" He was jumping into the air and waving his arms. "Go, go, go, Baby, GO!"

Dudley's heart went into his throat as he stood bolt upright and watched the missile roar offshore and out over the blue Gulf. He still wondered if the on-board guidance system was really working. The missile settled on a steady course, made one false turn out to sea, then swung back directly toward the big Lockheed. In only a few seconds it caught the big bird and rammed into it.

First came the silent images. A blinding orange flash slowly dissolved into a black ball of smoke where the plane had been. Then the rain of debris and shrapnel falling slowly down and splashing into the sea. It was all surreal and distant. Only silence. Then came the booming report and the shock wave rolled past. The big four-engine C-130 had just evaporated.

Jabe and Juan were jumping wildly and slapping their thighs. Dudley couldn't believe his eyes. He gained a firm footing as Jabe raced toward him.

Jabe grabbed his friend and lifted him off the ground, "Did you see that? You big, beautiful, brilliant SonofaGun!" Jabe was laughing hard when he let Dudley back down to the ground again. "You did it! You damn sure did it!"

Dudley still had his philosophical look about him, "Well, like I always say, you have to be patient. It takes a few seconds for target acquisition. Just took a little longer than I'd expected, that's all. And I believe the term is WE, compadre. We did it! All of us together." Dudley let a grin creep across his face. And in an instant he and the whole outfit were laughing uncontrollably.

Far out to sea, the other Hercules had turned back for one quick pass over the wreckage of its companion in a search for survivors. There were none.

This was an expensive loss for the drug runners. And Jabe well knew it would not go without retribution.

25

In Washington, Wade Breggard sat alone in the communications room deep in the basement of the Old Executive Office Building. His brisk conversation with the headquarters of General Mendoza, somewhere in the Yucatan, was coming to a close.

"I'll get back to you as soon as I can, General. Adios." Slowly, Wade pulled off his earphones and laid them on the radio desk. He switched off the transceiver and scribbled a hasty note.

He walked slowly upstairs avoiding the elevator on his trip up to see his boss. He thought about his fifteen years of government service and wondered how he had gotten in this fix. He had started out with the best of intentions, just like all the other beginning young government bureaucrats.

But, somewhere he had fallen away from his intended course. One thing had led to another as it often does in these situations, and he found he'd had to do things he never set out to do, just to keep his job. He had been hand-picked by the Administration to serve in his present position and he had been awed by the power and authority of those in office.

Back when he was new at this, he had been quite excited about the many possibilities that lay before him. Then he'd found out the truth about where a lot of the money came from. But, all things considered, he had made the decision to stay on just the same. He'd figured that if the American people really wanted drugs, they'd get them somewhere. The rationalizations had been easy for him. But, now it had gone too far. People were actually getting killed and he was deep in the midst of the whole operation.

Halfway down the hall, he turned and walked through a great oaken doorway over which hung a gilded plaque hanging from brass chains. It bore the simple words, "Vice President of the United States." Wade passed through to the inner office in time to hear his boss finish a telephone conversation, ".....and I don't care how it affects your Mexican connections. We can take your entire production and guarantee same-day payment."

Jefe motioned for him to take a seat. Then went on, "What?..... Of course I can........ You let me worry about that. I won't tolerate that kind of interference. Anyone down there foolish enough to try and mount serious competition against us will be swiftly dealt with, and I can assure you of that. You just make sure Mendoza keeps our fueling operation and crew accommodations at the half-way point secure, that's all I need from you. You tell him 'El Jefe' said that. My people will handle all the rest.........Si compadre. Y usted. Adios."

The VP hung up the phone, lifted a smoking cigar off the ashtray and tipped off the ash. He took a long pull at it and turned to his assistant. "Well, my boy, we're on our way up in the world. At this rate, I'll have enough of a war-chest to take on the whole World Order, much less the White House. What's on your mind?"

Wade didn't quite know how to break the news. He simply said, "Sir, we're snake bit again."

"What? That airstrip out West is operational, isn't it? Papa Bear losing control out there again?"

"No sir, the problem isn't in New Mexico. We've got full control of that high mesa now. As you know, we've landed four of the big transports with full loads in just the past two days. Our problems have shifted toward the south."

The VP leaned forward in his chair and drummed the desktop with his fingertips, "Okay, Wade. Then what is it?"

"There's another one down, sir. I just got off the radio with our man Mendoza. Something fishy going on down there. And this time we've lost one of the big transports."

The VP sat upright, "The hell, you say. That's two hundred million dollars' worth of hard-earned American taxes. What in hell happened to it?"

"It was part of a two-plane flight due for arrival today, sir. Only one of them made it up here. We've talked with the crew, but all they can say for sure is that the other plane just went down in a ball of flames. They circled the wreckage for survivors, but there was no sign of life. Mendoza's men are collecting the pieces washing up on the beach to make sure no sign of the cargo shows up in the wrong hands."

The VP just stared at his assistant.

Wade went on, "It doesn't make a lot of sense, Sir. Either that plane was sabotaged, or it was shot down."

"What in hell-fire and damnation is going on down there? The people running the half-way point are all well known to us. I can't see how anyone could get in there and sabotage a flight. Security is too good for that. What about a shoot-down, Wade?"

"That's what has me puzzled. Mendoza says there is no way it could be that guerrilla band. Gomez's jungle force has run them out of that part of the country."

The VP briskly exhaled a lung-full of thick cigar smoke, "But, there is one other explanation, isn't there my friend?"

Wade Breggard looked quizzically at his mentor, "You mean that fellow the contractors had trouble with out on the reservation?"

The VP cocked his head slightly, "Precisely, my boy. Although I don't see how one man could be causing all of these problems for us, couldn't it be him? Now refresh my memory on all that again."

"Well sir, after interfering with the construction crew, he was traced to…right here in DC. What he was doing here, we were never able to find out. He slipped our trap here and then our people almost caught up with him back in Galveston. He had to leave there in quite a hurry. He took off in a light plane and disappeared out over the Gulf. Probably went down at sea, Sir. It appears he didn't make it back to the beach. And he hasn't been seen out on the reservation, so we think we're rid of him."

The VP was not convinced, "Perhaps he crossed the Gulf and landed in Mexico. Ever think of that?"

"Oh, no sir, that's quite impossible. That little two-seater airplane was a rickety home-built job. No way could it do seven hundred miles. They're lost at sea, Sir, you can bet on that."

"What's this *'they'* stuff? I thought he was all alone. Now there's two of them we have to worry with?" The VP didn't miss a thing.

"The aircraft was the property of the hotel night clerk where the Indian stayed in Galveston. We've tried for an ID on him, but he's not in any of our systems. Probably just another waterfront bum. Not likely he had any special talent that could take out a C-130, sir."

"So right now, he's an unknown quantity?"

"Well, yessir."

"Just what we need. Nothing to worry about. Just a couple of waterfront bums who are somehow capable of blowing freaking *four-engine turboprop transports out of the sky!*"

The VP leaned back and began to blow smoke-rings again. Wade hated when he did that.

"Let me see if I've got it all straight, Son. We were losing about an aircraft a month to rifle fire from some renegade guerrilla band down there in the Mexican jungle. So, we sent in Mendoza. He agreed to put the guerrillas preying on our contractor flights out of business, right?"

"Right, sir."

"So, the guerillas don't have the easy targets they once had, because we're flying the big transports over water now. Correct?"

"Yessir."

"Okay. Then who is knocking down our C-130s, Wade?"

Wade was silent, "Who, sir?"

"I'll tell you who. It's that damned Indian and his friend, that's who. He got clean away from our people out on the rez. Then he avoided capture here in D.C. and slipped out of our hands again down in Galveston. Have I missed anything so far, Wade?"

Wade was amazed by the clear thinking and sharp memory of his boss, "No Sir, that's about the size of it. But how in thunder is he able to knock down a heavy transport like a C-130?"

"Because he's somehow got hold of heavy ordinance, that's how."

Wade was stunned, "I don't know how he could be doing that, Sir. He'd have no place to get such a thing."

"Well it doesn't matter much just where he got the damn stuff. What matters is that we stop him right now, before he can do us any more damage. If we don't, it'll get so hazardous those pilots will refuse to fly another load. They won't be willing to die for amnesty. They can just go back to the Fort Worth Pen and finish out their time. And the money is immaterial if a man's not alive to enjoy it. We're gonna have to rethink some strategy here."

The VP's telephone ran. He picked it up and said, "Yes Julie, what is it? Who? Okay, then put him on........... Yes, this is the Vice President.........Oh yes, hello Mr. Samuelson......." He looked up and winked at Wade. "Oh, it's no bother whatsoever. Now what can I do for you?........... Yes, we know about the loss of a Lockheed Hercules. Well, my information is that we have some aircraft down there doing humanitarian work. They're transporting medical personnel and supplies into the area hit by the recent floods.........Yes, I think they have made a significant contribution to the international effort down there.......... No sir, we don't know any more than that. Well, thanks for your interest. I'm glad I could be of service. Good day."

Wade was a little stumped, "Humanitarian effort, Sir?"

"That guy is fishing for a news story and I think I'll give him one. Rule number one, my boy. Don't ever miss a chance to make points with the public. I'm going to paint a very gruesome picture of that Indian kid for public consumption. Then I'm sending in a crack military team to take him out once and for good. After all, I can make the argument that this would never have happened if the President had been doing his job tending to the affairs of state instead of those endless rounds of golf and foreign vacations. Yessir, my boy. We'll turn this into a landslide victory for Yours Truly, alright. There's no telling how far this will take us. Just you wait and see." The VP chuckled at his own genius.

Wade asked, "Sir, what shall I tell Mendoza?"

"You can tell that no-good counterpart of ours that he'd better take care of those jungle guerrillas and that outlaw Indian, and pronto. Tell him there's a hefty bonus in it for him. That Indian has become a menace to the New World Order. I'll see to that. If Mendoza can't take him out, tell him I will. He's got one more chance, got it?"

"Yessir, I do. I only hope Mendoza gets it, too."

Now it was official. Like it or not, Jabe Rainwater had finally earned the title of a recognized international villain, courtesy of the U.S. Vice President himself. He was being dubbed a menace to world peace with a price on his head. He was a real outlaw now.

26

A couple of hours had passed before the little band of jungle fighters had rested themselves enough to think of moving out. Juan and his men inspected the launch site for any sign of smoldering embers left by the missile launch that could start a brush fire and Dudley retrieved the launch module and packed the equipment for the return trip.

Jabe slapped Dudley on the back, "Can you believe that? It actually worked, Cap'n!"

Dudley was still in awe of the fact. "Just like clockwork." But, he could hardly believe it had all been so simple. He was thinking like a military strategic planner.

"At this rate, with all the missiles we've got in reserve, we could actually be a real deterrent to those bastards running the drug trade. At least until we can get out of here and back home. They'll be coming for us, J.B."

Jabe was in agreement. He was already seeing a clear picture of the type of destruction he and Dudley could bring to bear on this immoral and deadly bunch of thugs. But, this business wouldn't be without its risks. They certainly would not route any further shipments over this part of Juan Goyona's domain. The missiles would have to be used much closer to their air base. And that could get dicey.

Jabe began to get an uneasy feeling. He gathered his own gear and helped Juan and Dudley get loaded for the trip back, "We'd better get back to the camp, old Pard. You're right about something. They'll be sending their people in here to get us after suffering that big of a loss."

They all took the march for the beach and reached the rise above the caves in clear view of the ocean. From here it was a short walk back to the airstrip.

Dudley had his binoculars to his eyes and was scanning the ocean. Jabe noticed his diligence, "See something out there, Cap'n?"

"I though I saw a glint. Maybe the sun reflecting off a big wave. Maybe just some wreckage glistening in the sun."

Jabe studied the sea horizon, but saw nothing other than a few large waves. Then he thought he saw a speck just off the water.

Dudley lowered his binocs, then raised them again. "No, there it is again...Damn! It's those two choppers and they're headed straight for us."

Everyone jumped at once.

Dudley said, "They'll be heading for the airstrip, J.B." Then he scrambled to catch up with the others who had already bolted down the trail.

Juan took the running lead back toward the airstrip with Jabe and the rest close on his heels. They had made only a few hundred yards when the choppers roared over. Even at a dead run, they would be too late to meet the landing. Domingo would have his hands full until they could get there and Diego's force would just have to catch up the best they could.

From the direction of the airstrip, the crack of rifle fire echoed through the jungle and Jabe could hear the excited voices of the invaders calling to each other. Approaching the airstrip, he heard the staccato bark of machine guns.

Domingo was pouring rifle fire into one of the choppers as it sat on the ground. It started smoking and the rotor blades slowed considerably. Jabe saw the muzzle flashes coming from the helicopter as the airmen were returning fire, but it looked hopeless for them. Domingo had the advantage of cover, and the chopper was just a sitting duck. The steady roar of gunfire was deafening.

Just then, Jabe saw the second chopper lift off from behind the Quonset huts and head out toward the interior.

The men aboard the crippled chopper began to abandon it and run for the cover of the jungle. Gunfire erupted from the jungle just ahead of them and they stopped short before they could gain the cover of the brush. With a shout, Diego and his men ran out of the jungle, surrounded them and forced them to the ground. This chopper and its crew were going nowhere.

Jabe dashed forward, outdistanced his friends and was the first to arrive at the crippled chopper. Domingo left the cover of the Quonset hut and headed toward Jabe. Diego's men already had the captives face down with their hands behind their heads.

A grinning Diego came toward Jabe with his rifle held high above his head. "Today, the fox was to have been eaten by the chicken, no?" He gripped a bloody spot on his shoulder and winced. His men jerked the captives to their feet and Diego inspected them as Juan came up.

"That rascal Gomez has gotten away in the other airplane."

Juan only laughed, "And it looks as though the fox has clipped the chicken's wings as well. We better have a look at that shoulder. Now that he has seen you fighting on my side, I do not think he will be giving you any more of his gold, my cousin."

Domingo arrived and shouldered his weapon. He seemed to recognize one of the captives, "Well, if it isn't that old coyote, de la Cruz." The fellow he addressed was wearing a red beret. He stood erect with his hands on his head, but he smiled wryly at Domingo and said something in Spanish.

They interrogated this man briefly and then Juan translated for Jabe and Dudley. "I know this man. He fought with us in the Sandinista War. He was trained to fly helicopters by the gringos. He and his crew were pressed into service by Gomez. They have been treated badly and are glad to have been captured alive, so they may return to their families. Gomez will think they have been killed and will not likely return to see about them. They are perfectly expendable to Gomez."

Jabe was eager for their help, "What can these men tell us about Gomez' base of operations and the drug shipments?"

Juan was hopeful, "Perhaps we can find out many things. We will see what they can tell us. I would like to find a way to rid this jungle of that Gomez and his fellows for good. I do not believe Gomez will be satisfied now until he kills me."

Dudley was getting cranky as well, "I'm damn tired of running a defense from the likes of 'Gomez & Company.' Maybe we can take the fight to him this time. And with any luck at all, we might even find enough avgas to get us home, J.B."

Jabe was thinking as he viewed the downed chopper. It sat there on the airstrip still smoking, but not yet on fire. "Hell, Cap'n. Our gasoline is right here in this chopper. But we'd better get to it before that smoldering fire does, or it'll all go up in smoke."

"Damn! You're right, Pard." Dudley was a blur of action as he realized the urgency of the moment. He dashed into the hut and returned with two empty Jerry cans. "Boy, you're right about that, J.B. These old H-34s have piston engines and burn first grade avgas. I wonder if there's enough to get us home."

Diego had found the aircraft's fire extinguishers and dowsed the fire, while his men fetched more gas cans. Jabe had already found the fuel dump valve on the chopper's belly and turned it on as Dudley held the Jerry cans in place to receive the precious liquid. The blue tint of the fuel clearly identified it as 100-octane avgas.

When the flow diminished, they had collected eleven cans of gas. Dudley was elated, "Hot damn. That's fifty-five gallons. This is what we've been needing, Juan. Now we're fixed to get back home."

Jabe was smiling as well. He hadn't expected they would have found their badly needed avgas so quickly. He thought about how fortunate this had all been. "Did you lose any of your men, Juan?"

Diego gave the answer. "No, senor, by the grace of God. Only a wound here in my shoulder that was put there by that madman Gomez. He was trying to kill me!"

Juan turned to Domingo and asked, "And you, mi amigo. Are you unhurt, and Juanita as well?"

"Si, Capitan. We are safe." Domingo smiled his apparent satisfaction. "But, we had, how you say, a close call from these unwanted visitors here. When they landed, we went into the little hut to take cover. They began to shoot at us and Juanita was so frightened, she ran out the back door into the jungle. So I am sure she is safe and sound."

Jabe felt tightness in his stomach at this revelation. "Domingo, where is she now. Did you see her come back? We saw the other chopper take off from behind the huts as we ran in." Jabe broke for the hut at a dead run.

Domingo went wide-eyed, "Another aeroplane, senor? We saw only this one."

Juan ran after Jabe, "Madre de Dios! Juanita!"

Everyone took up the search at once. Juan and his men went into the jungle calling out her name, but there was no answer. Jabe made a beeline for the spot where the chopper had lifted off. He arrived in a small clearing sixty yards or so behind the huts. There on the ground was the red scarf she had been wearing. Jabe picked it up and felt his whole body go numb as he realized that Gomez had kidnapped her

The camp was silent that night as the men munched cold C-rations again. Jabe missed the home-made tortillas, the green chili stew, the carne adovada…and, most of all, he missed Juanita. The numbness in his innards was slow to abate. His jaw was set and he unconsciously ground his teeth. He could only imagine the feelings of his friend Juan.

Domingo cried big alligator tears as he tended the coffee pot. He turned to Juan and lamented, "Mi amigo, I had no idea she was in danger. I would have died to keep her safe. Aye, Juanita!"

Juan was nervous and distraught, "Domingo, you are not to blame. I know how much you do for our cause, and I could not do all I have done without you by my side. Aye Chihuahua! I cannot believe they got away with her." He rose and put a hand on Domingo's shoulder. "Domingo, I blame only myself. I should have kept her beside me. But now you will come with me and we will go and bring her back. You and I together, Domingo." He hugged his comrade and patted his back. "Together, no?"

Turning to Jabe, he continued, "Senor Jabe. Now that you have some gasolina, you and your amigo must leave us. You can now return to your own country. You must leave here at the first light of the sun, or that Gomez will come back here and find the little airplane and destroy your only chance to get home."

Jabe liked the idea, but he wasn't sure it was the right thing to do. How would Juan get his Juanita back? Jabe felt he had a vested interest. There was an old wound in his heart that Juanita had reopened. He wanted to close it again, and this time for good.

Juan wanted to post some of the men at the caves in order to watch for any attempt by Gomez from that direction. Jabe and Dudley joined him outside and they started for the beach. Domingo was more than glad to join up for the trip.

When they arrived above the caves, the moon was up and Dudley and Domingo set up the watch. Jabe wanted to see the beach again and started down toward the sand. Although he hadn't said it aloud, he wanted to be where she had been with him only a day before. Juan followed along behind him.

The salt air in Jabe's face felt refreshing and brought a release from some of his pent-up tension. It made him want to run off some energy he didn't know what to do with.

"Come on, Juan. Run with me." Jabe began to trot along the beach and his companion fell into stride alongside him. In a half-mile or so, Jabe picked up the pace. Juan stayed even and began to chuckle. He even pulled ahead some and looked back as he broke from a gallop into a full run. Jabe put on some steam, but he gained very little. Juan had some steam of his own.

By this time, Juan was laughing out loud. The Indian runner in Jabe came to the surface and he pulled out all the stops. Juan had a few steps on Jabe, but his lead vanished and he fell steadily behind as the two of them made another half-mile before Jabe let Juan catch up.

Jabe thought, 'Man, this Mexican can run! He must be part Indian.'

Juan followed Jabe up a low dune and the two friends fell into the soft sand in hysterical laughter.

"Senor Jabe. You run like the Tarahumara. You are an Indio, no?"

"Indio, yeah. And you must have some Indian blood as well, Juan."

"Oh, si. I am part Indio myself. And where is your home?"

"I come from New Mexico, Juan."

"Oohhhh, Nuevo Mejico. You are a cousin! I thought you were funny looking for a Mejicano, senor."

The two caught their breaths and began to walk back up the beach. Juan talked of his Juanita and was naturally anxious to be off to find her.

"Senor Jabe. You and your friend must be off in your little plane very early in the morning. Then I will go and find my Juanita. It has been very good to have you with us here in the jungle. We have fought very well together, no? But, now you must leave us and go back to your homes. I will miss you very much."

They found the trail and started up to find Domingo and Dudley. Jabe asked, "Where will you look for her, Juan?"

"Oh, I believe they have taken her to the airbase they have in the jungle. I will go there and see what I can do to get her back." Juan hung his head, "She has been with me every step I have taken for many long years." He looked Jabe straight in the eye, "I will get her back, senor Jabe. I will have my Juanita back by my side, or I will die trying. I only wish you could be with me when we get her back." Juan drew the dagger that he carried on his hip. He held it at arm's length and waved it around, "And if they have hurt her one little bit...."

"Juan, I know you will find her. I would do the same thing if I were trying to rescue my own wife. Maybe Dudley and I......."

"Mi esposa?" Juan had a look of curiosity. "No, Senor Jabe! Juanita is not my wife. She is my seester."

Jabe froze in mid-stride. "Sister? Juanita is your sister?"

"Si, senor. I thought you knew. She has liked you from the start. And you could not tell that I approved?"

Jabe was stunned. No wonder Juan had not reacted like a husband when she had held Jabe's arm on the ridge up by the caves. No wonder he had not come looking for them on the beach. No wonder! This changed everything.

Domingo and Dudley called from up the trail. They had posted the required lookout and waited for Juan and Jabe to catch up and soon the four compadres were back in camp.

"Dudley, old Pard, guess what!" Jabe asked his buddy.

"She's his sister, right?"

"Well, how the hell did you know that?"

"Domingo here told me."

"And when was that?"

"Several days ago."

"You mean......?"

"Yeah, I knew it before you did, alright. But, I thought it was best if you didn't know. It would be hard enough for you to leave here as it was, and I know you have to get back to the pueblo."

"Righto. But, this kind of changes things for me doesn't it. Juan and I are going after her, first thing. I can't let him go it alone. They'll damn sure be waiting for him to come after her, and if I can be any help at all....."

Domingo got their drift, "Si, senor. Gomez knows that Juan will come for Juanita. And then he will try and kill us and you as well, as sure as the pig eats the cabbage."

Dudley was quick to correct, "That's how the *cow* eats the cabbage, Domingo. Not the *sow*."

Juan was unmoved, "Sow, cow, goats, pigs; it is all the same, senor. They all eat up my garden when the gate is left open. And this Gomez will come in here as if the gate is open and eat up our lunches."

Jabe chimed in, "Well, this gate is closed, Domingo. I wonder if Gomez has remembered to close his own gate. Juan, do you think we can get up to that military airbase undetected?"

"Perhaps, if we go in the night-time, senor. But if Gomez finds us close to his compound, it would be a thing that could put us all in the grave."

Dudley was incredulous, "Well dang me for sure! You two are actually going up there, aren't you?"

"Any other suggestions, Cap'n?"

"Well, you've got that look of determination and I'm sure you can't be talked out of it. So, maybe we could surprise them on their own ground."

"Maybe...," Jabe was not surprised to hear his longtime buddy so quickly volunteer to help.

"But, I've still got to get the Lancair out of here at first light, J.B., and find her a safe haven. Then I can rest easy knowing we can leave here as soon as we can get this settled. Maybe I can get back here in time to help out. And besides, this time we won't be going in with just our rifles. We've got some heavy ordinance to work with. Maybe we can get close enough to do some serious damage. Wouldn't that put a crimp in their style?"

"After we get Juanita back, old Pard. I don't want to put her at any more risk than need be. Juan, if your folks will bring up several of those rockets from the bunker, Dudley and I will get the launchers ready and meet you back here at the airstrip. I'll help Dudley get the plane fueled for an early start in the morning. Amigo, you won't be alone in your search for Juanita. I'm coming with you."

27

Dudley had the Cloud Dancer fueled and warmed up long before daylight. While the night guard was changing just before dawn, Jabe placed a few food rations under the right-hand seatbelt beside his partner.

"Take good care, old Pard," Jabe cautioned Dudley. "And put her somewhere safe."

"I'll get back here just as soon as I can. And you take care of yourself as well. Don't try anything foolish while I'm not around to take care of you, ya hear?"

The blackness was turning pale toward the east and at first light, Dudley cranked up and waved goodbye to Jabe and Juan, then taxied out and took off. He stayed low over the treetops and made for the Gulf.

He could make good time up the beach and with any luck at all, Jabe thought Dudley could find a safer place to hide Cloud Dancer. If Gomez could surprise them here once, he could do it again. And he'd be sure to find and destroy the Lancair the next time he came. This way, Cloud Dancer might live to fly another day and maybe even get them back home again.

Jabe made a beeline for the Ops hut with Juan close behind. He dragged a large wooden crate away from the wall and lifted the hinged lid. "Juan, give me a hand with this, will you?"

The two men lifted the big transmitter out of the crate, connected the microphone and positioned the rig on the makeshift workbench that Dudley had set up. Then they placed the receiver next to it and wired up the connections.

Jabe anticipated Juan's question, "We're going to need as much help as we can get, Juan. I'm going to try and contact a friend of mine back in the states, if I can raise him."

Juan looked at the big short-wave rig and declared, "And now if only you had the power to run this thing."

"Oh, these truck batteries will work just fine, Juan. But I'll need a long-wire antenna hung in the trees over there."

Jabe rummaged through the boxes and came up with a roll of antenna wire, connected the free end to the rig, ran the free end over the window transom. Juan motioned to Domingo who was standing outside and in an instant several men materialized in the doorway. "Por favor, Domingo." Juan took the men outside and moved away from the Ops hut unrolling the spool. They ran it out as far as it would go and hung the far end in the trees.

Jabe had the batteries wired up in no time. He hooked them to the DC input terminals on the rear of the radios and was set to go.

"How will your friend know to turn on his radio, senor?"

"Oh, that's easy, Juan. He's a ham operator and he never misses his scheduled 0900 hours rag-chew with his buddies on 20 meter phone. Franklin and I got our ham radio tickets the same day way back there in ancient history. He's got a rig right in his office, and with some luck he'll hear me when I check into the net. I only hope this old rig will get out there on the ether today." Jabe checked his watch; 0740 local time.

"It's 0840 in Washington. If I don't miss my guess, he should be on the air in about 20 minutes. That'll be time enough for the tube filaments to heat. Let's have some breakfast, Juan." Jabe switched on the radios to allow them to warm up and they went for a quick bite.

"Si, we will have a cold breakfast of rations, senor Jabe. But, it will have to do until our Juanita returns to us." Juan appeared quite sad to be fixing his own breakfast as he broke out a fresh ration and shared it.

Back at the radios again, Jabe tuned the receiver through the 20 meter band and heard voices from all over the world, loud and clear. He marveled at the reliability of these old vacuum tube rigs. After all these years, the old transmitter tuned up right on frequency. He scanned the voice traffic and listened carefully to the ongoing conversations on the 14 Megahertz band.

As he swept the receiver dial slowly through 14.150 Mh he heard the familiar call, "0900 net control. Who is checking in?"

"W5GLB checking in. Good morning, fellas." It was Franklin Gilmer checking into the net from his Washington office—right on cue!

"How about that Gilmer? He's predictable as a grandfather clock." Jabe carefully dialed the frequency into the transmitter. "Old Ten Eagles used to say Gilmer was so predictable he could read the boy's mind."

Juan looked puzzled, "Que, senor Jabe?"

"Nothing, Juan. Stand by for a second." Pressing the mike button, Jabe intoned, "W5GLB, Whiskey Five Golf Lima Bravo, this is W5GLC, Whiskey Five Golf Lima Charlie. How do you read? Over."

Franklin came right back, "W5GLC, Whiskey Five Golf Lima Charlie, W5GLB. Go to 14.120. Over."

Jabe snapped his fingers. "I got him! Good old Gilmer. Good old radio!" he said patting the transmitter cabinet softly. He quickly moved his radio frequencies 30 kilohertz and called again. Franklin was there waiting for him. Gilmer called back using their native tongue to signal he wanted to converse in their "special code" this time. He and J.B. had made it up on the reservation when they had been just boys looking for a secret cipher. Now it would come in very handy indeed. Nobody in this living world could decipher Pig-Latin Pueblo Indian.

"J.B. is that you? Are you back at home, or is that you who is causing all that trouble down south there?"

Jabe took his cue and answered the same Pig-Latin code. It would be gobbledygook to anyone listening in.

"Hell yes, it's me. And no, I'm not at home. Can you let them know I'm okay?"

"I was just out there and your Grandfather is quite fine. He was asking about you, so I lied all I could for you. Told him you were staying with me so he wouldn't worry. You got a means of communicating here on a regular basis?"

"No, nothing of the kind. I've got to stash this rig in the woods and get the hell out of here. Franklin, we're in a helluva pickle down here and I need some help."

"Yeah, you're certainly in a pickle alright. You know that airstrip they were building out on the home place is operational now. There's been a plane a day into there and now they'll be trying for two or three shipments daily.

"Franklin, how in hell can they cover such a big operation? I know they own the airplanes, but who would they get to fly them and keep their mouths shut about it?"

"Oh, that's easy. Their pilots already know the business and the routes as well. They're using inmates from the Federal prisons who are already doing time for drug trafficking. They were flying drugs for a living. Now they must be getting paid big bucks to fly the Customs C-130s. I've been keeping track of this, and virtually all the drugs coming into the U.S. now are being moved by Customs."

"That's some monopoly. How did they manage that?"

"They've squeezed out the little guys by having their South American friends refuse to sell to them. It's some kind of a political move and it's making billions for them. Last night, one of their C-130 shipments didn't arrive and they're hopping mad about it. You have something or other to do with that, too?"

"Something or other. We found a weapons cache in an old bunker and I'm prepared to do major battle down here."

"Man, what've you got yourself into? I knew you and Dudley must've been responsible for stopping their deliveries. The Mexicans have lodged a formal complaint at the UN saying you're a menace to world peace. There'll be all-out war down there till they eliminate you as a threat. Not only that, but the VP went on television last night and claimed you shot down a mercy mission. He declared you were an enemy of the New World Order. Didn't mention your name, of course. Said he was sending in troops to flush you out. That'll mean he's sending in a personalized assassination force. Don't you think it's time for you to come home?"

"Soon as I can get there, old man. First, I've got some business to tend to. I'm going to personally wipe those drug- running sonsabitches out. You just keep your regular net schedule and I'll contact you as soon as I can, okay?"

"Oooookay, fine. You'd better close it down now in case they're homing in on you. Good luck, Pal. And I'll see if I can get you some help. W5GLB clear."

Jabe was all too aware of the capabilities of swift direction finding equipment, so he shut down immediately. He was careful to move the dials off frequency and then repacked the radios into their crates. Domingo and Diego retrieved the antenna wire and came inside. They gave Jabe a hand and moved the boxes out of the Ops hut and into the shelter of the jungle and covered them with soil. Better to hide them now before things got too busy.

"Senor Jabe. It is time we started after Juanita, no?" Domingo was anxious to be on the trail.

"Domingo, you can read my mind. We need to vacate this place before Gomez comes back. Let's move out as soon as we can. We'll need all the ordinance we can carry. You have men enough to carry three of the missiles plus the batteries, and Juan and I can take the rations and extra ammo."

"Si, señor. But where have they taken her? Señor Jabe, do you think we can find Juanita and get her back safely?" Domingo had a sad look in his eye.

Jabe could see his concern and reasoned, "Mi amigo, they have taken her away in an airplane, right? I'm betting that chopper has to be stationed up at that airbase. Juan said there are no roads in or out of there. And they know we will come for her, okay? So where else would they take her except to their strongest location? Domingo, that's where she's being held alright, and you can bet your burrito on that!" Jabe headed outside and Domingo and the others followed.

"Si, then we know where to find her. But, can we get her back safely again?" Domingo wanted a guarantee that Jabe couldn't give him.

Just then, Juan arrived to answer the question, "Amigos, we will do that very thing. I do not yet know how we will do this thing, Domingo." Juan placed an arm around Domingo's shoulder, "But, with the help of my Domingo, we will find her and get her back. Do you not believe we can do it together, Domingo?"

Diego was ready to help as well, "Domingo, that old fox Gomez has been sleeping all of his life. We have outsmarted him ever since he came into our homeland. We have found him time after time. Can we not now find him yet again and get our Juanita back?"

Domingo's face brightened, and he appeared to relax a bit, "Si, if you say so amigos, I will not worry so much any more."

Juan was ready to depart, "Bueno, Domingo, muy bueno. Now, mi amigos. We go to find our sister Juanita and bring her back. Vamanos!"

The men held their rifles high and gave a cheer for their Captain. Then, at Juan's order, they fell to grabbing their gear and headed out behind Diego and Jabe. They made a stop at the bunker and selected three missiles. All loaded now, they took the trail for the beach.

Jabe could see that these men were exhausted. They had been fighting Gomez and his men for months on end and they were near the end of their ropes. How long would it be before they would get any rest?

Jabe looked over his companions with their load of military ordinance and said, "Juan, we're loaded for bear." He could not have known how correct that observation would prove to be.

28

The march along the beach was a bit risky due to the boot prints they left in the sand and the deep hoof prints left by the heavily loaded Cimarron. Diego had offered his Mustang for pack duty and the missiles had an easy ride.

So, Juan led the column into the edge of the surf so that the waves erased their tracks. It wouldn't do to have Gomez track them as easily as he'd found the tracks of Cloud Dancer.

Jabe welcomed the brisk sea breeze that blew over the beach providing a welcome refreshing to his tired companions. The sky toward the ocean was light blue with the regular scattering of puffy cumulus clouds, the portender of fair weather. By mid-afternoon, they had covered better than 20 miles and they stopped again under the palms to rest. Jabe scanned the sea horizon with his binoculars and paid particular attention to a patch of haze very far out. He sat down and enjoyed a cool drink from his canteen. A solitary Domingo was pacing the beach with both hands in his pockets and kicking shells around.

Juan came up and glanced in the direction of the haze out in the distance. "It is the smoke of a ship, no?"

"Oh, it's a ship alright. Just don't know what kind yet. We'll get a better look at her in about an hour, if she's coming this way."

Back on the trail again, the inland terrain began to rise in a series of undulating hills. By early evening, the sea breeze had swung and the wind was along the coast now. Jabe lifted his binocs and checked the seaward horizon again. The ship had hove in view. She had the outline of a coast cutter and was making heavy smoke. She was doing 40 knots or better and was heading in to shore. The angle on her bow suggested she should make landfall somewhere a few miles up ahead. As they continued their march, Jabe wondered where the harbor lay that she was steering for. In another few minutes, she rounded the curve of the beach and disappeared around the bend.

Just at twilight, the small column rounded the curve and came in view of a harbor breakwater. The installation beyond appeared to be a coast patrol base and three gunboats were tied up along the pier, some crewmen lounging on the decks. And there stood the cutter at the wharf. Her crew was busy tending hoses and pumps. A uniformed officer standing on the wharf appeared to be supervising the whole affair. Jabe studied all this through his binocs in the dim light of dusk.

"What flag does she fly, señor?" Juan was staring into the gathering darkness. Just then, the floodlights along the wharf came on and Jabe had a clear view.

"U.S. Customs, the cutter and the gunboats, Juan." Jabe could see that the hoses connecting the cutter to the wharf ran to a fueling manifold that led into a battery of pumps, valves and onshore tanks.

"She's heavy in the water, Juan, and appears to be offloading fuel. We better wait until full darkness and then have a closer look."

"She is bringing the fuel for the aeroplanes, no? That is the pipeline leading to the airbase up in the hills." Juan was pointing to a clearing in the brush that led inland.

"How far away is the airbase, Juan?"

"Only half a day on the march, I think."

Jabe would have given anything not to have heard that. He was physically running out of steam and needed a long rest. He worried for the rest of the men. If he was this tired, how must these men feel? And having to eat military field rations instead of the hearty fare provided by Juanita didn't help any.

Just past nightfall, the men moved forward along the beach and bivouacked under cover of a palm grove just outside the harbor compound. Juan selected a guard for first watch and then joined Jabe for a closer look at the harbor.

They moved down to the edge of brush cover and took a position that commanded a view of the harbor, the gunboats and the cutter. Jabe knew the fuel delivery was nearing completion now by the way the cutter rode high in the water. Directly, the crew unhooked the delivery hoses and came back aboard. She was untied and began backing out. The gunboat crews disembarked and filed up the wharf. The shore crew secured the pump station and cut the lights. Then they all climbed aboard a deuce-and-a-half troop transport and roared off. The harbor lay dark and deserted. Not a single sentry in sight.

When the cutter was well away, Jabe and Juan carefully crept along the beach and down to the wharf in the darkness. The fuel tank battery was fenced and locked. Seeing no lights and satisfied the place was deserted, they walked silently out to the gunboats for a closer look. Each of them flew three flags; Mexican, American, and U.S. Customs.

Jabe stared at the whole installation in disbelief, "Well, would you look at this! Who ever heard of a coast patrol base just lying deserted? No guards, no crews, no night lighting! A whole drug interdiction setup just lying here deserted. I don't even see any crew quarters. No harbormaster, no warehouses, no nothing! It ain't right, Juan."

Jabe began to pull off clothing. Juan watched him, and when Jabe got down to his shorts, he asked, "What will you do, Señor Jabe? Go in for a swim?"

"I want to see the hull of this gunboat for myself." With that, Jabe took his flashlight in hand, slipped quietly into the water alongside the wharf and dove under. When he was fully submerged, he snapped on the light and quickly inspected the hull. Then he surfaced and climbed out.

He sat down on the wharf, removed the lens of his flashlight and tipped it to empty the seawater that had seeped inside. He carefully dried the batteries and parts, reassembled it and sat back against the wharf railing. Juan watched him in anticipation.

"It's just as I thought, Juan. Their hulls are covered in sea moss and barnacles. They haven't been out of the harbor in months."

"What does it mean, Señor Jabe?"

"They're only decoys, Juan. They're here for the benefit of those sailors on the cutter who think they are delivering fuel for these gunboats. Those Americans have no idea they are delivering fuel for the drug shipments. Somebody is manipulating these Customs boys from the top down. It's quite a setup."

"But, señor. The gunboats can use the same gasolina as the aeroplanes?"

"Yep, they sure can, Juan. These patrol boats are powered by turbines. They use the same fuel as a turboprop airplane or a chopper. The military has standardized on one fuel for everything they've got. Except for the big nuclear warships, everything that moves runs on kerosene. And if you're right about that pipeline running up to the airbase, those U.S. Customs sailor-boys don't have a clue as to what the fuel they deliver is really being used for."

Back at the bivouac, they found the men fairly whipped after the day's long march. They decided to eat a ration and rest for a while before moving out for the airbase. Jabe checked his watch. It was nearing 2200 hours and the waning full moon had risen and provided adequate light for the long march ahead. The troops were weary and the moonlight would encourage them. They would have to cache their rations and other supplies here as the trip into the hills was too arduous for them to carry all that gear in addition to the arms and ammo. But, the sure-footed Cimarron would carry the missiles with ease. Jabe wasn't going in there without the missiles.

Domingo rousted the men from their naps and Jabe and Juan led out on the trail toward the airbase. The others followed in single file and this time Diego took up the position of rear guard leading the Mustang.

The moon had passed the zenith by the time the column had moved well inland. They had gained the top of a low hill and Juan said he was sure they were near the airbase. Up ahead, Jabe could see the familiar glow of mercury vapor lamps filtering through the jungle. The lighting was military specification alright; no civilian village in this part of the world had any of those. They left the trail and cut their way directly through to the perimeter fence.

At the edge of the jungle cover, Jabe let his ammo pack down to the ground and lowered his aching body to the earth alongside Juan.

Man, what a relief!

The rest of the column did likewise and reclined in the soft jungle vegetation, bugs or no. Everyone was plumb winded. If human bodies had been equipped with built-in odometers, Jabe was sure his had passed the million-mile mark by this point in his life. The others were in no condition to move another step and were fast asleep within thirty seconds. No one stirred for a half hour. Jabe felt himself slipping under as well. Anyway, it would be several hours before dawn and they could do nothing constructive until they had light.

Jabe's eyes opened slowly. He felt a wave of pain sweep over his aching body, but quickly shook it off. The first pale glow of dawn colored the eastern sky. Jabe knew only too well that these men were all dog tired and long overdue for a two-week liberty in a resort town. Maybe soon, but not now. At least not until they had recovered Juanita.

Across the perimeter fence, the mown grass reached to the asphalt runway and then continued beyond to a row of barracks. There were lookout towers on both ends of the compound. Jabe could see they were armed by machine-gunners. From the towers, every inch of the installation was clearly visible. Anyone crossing the base on foot from any point on the perimeter would be an easy target.

Across from the middle of the runway stood a huge maintenance hangar and there on the ramp in front of it sat three C-130s. Jabe surveyed the entire base with his binocs, then handed them to Juan who continued the surveillance. Somewhere in this inland fortress was a very frightened young woman and Jabe was determined to find her. They needed to locate where the soldiers were holding Juanita as soon as possible.

Jabe thought about the circumstances that had brought him into this drug war that seemed to go on forever. The small seizures that were reported in the news were always offset by a step-up in drug deliveries. It all seemed to be choreographed. Each little bit of forward motion was followed by yet another setback. It was sort of like dancing the Texas Two-step—one step forward, two steps back. Those folks back in the States who were actually serious about fighting the cartels and the politicians were little more than a nuisance to this evil business. Public opinion didn't make one little bit of difference to those in power. There were too many officials in very high places who could counter a citizen's every move. Each new "Drug Czar" either did nothing, or was soon rendered ineffective. The bureaucrats always saw to that. No real progress had been made in decades. The drug situation had only gotten worse and worse—all the rhetoric to the contrary. Eighty percent of the world production of illegal narcotics came in from Columbia. And now, here he was at the through-point for virtually all the drugs entering the U.S. It all came through here. He might never again get a chance like this to make a difference. Suddenly he wasn't as tired anymore. This is what he'd been waiting for. For Jabe and this little band of anti-drug guerrillas, it was now or never.

Jabe wondered how Dudley was getting along. Had he made it to a safe port? Knowing Dudley, surely he had. Would he try and catch up? Probably not. How would he know where they had gone? He couldn't. Would he be missed? Absolutely. But, Jabe had paid attention to the missile launch setup when they'd brought down their first Hercules and he could rig up these three birds the same way without any difficulty. All he would need would be a launch pad, and....launch pad! That one thought brought everything squarely back into focus.

Jabe gently shook Juan awake, "Juan, wake up. We're gunna need launch cradles, three of them, in order to fire the missiles. And pronto!"

Juan aroused instantly and sprang forward on his knees. He gathered several of the men and led them back into the jungle. The early light was sufficient for the work and they had the makeshift cradles fashioned in short order. Jabe had the men place them pointed out along the runway departure heading toward the south. He and Juan laid in the missiles and then he wired the batteries, a launcher and a firing switch to each of them. When he returned to his perch alongside Juan at the perimeter fence, the crews were boarding the planes and he realized they had arrived just in time for a crack at these big babies. But, one shot might be all they'd get. As soon as he launched the first bird, the guards would see it and pour in fire from the lookout towers. Then they'd all have to retreat in a hurry without firing the remaining missiles.

Juan must have been reading his mind, "Señor Jabe, we cannot stay here. The little bird will call attention to our position when she flies, no?"

Of course, he was right. They would need a diversion of some sort to attract the fire from the towers away from the launch point.

Jabe considered that, "Juan, maybe if we send Diego…." When Jabe looked around, Juan was already in conversation with Diego, who then pulled out with his men heading back toward the north end of the runway. They kept low in the brush to cover their movement. Juan kept Domingo and two of his men behind for cover.

Juan explained, "Diego will post his men in position to shoot up the north tower as soon as we fly the little bird."

That sounded a lot less reassuring than Jabe had hoped. As soon as the missile flew, they'd be caught in a rain of bullets unless Diego's men could bring effective fire against those towers. And he'd have to do it fast, if Jabe and the men with him were to survive.

Juan seemed confident enough, "This is a stopping place for the big airplanes, no?" Juan was on edge and keen as a jaguar. Though he had to be exhausted, he hadn't even shown a hint of fatigue. Jabe was sure now that there was more than an even chance that Juan was all Indian instead of only part.

"Exactamundo, compadre. They have to carry huge quantities of dope, so they can't take off in Columbia with full fuel loads. That severely limits their range. Then too, they're travelling such great distances, their crews need a stopover for rest about half way to the states. And this is it. It's right on their route and it's the halfway point between their South American departure base and my house." Jabe could see movement around the Herkybirds. Their crews would soon be boarding.

Juan surveyed the installation once more, and asked, "Su casa? They go to your home, Señor Jabe?"

"Yes, they most certainly do amigo. Since they started using these bigger airplanes, they have been going there for several days now. The airplane we shot down was heading there to my pueblo in the mountains of Nuevo Mejico. They have been landing and unloading their poison right there on a mesa-top on my home reservation. And that's where these three are heading right now."

Juan handed the glasses back to Jabe. He scanned the scene once more in search of some sign that might indicate where they were holding Juanita. He could see many fatigue-uniformed troops and the blue-suited flight crews moving around the hangar area. Then he caught sight of a crewman of much smaller size dressed in a blue flight suit and studied him closely. This pilot sported a bouncing red-auburn pony-tail and a trim figure. This was no guy—it was a woman! But, Jabe knew by her figure it wasn't Juanita.

This woman had a crew of three Federales following her around. She moved in and out of the hangar along with her entourage and then was taken to a small blockhouse he hadn't noticed before. It was situated far over on the distant end of the installation, well away from the hangar and barracks. It appeared to be a pump-house of some sort, possibly for the pipeline operation. Jabe wondered who she was and why she looked so important. None of the others had their own bodyguards. Maybe she had flown up on the first leg and would not be flying the next leg. Could it be Lia?

Jabe watched as the crews prepared to board their transports. Leading one crew was a large black man of middling age. Jabe watched him as he stood by the door assisting his crew into the big Lockheed. He was wearing a blue shirt with the work KODIAK across the back. He recognized his nemesis from the Texas landing strip and hoped against hope that the Bear would be piloting today. And Jabe was loaded for Bear.

Jabe handed the glasses back to Juan, "Take a look at those rotten bastards, Juan. If we can pull this thing off, they'll never see the light of another day."

"Si, Señor Jabe. And the drugs they carry will die along with them, no?"

Jabe began to feel his temper rising and his blood rushing. He wanted nothing more than to blow these bastards to hell right now. But, he was still concerned for the convict pilots who were just trying to stay alive to see their families once again. But, that was a sacrifice he was more than willing to make. He just didn't dare loose off one of the missiles until he knew where they were holding Juanita. What if they had her aboard one of the transports?

Juan glanced back at the missiles, then turned and asked, "Señor Jabe. Juanita!"

"Juan, we will not fire at anything until we know where she is located and that she is safely out of the way."

Juan continued to scan the installation and Jabe knew he was looking for his sister.

"She is not with the ones who get into the airplanes, amigo."

Jabe didn't expect they would move Juanita away from this installation. She represented a pretty nifty insurance policy against its destruction by the guerrillas.

He saw some movement near the small blockhouse, tapped Juan's arm and motioned for the field glasses. He raised them to his eyes and was astonished not to have to refocus the center wheel. Juan had perfect eyesight equal to his own. Yep, Juan Goyona had to be all Indian for sure.

Then he saw something that made him catch his breath. It was the small frame of a woman, alright. She was headed to a nearby latrine with a Federale guard in tow and she appeared to be giving him a piece of her mind. It was Juanita!

"Juan, I can see Juanita. She is way over there on the far end." Jabe handed the binocs to the excited Juan, who quickly confirmed the news.

"Señor Jabe! We have found my Juanita!"

Handing the binocs back, Juan announced in a whisper to Domingo, "Amigo, Juanita is safe. I can see her there. She is okay. Domingo, we will get our little sister back home again, sound and safe."

Dudley would have had a field day with that one, but Jabe felt his aches and pains vanish and a new rush of energy at this revelation. Those bumbling Federales had not bound or handcuffed her. And that could prove to be an expensive omission.

The force that had been gripping his heart since the kidnapping began to let go now and he breathed a little easier with the thought that they now had a chance to get her back.

Domingo raised his rifle high and grinned at this news, "Si, mi amigo, we have found her," he whispered. He seemed unable to say anything further. Big alligator tears rolled down his cheeks again, but this time they were the tears of intense relief.

Fueled and loaded now, the big transport nearest to them cranked up and began to taxi out to the far end of the field. Jabe didn't even have to change his position.

He had the firing switch in hand as he grunted, "Attaboy, fellas. Bring it on. Fly that big fat baby full of drugs right off my end of this runway. Come on, now. I've got a surprise for you boys that'll fly right up your ass end."

Then the other two Hercules fired up and followed. Jabe gulped at this turn of events. They wheeled onto the runway and lined up for a three-ship formation takeoff.

"Madre de Dios! Señor Jabe, how will we stop the three of them?" Juan was getting greedy now. One shot might be all they could get, and Juan seemed disappointed that they might not be able to bring down all three.

29

The morning sun was just peeking above the horizon as the three big transports prepared for takeoff. The first two were heavy on their wheels with contraband and the third was sporting a great deal of fire-power. Being lightly loaded, it could maneuver with ease in protecting the other two. He could plainly see that the side doors were now open and gunners were standing in the doors, each manning a weapon that was very familiar to him—a mini-gun! These were the fast 7.62mm electric Gatlings that could deliver 4000 rounds per minute. This bird would bear a close watch, indeed.

The pilots held their brakes on and brought the engines up to full military throttle. The whirling prop blades reflected the rising sun and made each a gleaming disc of golden-yellow against the green jungle beyond. The high-pitched whine of a dozen jet turbines at full throttle pierced the morning air. Heat from their exhaust made the jungle vegetation shimmer, as if rustled by an unseen wind.

"Señor Jabe. They all leave together, no?"

Juan had stayed close to his Indian comrade and stood fast in the face of the impending danger. He'd made no move whatsoever to run away from a bad situation. Jabe wondered if any other man in the outfit would have stayed with him right down to the line like this jovial jungle guerrilla did. Never mind the risk, Juan seemed to actually enjoy the excitement and Jabe was glad for his company.

"Looks like a formation takeoff, amigo. Keep your head down. They'll rake the whole perimeter with gunfire as soon as these little birds fly—you can bet on that. Have your men here hold their fire. That'll give Diego the chance to draw attention away from the missiles."

Juan passed the word.

Jabe weighed his chances for success. All the trouble he and Dudley had been through—- his scrape at the pueblo, the shootout in Galveston, their escape across the Gulf, all their trouble with Gomez, and now the situation Juanita was in——- and after all their recent efforts to stop the drug flights, he just wanted to do maximum destruction.

So he carefully planned his next move. He was sorely tempted to fire all three missiles at the same time. But flying them all at once could prove counter-productive. They might all lock-on to the same aircraft and the other two would escape. Or at best, he might only get two of them. But, now with Juanita safely out of harms way—call him greedy, call him a fanatic—Jabe Rainwater wanted them all.

Now in unison, the three heavily loaded transports began their takeoff roll. They accelerated quickly down the runway toward the waiting missiles—right into the mouth of the trap. From his semi-prone position in the grass, Jabe watched this scene in wild anticipation. His shirt was soaked with sweat and his adrenaline level was about 80-proof. He had his hand on the launch button for the last missile in line; two more buttons lay nearby. Half-reclining in the brush alongside the perimeter fence, he held his fire until the transports had passed him and went airborne.

As their wheels cleared the pavement, he pressed the button and waited while they climbed out. Target acquisition took several seconds; he remembered that. The two lead planes climbed out straight and level, but the third lagged behind a bit. Its pilot was no beginner at providing cover.

Then,.....WHAM! The first missile made a trail of smoke as it leapt into the clear blue sky and headed straight for the departing formation. The roar of the missile's solid-fuel rocket drowned out the steady drone of the turboprops.

Jabe held his breath.

Within seven seconds if rammed into the leading C-130 and exploded into a thunderous red fireball.

"WHOOO BOY! Atta Baby. Way to GO!" Jabe felt his chest tighten and his blood ran hot.

The two remaining transports banked sharply left and began a panic turn to clear the area. Jabe waited for the fireball to die, so that its heat didn't divert his next shot.

In an instant the two gun towers came to life and raked the perimeter with machinegun fire. Much of it came too close for comfort. Jabe crouched low to the earth and heard the answering fire from Diego far down the perimeter fence. This drew the attention of the tower gunners long enough for him to launch another missile, but his target was quickly moving out of range. He pressed both the launch buttons and hoped for the best.

Debris from the first transport was still raining into the jungle as the second missile fixed its target and launched, just as the first one had—true on course. Jabe watched the second transport dive toward the treetops in an attempt to avoid the inevitable, but it was too late. The impact and fireball shook the jungle like an earthquake. He felt like jumping straight up, but had to be satisfied to lie flat on his back.

"Did you see that, Juan?"

He had anticipated the launch of the third missile, but it had not fired and he could no longer see the Lockheed that had lagged behind. Where had it gone? Then he heard the roar of its engines right behind him. While he had been intent on his quarry, its pilot had reversed course, circled the field and was now behind them and circling in for the kill.

Instinctively, Jabe jumped up, wheeled around and looked face-on into the jaws of sudden death. His blood went ice-cold and he froze in his tracks. Had he finally made the mistake of an amateur and blown it? The C-130 gunship with its famous mini-guns had proven its worth in countless battles and now he was looking right down the wrong end of its barrels.

"Aye, Chihuahua! Señor Jabe!" Juan yelled from over his shoulder as he dashed for the cover of the jungle. Jabe hoofed it after Juan and his men. He didn't stay around for the last missile shot.

What the hell? It wouldn't have mattered much, anyway. The pilot would surely break away after his strafing run had destroyed them all and the missile would never attain target acquisition.

By this time, Juan and his men were already into the jungle. Jabe hurried to catch up just as the gunners opened fire.

Jabe sensed his goose was cooked, but the gunners were wide of their mark. In their excitement, they over-corrected for the deceptive speed of this limber Indian and their bullets tore up the earth just ahead of him. The vegetation fell flat and flew into shreds as if knocked down by a bulldozer.

He dove for cover as the gunners swung back and plowed up the ground he had just covered. He actually lay in a circle of undisturbed brush barely three yards in diameter. Like a deer fawn that has wandered away from its mother, he lay frozen to the ground and motionless as the plane shot past and the gunners lost their chance for a kill.

The pilot pulled up and banked sharply around for another pass, but in his excitement he had put his airplane in jeopardy.

Jabe regained his footing and made a dash for the launch button. The Hercules went rocketing outbound on the runway heading—then pitched up hard and banked again as the pilot realized his mistake. Its position wasn't perfect for the missile to lock onto him, but Jabe was out of options.

One last try for an infield triple! You don't shoot at ME and get away with it.

Jabe arrived at the perimeter fence and could see that Diego was in a fierce gun-battle with the tower gunners. He grabbed the launch button and yelled, "You're dead meat now, Charlie."

Then he grinned as he pushed the button once, then again for good measure. The plane arced over and down toward the treetops once again in a tight turn for another pass. Jabe waited and expected to feel the jolt of the launch, but the missile just sat there. Nothing. This bird was going nowhere. And Jabe was trapped out in the open.

Normally, Jabe would have settled for two-out-of-three kills on any day of the week. But this time the one that got away was going to be his undoing.

Diego's men had pumped an effective fire into the gun towers and they had gone silent. But, his rifles were no match for the firepower of the gunship.

He looked in Diego's direction and saw the men scattering in full retreat across a brushy opening that separated them from the thicker covering of the jungle. They got there just in time, but the gunners poured in fire for good measure.

Jabe felt a chill go up his spine as the big bird rolled level and began a shallow dive toward him. Closer it came, as the door-gunners prepared to open up. He was dead meat!

Through the windshield, Jabe could clearly see the pilot's head. It was the face of the black man he had seen on the tarmac. It was the Bear and he was smiling as he reached up and pulled down his helmet sun goggles. If it weren't for those eyeshades, Jabe was sure he could have seen the whites of his eyes.

The whole scene seemed to freeze in Jabe's brain. What he wouldn't have given to have just a .30-30 rifle to use! Just like old Ten Eagles, he would have raised his Winchester, taken careful aim between the pilot's eyes and squeezed off a single round, slow and sure. Who knows? That one shot might have saved them all in the last split-second.

But now, as he watched the big bird arriving at better than 300 knots, his stomach tightened in anticipation of the bullets that were about to come ripping through him. He stood straight up and held his defiant fists above his head. He had cost them dearly and he couldn't blame them for trying to defend themselves. It was human instinct, after all.

Just at the last instant, the Bear jerked his head to the side as if instinctively dodging some unseen object and the Hercules heeled over and banked nearly vertical in a panic turn Jabe could never have expected. Her left wingtip was clipping the brush and the belly of the big transport flashed by barely thirty feet over his head. Jabe felt the wind from the turboprops across his face as she passed him.

Then he heard the screaming of a small piston engine at high revs. Curious, but he thought he'd heard that sound somewhere before. On its first pass, Jabe only caught sight of it out of the corner of his eye.

It was FAST! It was RED! It was CLOUD DANCER!

DUDLEY WAS BACK! And he flew with a vengeance.

Jabe jumped into the air and waved Dudley on, "Whoooooaah, go get 'em Dudley, old Pard!"

Jabe broke into an Indian War Dance and yelled to nobody in particular, "Praise the Lord and pass the ammunition."

He looked skyward, "You rascal. I'd about given up on ya."

Jabe hoped that Dudley could distract the gunners long enough for them to get away. What else could a little two-seater do against the might of a Lockheed Hercules bristling with mini-guns?

Able to turn and maneuver Cloud Dancer much quicker than the Bear could handle the big Hercules, Dudley wheeled the Lancair through a tight turn that put the departing Hercules a short distance off his left wing. Coming around parallel, the mini-gunners opened fire on the Lancair with a two-second burst. A cloud of tracers leaving a trail of smoke and light reached out toward Cloud Dancer. Dudley was expecting it. He had pulled the nose up just in time. The tracers flew by only a yard or so beneath him.

Jabe could see Dudley slide back the canopy and hold up what looked to be a missile launcher. Where in hell did he get that? Dudley fired and a single bright-tipped trail of smoke shot toward the transport. At the same time, the gunners let fly with another burst. Their bullets passed the missile at the midway point, but Dudley had already put the Lancair into a power dive. The gunners missed again.

But Dudley didn't.

The heat of the mini-guns had attracted the missile and it flew straight into the open cargo door. A bright flash temporarily blinded Jabe and a muffled report came quickly after. But, an instant later he could still make out the Hercules.

Miraculously, it was still flying. It trailed a thin line of gray smoke that grew thicker with every passing second. Then she began a slow descent toward the airbase. Out of the battle now and mortally wounded, The Bear was trying to bring her in for a landing.

Jabe heard the rattle of a machinegun. A string of bullets that ripped up the ground a few yards outside the perimeter fence forced him to hit the deck again. New troops had reinforced the towers and the gunners had come awake from watching the air battle. With the threat of the transport's mini-guns, Jabe had completely forgotten about the gunners in the towers. That kind of a mental lapse could get you killed!

He watched as the burning Hercules made a botched landing and bounced down the runway with smoke and flames pouring out of every opening. The wing tanks exploded and the big bird began to shed engines and pieces of its wings all along the runway. The heat of burning fuel touched off the ammunition and one great shuddering explosion enveloped the fuselage from nose to tail as the big transport disintegrated in a shower of debris. The entire airplane just disappeared in a ball of orange flame and black smoke. Bits and pieces of flaming wreckage were littered along the entire length of the runway.

Angry tower gunners took aim and fired long bursts at the departing Lancair, but Dudley had kept himself well out of range. He turned Cloud Dancer out over the jungle and waggled his wings at Jabe, then dived to treetop level and flew off toward the coast.

Jabe made a dash for the jungle and caught up with Juan, Domingo and Diego on the trail back toward the beach. Juan had sent the rest of the company on ahead to safeguard their food cache and see if they could secure an area where they could hide out. After the week just passed, they were entitled to some much-needed rest.

Jabe caught hold of Diego's shoulder, "That was some fancy shooting back there, Diego. You really kept those tower gunners busy so we could man the missiles."

Diego grinned his appreciation.

Juan, who was just ahead, turned with a look of concern.

"And you, señor? They shoot at you pretty good, no? You knocked down the aeroplanes they send to the Norte. All three! Are you okay?"

"Yeah, I think so. If it hadn't been for Dudley, that gunship would have gotten us for sure. I guess we made them a little mad, amigo."

Juan agreed, "Oh si, señor Jabe. They will be out of commission for a while now, and it will be very hard to catch them asleep again. I do not think they are all as slow in the cabeza as that Gomez."

"Were any of your men hurt, Juan?"

"Thanks to you, señor, we are all okay here and no one is hurt," Juan said with a shrug. "Only Diego's feelings."

"What is this about Diego's feelings?" Jabe inquired.

Juan tried to hide a creeping smile, "Oh, just that he had to shoot twice to get the gunners in the towers. Poor Diego. Now he is feeling like he needs a long rest in order to improve his aim and regain his dignity."

Diego replied in an appealing tone, "Si, señores. All I ask is a month or two in the cantinas in Cozumel for me and my men. When we are rested, then we can continue this war. And as for me, Capitán, my aim is as good as it ever was. That gunner simply duck the first time. When he look up again, I shoot off his ear."

Everyone laughed, except Domingo, "But they still have Juanita, señores." And he was right.

30

On the march back to the gunboat base, Jabe fell in dead last in the column. He felt gladness and sorrow at the same time. He was glad to know that his pal Dudley was safe. And he was certainly thankful to him for saving his life. But, he also had a very heavy heart knowing Juanita was still in captivity. He felt the same way Juan did when he held out his dagger. If they had harmed her in any way, he would personally send them all to hell. He only hoped that he and Juan could find a way to rescue her soon.

After a half-day hike, the harbor came into view. Jabe could see Diego and his men running up the beach to greet another man who was walking toward them and carrying something over his shoulder. It was Dudley. Jabe could see Cloud Dancer parked down the beach under the palms.

Jabe said with obvious admiration, "Juan, that's quite a man down there!" They hurried to join the happy crowd.

Juan was right beside Jabe as they ran up to the throng of cheering men.

Juan was excited, "Señor Jabe, your compadre is a hero today, no?"

"You can say that again." Jabe, grinning widely, grabbed Dudley and lifted him into the air as the men gave him a cheer, "Hot damn, that was some fancy shooting back there, Cap'n."

Dudley laughed, "Well, it was the least I could do for an old pal. Seems every time I let you out of my sight, you get yourself in trouble. Somebody has to come and get you out of it, don't they? Now, put me down!"

"I guess that's so, Cap'n. And your timing couldn't have been better. How did you know where to find us and where in hell did you get that missile launcher?"

"Well, now that's quite a story. I flew out west along the coast looking for a safe haven, but there's not an airstrip for two hundred miles up that way. I made a detour inland and found a lot of the same thing, nothing. So, there I was—half my avgas gone and nothing to show for it. So I says to myself, I says, 'Self? What would a good Indian do, now?' And self said, 'Land on the beach and cool off. Then go on back to the old airstrip near dark.' And that's exactly what I did. Got there just at dusk and hangared the Dancer. Then I got to thinking I'd look through that bunker again, and guess what I found stacked against the back wall out of sight?" Dudley held up the spent launch tube.

Jabe held it up to his shoulder and looked through the flip-up sight. "I know what it is, but what's it called?"

"Old Pard, behold a wonder of our modern age. It's a Stinger missile. Shoulder-launched and guaranteed to pack a whollop at whatever you point it at."

"A C-130, for instance?" Jabe lowered the weapon and handed it back to Dudley. "I've heard about Stingers, but I didn't believe they could be so effective."

"Oh, they've got a kick, okay. Not nearly as powerful as the big ones we found, but pretty trusty. Good thing those door gunners were persistent. With all their fire-power, I guess they got a little over-confident. But, they sure provided the heat-target this baby needed. If they'd held their fire another instant, I'd have missed them completely."

"Well, they were hardly expecting any trouble from a little two-seater like the Dancer.

Dudley waved his hand toward his audience, "Well, as I was saying—there I was this morning. All wired up and armed to the teeth with nowhere to go. I figured you guys must've gone out to the east, so I flew down here to investigate. I landed right here about sunup and found your cache over there. The thing that puzzled me is that gunboat base and the fuel pipeline going inland. So, I put two and two together, took off and followed it up there to the airbase. When I got there, I could see you guys were under heavy fire from that gunship. So…"

"So you saved my skin, you son-of-a-gun!" Jabe slapped Dudley on the shoulder.

Juan chimed in, "And the skins of me and my men, señor."

Diego had caught the spirit of it all, "And the little aeroplane, señor. It is a little lamb that bites like the wolf, no?"

The whole crowd burst out laughing, but Diego had nailed it. Dudley had to let this one pass. He was quick to inquire about Juanita and Jabe filled him in.

"Juan and I are going back up there as soon as these men have had enough rest to come along. This time I'm not coming back without her. You'll give me a hand? We can expect a welcoming committee when we go back up there."

"You can count on me, J.B."

"Thanks, I appreciate that. When we've rested, I want to show you their setup. Then we can plan our next move."

Jabe pitched in to help Juan and his men cut palm fronds for camouflage. Dudley directed the effort and Cloud Dancer was completely hidden in a few minutes. With guards posted in every direction, the weary band settled in for a rest and a meal of cold rations. As soon as they could regroup up at the airbase, it wouldn't take the Federales long to launch a counter-offensive.

During the afternoon the men took turns sleeping. Jabe hoped they could enjoy a respite before they were bothered again. After inflicting such a heavy loss on the enemy, those drug-runners back at the airbase were sure to come looking for them soon.

Late in the evening after a long nap, Jabe and Dudley strolled down to the deserted wharf to have a look.

Dudley was amazed at the elaborate setup, "This is something, old Pard. They get their fuel delivered by the Navy and the U.S. Customs Department. Then they pipeline it up to the airbase—pretty slick."

"Yeah, I'd say it's pretty gutsy myself. When we were up there today, I could see the personnel who manned the transports and they've got the look of Customs people alright, just as Franklin suspected."

"Franklin knows all about this, does he?"

"Sure does. That Indian is well connected for sure. By the way, Cap'n, I wonder if these gunboats have any decent radio equipment on board. I'd sure like to contact Franklin again. See if he can give us an update on what we can expect."

Dudley was just as curious, "Let's have a look-see."

Onboard one of the gunboats sporting a tall vertical antenna, they found a complete set of marine radios. Jabe spun the dials to check their frequency capabilities. He smiled a satisfied look, "Yepper, these babies can operate on 20 meters."

He tried the switch, but nothing happened. He glanced back at Dudley, "But we'll need power to get them on the air. Will you see what you can do?"

Dudley went below, found a breaker panel and switched on the power. He called up to Jabe, "See if you can fire them up now, J.B."

Jabe tried the switches and the rigs lit right up. "Jackpot, Cap'n. We'll give Franklin a call in the morning, and see if we can raise him."

Back on the wharf now and moving back towards the bivouac, Jabe heard a whine coming from the direction of the pump shed. They walked over and found the noise was coming from a pump inside the shed. But, there was a padlock on the door.

Jabe said, "We'll need a key, Cap'n"

Jabe whistled to Juan who came on the run. "Como se va, señor Jabe?"

"I need to borrow your key, Juan."

"My key?" Juan didn't have a clue.

"This will do just fine, Juan," Jabe said, taking Juan's Browning. "This here's a key that'll open any lock those guys can come up with." Jabe pointed the 12-guage at the padlock while Juan and Dudley ducked for cover. BOOM! One round was all it took—the lock just vanished.

Inside, they found the transfer pump running at full gallop. Jabe unloaded a second round into the breaker box and the pump went silent. Dudley closed up the pump shed while Juan retrieved his weapon.

"How long do you think that thing was running, J.B.?"

"Must've just started. It wasn't running when we passed here going down to the gunboats. I'll bet they're out of fuel up there, or they wouldn't need to activate the pipeline."

Dudley smiled, "Bad timing, I'd say. They must've let their tanks go bone-dry up there. Imagine that! They've got what's left of a fleet of airplanes, but we've got control of their fuel supply. Without fuel, those planes aren't going anywhere."

"Righto, Cap'n. But, they'll sure as hell come down here to set things right again, and you can bank on that in Denver." Jabe was already moving back toward the bivouac.

That night, Juan stationed a strong guard a few hundred yards up the pipeline to protect against surprise visitors from the airbase. Just past midnight, they had a brief fire-fight with a Federale recon patrol that quickly retreated.

After that, things went quiet, but Jabe expected they'd try it again at first light. And this time they'd bring a reconnaissance in force. How he'd ever get back up there to rescue Juanita, he didn't have a clue. All he knew was that he wasn't leaving without her.

31

Early next morning, Jabe and Dudley were in the gunboat manning the radio and checking into the net. Franklin heard Jabe just as before. They moved to a clear frequency and resumed their conversation in pueblo pig-latin.

Franklin's signal was strong, *"Jabe, its good to hear you're okay."*

"We're fine, Franklin. Having a real party. Wish you were here."

"Yeah, I'll just bet. You certainly got the notice of the Vice President. He's been looking for a way to take you out. I guessed right about him sending in an assassination force. He's hand-picked the unit himself, and guess who's coming to dinner?"

"Maybe you could talk the VP into coming here and trying it himself? I'd like nothing better than to meet him up close and personal."

"Not a chance. That lily-livered bastard wouldn't meet anybody in a fair fight. I got orders to alert Seal Team 21. The C.O. is Commander McPherson."

"Jack McPherson? I know him well. We were in training together."

"I knew that, so I briefed him myself, J.B. You'll have to convince him about all the rest when he arrives."

"Will that be soon?"

"They flew down and joined the carrier Saratoga early yesterday. Should have arrived on station by now. I'm sure he'll be along. Just be sure those guerrillas of yours don't gun him down by mistake."

"Right you are, Franklin. Thanks for all your help."

"Good luck, and come home safe, J.B.……. W5GLB, clear."

They shut down the radio and Jabe briefed Dudley on the news as they headed for the beach. There they met Juan wearing a very raggedy straw hat and Jabe gave him the news as Dudley made toward the Cloud Dancer.

Dudley had the camouflage removed when Jabe arrived. "What's up, Cap'n?"

"I brought along some extra ammo here, in case we need it." Dudley lifted a Stinger missile out of the passenger seat and handed it to Jabe. Another two remained in the cockpit.

Jabe hesitated, "Better give me a quick check-out on this thing, Cap'n."

Dudley held the launcher up to his shoulder, then flipped up the sight, "Well, it's pretty easy. Just take a bead on your target through here, flip the safety off, and....... Oh, you'd better make sure nobody stands behind you, Pardner. The exhaust end of this thing will set you on fire. Here's the launch trigger," Dudley indicated the red button as he handed the weapon back to Jabe.

Jabe took the Stinger and sighted it toward one of the gunboats in the harbor, "Think it would work at this distance, Cap'n?"

"Oh, they're good up to a few thousand yards or so. Any farther than that, I don't know. You pays your money and you takes your chances, old Pard. What did Juan have to say about that fire fight last night?"

"He and Domingo were out on guard up there on the pipeline and some of those Federale soldiers tried to sneak up on them. Juan heard them creeping in. I swear he's got the senses of a brother Indian. Anyway he propped his hat on a log, then slipped off a ways and waited until they opened fire on it. He got an instant bead on their muzzle flashes and it was over in a twinkling. He's got his whole crew up there this morning. Those Federales will be back down here gunning for us, okay."

"The hell, you say. Propped his hat up on a log? No wonder that old hat of his is a mess. He must have gotten that trick out of an old Hollywood western." Dudley found it humorous.

"No way, pal. It's an old Indian trick. Where in hell do you think Hollywood got it in the first place?"

Just then, the crack of rifle fire erupted out along the pipeline. It was coming from a good distance away—then came the rattle of machineguns. Juan and his men were under attack.

Jabe leaned the Stinger against a palm tree and returned to help Dudley with the Lancair, "Looks like they're here, Cap'n. Time to say goodbye."

"Yeah, I'd better get this bird airborne pronto, just in case they break through to the beach."

Dudley grabbed a wing and began to push the Cloud Dancer out of hiding. Jabe helped him get her ready for takeoff. They pointed her nose down the beach away from the harbor and Dudley climbed into the cockpit.

"CLEAR PROP," called Dudley out of sheer habit.

"Better put her in high gear, Pardner." Jabe was pointing toward the harbor and two Federale helicopters that were coming at them from up the beach. Jabe recognized their tactics—a classic pincer movement. Their frontal attack down the pipeline would have to be supported by an end-run at the guerrilla's flank—and here it came.

Dudley lost no time. He pulled the starter and the engine came to life. He buckled up and pushed the throttle open. No time for a warm-up. Dudley would have to force the Lycoming to full power while it was still stone cold. He hated to treat her engine that badly, but this time Cloud Dancer was running for her life.

Dudley got a lucky break. The chopper gunners apparently didn't see him there beneath the palms. Their attention was drawn away toward the fighting on the ground and the choppers made a low pass, their gunners firing at the band of guerrillas.

But, this was nothing new to Juan and his men. They returned fire and their aim was accurate. The choppers broke off and headed back out over the water.

Dudley had Cloud Dancer at full throttle down the beach. Seconds later he was airborne. He stayed low to gather airspeed before climbing out. The choppers turned out over the water and began a turn for another pass at the fire-fight. They apparently hadn't even seen Dudley's take off.

Jabe retrieved his Stinger missile and aimed for the lead chopper. He followed it around with the sight's cross-hairs dead on the cockpit. He waited until it had completed its turn and had lined up for its next pass. That would bring it right toward him. It made an easy target as it bore straight in on him. He inhaled and then held his breath as he squeezed the trigger.

He was surprised at the gentle recoil as the missile left its launch tube with a hiss that reminded him of a sky rocket taking off. He watched the bright-tipped trail of smoke converge on the target and instinctively blinked to avoid the blinding flash that followed. When he looked again, the chopper had come completely undone and he heard the sharp report as the shock wave passed onshore and rolled into the jungle beyond.

The fuselage had broken into a half dozen pieces that were falling into the surf. Strangely, the rotor blades went right on flying. Still connected to the hub, they sailed along as if the chopper still owned them and headed right toward the fire-fight like a Frisbee programmed for a direct hit. The soldiers on the ground all scattered as the rotors made impact and took out a sizable swath of jungle vegetation. That ended the fire-fight.

The doomed chopper's companion had taken the hint and its pilot was beating a hasty retreat away from the beach. But, Dudley was hot after him. No way could the chopper outrun Cloud Dancer. Dudley raced after him well out to sea. Then he let fly at the chopper. The two airplanes were just specks above the horizon when Jabe saw that familiar flash.

"Good old Dudley," Jabe said to himself as he sat down under the palms and waited. Directly, Juan and Diego came down to join him.

Juan certainly appreciated the position they were in. "Señor Jabe, the Federales. We can expect them to come back again, no?"

"Oh, I believe we can, Juan. They won't give up until we are completely out of the picture."

Diego was looking toward the sea, "And here they come again, señor."

Jabe jumped up and scanned the sea horizon. Sure enough, there was another chopper circling in for an approach. This one was twice the size the others had been. It seemed they were throwing in all the firepower they had. And this time, he had no Stinger for the reception.

So, they all dived for the cover of the jungle and hoped Dudley could do his magic again.

32

Jabe wondered if Dudley would see the arrival of this new threat and come back. He needn't have worried. He'd no sooner thought of that when he saw the Lancair streaking in toward the intruder. Dudley didn't miss much. You had to get up real early in the morning to get ahead of the Cap'n!

But, curiously, Dudley didn't open fire. Instead, he circled the big chopper and brought the Lancair up alongside taking a parallel position in *formation* with it. Dudley waggled his wings to let Jabe know it was a friendly.

As they neared the beach, Jabe could see the Navy markings on the big blue chopper. The Seals had arrived!

Dudley peeled off and circled for a landing on the beach. The big Sikorsky slowed and settled to a smooth touchdown on the sand not far away from Jabe and the others. Its huge side door rolled open and out jumped several Navy Seals draped in full battle gear. They took up defensive positions around the chopper.

The tallest of the team walked straight over and addressed the ragtag group of guerrillas, "Who's in charge here. Donde es su Capitan? Comprende?"

Juan stepped forward and saluted, "I am the Capitán, senor. I am Juan Goyona and this es mi compadre from Nuevo Mejico."

The Seal returned the salute, "Commander Jack McPherson, U.S. Navy." Juan and the Commander shook hands.

Jabe offered his own hand, "Hello, Jack."

The Commander straightened his frame and grinned, "Well, J.B. Rainwater. I was told you were down here raising hell." The Commander took Jabe's hand and gripped it.

Jabe was surprised at the warm greeting, "It's good to see an old friend like you, Commander." Jabe introduced Domingo and Diego.

The Commander glanced up toward the hills, "Are we secure here fellas?"

Juan answered up without hesitation, "Si, señor. My men have had a little shooting practice this morning. But it is of no concern to us. We are always having to shoot some of those drug-running bastard peoples."

The Commander turned and gave a signal to his men, "Well, Captain Goyona, my men can help with the security here until I can find out what's going on." Then to one of his men, "Ensign Bridger?"

Juan turned to his companions, "Diego, if you will come, por favor." Juan and Diego led the Seals out to reinforce Domingo's men to ensure they were ready if another attack came.

Dudley landed and climbed out of the Lancair. He hustled over to meet their visitors.

"Commander, we're glad you're here."

Jack McPherson nodded and shook hands with Dudley.

"Yeah, I've been hearing a good deal about you guys. I didn't believe much of what I was told. Never do, 'til I can see things for myself. Maybe Mr. Rainwater here can fill me in. Take a walk with me, Lieutenant."

Jabe and the Commander took a stroll down the beach and Dudley hustled off to join Juan and Diego.

The Commander took a long look at Jabe and continued, "I've got orders to come in here and take out the people who are shooting down our U.N. mercy missions, J.B. But, Franklin Gilmer sheds a different light on things. I've known him about as long as I've known you, and he's in a position to know a lot more about what's really going on than most of my superiors."

Jabe reacted, "Mercy missions? The hell you say. This is about nothing other than drugs moving into North America, Jack. I was run out of my own pueblo so these clowns could land C-130s full of narcotics on a deserted mesa without being detected. They're moving sixty tons at a time now, not just a few hundred pounds. These Mexican guerrillas have been killed and wounded over the past six months trying to run this business out of their country. Do you think they'd react that way to a mercy mission? Hell Jack, these damned drug-running politician sonsabitches are making so much money on the drug trade, they'd say or do anything to cover their asses. Did Franklin tell you about the Customs connection?"

"Yes he did, J.B. I even saw those news clips that WNN ran. That guy Don Samuelson broke the news story of the century. But, there hasn't been another peep about that story—no response whatsoever. And I'm not sure there will be. Just like there was no proper response to those mysterious 'suicides' a while back. And I know how crooked those boys in Washington can be. There have been stories of drug dealing by the high-ups for a long time. But, it's really hard to believe that kind of thing could be kept quiet for so long. Hard to conceive they'd really go that far. Do you have any real proof that drugs are moving through here or that Customs is connected with any of it?"

"I'll tell you what, Jack. I know you've got your mission orders and a job to do here. And I respect that. When I was in the service I had as much esprit de corps as any man ever had. But, I've had a rude awakening over the past couple of weeks that I would have never dreamed about in my worst nightmares. Have you got a little time to go for a recon up to that airbase with me?"

"Airbase? What airbase?"

"Uh-huh. I thought they'd overlook telling you about that little item. I'm talking about the airbase up the hill here. It's where the Customs drug shipments make a pit stop on their way up from South America—the one where they spend the night and rest and refuel for the hop to the states. That airbase."

"Okay. That'd be the landing strip they're claiming is a Red Cross operation?"

"Landing strip my foot. It's a fortified secret compound. You'll have to see it for yourself, Jack. What are your orders, anyway?"

"All I was told was to land on the beach, deploy into the jungle and hunt you guys down. The Vice President made a special point of ordering me to shoot you on sight, J.B. What got me wondering is that he named you personally. I didn't dare tell him that I was acquainted with you. I knew you were the last person in the world to be involved in terrorism. And, they didn't want any prisoners, either. He made that perfectly clear. I've never had an order like that in my life. If any of those goofballs had ever had any military training, they'd have known better than to give a stupid order like that. Then, after we took you out, we were to find the weapons cache and take that out so the guerrillas couldn't use it."

"Yeah, they're pretty thorough aren't they?"

"That's when I decided to meet with Franklin. I called him back and asked to see him. I didn't want to leave on this mission without talking with someone at Naval Intelligence. They're the only people I really trust anymore. I don't like being the chosen executioner for some politician's personal dirty-work."

Jabe gave the Commander a quick history, "When Dudley and I started out on this campaign it was just plain war. Them against us. I didn't know much about what we had gotten into until I talked with Franklin. When we got down here we met Juan Goyona and his men and threw in with them and we've made an effective team. But, then those clowns went and made it personal. They've kidnapped Juan's sister and they're holding her at that airbase."

"Just how personal is it, J.B.?"

"Well Jack, I'm going back up to get her out of there, or I'll die trying."

"That's pretty personal."

"Jack, does your team know what their orders are yet?"

"Nope, not yet. No way I'm giving any search and destroy orders until I'm sure what the objective really is, J.B. When some politician involves you in a mission with too many unknowns, you've got to reserve some strategic decisions for yourself."

"They didn't teach you that in Seal School, Jack."

"That's for sure. But, those Seal instructors were trained in a different time, before Viet Nam. Back then, the objectives were clear as a bell. Not that way any more, is it?"

"I'm glad you talked with Franklin. But, he hasn't seen what I've seen down here. Will you come up the country with me on a recon?"

"Yeah, you bet I can. Soon as we've unloaded our field gear and I can send that chopper back to the carrier. The Task Group Commander aboard the Saratoga gave me full authority for this mission, but he doesn't know about my secret orders from the V.P. and I didn't tell him. He'll insist I keep in touch with him by radio. But, I want to go up there with you and see this for myself. What kind of help do you get from that Juan fellow?"

"The very best there is, Jack. He and his men were trained by our people back during the Nicaraguan conflict. You won't find any better."

The two men moved back along the beach. The Commander stopped for a look at the Cloud Dancer. "That's the cutest thing I've ever seen sporting wings, J.B. You guys cross the Gulf in this?"

"You bet we did. And she has served us very well since we've been here. If it hadn't been for Dudley and this little bird, I wouldn't be standing here talking with you."

The Commander bent over the open cockpit and touched one of the Stingers, "Damn, J.B. Where'd you fellas get these things?"

"I'll tell you all about it on our way up the country. We'd better get started." Jabe was anxious to show his old comrade the drug operations at the airbase. Commander Jack looked like Jabe's only ticket to freedom, and he hadn't arrived any too soon.

They took a quick tour of the gunboat base and the fuel depot. When they arrived back at the chopper, Seal Team 21 had already unloaded the gear and was ready for deployment. The big Sikorsky lifted off and headed back to the carrier as the Commander laid out the plan to reconnoiter the airbase up in the hills, "Gentlemen, we are going up-country to have a look at an installation that may be manned by unfriendly forces. Don't let friendly uniforms fool you and don't fire back at anything until you have my order. Now let's move out."

Dudley looked worried, "J.B., I'd better stay behind and get the Dancer covered and out of sight. I can catch up with you guys on the trail."

"Okay, Cap'n. But, if you hear one of those gunships open up on us again, better come a-runnin. I might need you like I did before. And don't forget to bring that Stinger with you when you come."

Jabe and the Commander took the point and led out toward the south. Passing the scene of last night's fire-fight, they found plenty of blood, but no bodies. When they reached the halfway point up to the base, the Commander signaled a rest and he radioed his boss back on the carrier. He reported he was on a routine recon patrol and would maintain contact, then he signed off and packed up the radio.

"No need to tell him very much at this point. I need to see a lot more than just that fake gunboat base and the pipeline, J.B."

"Oh, I think I can provide you with all the evidence you're going to need. We'll divert around toward the far end. You can help me check out the crash sites of those Herkybirds we took out yesterday. Are you up on your crash site investigation techniques, Commander?"

"You took out some airborne 130s?"

"I'll show you how we did that too, Commander."

"Are you sure we can get in there undetected? If there's a fire-fight, I can't order my men to help you against those people until I have the evidence I need."

"I understand perfectly, Jack. It's in the code of military conduct and I've read the manual. I think the two of us can get in there for a quick look-see and get back out again without attracting attention. But, you'll have to be a good Indian. Move fast and keep out of sight."

Jack McPherson only grinned and nodded his answer.

After a brief rest, they started out again. After a few more miles on the trail, the steady drone of a Hercules somewhere up ahead signaled that they were getting close now.

Gaining a hilltop overlooking the base, Jabe brought the column to a halt and the troops fanned out and took cover. Jack and he scanned the base using their binoculars. The wreckage of the burned Hercules was being dragged off the runway and stacked in a ragged pile beyond the crew barracks. The men working at this task wore the camouflage uniforms of the Federales. Jabe could see a column of trucks and armored

Jeeps parked alongside the barracks. One of the Jeeps had a white star painted on its doors. That was the emblem of a General Officer.

Jack asked, "That wreckage over there in a pile. Is that the remains you left on your last visit?"

"That there was Dudley's doing. And if he hadn't come along when he did, I wouldn't be here talking with you Commander. That thing was bristling with mini-guns."

"Why would a mercy mission need those?"

"Yeah, uh-huh. You can see where they took out a stand of the perimeter fence over there." Then Jabe warned, "We can expect to run into their perimeter pickets from here on in, Jack. The last time we were here, they had neglected to post any. I'll bet they haven't overlooked it this time."

"You mentioned downing some other 130s as well. Any chance you've made a big mistake here, J.B.?"

"Maybe you ought to see the other two birds for yourself. One is down south and the other is out east of here. I think you'll have all the evidence you'll need that this isn't any Red Cross operation."

They crept out quietly through the jungle keeping low as Jabe led the way. He took the Commander on a course that put them wide of any pickets that might be stationed around the base. Jabe estimated the distance to the crash site of his first kill at about four thousand yards out. About half way to the site and well downwind, he circled in until they caught the scent of turbine fuel.

The Commander had a nose almost as keen as Jabe's, "That's the smell of jet fuel, J.B."

"Just what we need for a homing beacon, Jack." In another 200 yards, they came to the edge of the crash zone. Without speaking, Jabe took the Commander in close and they sat down and remained still for a few minutes as they watched for any movement. When he was satisfied there were no guards posted, Jabe took him in for a look.

The burned-out hulk of the fuselage had been picked clean of evidence, but several yards into the underbrush around the perimeter they found bits of brown plastic wrapping. Jabe knew the clean-up crew would not have been thorough enough to have found and removed every single trace of evidence. He saw the remains of several sacks of dope himself, but he wanted the Commander to find the evidence he needed on his own. Then there wouldn't be any reason left for Jack to doubt what was going on here.

Directly, the Commander pushed back a knot of vegetation and retrieved an unbroken brown package from beneath it. He whistled softly for Jabe to come over.

McPherson slit the plastic with his service knife and tasted the contents, "This ain't medicine, J.B. It's heroin!

Jabe only cocked his head.

"Now all I need is a connection between this dope and the base down there. Can you show me what I need to see?"

"That's going to be a little harder, Jack. Let me think on that."

"No wonder they want you dead, J.B. I'm here to help you all I can." The Commander tucked the bag of contraband under his arm as they started back out the way they had come.

Jabe was less than hopeful, "I don't know, Jack. I'm grateful for any help you can give us, but this thing goes all the way to the top. I'm not sure I'll survive this adventure. They know I'm the one responsible for their losses and I'm not sure you can give me the kind of help I'm going to need."

Getting back, they rejoined Juan and the others on the hill overlooking the airbase. A constant stream of pickets wandered the fence-lines. The installation commanders were trying to avoid being surprised again.

Out toward the north, a solitary Hercules was on approach. It made a normal touchdown, then its pilot gunned the engines and took off again.

The Commander observed, "I've been hearing that Lockheed ever since we first got here. Must be a training flight, J.B. She's been doing nothing but touch-and-go."

"Yeah, they're bringing in more aircraft and probably some new crews. The new pilots have to be checked out in the 130s. Looks like they've also brought in more troop reinforcements. There are some new-ly arrived vehicles down there, too. They'll want to protect themselves better this time."

The Lockheed made another landing. This time to a full stop, then she taxied in and parked on the ramp. Jabe watched as the crew de-planed. Then he saw that same redhead with the pony-tail. She had her entourage in tow behind her. They were all wearing the blue Customs jackets and caps.

Dudley came from up the trail, "What's up guys?"

Jabe said, "Well, Cap'n, the Commander here just got an educa-tion into what's been going on."

McPherson presented his package for Dudley's inspection. "As soon as I can be sure this came from that C-130 operation down there, I believe I'll have enough evidence to back you guys up on just about any-thing you want to do."

Dudley just smiled, "I'm glad to hear that, Commander."

Jabe had been watching the redhead and following her movements around the ramp, "That redhead must be somebody real important, Jack."

The Commander put his binocs to his eyes again, "Must be. And from the look of those uniforms, you're right about this being a Customs operation. Wonder who she is?"

Dudley was curious at this, "Mind if I have a look?"

Jabe handed him the binocs.

Dudley scanned the installation and stopped dead on the redhead. "Well......so that's.........I'll be damn!" He lowered the binocs and looked straight at Jabe.

Jabe queried his pal, "You know who she is, don't you?"

Dudley put the glasses back to his eyes, "It can't be." He studied the trim frame of someone he knew very well. "J.B., I'm almost positive that's Lia MacTaggart, my old flight instructor."

"MacTaggart? Your flight instructor was Lia MacTaggart?"

"You mean you know her, too?"

237

Jabe was stunned. "Yeah, I know her alright. She was in the pen with me up at Fort Worth Federal."

Jack McPherson snapped a quick look toward J.B.

Dudley was still studying his old sweetheart, "But, what in the hell is she doing down here with these drug-runners?"

"Well, they framed her and then forced her to fly for them the same way they did me."

"No wonder I never heard from her again." Dudley seemed deeply troubled at this turn of events.

Jabe scanned the blockhouse where he'd seen Juanita the day before. There was the guard standing duty. They still had her there. Lia was marched up to the blockhouse and put inside as well. He handed the binocs to Dudley.

Dudley was somewhat relieved to see this, "They must have the girls bunking together over there in that blockhouse, or whatever it is. That could mean Lia's clean and needs watching, too."

Jack saw the same thing and asked, "Any way we can get word to them that we're here, fellas?"

Jabe answered, "Well, we certainly can't show ourselves, or they'd shoot on sight." Then to Dudley, "Cap'n, I think its time you and I made a deep recon penetration. Are you up to it?"

"To that blockhouse, right?"

"That's what I had in mind. Juan and his men can cover us if we're detected. The Commander here can come along if he's got a mind to. What do you say, fellas?"

Commander Jack was on board, "Well, a mercy mission couldn't very well object to the presence of the U.S. Navy, now could it?"

Dudley said, "Let's go for it, J.B."

Jabe and Dudley laid out their plan and the Commander posted his men with Juan's. Juan gave his men orders to provide whatever covering fire came to be needed. Jabe felt his stomach tighten as he considered their next move. Everything the Commander needed to see was just a couple hundred yards away. But, he and Dudley would have to be fast and crafty if they had any chance at all to recover Lia and Juanita. They planned to move out right after dark.

33

Jabe and Dudley were ready to start just at sundown. Commander Jack McPherson joined them after directing his men to their positions as primary backup to Juan's little band. Their combined fire-power was quite enough for the job at hand.

"You ready, Commander?" Jabe asked.

"I'm ready to rock and roll, J.B. This whole thing has got my curiosity up, and it's about to get my dander up as well. I haven't had such an adrenaline rush since way back in '64 when I was aboard the Maddox and those Commie gunboats gave us a two-day chase in the Tonkin Gulf."

"Yeah, you told me about that, Jack. But, the politicians in Congress insisted you guys made the whole thing up, as I remember. Got your skipper canned. And they'll try and do the same about this whole mess as well"

"Lousy, self-serving bastards. Don't get me started, J.B."

Jabe was glad to have the Commander's company. A better warrior was nowhere to be found.

"Things could get a little dicey in there, Commander. Juan will cover us by taking out the gun-towers if they open up on us. But, we may have to fight our way out of there against the ground troops."

Jack McPherson was not deterred, "My gunners have orders to cover anything that Juan's men can't. We'll have only about an hour and a half of complete darkness after sunset and before moonrise. Then we'll lose the advantage."

"Right you are. We'll make contact with the girls first thing. Dudley thinks he can communicate with Lia, so she and Juanita will know we're coming in. The last thing I need is to get bushwhacked by two very frightened women."

The Commander was more than ready. He was also well supplied. "I brought you some added protection, just in case we come up against some of their infantry. Better put these on." He handed Jabe and Dudley Kevlar™ flak-vests. These could stop even a .357 magnum slug at close range.

"Don't mind if I do, Commander." Dudley responded.

Jabe donned his vest, checked the clip in his Colt .45 and made sure he had plenty of extra full clips on his ammo belt. Then he paused to consider their situation.

The objectives were simple enough. All they had to do was to infiltrate a heavily armed and well-guarded military compound, find and rescue two frightened women in the dead of night, steal a sample of the goods being transported right out from under the noses of the Federales, and then the whole bunch of them would have to get back out across the runway into the cover of the jungle before they were detected. It was all simple enough.

Yeah, right! He weighed the chances for success. Here were three of the best-trained military men his country could produce. Dudley was cool, capable, absolutely trustworthy and quick on his feet. He was a superb outdoorsman, crafty, lightning fast with his hands, and he thought like an Indian. Jabe was pleased to have him along.

His old shipmate and fellow-Seal Jack McPherson was all a man could ask for in a battle companion. He had seen action in every conflict in which his country had been involved over a span of thirty years—a seasoned combat veteran. Deadly stealth was his craft and trade.

Still in Jabe's estimation, their chances were fair to poor at best.

Just after sunset in dim twilight, Juan's men and the Seals moved off the hilltop and filtered down through the brush toward the perimeter fence. They took positions in the edge of the brush at both ends of the facility in order to establish an effective cross-fire, if events called for it. When he saw they had reached their positions, Jabe led Dudley and the Commander down to a gap in the torn-up fence line as the twilight faded into darkness.

They had a clear view of the airfield. Through his binoculars Jabe could see some loading activity out around the Hercules. A column of troops had formed a line from the hangar to the C-130 on the ramp and they were passing the familiar brown plastic packages down the line by hand.

This shipment would be departing soon. Just how soon, Jabe could only guess. He and his companions lay back in the shadows as the search-lights atop the gun towers played up and down the runway and across the field to the perimeter fence.

After a quick appraisal of the scene ahead of them and making sure the roving patrol wasn't a factor, Jabe took a deep breath, moved silently through the fence and scurried out keeping low to the ground. Dudley and the Commander followed him in.

Here in the hour before moonrise, the darkness was complete. They moved in short dashes between periodic sweeps of the searchlights, then made a long sprint across the runway and took cover behind an electrical box about thirty yards from the blockhouse. Two guards in lazy conversation were stationed by the door. They wore the camouflage fatigues of Federales.

All was quiet inside the blockhouse. Jabe hoped the girls were not already asleep.

What followed had been carefully planned in advance. He patted Dudley's shoulder and then Jabe and the Commander crawled around to the rear of the blockhouse. When they were in position, Dudley gave a series of soft single-note bird calls. They went unnoticed by the guards.

Dudley's signal was the call of a night-hawk. It was an old Indian method of announcing the arrival of help. Lia knew the signal. Dudley's South Texas nasal twang was the perfect mechanism to reproduce it, and he'd had many years of practice at it.

Dudley stopped and listened for a reply. He resumed the call and then listened again. The guards stopped their talk and listened as well. This time, Jabe could hear the answering call coming back to Dudley from the blockhouse.

Now that he'd gotten an answer, Dudley gave the call again. The guards took the bait. When they rounded the corner, Jabe and Commander Jack came from behind and took them down hard, but without a sound. The guards were quickly gagged and bound although they would be unconscious for quite a while.

In an instant, Dudley was gently tapping at the door and giving his bird call. Back came the call through the door again. The door was secured on the outside by a single deadbolt. Dudley threw the bolt open, went into the dark interior and fell right into the arms of Lia. Jabe followed him in, snapped on his flashlight and was met by a smiling Juanita who fairly jumped to meet him. She was beside herself and gave a muffled shriek, "Señor Jabe! Esta usted?"

Lia was incredulous, "Dudley! I never thought I'd see you again. But, Juanita said you two would be along and from her description, I figured it could only be my Dudley. J.B. it's been a while, but I should have known you were behind all this. I thank God I wasn't in the pilot's seat of one of those birds you knocked down."

Not one to show much emotion, Jabe took Juanita's hand and broke up the reunion, "Nice to see you again, Lia, but there really wasn't any choice in the matter. We'll have to move quickly if we're going to get out of here alive." Juanita wore the biggest grin Jabe had ever seen, but they'd have to save the conversation for later.

Commander Jack had been busy outside. He wore the hat and uniform jacket of one of the guards and handed the other hat and jacket to Jabe as he came out, "Better put these on, J.B. We'll have to keep up appearances."

The searchlight was making a slow swing in their direction and Jabe had to jump back inside the door to avoid being seen. He fumbled getting the jacket over his flak vest and had just closed the door when the beam illuminated the building. The Commander straightened to attention outside, as the beam swept past. It hadn't gone much farther when it stopped cold and swung back. Jabe had only a split second to slip through the door and take up his position. After all, the blockhouse was supposed to have TWO guards.

The beam snapped back and stayed a few seconds—long enough to reassure the tower guards, then it continued its lazy sweep.

Jabe ducked back inside and hustled Dudley and the girls on their way out to the perimeter fence. He caught Juanita by the arm and gave her a quick kiss, "It's always hello and goodbye again for us, isn't it?"

"No, mi amor. Por favor, ben para aca," she frowned.

Dudley was in a hurry, "Juan will be along shortly, Juanita. Lia, make sure you two stay right on my heels. We're going to be moving fast." They waited for another sweep of the pesky searchlight and then they moved out.

Jabe and the Commander watched Dudley and the girls make for safety, then worked their way toward the back side of the hangar. They walked slowly around toward the loaded C-130 parked on the ramp. They blended in perfectly with the other Federales milling around the ramp in pairs. No one even challenged them. They waited under the wing for their chance.

Walking up and peeking through the side windows, Jabe could see the neatly stacked rows of packages wrapped in brown plastic. Jabe nodded for the Commander to have a look for himself.

McPherson peered in at the cargo and then whispered, "I still need to get inside and inspect that cargo, J.B. No way can I assume those packages contain drugs. I've got to verify it personally."

Jabe was getting anxious, "Well, we can't hang around here very long. It won't take those guards in the towers long to realize the blockhouse guards are missing."

Jabe surveyed the area and assessed their chances for the Commander to have a look inside the transport. It seemed that all the other Federales were intent on their own conversations to notice anything Jabe and the Commander were doing. So Jabe flipped the lever and slid the door back slowly. Jack hopped inside and was out again in a couple of seconds. "I've got one J.B. Let's beat it."

"Oooooookay, fine," Jabe whispered.

Dudley had eluded the search lights and taken Lia and Juanita out across the runway. They were making for the safety of the perimeter fence when Juanita slowed up and cast a worried glance back over the field looking for Jabe and the Commander. She instinctively felt for the silver chain and eagle that she had worn around her neck. But, it wasn't there. She stopped in her tracks. Now, she looked back across the field toward the blockhouse and remembered that the guard had taken it.

Dudley and Lia continued their headlong dash for safety and didn't notice that Juanita had dropped behind. Then she bolted back across the runway just as the searchlight beam arced toward Dudley and Lia. They hit the ground as the beam swept across. Then they made the final sprint to the perimeter fence.

Confident that Dudley had the girls safely out of danger and back into the jungle, Jabe and the Commander had taken a circuitous route and were walking nonchalantly down the runway toward the crew barracks. When they were far enough away, they made a quick dash for the fence.

Back safely across, they were met by Dudley and Lia, both breathing hard.

Dudley greeted his pals, "You get what you needed, Commander?"

Jabe answered, "Well if he didn't, it's too late for another look, old Pard. Where's Juanita?"

Lia looked around for Juanita, "Where did she get off to now?"

Dudley glanced around and saw Juanita making for the blockhouse. "Oh, for God's sake, there she goes. She must have gone back for something."

Jabe's heart sank as he watched the spectacle. Juanita ran like a gazelle. She was a woman with a purpose and nothing would prevent her getting that precious pendant back. The searchlight beam moved along behind her at the same rate she was running, but she was fast enough to stay just ahead of it. She ran straight up to the unconscious guards and rifled their pockets. Just then the light beam caught her square and ceased its swing.

She retrieved the pendant and made a dash for the fence, but the Federales were wide awake this time. Jabe felt that old tightness in his gut again as three of the Federale guards came running up and tackled her in the grass.

34

There was that sinking feeling again—there wasn't anything Jabe could do. Was it bad breaks or just dumb luck? What had made Juanita run back? He could only wonder.

Jabe, Lia, and the Commander could only watch as Juanita was taken back to the blockhouse from which she had only just been liberated. This time an entire platoon was placed on guard and a roving picket was set to patrolling that end of the facility.

Jabe sent runners to retrieve Juan's men and the Seals from their positions on the perimeter fence. Juan arrived with Domingo and his men expecting to see his Juanita. Apparently Juan had not seen her go back in.

Juan was smiling, "Ah, señores. And where is my little Juanita?"

Jabe told him straight out, "We didn't succeed. Dudley had them almost all the way out when she went running back."

Lia shed some light on matters, "I only know that eagle pendant Jabe gave her meant a lot. I think she went back in to get it."

Juan's face went sullen, "Aye Chihuahua! Señor Jabe!"

Getting the bad news Domingo asked, "Señor. We can go back in there and get her tonight. You will go back in there with me, no?"

Jabe could understand his frustration, "I'm sorry Domingo. As much as I want to go with you, I don't think anyone could survive another attempt at it tonight. But, don't worry. We'll figure a way to get her back. We're not leaving here without her."

Just as the Seals arrived back on the hilltop, the gunners in the towers sent a thunderous burst of machinegun fire into the brush along the perimeter. A concentrated stream of tracers riddled the positions the guerrillas had held only minutes before.

Everyone took cover in case the hilltop came under attack. They fortified their position and waited. The big transport sitting on the ramp was ready to go north, but they had no way of stopping this one.

Jabe and Dudley sat behind a boulder they had taken for cover and quietly stared at the C-130. Jabe's face was sullen and blank of expression. When he was in deep thought, he hardly ever moved or showed any sign of life at all. His thoughts were on his Juanita.

"Any ideas how we can get her back, old Pard?" Dudley ventured.

After a moment, Jabe stirred, "I've been thinking on that, Cap'n."

Jack McPherson came over and sat down, "Helluva situation, gentlemen."

Jabe allowed, "Well, we're no worse off than we were yesterday and we got Lia out. They've still got Juanita, but they're afraid to try another flight north until they've eliminated us as a threat. They have no way to know how many more of those missiles we might have here, Jack."

"So, you think they won't try to fly that baby out of here, J.B.?"

"I'm thinking they won't launch her until they can make damned sure we aren't a threat anymore. They can't afford to lose any more shipments. So, they'll come up here looking for us. Probably send some recon patrols up here before sunup."

The Commander had studied the situation, "They could fly her out any time they wish. The crews can get aboard without our knowing it. They're shielded by the transport. We could try and get back inside. Maybe try and sabotage it."

"I don't know how we could ever get back in there again, Jack. It would take a miracle."

"All we have is that Stinger and I don't know if it would penetrate. And we don't have any other fire-power that is heavy enough to be effective against the likes of that Lockheed."

Jabe and Dudley looked at each other and clicked at the same time. Dudley was getting up as Jabe said, "Hey, how about........."

"......the missile that misfired on you?" Dudley answered. "I'll take some help and check it out right now. If these Federale boys haven't discovered it, then maybe we still have some fire-power we can use against that transport, Commander." Dudley took Juan and two of his men down the hillside toward the departure end of the runway to retrieve the missile. It was their only hope of keeping that Lockheed from moving another planeload of dope to the States.

Jabe and the Commander set to work on a new plan. If the Federales hadn't found the missile and they could get it set up before sunrise and avoid the morning patrols, they just might have a chance to destroy the transport before it could get away. In the confusion of the explosion, they might have a chance to get Juanita out of there. It would be a tough undertaking, but Jabe was ready to try anything.

Dudley and Juan were gone almost an hour. When they returned, Dudley approached Jabe and the Commander. He was swinging the launch mechanism by its pigtail wire. He pitched it over to Jabe, "No wonder that missile refused to fly. The steady current from those wet cells fried the solenoids. I inspected the other two launchers, but the surge current on launch smoked them as well."

The Commander spoke up, "No way at all we can fire off that bird?"

"Not a chance, Commander. Sorry."

Dudley and Lia retired to a far corner of the hilltop to get reacquainted.

The Commander called for his field radio. "I've got to call the Task Force, J.B. Gotta give an update on the mission before they get tired of waiting and send in more troops. At this point, that would only complicate matters."

He radioed the carrier and reported that he was in position to observe the operation in question. Then almost as an afterthought he said, "Have Squadron 3 stand at the ready, just in case we need some air cover. I plan to be done here a little after sunup. I expect to extract by early tomorrow. Then we can all breathe a little easier, sir." The Commander signed off and stowed the radio.

Then he continued, "I've got the feeling you're right about us having some unwanted visitors up here by morning, J.B. If that happens, I'm going to call in the Tomcats. No way am I taking any fire from the likes of a bunch of drug runners without some help. If it's a fire-fight they want, they're damn sure going to get one."

Jabe was concerned, "We're inside a sovereign nation, Jack. This here is Mexico. Can't that open you up for some severe criticism? Maybe even a court martial?"

"Nah, I don't think so, J.B. The Captain of the Task Force can't launch an air-strike from the Saratoga unless he gets a clearance from the Joint Chiefs. Well, he's already got the okay. So that means the White House is in the loop, maybe even gave the order. It would also depend on the Mexicans making a formal complaint. They'd have to say we invaded sovereign soil for no good reason. But, I think I've got a pretty good reason right here. Got a couple of bags full of good reason. I don't think they'd be stupid enough to take a chance on blowing their cover."

Jabe eyed the bundles. Then he said, "You've got more confidence in the system than I do, Jack. If only a fraction of what Franklin Gilmer says is true, the Administration would fry your hide in a nanosecond to cover up the drug connection. They sent you in here to kill me, didn't they? Probably claim it was all some vast plot conjured up by the opposition party to incriminate the White House. And what's worse, the American people would believe it. Those same sonsabitches have already tried to take me and Dudley out more than once. And I'm damn sure going to hate it if I end up getting killed over this thing."

The Commander laid the bundles on the ground and gave them a pat. He shrugged his shoulders, "Well, you might be right. Let's just hope it doesn't come to that, J.B. I'm going to do my best to see this thing through with you and I'll be damned if I'm going to sit by and let any more of those drug flights out of here. I think we'll both be lucky to get out of this thing alive."

35

Back in Washington, it was nearly midnight when Wade Breggard entered the office of the Vice President wearing a smile of confidence. The VP was in conversation with the Chief of Naval Operations, Admiral Wayne Faragut.

The VP had assumed his stern authoritarian demeanor as he continued, "Admiral, it is imperative that your people follow my orders explicitly. The President has given me full authority to deploy whatever force is necessary to protect those Mexican food and medical shipments."

The Admiral leaned forward in his chair, "I intend to give you all the support you need. I'm just saying that my intelligence people aboard the Saratoga and forces on the ground can only confirm the activity of a band of jungle rebels down there. What makes General Mendoza think this Rainwater fellow is involved?"

The VP turned and nodded, "Mr. Breggard here can fill you in on that account. Wade?"

"Well Admiral, I've just been on the radio with the General. He still maintains that the rebel leader is one Juan Goyona. But, he also confirms that this Rainwater fellow has joined Goyona and the two of them are behind all the troubles down there. His field commander, Colonel Gomez, has captured a member of the rebel gang during a skirmish they had down there. Gomez reports the guerrillas are presently camped out on a hilltop overlooking the medical supply base. They're knocking down every shipment he tries to fly. He doesn't have enough of a garrison to defeat their fortified position and he doesn't dare try to fly any more relief supplies until those rebels are eliminated. That's why we need your help."

"Well, my people tell me pretty much the same story. We have a Seal Team in there now and they have the situation under surveillance.

They say they might need some air cover and I expect we may have some action down there come morning."

The VP cleared his throat and stood up, "That's wonderful, Admiral. The President knew he could count on the Navy to come through. This humanitarian effort is very high on the President's priority list in improving our relations with the Mexicans. You just make damn sure that Seal Team gets everything they ask for. I don't want any more trouble out of that bunch of jungle hooligans. And the Mexican government will be doubly grateful." He shook the Admiral's hand and Wade showed the Admiral out.

"Wade, my boy, we're back in business. All we need is a press release ready to go out tomorrow explaining things. You can write up a draft for my approval. Make sure we credit all those involved and the Mexicans, without whose help we could never have put a stop to the threat, etcetera, etcetera. This will make us big points with the public. I think I need a good night's sleep. I'll see you tomorrow."

"Yes sir. It will be on your desk before I leave the office tonight."

36

The night air in the jungle was finally beginning to cool down and the haze was turning into fog. The whole company was just whipped. Jabe and the Commander tried to get some rest while Juan and his men took turns at night watch.

The tower gunners kept up a sporadic fire during the night to keep the guerrillas edgy and prevent them getting any sleep. Just past midnight, Juan's men had engaged a Federale patrol creeping up from the south and sent them packing. Then everything settled down again.

Every time he tried to rest, Jabe had felt the aching in his body. He had tried to relax by staring up at the stars and once or twice he had actually closed his eyes. Every now and then he had trained his binocs on the blockhouse, but had seen nothing except the changing of the guard.

Now, just before dawn, Jabe roused himself. He stretched his muscles and began moving about the hilltop in an effort to get his tired body functioning again.

He found Dudley and Lia still in quiet conversation. "You two get any rest? Looks like you must have talked all night long."

Lia looked up and smiled, "I've been catching Dudley up on my whereabouts over these past few months." Lia laid her head back against Dudley's chest. She looked up at her old beau and touched his cheek. "I imagined I'd never see him again."

Dudley took up the explanation, "No wonder I never heard from her, J.B. The Feds had her up there in that Fort Worth Pen. She was arrested by Customs agents and summarily slammed into the pokey as a material witness against some folks she knew about. Then they had her flying for them, just like you."

Jabe acted surprised, "I didn't know they could do that."

Lia's look turned cold, "They do just as they please. And they can do anything they want to do, as long as the public lets them get away with it."

Dudley continued his unnecessary explanation, "They told her she'd witnessed or participated in key activities in a drug smuggling operation and that if she didn't cooperate she'd be prosecuted as an accessory. It was pure blackmail, J.B., and now they've brought her down here to learn to fly the C-130s."

Jabe was silent for a moment. "I know what they told me. But, what was the story they gave you, Lia.

"Well, J.B., that bunch you and I were flying for, they had that whole fleet of light twins bringing in South American smack. They said it was all a big sting operation designed to trap the kingpins and put them all in prison. That way Customs says they can eventually stop all the drugs coming into the U.S. What a laugh."

Jabe picked up the story, "I always wondered why they'd have to blackmail pilots into flying for them if it was a legitimate operation? And what happened to all the kingpins who were being set up? It's just another pile of government bullshit. They've moved several billions of dollars in drugs over the past three years. It goes on the streets in Houston, Galveston, Dallas and who knows where. They've got a whole network in place to dispose of it. With these C-130s they're bringing in, they can control the entire U.S. drug trade."

"Then you know where they're landing in the States?"

"Things were heating up for them in south Texas when I went down short of the runway on South 59 and the locals got involved. Well, the big transports don't have a safe haven there. Now they swing through northern Mexico and cross the Rio Grande at the Big Bend and land on my reservation in New Mexico. MY PUEBLO!"

Lia, continued, "I'm not surprised, J.B. They seem to be taking their orders from someone way at the top."

"Who was piloting those 130s we took out yesterday, Lia?"

"Those guys were all Customs people. They don't have any of us jailbirds trained yet—except for Al Summers. Al is an old hand at flying the big Lockheeds. They brought him down here to train the rest of us. They promised to get us out of jail if we'd fly for them. Al and I refused, but they made it clear what would happen to us if we tried to cut loose."

She looked at Dudley, "That guy who flew the gunship was the worst. Called himself 'The Bear.' I just called him Blackie. I thought he'd be the death of me, but you took him out, Sugar."

Jabe shuddered at the thought, "Yeah, that guy had me cold in his sights when the Cap'n here showed up unexpected. I can't wait to see the Commander's face when you tell him what you've just told me."

Lia's eyes softened as she changed the subject, "There's a woman being held against her will down there who'd like to tell *you* something. She's more concerned about your safety than she is about her own."

Jabe felt his belly go tight at Lia's words. He glanced toward the horizon for signs of first light. "I'm going to try and fix that situation. They've been playing us like a cat plays a mouse. I'm ready to take whatever gamble it takes to get her back and I'm damn tired of playing a lone hand against the house."

Dudley offered, "Anything we can do to help, J.B.? You just let us know."

"You just keep Lia safe, old Pard. She's done quite enough already. Better a lone Indian takes over from here on. But, thanks just the same."

The sky had paled toward the east as Jabe roused the Commander who had been fast asleep. He wondered how the hell Jack could just fall asleep like that.

"Better get ready for some action, Commander."

Jabe and McPherson gathered the little band of guerrillas around them on the hilltop. Commander Jack filled in his men about the cargo being carried aboard the C-130s. The bags of cocaine were quite enough to convince them—all but one.

"Aw, Commander. You know as well as I do there are plenty of Americans who just want to do drugs and be left alone. I think it's a fine idea to go ahead and legalize the stuff. The prisons don't have enough room for all of us."

R. Barry King

The Commander cocked his head. "So, you think only adults are involved here, do you? You're quite a macho guy, son. Real modern and thoughtful. Not the kind of a guy who lets the death of innocent children bother him? Is that what you're trying to say?"

The sailor hung his head, "I never looked at it that way, sir."

The Commander grunted, "Yeah, uh-huh."

Juan was still worried, "Señor Jabe. What can we do now? The aeroplane can leave whenever it wants to, no?"

Domingo piped up again, "And they still have our little Juanita. Aye, Chihuahua."

Jabe answered, "I don't know, amigos. We'll just have to wait and see." He was all out of bright ideas.

Jabe and the Commander lifted their binoculars and peered through the early morning light. Down on the runway, they could see a burst of activity through the breaks in the fog. Several of the Federales were converging on the blockhouse. They unlocked the door and emerged with Juanita. They began marching her toward the waiting transport.

Jabe's mouth went suddenly dry. His first reflex was to run down there at full speed and take her back. Just how he'd accomplish that, he didn't have the slightest idea.

He quickly checked the gun towers for any sign of life and saw them bristling with gunners at the ready. The tightness in his stomach turned into a fiery pit that almost doubled him over.

Commander Jack saw the same thing, "Looks like they're planning to fly her out in the transport, J.B. They know you and Juan won't try and knock this one down with Juanita aboard. And we don't have a thing to fire at them but that Stinger."

Jabe felt his body go limp, "Dammit. They're sure as hell taking her out of here. That's all I need. Son of a bitch." His shoulders slumped visibly.

But, in the next moment, Jabe jumped up and took off for the perimeter fence.

"Hey, where you going?" The Commander went right after him.

"I don't know, Jack. But I can't just sit here and watch. I don't expect anybody to come along with me. This is my fight."

254

The Commander understood. "Well, you never can have too many of these," he said as he handed Jabe his own Colt automatic. "When it comes to sidearms, two is definitely better than one."

Juan and Domingo had been watching the action down on the base.

Juan said, "Señor Jabe. We will go along with you. Maybe, with a little luck, we can get Juanita away from them, no?"

Jabe stopped to console his friend, "Amigos, this time I have to go alone. If they see all of us coming, we won't stand a chance. They'll just gun us all down for sure."

Domingo complained, "But, Señor Jabe. We cannot let you go down there alone. Juanita is one of our own."

"Domingo, the only chance you have to get her back is for me to go in there alone. It's me they really want. If they see me coming in alone, they won't harm the rest of you. That's the only chance we have. Whatever happens, I'll have to do it on my own."

Juan was incredulous, "But, what will you do, Señor Jabe?"

Jabe just shook his head, "I'll let you know just as soon as I can think of something, Juan."

Jabe had that lost feeling deep down inside again. He tried to think of every trick he'd ever learned, but he didn't have a clue what he would do next. His mind was clouded by his concern for Juanita. He knew they were just using her to get to him.

He thought of his Grandfather. What would Longrifle tell him to do now? Juan and every one of his guerrillas depended on Jabe for their safety now. And Juanita? None of this had anything to do with her. She had never done anything to these Federales. She'd done nothing to deserve the trouble she was in. She'd had nothing to do with their losses in drugs. She had never pulled a trigger against them. She wasn't even a true guerrilla. She was only the cook. Except to Jabe, that is.

Diego approached Jabe. He had a very sad expression. He was leading his little black Mustang stallion.

"Señor Jabe, por favor. You will go back in there again, no?"

"Sure will, Diego."

"You will need a way to get her safely back to us. She likes to ride my little Cimarron, and he is pleased to go in there with you, amigo. Even if he does not return. I have already asked him. And he said 'yes'."

Jabe watched as the tears streamed down Diego's face. It was clear that this faithful jungle guerrilla was willing to sacrifice the Mustang he dearly loved for the safety of his blood cousin. Every one in the group loved Juanita like a sister. She was very dear to each one of them and Jabe had never known a braver woman. He marveled at their family loyalty and the simplicity of it all. Just like the folks back home in the pueblo.

Jabe took the reins and stroked Cimarron's forehead. He considered Diego. How could he refuse the offering of such a brave heart?

"Maybe that's a good idea, Diego."

Diego's voice quivered as he stroked his loyal stallion, "You and El Cimarron will bring Juanita back to us, señor." He handed the reins to Jabe and threw his arms around the pony's neck.

His voiced broke as he addressed his faithful pony, "Vaya con Dios, amigo. One day I will see you again."

Every one of the guerrillas had been watching. They repeated the farewell in unison, "Vaya con Dios, amigos."

Then Diego turned and walked away.

Jabe mounted Cimarron. He pulled his Colt .45s and checked the clips. Then he said, "I'd appreciate any cover you boys can give me."

Commander Jack McPherson stepped up and handed over his flak vest. The look on his face said it all. Jabe took it in silence and hooked it on the saddle horn, then turned to go.

The Commander said, "J.B., I'm calling in the Navy's best. If you can distract them down there long enough to gather up Juanita, I'm damned if I'm going to let them get that Hercules off safely. It'll make me feel a lot better having a flight of Tomcats about half a minute away out over the jungle, just in case we get the chance for a clear shot."

Jabe shook his head in agreement and saluted, "Aye aye, Commander. It'd be a comfort."

Then he reined the little Mustang around and headed down toward the perimeter fence.

37

The first rays of sun broke the jungle shadows overhead as Jabe made his way down through the wooded hillside. He felt a shivering cold creeping up his spine that reminded him of the time when, as a child, he had been gathering winter firewood and he'd lost his footing in the snow and tumbled over backwards into the half-frozen creek.

Then the sensation left him as suddenly as it had come. He was feeling an insidious swirl of mixed emotions. The only thing Jabe knew was that right now, nothing he was doing felt right to him. And he also knew that an Indian is never supposed to feel that way. An Indian never makes a move without a plan. But this time, Jabe had no plan at all.

He had always been in control of his life. Even when he'd lost his wife, he had been able to come to a peace about it and go on. But today, he didn't seem to have a clue about what he was doing. How in the world could he get Juanita out of danger? He could only wonder what the new day would bring.

His trip down the trail covered a mix of soft sand, rock rubble and the slickness of solid polished sandstone, but the little pony glided over it all with ease. Cimarron had the sure footing of a mountain goat. The little Mustang seemed to sense an adventure at hand. He breathed an irregular and impatient snort and gave an occasional tremble as he stepped along.

Near the perimeter fence, Jabe reined up and sat his horse looking out across the wet grass toward the runway. The early morning dew dripped off the vegetation and he remained hidden behind a thicket of pampas grass while he surveyed the facility. A layer of morning haze still hugged the ground. Jabe had trouble making out the shadowy forms of the flight crew as they moved about the huge transport.

He held Cimarron quiet as he took in the situation. He would wait until he had a clear lay of things before he moved in. There hadn't been many times in his life when he had found himself at a loss like this. He simply didn't know what to do. Another chill down his spine suddenly sent his thoughts way back to a cold winter morning far away on his home pueblo.

Longrifle had been stoking up a fire in the kiva long before sunup. The firelight had played across the old man's face as he sat cross-legged and studied the flames. Jabe always sat still and waited for his Grandfather to speak first. That was just plain courtesy.

At last Longrifle had said, "Joe Bob, there will be times in your life when you will not know what to do. One day it will happen. All the things you have learned will be of no use to you. Do you know what you can do when that happens to you, my son?"

Jabe had admitted, "No, Grandfather. What?"

"That is when you must ask the animals."

"The animals? What can an animal tell me?"

"They can tell you a lot if you know how to listen. Maybe you get lost, or something. Maybe you are out late at night and you do not know which direction to take. If you see an animal, you can ask it what you should do. If you see a coyote, sometimes they can help. Just ask the coyote what she would do."

"And what would she have to tell me, Grandfather?"

Longrifle was quiet for a moment. "She would expect you to go where she goes, my son."

"And where does she go so late at night?"

Longrifle waited while he stirred the fire, "She probably goes home where she belongs. But, sometimes she also knows where you should go. If you listen, she will tell you how to come out safe and sound. If you follow her, she will show you."

That didn't make a lick of sense to J.B., but he found the idea interesting.

"Are the animals always right, Grandfather?"

"That's what Ten Eagles always says."

"What does he know?"

"Almost as much as I do. I heard him tell about an old mother coyote one time. He had been on the hunt for about a week and had nothing to show for it. It was a bad time for hunting, and the pueblo was without enough food. He didn't know what to do.

"He was camped on a ridge over the river and this old mother coyote came into his camp one morning. She stood and looked at him for a long time and then she lay down in the dirt. It was a bad time for her, too. She was quite thin and he could see she had a litter of pups. He had nothing to give her and he was about to starve for something to eat himself. Then, he asked her what she would have him to do."

"But how can a coyote answer a question like that, Grandfather?"

"The animals have their ways of talking to us." The Cacique had put another piece of wood on the fire, "In a little while, she got up and gave a little bark and ran off toward the south. Ten Eagles understood what she had said and went after her. In less distance than a rifle bullet can travel, he came on the tracks of an antelope. He followed them up and killed a nice fat one that fed the pueblo people a nice feast."

"What makes you think the coyote had anything to do with that?"

"When he got that antelope back to his camp, that coyote was there waiting for her share. So he shared his beef with her. And for the rest of that summer, when all of the Indian Country was hungry, Ten Eagles went out hunting and camped in that same place. And every time he did that, the coyote came and led him to a kill.

"That coyote and our pueblo made it through the summer in fine shape and she was able to raise her pups. They did it together, that coyote and Ten Eagles. You must learn to trust the animals. They have been here longer than we have."

Jabe could still hear the words of his Grandfather as a slight breeze began to blow the haze off the runway and after a minute or two Jabe could see people moving in the distance.

His vision of home faded and he stroked the neck of the spirited little Mustang.

R. Barry King

"Well Cimarron, what should we do? Have you got anything to tell me? If you can help me out, now is the time, little Pardner."

Cimarron stamped a foot and pitched his head back. He was an impatient mount and was ready to get started. Jabe patted the pony's shoulder, "Okay boy, we'll go in just a minute."

Jabe watched as a group of Federales approached the aircraft. Someone in their midst was a head shorter than the rest.

Jabe studied the situation, still at a loss for some kind of move he might make. He felt a tugging against his leg, but ignored it. Then it came again, sharper this time. Cimarron had turned his head and had the flak vest that hung from the saddle horn firmly in his teeth. He shook it again and Jabe lifted it off the saddle horn. Now it was a tug-of-war.

Jabe held it fast while the Mustang shook it, "Okay now, let it go. I'll get it off your neck." There was nowhere else Jabe could put the thing, so he slung it over his back.

"Maybe I'd better wear this thing on my back. If I'm lucky enough to get in there again, I'll need to cover my backside coming out. Is that it?" Cimarron looked back over his shoulder and began shaking his head in the negative. This was incredible. What can a horse know about what he should do?

Then, Jabe caught the clue, "No? That the wrong way to wear it?"

Jabe took it off and began buckling it over his chest. The Mustang whinnied his approval.

"Oooookay, fine. If you say so. But, I still say I'm going to need it on the way out." Jabe couldn't believe he was actually carrying on a conversation with a horse.

Then he heard the Cacique's words again, "That is when you must ask the animals." And Jabe knew better than to question the wisdom of his elders.

"If that don't beat all. I'm going to need all the armor I can get to cover my backside on the way out of there and you've got me wearing this damn thing frontward." Cimarron just shook his head again.

This time Jabe began to get the message as he felt the same old adrenaline rush he'd felt so many times before. Just like jumping off on

260

another mission. A moment before, he'd been plumb out of ideas. But, now he knew exactly what he was going to do.

He buckled the vest over his chest and shoved his Colts down the collar behind his neck. He was going to give them something they'd never expect.

The fog had lifted clear and he could see the whole scene before him now. The flight crew began to board the Hercules. They wore blue and were clearly distinguishable from the camouflage uniforms of the Federales.

Jabe recognized one of the soldiers. It was the familiar form of Colonel Gomez. He and his men were pushing Juanita toward the open door of the transport. They were heavily armed. He could see the gunners in the towers. Everyone in the installation was ready and waiting for..... his next move. Going in there would be like walking straight into hell.

Jabe felt his chest tighten as Juanita resisted her captives. She pulled and tugged to get loose while she unloosed a tirade of epithets against them in perfect Castillian. She looked out in Jabe's direction as if searching for some sign of salvation. The soldiers shoved her nearer the plane and Jabe felt his heart skip a beat. If they got her aboard, how would he ever get her back out again?

Just before reaching the open door, Juanita tugged loose and bolted straight for the perimeter fence. She dashed a full twenty yards before the gaggle of stunned Federales could take up the pursuit.

Jabe instinctively spurred the pony through the open fence and into a gallop fully exposing himself. Juanita saw him and poured on the speed. She had crossed the runway before the soldiers caught up and tackled her in the grass.

Now every eye was on J.B. Rainwater.

The soldiers had Juanita standing erect when Gomez ran up and grabbed her from behind. He looked straight at Jabe as he bent her arms behind her and held them there.

Jabe slowed Cimarron to a walk. Then he reined up the pony a scant 30 yards' distance away and waited for his chance. He and Gomez were finally face to face. The whole lot of Federales was frozen in place. The astonishment Jabe saw in their faces made the scene complete. They never expected Rainwater would show himself all alone like this.

Gomez' face was cold as stone. Jabe could see the look of murder there. The Colonel smiled as he reached around and ripped open Juanita's shirt. Then he drew a sizeable hunting knife and held it between her breasts, the blade pointing upward.

This move was undoubtedly designed to divert Jabe's attention away from Gomez and make him concentrate on Juanita, but it didn't work. Jabe felt a flash of numbness creep in. Just as fast, he consciously threw it off and concentrated on the Colonel.

Gomez looked at Jabe for a moment. He wore a sinister grin. It told Jabe that Gomez thought he was in full control of the situation. And, that was the look Jabe had been waiting to see. Overconfidence would be Gomez' downfall.

Gomez reached up and pulled a handful of her hair to force Juanita's head back and held the blade tight against her skin. Then he taunted Jabe as he yelled, "Oyaaaaayy, Gringo. You have come for the señorita, no?"

Jabe didn't answer.

Juanita squirmed and tried to lose her feet, but the Colonel held her tight, "Maybe you will come and take her away from me."

Jabe moved forward again and walked the Mustang closer to Gomez and the Federales. He held his hands in the clear so they could see he had no weapon. Gomez and his men just stood there and stared as he approached.

The Seals and guerrillas back on the hill looked at this scene in disbelief. There went a lone horseman against the might of a hundred guns, any one of which could easily pick him off with a single shot. Apparently, Gomez had given the order that he would take the Indian out personally. That was just another thing Jabe had counted on.

He walked Cimarron slowly up within ten yards of Gomez and stopped. He couldn't miss from this close. But, neither could they.

Every Federale gun in the installation was trained on him. And every guerrilla gun on the hilltop had its own target. Juan and Diego's men sighted-in on the gun towers and the Seals covered the soldiers who were facing J.B. It looked like a stand-off. And in an instant, it would all be over but the shouting.

Jabe sat coolly and watched for his chance. Then he called to Gomez, "Why don't you come and get me. I'm the one you want. The girl is no use to you."

Gomez lowered his voice, "Oh, I think I can make you come to me, señor." He moved his blade and placed it to Juanita's throat. "I can see you are a gentleman who would not like to see the blood of an innocent girl."

Juanita screamed, "Nnnoooooo!"

Gomez only grinned.

Jabe lifted his hands in surrender. The Mustang was trembling all over in anticipation and Jabe gently urged Cimarron into a walk straight for the Colonel. The Federales watched in awe as the Indian approached and everyone held their fire. When Jabe was close enough that he could put a bullet between Gomez eyes, he pushed his arms straight up over his head. At this, the Colonel laughed, lowered his knife and relaxed his hold on Juanita.

It was just what Jabe had wanted. His next move was made with blinding speed. In a heartbeat, he reached back over his shoulders and drew his Colts. Instantly, Juanita lost her feet and hit the deck leaving the Colonel fully exposed. Jabe began blasting and Gomez was the first to hit the ground.

The relaxed Federales had been caught completely off guard. While they fumbled with their bulky rifles, Jabe took them down like dominoes. Juan's men opened up from the perimeter fence taking out Gomez's men, poured a steady stream of fire into the gun towers and the Seals raked the troops with automatic gunfire.

When Juanita stood up, her captives lay dead all around her. Without even a kick to his sides, Cimarron jumped forward and Jabe scooped Juanita right into the driver's seat. He planted her in the saddle, then whirled around behind her riding backward and began firing his Colts in quick succession as Juanita spurred the pony toward the safety of the jungle. Cimarron bolted like a quarter horse.

By now the Federales on the ramp had come alive and were firing at the pair on horseback. Across the perimeter fence every gun on the hilltop was ablaze as the guerrillas and Seals poured in a thunderous response.

But, Federale rounds were still finding their mark. Jabe's vest jumped and dust flew with every bullet that hit him. Yet he continued to fire until they jumped through the fence. Juanita ran Cimarron clear to the top of the hill.

Domingo was the first to get to them. Smoke from the gunfire burned his eyes so that he could barely see. Juanita reined in the Mustang and jumped to the ground just as Domingo caught her in his arms.

"Juanita! Madre de Dios. You are home again!"

Juanita looked over her shoulder, "Domingo, por favor. Señor Jabe."

J.B. Rainwater fell off the Mustang and landed in a heap. He lay there motionless. His flak vest was covered in blood and his long black hair shown crimson.

Juanita let out a moan and fell by his side. She stroked his hair and touched his face as she whispered, "Mi amor, mi amor."

Juan and the others arrived just as she raised her tear-stained face, "Juan, is he dead?"

In a single move, every man present removed his hat in reverence.

38

Commander Jack McPherson was next on the scene followed by his entire Seal Team and the others. He pulled the weeping Juanita to her feet and Juan came forward to console his sister. Then Jack kneeled at Jabe's side and carefully rolled him over on his back. Juanita gasped at the sight. Dudley and Lia were speechless. Jabe was a bloody mess. The Commander felt for a pulse in Jabe's neck. Everyone held their breath and waited for the verdict.

The Commander breathed a sigh, "Well, he's still alive. Just barely. Corpsman?"

The firing from the compound had gone silent as a result of the deadly accurate fire from the hilltop. The Commander stood up and stepped back. At a wave of his hand, his Seal Team Medic went to work. Juan took his sister aside and the entire solemn company of fighters, both Mexican and American, sat down in the dirt to watch like a gallery of medical students observing a surgery.

The medic and his assistant rigged an I.V. and deftly began cutting away clothing. Jabe's scalp had been creased by bullets directly above each eye so that he had two new parts in his hair. His right ear was cleanly pierced and a bullet had passed clear through the deltoid of his left shoulder. Another bullet had cut a gash in his right arm just above the elbow and a long ripping wound ran across his left thigh. His flak vest was an indescribable mess of torn fabric and he was bleeding from a dozen assorted wounds.

Juanita didn't have a scratch.

But Cimarron did. Just like Jabe, he was shot through his right ear. He also had a slug in his hip. Diego wiped off the blood and pulled the trembling Cimarron to the ground. It would be a while before the medics got done with J.B. Then it would be Cimarron's turn for treatment.

From down on the field, they heard the sound of a turboprop. The Commander turned his gaze toward the field as Diego approached.

"Señor, the plane. She is getting ready to leave."

The Commander lifted his binocs and saw that the C-130 crew had started their left inboard engine. The right inboard prop began to swing as he called for his field radio. This Herkybird would be ready to taxi in another few minutes.

"Ring up the Saratoga for me, son. Let's see if we can get a little help in here."

The radio operator dialed a frequency and called, "Rubber Duck calling Mother Hen. How do you read? Over." And a moment later, "Okay, I read you five by nine. Stand by, one." He handed the microphone and headset to the Commander.

"Mother Hen, this is Rubber Duck. Scramble the chicks. I say again, scramble the chicks. Have Red Leader meet me on TAC Channel One, over. Ooooookay, fine. Over and out."

The Commander secured the radio and pulled a fine meerschaum pipe from his shirt. He unzipped a shirt sleeve pocket, retrieved a tin and stuffed the pipe bowl with tobacco. He was lighting up when Dudley came over and stood beside him.

The Commander looked over toward the medics and nodded, "Your pal is pretty shot up. How's he doing?"

"He's breathing."

McPherson shook his head, "It's a wonder he even got back to the fence."

"Yeah, he's lucky alright. Seems to get away with a lot of that kind of stuff. I didn't have any idea what he was up to."

McPherson jerked his head toward the airfield, "Neither did those hapless Federales. That was the damnedest show I've ever seen. Went right in there all by himself. Rode right up to 'em. Just like those Federales, I couldn't for the life of me figure out what he was going to do down there. What was that anyway, some kind of a cavalry maneuver?"

"Well, Indian cavalry, I guess. It's not in any of the war manuals I ever read. I think he makes it up as he goes along," Dudley chuckled.

"Well, he damn sure had a plan. No way could that have been the result of chance. It went down way too smooth for an after-thought."

Just then a rattling fire erupted from the gun towers as the gunners recovered from their momentary lapse. They raked the perimeter fence to discourage any last-minute attempts by the guerrillas to rush the transport.

The Commander continued, "They're still a bit edgy after that chivaree J.B. put on down there." He lifted his foot and placed it on a rock. He folded his arms across his knee, leaned forward and drew heavily on his pipe.

The Lockheed began to taxi away from the ramp as Dudley tapped the Commander's arm and motioned toward it, "There they go, Commander."

Jack McPherson surveyed the field and was just eyeing the gun towers when he caught the spark of muzzle flashes. The rocks and brush around their hilltop position exploded as the rounds poured in. They all hit the deck as stone shards and shredded vegetation went airborne. Bullets ricocheted in all directions.

Commander Jack settled back against the cover of a rock. "Just like being inside a corn popper, huh?"

Then all went silent again.

Dudley got to his knees, poked his head up over the rock and regarded the taxiing Lockheed, "That Herkybird will be off and gone before those Tomcats can get here, won't it?"

"Oh, I don't think so," the Commander glanced at his wristwatch. "That C-130 crew will probably take their sweet time about it. They probably won't be in a big hurry to leave. They know we would have already blown up that transport right there on the runway, if we'd had anything to use against it."

Dudley argued, "Well, they damn sure know that carrier is out there, don't you think?"

"Oh, sure they do. But, they'll expect any help that arrives will be coming for their benefit. I don't think they'll be expecting what I'm going to send them. And those jets ought to be along here pretty soon now."

"Well, they better make it snappy, Commander. You sure they understand the urgency here?"

"I'm way ahead of you, pal. While you were catching 40 winks last night, I radioed the carrier to make sure they had those F-14s warmed up and placed on the catapults before first light. Those pilots have been sitting in their cockpits since sunup."

"You put all that in place last night?"

"Roger that. Ain't radio wonderful?"

Juan scurried over and took a spot beside Dudley. "Señores. The plane."

Dudley still seemed worried, "So you think those jets are really on their way in here?"

Jack McPherson checked his watch again. "They launched about three minutes ago and they can accelerate to Mach 2 in about thirty seconds. At that rate, they can cover maybe 20 miles a minute." Then, beckoning to his radio man, "They'll be coming in right over this hill."

The Commander knee-walked over and joined Juan and Dudley. "Her Captain has been keeping the carrier about 40 miles offshore and we're about another twenty miles in from the beach. So, they should be right along now."

Dudley watched the Lockheed make her turn onto the runway and regarded Jack McPherson with a concerned look, "So you still think they'll get here in time? That C-130 will be airborne in another minute, Commander."

The Commander motioned for his radio, "Well, let's just check in and find out. What do you say?" He took the headphones and mike, selected a new frequency and called, "Red Leader, Red Leader, this is the Rubber Duck. How do you read? Over."

Hearing the reply, the Commander gave orders. "Combatants have boarded a C-130. That's a Charlie One-Three-Zero. Do you read?" A moment later, "Roger, Roger. Target is a Herkybird on the runway. Entire facility is armed and hostile. Rubber Duck is located on the hilltop west of the runway. Make your approach from the west. Read it back, over."

Jack McPherson listened intently to verify a proper read-back. Then he signed off and looked toward the west. Dudley and Juan followed his gaze skyward. Four specks were clearly visible arcing in from the northwest through the bright morning haze in the distance.

The Commander slapped his thigh, "Right on time." Then he addressed the group, "Better lay low for this, ladies and gentlemen." Everybody took cover. Then he settled back down beside Dudley and Juan.

The Tomcats came in low over the hilltop in formation echelon left and made a single pass over the airfield at terrific speed. Their wings were swept fully back as they thundered by. The rocks and brush trembled from the crackling roar of their afterburners. They made a straight run over the facility, pulled up and peeled off, two to the north and two toward the south, then began a circling approach for their ordinance-delivery runs.

At this, the Federales whooped and shouted in glee. The Commander watched as they jumped into the air and waved their arms. Some ran down the taxiway toward the transport and pointed at the approaching Tomcats to let the Hercules pilots know that help had finally arrived. Every man on the facility came outside to watch the action. They were clearly thrilled at the expectation of seeing the extermination of the guerrilla garrison on the hilltop.

The first two Tomcats arrived from the south end of the runway. They began firing from well out over the jungle. Their 20mm rounds chewed up the runway ahead of the transport and the Tomcat pilots walked their fire right into the big Lockheed. The cheers from the troops faded as the Hercules shook and trembled as she absorbed a terrific punishment.

Shards of metal and Plexiglas flew in every direction. Every round that struck her gave off a shower of sparks and flame. The impact flashes covered her like lights on a Christmas tree. Suddenly, her engines ignited and set fire to the wings. The 20mm tracers penetrated into her bowels and set fire to her entire load of contraband. The F-14s pulled up and over as a ball of fire engulfed her from nose to tail. Her entire cocaine cargo was left burning.

McPherson could feel the heat from this inferno on his cheeks and it reminded him of the white-hot core of the nuclear reactor that drove the Saratoga.

The ground troops had watched all this frozen in horror. No sooner had the first two Tomcats roared away than two more swept in from the north. The tower gunners trained their fire on the two incoming F-14s and the Federales ran for the cover of the hangar. It was a bad decision.

Juan had been arranging a reception party for the F-14s. From their hilltop position, his men opened up on the south gun tower as the Seals poured their fire into the tower on the north.

Their fire was effective and the tower guns fell silent as the two Tomcats arced across the facility and delivered an enfilading fire into the hangar facility. The hangar was left burning from end to end. Smoldering Federales escaped this inferno in every direction. Only the barracks were left standing.

The Commander surveyed the damage and called off the raid. He bid the Tomcats farewell, "Red Leader, this is Rubber Duck. We'll take it from here, fellas. Have a good flight home and tell your Momma hey."

He noticed with some trepidation the thin trail of smoke in the wake of one of the Tomcats.

Diego and his men jumped out over the perimeter fence and rushed the gun towers. The confusion on the field was complete. Smoke poured from a dozen fires that dotted the facility. The entire hangar lay in ruins and the transport on the runway was only a pile of smoking rubble. Diego and his men rounded up what remained of the Federales, disarmed them and herded them toward the center of the field.

Commander Jack moved out with Juan and Dudley close alongside and the Seals fell in behind them. Diego met them at midfield.

Juan greeted his cousin, "I see you have made some new friends, amigo. Be sure that they do not shoot you in the back."

Commander Jack made a fast count. Then he moved out toward the barracks. Approaching the buildings the Commander stopped and yelled, "Ahoy the barracks!"

A face appeared in the window. Then the door swung fully open. "Ahoy yourself, Commander. Come on in." Pilot Al Summers stood in the doorway and greeted his visitors. He had an AK-47 slung over his shoulder.

Entering the barracks, Jack McPherson was met by a peculiar scene. A Federale General sat in a chair in the middle of the room. Several high-ranking officers of the Army of Mexico stood behind him.

Al Summers introduced himself. Then he said, "The General here, with a little help from his friends, has been running this smuggling operation for quite a while, Commander. Do you know what was in that transport your fly-boys just hit out there?"

"Yep, sure do. And just where do you come into the picture, Mr. Summers?"

Just then Lia McTaggart came through the door. "I can vouch for him, Commander. He didn't volunteer for this duty station."

She ran over and hugged Al. "Good to see you're okay, Al."

Then she turned to Dudley, "He was recruited the same way I was. He checked me out in C-130s, the same way he's been made to train the others. Said I was too green to fly the missions this week."

Al retorted, "She's plumb dangerous in the pilot's seat. I couldn't risk a whole load of hash with a pilot like her. Thought you boys might be showing up here soon."

Lia's voice softened, "Saved my life. That's what he did."

Dudley nodded, "I'm grateful for that, Al."

The screech of rubber on concrete echoed through the open barracks window. The Commander bolted outside and ran toward a smoking F-14 rolling along the runway. It turned off and taxied to the ramp. Its pilot shut down the engines and raised the canopy.

Jack McPherson vaulted up on the wing and began unbuckling the pilot who offered, "Two thousand dollars worth of premium and wipe the windshield, my boy."

"How about I put out that engine fire for an extra tip, Sir? Did you catch some flak or just suck a palm-frond into the turbine?"

"Damned if I know. I hadn't even noticed that."

Diego had seen it all. As the smoking Tomcat had approached for a landing, he had found one of the large wheeled carbon dioxide fire extinguishers that was standard equipment on any aviation facility and was arriving on the run. Diego quickly had the fire out.

"Where'd he come from, Commander?" The pilot was impressed.

"I don't know, but he's always around whenever you need him. Good old Diego. Muchesa mas gracias, amigo."

Diego looked up at the Tomcat, "Madre de Dios. It is so beeg!"

They left Diego and his men walking around the Tomcat and regarding it as if it were some kind of an alien spacecraft. The Commander walked his Navy flier friend back to the barracks.

Inside again the Commander introduced the pilot, "This here's the sorriest fly-boy in the entire Navy. Thought this runway out here was the flight deck of the U.S.S. Saratoga. Saw that burning transport out there as some kind of signal fire specially lit just for his own personal guidance to a safe touchdown. I just don't know where the Navy finds this kind of trash. Meet my nephew, Lieutenant Jon Kenneth McPherson."

Everyone laughed and shook hands.

The General spoke up, "Perdona mi, señores. But let me introduce myself. I am El Jente Jeneral Jorje Alfonso Mendoza de la Garza y Chavez de la Cruz, Commandant of the Federales in the Mexican State of Quintana Roo."

"Damn!" said Pilot Al. "Say that three times fast."

The Commander regarded the General and suggested, "I think we'll just call you 'Roy' for short."

Diego was the next to speak, "Si si, señores. This is the man who sends the likes of that fox, Colonel Gomez to kill us in the jungle. This is the man who is to account for all our troubles. But, now the fox he sent to kill us is himself dead of lead poisoning."

The General protested, "I have only acted according to my orders. You would have done the same."

Diego started for the General, but Dudley caught and held him back, "Wait a minute, Diego. We're going to need him as material evidence."

"And you, señor." Mendoza was addressing Jon McPherson. "Are you a part of the American conspiracy to destroy my country?"

Jon reacted, "Who, me? What the hell does *that* mean?"

The General stood up and walked over to face the Tomcat pilot, "You are the pilot of that airplane just outside of here, are you not?"

"Well, sure. But, I was only following orders, General. Just like you."

"And who gave you the order to attack the sovereign nation of Mejico. Can you tell me that?"

Commander Jack stepped in, "General, I'd advise you to shut up and sit down." He pushed the General backwards and shoved him back into his chair. "If I have my way, you'll stand trial in a U.S. Federal Court for drug trafficking and do twenty-to-life in a state-side penitentiary."

The General glared at the Commander. "Señor, you have no legs to stand on. You and your compadres have invaded the peace and tranquility of the Mejicano people right in their own homes and there will be a price to pay, señor."

"Seems like you folks are the ones who ordered the attack. Didn't you request the assistance of a U.S. carrier task force to come in here?"

"Si si, señor. But, we needed protection from that man Juan Goyona. This is a medical assistance base operated by the Federal Mexican government and the United Nations. We only try to help the poor and the unfortunate flood victims who have no food or medicine. That Goyona and his men have been pestering us for months."

The Commander replied, "Oh you've been delivering the medicine okay. Bad medicine. Bags full of it. And it all travels to the States. I got a look inside that transport out there on the runway and sampled the goods myself. And don't act like you didn't know what it was carrying."

"Señor, you are the guilty parties. You have interfered with a mercy mission of the United Nations. And for that, you will........."

"Mercy mission?" Dudley spoke up. "The hell you say. I know good and well what kind of mission this is. You've cut a deal with some American Customs people to move drugs through this hidden airbase.

Here are two of the pilots you forced into service and we have enough evidence here to make an airtight case."

Jack McPherson was getting mad now. He motioned toward Jon, "As for this man's orders, he was simply following directions. I'd say it was just another military snafu. In all the confusion, the radio might have gotten garbled. Maybe the transmissions were faulty and the pilots got a twisted sense of the intended target. Maybe my compass went haywire and malfunctioned. It was all just an unfortunate mistake. You were the victims of friendly fire, General."

The General snarled, "Friendly fire? You killed many of my men, señor. But, it is not only you who will pay for this. I will see that Mejico gets her fair compensation for these atrocities from your government."

Jack McPherson felt his blood begin to simmer, "Friendly fire, General. That's the easy way out. If I were you, that's the story I'd tell, cause that's the story I'm gonna tell. Otherwise, you'll have to face the consequences. I'll make you wish you'd never SEEN me."

One of the Seals stuck his head in the door, "Commander, the Captain's on the horn and he's asking for you."

The Commander regarded the General for a long moment. Then he said again, "Friendly fire, General." He slowly turned and headed through the door.

Outside, the Commander joined his radioman and donned the headset, "Recon One, go ahead."

It was the Captain, "Hello Jack. You got one of my birds up there? Red Leader came aboard one short."

"Yessir. Lieutenant McPherson took a hit and had to land."

"Did you get your money's worth out of Red Leader and company?"

"Oh, you betcha we did, sir. Can you send me some help? We're going to need a little road service before we can get Jon out of here and back aboard the Saratoga. He fried his fuel lines on the starboard engine."

"I'll launch a chopper right away. Better make sure you're secure there, Jack. And watch your backside. Don't let any of those insurgents creep in there."

"The base is secure, Captain."

"Okay then. I'll send a flight of mechanics in there at once. Jack, I got an urgent signal from CNO. We can't come home until you've either taken out that Indian or we have him under arrest. I don't know why they're so paranoid about him. You going to need any more help to accomplish that?"

Jack McPherson swallowed hard and his forehead broke a cold sweat, "Negative, sir. I believe I have this about wrapped up. You can expect me back on board as soon as the Lieutenant is airworthy and out of here. We'll ride back with the mechanics."

"Okay, son. I knew I could count on you."

Jack McPherson was stuck. He was an officer of the United States Navy, sworn to obey his orders to the death. But, now he had a set of orders he severely disliked. He had to take Jabe Rainwater into custody and deliver his friend to the carrier for transport back to the States. Those high-binders in Washington would nail Jabe's hide to the wall to save their own necks. Jack also knew that this whole Mexican thing was a covert drug operation supported at the highest levels of his own government. Now that their plans had backfired and their main transfer base was a burning wreck he knew what those in power would be looking for—a convenient scapegoat.

And Jabe Rainwater would be just the ticket.

39

Just before noon, Admiral Wayne Faragut strode down the hall and turned into the office of the Vice President. He was received directly into the inner office.

The VP was seated at his desk and was just finishing a telephone conversation. He motioned for the Admiral to be seated.

"Okay Wade, thanks for the update. The Admiral has just arrived."

He hung up the telephone and greeted his visitor. "Glad you could come over right away, Admiral. What have we got?"

"Well, as you know, the USS Saratoga has been on station for a few days now in the Bay of Campeche. I've just been on the horn with the Task Group Commander down there. He reports the mission is nearing completion. I gave him clearance to utilize any amount of force he needed, just as you instructed."

"The Seal Team deployed yesterday and has had the situation under surveillance. When they called for an air strike this morning, we sent in a flight of F-14s that engaged the subjects and took out the threat. The Seal Team commander in the Yucatan is flying back aboard the carrier shortly and then we'll have the full report."

"That's good news, Admiral. Any casualties?"

"We may have lost a Tomcat, sir."

"What do you mean *may have?*"

"The pilot had an engine fire and had to land on the runway at the mission facility. Funny, but those jungle airfields usually have a pretty short strip, but this one had a runway long enough to accommodate a military fighter."

"I suppose that was fortunate for the pilot."

"The Task Group is sending in a repair detail by chopper. Not any jungle strips I know of can receive a Tomcat. I'm not sure yet what our pilots were up against, but it just seems odd that landing strip being such a long one. I'd just hate like hell to lose one of my pilots."

The VP squirmed in his chair and reached for a cigar, "Can we get that F-14 back out of there, Admiral?"

"Don't know yet, but I hope so."

"Dammit to hell, Admiral. What if the pilot can't get that Tomcat back out of there? That could cause me a world of hurt."

The Admiral cocked his head and looked askance at the VP, "Not to mention the hurt that could have befallen that brave young pilot? He's one of my men. One of my boys."

"Well sure he is, Admiral. I'm sure we'll do what's right by him. But, I'll feel a whole lot better when we get that fighter off Mexican soil and back aboard the carrier. This kind of thing can lead to a lot of embarrassment for us. I want to be kept informed about the situation out there minute by minute."

The VP stood up and the Admiral took his cue to leave. He turned to go and then said, "I should be hearing something soon. Oh, by the way. What has the President got to say about all this?"

The VP grinned and took the Admirals hand. He gripped it harder than usual, "He's leaving it all up to us, Admiral. Just you and me. You'll be in touch?"

"Yessir, I will."

The VP showed the Admiral out into the hallway. Then he turned to his assistant, "Wade, will you come in here?"

The VP continued as Wade Breggard followed him back into his office, "I want you to write up a press item for immediate release. The Navy has apparently taken out that bunch of rebels down there. Damn, but he hurt us a lot. We'll say that the USS Saratoga has participated in a mission to protect the pilots and crews of airborne U.N. mercy missions operating in Mexico. As soon as the Admiral gets us the details, we can spin the story so that we get the credit for restoring peace down there. Be sure and mention the help provided by the Navy and the Mexican authorities, etcetera."

Wade broke a thin grin, "Sounds like a plan, sir."

The VP lit his cigar and pulled at it easily. He sat down and reared back in his chair. He placed his hands behind his head and smiled, "Maybe with some luck, we'll be back in business by tomorrow, my boy."

40

It was just past mid-day when the still air of the jungle was vibrated into movement by a helicopter on approach. A column of smoke from the burning hangar rose high into the sky as the big blue Navy Sikorsky swooped down and landed close by the Tomcat sitting on the ramp.

Jack McPherson and Dudley walked up just as several sailors emerged from the cargo bay of the giant bird. The sailors lined up in a brace and stood at attention as a Navy Captain deplaned and made straight for Dudley and the Commander.

Jack McPherson snapped a salute, "Good to see you, sir. I didn't expect to see you come in here personally." Now he'd have to come clean with his boss.

"You've got quite a mess up here, Commander, and I wanted to see it all for myself. What in heaven's name has been going on? I've had one emergency communiqué after another all morning. The CNO wants a full report, so I thought I'd better have a look up here myself. He keeps saying we responded to a plea from the Mexicans for help with a bunch of guerrillas who were harassing a medical mission. But, this place damn sure doesn't look like any Red Cross outfit *I* ever saw."

"Roger that, Sir. As you can see, this place is certainly no mercy base. This facility is the refueling point for drug planes coming up from Colombia. It looks like about every kilo of cocaine going into the U.S. comes through here."

The Captain's face turned visibly pale, "Wait one minute, Commander. I can't believe the Navy is being called in to assist a bunch of drug runners. You want to clarify that?"

"Yessir, I certainly will. Let us show you around. This man here can tell you a lot more of the history than I can."

Dudley filled in the Captain on the whole story from the start. They took a tour around the burned-out hangar and came to the wreckage of the Hercules out on the runway. Near the rear of the aircraft the runway asphalt was covered by white powder about an inch or so in depth. The Captain knelt down and examined the material.

Dudley knelt by his side and ran his fingers through the crystalline contraband, "This here Hercules was filled with thousands of packages of the stuff. Here's all that's left of the load. Would you recognize cocaine if you saw it, sir?"

The Captain answered, "No, not me. I've never even seen the stuff. But, I've got a pharmacist's mate back aboard the Saratoga who knows the difference. Got anything I can use for a sample container?"

"Sure do," Jack said.

The Commander emptied his tobacco can into a pocket on his sleeve. Then he handed the empty can to the Captain. "I was able to liberate a couple of bags of the stuff from this very aircraft before she taxied out here, sir. She was carrying thirty tons or so."

The Captain gathered his sample and stood up. He slipped it into his pocket and looked at Dudley, then the Commander.

"And so you gave the order for my F-14s to attack this transport?"

Jack swallowed hard, "Yessir, I did. Then that hangar over there where they had a lot more of it waiting to go north."

The Captain slowly eyed the burning hangar and compound, "McPherson, you were the officer in command of this mission. It was your call. And if you're right about all of this, I'll go to the mat for you." Then he hesitated and looked straight at the Commander, "But, if you are wrong about any of it, I can't defend you."

"Yessir, I understand."

They walked back toward the barracks and past the mechanics who were busy with the Tomcat. The fighter's side panels lay scattered all over the ground. The chief mechanic's upper torso was deep inside the engine compartment and two sailors stood close by to assist their boss. The Captain walked over, tapped the Chief on the back and inquired, "Having any luck with her, Chief?"

The startled Chief jerked and bumped his head, "Dammit!" The Captain took a quick step backwards, "Sorry about that, son."

The chief pulled himself out of the jet's innards and backed away from the F-14 rubbing the back of his head. He saw the Captain, but didn't even attempt a salute.

"Yessir, we've about finished here. She took a couple of rounds down the throat. Nicked a fuel line and started a fire. But, they doused it before it could do major damage."

He stopped rubbing and inspected his hand as if looking for any signs of blood on his fingers.

"We've been busy fitting new fuel lines and I think she'll be able to fly out of here on her own." The Chief went back to rubbing his head. "Anything else, sir?"

"No, no. Nothing else, Chief. I didn't mean to startle you. I'm sorry about that. You go right ahead with your work there. Good work men. Nice job. I'll be grateful just to have her back aboard safe and sound. That's all. Carry on."

The Captain turned toward the barracks.

"Come on, Jack. I want to meet this General Mendoza I've heard so much about."

Lieutenant Jon McPherson popped a salute and greeted the Captain as he stormed through the door.

"Hello, Captain. Here's a fellow who wants to meet you. General Mendoza, meet my commanding officer."

The smiling General rose and extended a hand. "Excellency, it is nice to see that I am in such good hands. These guerrillas have treated me and my men badly, but now that you are here, I think we can expect......"

"You can expect nothing from me but justice, General." The Captain ignored the proffered hand. "If what my men tell me is true, then I don't think you will like the treatment you'll get from me either. You will remain under guard here, until I have decided what I will do with you. I will send my adjutant to take your statement. You may be seated."

On his way back outside, the Captain turned to Jack McPherson.

"Commander, see that these men are treated well and that they have some refreshment."

The Commander turned the Federales over to Pilot Al and then joined the others outside.

"Captain, if you please. I've got to check on my medic and the remainder of my team up on the hill. There's a wounded man up there who will need to go back aboard with us."

"One of ours, Commander?"

"He's the reason we're down here, sir. An ex-Navy Seal by the name of J.B. Rainwater."

"That the fellow we're supposed to arrest or eliminate?"

"The very same, sir. I should be back here in half an hour."

Back on the hilltop, they found Jabe sitting upright and talking with the medics as Juanita stroked his forehead.

Dudley walked up and sat down beside his buddy. "Well, if that bunch of mad-dog Federales can't kill you, then nobody can. I'm glad to see you're okay, old Pard."

Jabe grinned and winced as the medic tied the loose end of an arm sling.

"Oh, I'm in good hands alright." He glanced at Juanita. "These guys are pretty good Doc's. I can't wait to see the bill I'll get for a house call clear down here in the Yucatan."

The Commander reached for the shredded flak vest.

"You're awfully hard on government property, J.B. I don't know if I can afford to have you around here tearing up perfectly good GI equipment."

He gave the vest a good shake. Several spent slugs dropped to the ground and everyone's mouths dropped open. Everyone's but Jabe's.

"No wonder my chest hurts so badly."

The medic just shook his head, "I've got this man about as cleaned-up as I can get him, Commander. Plugged all the holes and used up all my plasma."

The Commander looked at Jabe, "You took out the whole lot of 'em, down there, Lieutenant. I counted eight in all. They had you eight to one. That the kind of odds a redskin likes?"

Jabe considered it, "Well, Commander McPherson, Sir, a redskin'll take any kind of odds he can get in a fair fight.

I say 'fair' in loose terms. They had me dead to rights. And because they were overconfident, I was the one with the upper hand. They just didn't realize it until too late. Truth is, the whole lot of those scumbags isn't worth the life of a single, harmless cockroach."

Commander Jack cocked his head, but Jabe offered no explanation. No one said a word.

The medic broke the silence.....Sir, I'll need to get this man aboard the carrier and into sick bay as soon as possible."

The Commander agreed, "Very well. Let's get out of here."

They made preparations for leaving and placed Jabe on a stretcher. At this, Diego tapped the medic on the shoulder and pleaded. "Senores, por favor. My little mustang has been waiting patiently."

Cimarron lay quietly on a bed of brush that the men had prepared for him. Juanita knelt down and held the pony's head in her lap. She stroked his quivering shoulder as the medic set to work.

The Navy corpsman worked with dedicated precision. He quickly dug the slug out of the Cimarron's hip, then disinfected the wound, sutured and bandaged it. He dressed and bandaged Cimarron's ear and stood up.

"Well, little fella, you got any more complaints?"

Cimarron only whinnied his thanks.

Diego got Cimarron to his feet and noticed he was standing uneasy. He lifted one hind foot and then the other.

"Aye, Chihuahua. He has had his shoes shot off." Cimarron was missing both his hind shoes. It was a wonder the bullets hadn't blown off both his hooves.

Jabe looked up from his stretcher, "Looks like he shared the punishment with me. Good horse. Cimarron really paid his dues today. I'd ride that pony to hell and back."

Down on the airfield, the medics placed Jabe aboard the Sikorsky while Lieutenant Jon McPherson boarded his Tomcat. The Captain was standing by the jet.

"Think you can get her back home safely, Lieutenant?"

"I'll let you know that as soon as I can get her airborne, Captain. If the landing gear is working and I don't catch fire again, I should be okay."

"Just don't bring her aboard if she isn't capable of a safe landing. I'd rather you ejected and put her in the drink than to take that kind of a chance, son. Got it?"

"Aye aye, sir." The Lieutenant saluted and dropped the canopy. Everyone moved back to give the fighter room to taxi.

Out on the runway, Jon McPherson maneuvered the big jet up close to the burned-out Hercules and turned her around into the wind. Toward the far end of the airfield, the men had just finished policing the runway removing debris as Juan turned and waved the okay.

The Lieutenant gunned the F-14's turbines to full military throttle and started his takeoff roll. Moving now at 60 knots or so, he punched in the afterburners and an orange-tipped blue flame shot out of the tailpipes.

He held her on the asphalt for maximum airspeed before he hauled back on the stick and was airborne just before he reached the jungle at the far end. He pulled her up and made altitude. He held her in a steep climb until he'd passed close to ten thousand feet above ground level, then pushed the nose over level and made a turn toward the north for the open Gulf.

Dudley moved toward the burned-out hangar. He busied himself investigating the smoking remains of file cabinets in the front office complex and started poking around in the ashes.

The Captain looked up after the departing jet, "I never get tired of seeing that. Gives me goose bumps all over. Godspeed, my boy."

The F-14 disappeared in the distance and they all waited until the jet noise had completely died away. Then the Commander approached the Captain.

"Sir, here's those packages I was telling you about."

The Captain hefted the bundles. "Heavier than they look, aren't they." He called to the team medic, "Come over here, son. Can you tell me what you think is in these bags?"

The medic came up and inspected the bundles.

He took a small taste and, surprised, said, "It's dope, Captain."

"Are you sure, son?"

"I'd bet my pension on it."

"That's good enough for me. Now let's have another talk with that Federale General, Commander."

They turned and entered the barracks. The Captain walked in and hefted the two bundles in plain view of his guests. He watched for their body-language or any changes of expression. The officers gave a noticeable jerk and began to mumble something to the General. The Captain placed the bundles on a table across the room. Then he addressed the General.

"Oh, General Mendoza, I believe these belong to you."

The General folded his arms and said, "I have never seen them before. Perhaps your Commander here has brought them along with him to try and implicate my country?"

The Captain continued, "Well, they have your name written all over them. Is this the kind of medicine you have been transporting through here?"

The General walked slowly over to the table and inspected the bundles. "Maybe it is medicine, maybe no. I do not know."

"So you admit you don't know medicine when you see it, huh? The Commander took these packages from that transport sitting out there in ruins. Oh, it's yours alright."

"Señor, do not try and play the cat and the mouse with me. I am El Jente Jeneral Jorje Alfonso Mendoza de la Garza y Chavez de la Cruz, Commandant of the Federales in the Mexican State of Quintana Roo. I am not a man to be trifled with."

"Well, I'd say you were at a temporary disadvantage, General."

"What do you intend to do with us? Just look at what you have done. You have kept me here against my will, a captive in my own country. You have blown up this facility and it is now in ruins. Haven't you done us enough damage for one day?"

R. Barry King

The Captain thought on that for a moment when Dudley came up the steps and ran into the room.

"Captain, I think you'll be interested in this."

The General fell silent and the color left his face as he recognized the item in Dudley's hand. It was a scorched ledger book. The corners were burned, but it was otherwise intact.

The Captain glanced back and noticed the change in the General's countenance as he reached for the ledger. Dudley flipped it open and pointed to some figures.

"These numbers were put down here this morning, Captain. And take a look at the signature."

The Captain looked through the ledger one page at a time. "Looks like a complete record of the tonnage going through here for the past six months or so. Dudley, my boy, you done good. These must be the aircraft numbers. This book will make things a lot simpler for us. And every entry is signed in large script." He looked up at the General. "Why, even a school child could read this."

The Captain read it aloud slowly.

"It says here, 'Jorge Mendoza de la Garza y Chavez.' Now, isn't that YOU, General?"

The General stammered, "Tha….. That is none of your business. That book……, Carrumba!" Then he regained his composure and blurted, "This is another of your lies, you Yankee swine. How dare you talk to me that way. I am the Jente Jeneral. You are the invaders of a poor country. Have you no shame?"

"What would you know about shame, General? You bastards don't know the meaning of the word." The Captain walked around the room and thought on the situation.

"But, you're in luck, General. I'm going to let you go. I've just got to make sure nobody kills you before I can get myself and my men back out of here. No way in hell I'm taking a murder charge for the likes of your sorry asses." Then he addressed the Commander.

"Jack, have we got their arms and ammo secured?"

The Commander responded, "Yessir. They can't throw anything at us but rocks."

"Then load 'em up and get 'em the hell out of here. I'm tired of looking at this trash."

The Seals and Juan's men rounded up all the soldiers, herded them out to their trucks and got them loaded. The General leaned out of his Jeep as it rolled away at the head of the column. "Death to all Yankee dogs," he yelled.

The Captain watched as the column departed, "Yeah, that's me alright. Nothing but an old meanie. Charming fellow, isn't he?"

Juan, Diego and Domingo were saying their good-byes to Jabe as the Captain approached the chopper. Juanita sat beside Jabe as he lay on his stretcher. Dudley and Lia were strapped into their seats and all ready to go.

The Captain shook guerrilla hands all around.

"Well, gentlemen, it's been good working with you. Thanks for all your help."

Juan took off his battered hat.

"Si si, Capitan. But, it is we who are in your debt for ridding us of that trash Mendoza."

Dudley retorted, "What makes you think you're rid of him, Juan. He has all the makings of a President. If you folks don't work hard for his defeat, you might see him get elected."

The three jungle fighters gasped at once.

Diego said, "Madre de Dios. We would have to spend the rest of our lives in hiding from that maniac."

Juan asked, "Capitan, por favor. My little Juanita say she no come home with us. She say she want to go with señor Jabe."

The Captain looked at Juanita, "That right, Juanita?"

"Si, señor Capitan." Juanita stroked Jabe's forehead.

Jabe said, "Is that okay with you Captain? I need a nurse real bad."

The Captain laughed, "Okay by me. Let's get started. Good bye Juan. So long Diego. Domingo."

Juan hugged Juanita once more and took Jabe's hand in his, "Señor. God has brought you to us and He will take you safely home. Vaya con Dios, mi amigo. I will see you again. One day."

Jabe shook Juan's hand, "One day, amigo. One fine day. Adios."

The big Sikorsky lifted off and slowly turned toward the north. A shout went up from the guerrilla fighters and they lifted their rifles in farewell.

The Captain ordered a landing on the beach near the Lancair and several of the Seals assisted Dudley. They took the covering of palm fronds off her and rolled her out on the beach. Dudley came over and thanked the Seals one by one. Lia climbed out and said good-bye to Juanita and Jabe.

Jabe stuck out his hand. "Where are you two headed, Cap'n?"

Dudley grabbed it, "J.B., old Pard. Lia and I are heading south. Thanks to you, things are still too hot for me in Texas."

"Where will you go, then?"

"I've got enough gasoline to reach Cozumel. I'll have time to go over this little bird feather-by-feather. We'll stay a few days and then head on down the coast. I've heard it's nice in Puerto Rico. And you? What will you do, J.B.?"

"Oh, I've got the entire U.S. Navy to take care of me. And then there's Juanita, here. I told you I wasn't leaving here without her. When you two get back to the states, you can always find us at the pueblo. I know the country up there and we'll be safe from anything that breathes. Come and see me?"

Lia chimed in, "One day, we might do just that, J.B. Take good care of yourself. Adios, Juanita."

Dudley and Lia threw their bags aboard the Lancair and climbed in. Dudley cranked up and turned the Cloud Dancer up the beach and into the wind. He and Lia waved a final good-bye.

Then Cloud Dancer rolled down the beach gaining speed, lifted off and climbed away toward open water. Dudley waggled the wings, then turned past a low-flying cloud and headed her south.

Jabe and Juanita passed the short ride to the carrier in silence. He couldn't remember when he had ever hurt this badly. It was twilight when they reached the carrier. Safely down on the deck, they were met by waiting corpsmen who took charge of Jabe's stretcher. Juanita followed them toward sick bay.

The Captain said, "Take good care of him, boys. I'll be down to see you directly, J.B." He disappeared up a ladder to tend to ship's business. Under his arm, he carried the two brown plastic packages and the ledger book.

Jabe was taken immediately into surgery and it was late evening before the ship's surgeon permitted any visitors. Juanita was the first to see him. She entered his small room and sat at the head of his bed. He opened his eyes and smiled at her. She had a look of deep concern on her face.

"Now, don't you worry about me, SweetiePie. It'll take a lot more than those Federales can dish out to whip me." He coughed long and hard. "But, they sure pounded my chest into a mess of bruises. I'll say that much for them."

A pharmacist's mate brought in a tray of pills. "You'll breathe a lot easier after you've taken these, sir."

Jabe looked at the tray, "I don't take pills."

"You do on my ship, sir. I can add this stuff to your I.V., but you wouldn't like that very much. Makes you quite nauseous when you take it that way. And I don't think you could take much of that kind of pain with your chest in the shape it's in."

"Better do as he says, J.B." It was the Commander who entered the room. "Pills knows what he's doing."

Jabe took the cup, "Okay Jack, if you say so."

The corpsman handed Jabe a glass of juice and he downed the pills all in one gulp. "Hey, that pineapple?"

"Yessir. Would you like some more? I've got plenty."

"I'll say. You can bring me about a quart of it. And another glass for my nurse here, if you please."

The Captain shoved his head through the door.

291

"Any room for the skipper in here?"

The Commander answered, "Sure is. Come on in, Captain."

"How's our patient getting along?"

The Commander continued, "This big Indian's just about to rediscover the high quality of Navy chow."

The Captain grinned, "Well he can have all he can eat. I keep my ship's company on proper rations."

The Captain said to the corpsman, "Pills, make sure he gets anything he wants and double portions for the lady."

"Aye aye, sir. You bet I will—as long as he takes his meds." The corpsman winked and ducked out.

The Captain closed the curtain and regarded his guests. "I've had the opinion of the Chief Pharmacist's Mate on the contents of those bags, Commander. He confirms your suspicions. It's cocaine alright. He wondered where in hell I'd gotten it. Had to swear him to absolute secrecy."

The Commander whistled.

The Captain continued, "Commander, I expect I'll be in for it when we arrive in Pensacola. I'm giving the CNO a report of your findings and observations in a few minutes. Any suggestions?"

"Sir, CNO takes his orders from the White House, doesn't he?"

"That's an astute observation, Commander. Of course he does."

The Commander paused, "And this is military information he'd be interested in hearing, right?"

The Captain cocked his head, but didn't answer.

Jack chose his words carefully, "Well, sir. You asked for my suggestions. The CNO's been ordered to have us come down here and take out the men who were obviously trying to stop the drug flights. And he gets his orders from the White House. I just don't think they're going to like hearing that we've busted up their game. You can't believe they are all innocent of this, can you Captain?"

The Captain folded his arms, "Go on, Commander."

"Well, the way I see it, we were just following orders. If it were me sir, I'd be able to make a convincing argument that the Federale installation was the unfortunate recipient of friendly fire when the Tomcats engaged those guerrillas. The jungle fighters were destroyed and the mission was a complete success. If Mendoza wants to open a complaint, let him face the ire of the Administration himself. If you report everything we know about this affair, I think you know what they'll do to you. Remember what they did to the skipper of the USS Maddox in that task group down in the Tonkin Gulf? And he only told the truth. Then, there was the commander of the USS Pueblo......"

The Captain paced the floor while shaking his head in the negative. As he paced, the shake turned affirmative.

"You know what, Commander. You might be right. It's not my problem. We did our jobs the best we could, you and I. Something just went wrong in there. Who knows what?" He smiled......"I like it." Then he walked out.

A half hour later he returned. He held a bottle of fine Scotch whiskey in each hand. "I've been saving these......"

"For a special occasion?" The Commander asked.

"Somehow, I don't think anyone will ask any more questions of me about this operation, Commander. As a famous Sergeant of the German Wermacht used to say, 'I hear notink, I see notink, and I know nnnnnnnot-tink!' Sometimes it's best to be just like him."

It was well past midnight when the last drink was poured. The Commander smoked his pipe and Juanita had gotten quite giggly. Jabe was very much enjoying the relaxation he'd been without for so long. He had taken his time in relating his entire story to the Captain.

The Commander verified he'd talked with Franklin and that he'd been told quite a bit about the drug smuggling operation before ever sending the Tomcats in there.

"I couldn't tell you about the allegations then, Captain. I was sworn to secrecy by Commander Gilmer. And he's with ONI."

"I understand, Commander. No sweat. I'd have done it the same way you did. J.B., you and Juanita have been through more trouble than anybody ought to have to endure. You two are lucky to be alive."

Jabe looked at Juanita and took her hand in his, "Baby, when I saw them taking you toward that transport, I didn't know what I was going to do. If they had gotten you aboard her and those Tomcats had appeared, I'd have had to watch them blow you to smithereens. And there wouldn't have been anything I could have done about it."

Juanita leaned down, squeezed Jabe's hand and half whispered, "Mi amor, it wouldn't have mattered. There's enough dope in one of those planes to kill half a million kids."

Jabe sat straight up in his bed, "You speak English!"

"Si, señor Jabe."

"Then you've understood…"

"Everything you've ever said to me."

41

The offices in the Old Administration Building were quiet at this early hour. The brisk parade of staffers and dignitaries up and down the hallways had not yet materialized when Wade Breggard brought in the VP's favorite cup full of steaming hot chocolate. He walked in and closed the door.

As usual, the VP was on the phone, "Thank you, Admiral. I appreciate the update......I've got the Mexican Ambassador here in my outer office waiting to see me, but I wanted to talk with you first........ Yes, I think I understand. It was just an unfortunate set of circumstances........ Yeah, I agree with what you're saying. They're the ones who asked us to come in there. And with that kind of a spontaneous operation, you pays your money and you takes your chances........ I'll have State look into this ASAP. I think they'll agree with your assessment. Thank you, Admiral." He replaced the receiver.

Wade placed the cup on the VP's desk. "Sir, the Ambassador is quite anxious to see you. What shall I say to him?"

"Let him sweat for a few more minutes, Wade. What did the Jente Jeneral have to say about all this?"

"I'm afraid it's not the good news we were expecting, sir."

"Yeah. Well, the Admiral said the Navy pilots who went in there got a little confused about their target. The ground commander was—how did he put it, 'imprecise' on his instructions to the Tomcats. What's in the General's report?"

"Well, I've got the decoded message right here, sir. The General puts a little different light on things. He says the whole facility was destroyed and a lot of his men were killed. He claims he is the victim of a Yankee plot to destroy his credibility. Says he was held under arrest. Claims the U.S. Navy invaded the sovereign nation of Mexico uninvited."

Wade waved the sheaf of yellow paper in the air. "He's claiming all sorts of things."

"That mangy bastard. He was supposed to provide cover for us on the ground. If he had done his job in the first place, we wouldn't have needed to bail him out. Let me see that." Wade handed the report to the VP. He read the entire report without a word. Then he dropped the papers on his desk. "Damn it all to hell. Can't this country's military ever get anything right? I've told that crank up there in the White House he'd better make the military a funding priority. And then his half-wit wife goes around cursing everyone in uniform. We're snake bit, Wade. If everything the General is saying is true, that facility is finished. They shot up the fuel depot as well. Dammit, it took me several years to put all that in place."

"Well, it may not be as bad as the General makes it sound. You know how he exaggerates things. Could be he's been dipping a little too much of his own nose candy, Sir."

"We can only hope you're right, Wade. If we lose that airfield and fueling depot, I'm finished. I can't operate a decent business without it."

"Decent business, Sir?"

"A figure of speech, my boy. The drug demand in this country is tremendous and getting bigger every day. Someone has to provide it. Why not you and me? We can't afford to have all of the profits going to those slime-balls in South America, can we? I just can't figure out what went wrong."

"It doesn't make sense, sir. With all the protection you had down there, I can't see how you lost the airstrip and all that hardware. There's a fly in the ointment somewhere, Sir."

"No fly, Wade. It's that Indian and his guerrilla friends. This time he's cost us dearly. We're down five C-130s and all of our pilots. The Bear was flying one of the birds they got. And he was my main man in Customs. The airfield is in shambles and the General's troops down there are scattered. Yessir, we're snake bit, and good. Out of business, that's what we are."

"How in the world was that Indian able to do all that, Sir?"

"This time he needed a lot of cooperation, Wade. He must have a network we don't know about. We need a helluva lot better information than we're getting. We better rethink our whole strategy here."

The red phone on the VP's desk rang. It was the direct line from the White House. He looked at Wade and scowled, "Now, what does that numb-nuts want?"

He picked up the phone, "Good morning, Sir......Yessir, I know. It's just like I've been telling you for the past couple of weeks......Well, I've been following your orders on that, Sir. We're in dealings with the Mexicans over that issue right now......Yessir, I take full responsibility for that. I'll need your authorization to involve State and the full coop-eration of the ambassador.........I don't think it's anything I can't han-dle....... Yessir, you'll come out looking quite good, sir.........Oh, yes. I'll handle it, Sir........ You bet I will."

The VP replaced the phone and looked up. He smiled, "That guy is really out in the ozone. If he had any moxey at all, he'd get his ass in gear and provide some real leadership for this country. As it is, I have to run the whole damned outfit all by myself." The VP smiled his satisfac-tion.

Wade said, "Well, we can be thankful he stays out of your hair, Sir. After all, he's really busy these days; trying to get Congress to bless his healthcare plan; jockeying for a position in the World Order; all those press conferences and people to see."

The VP chuckled, "Oh, he's got a lot of people to see alright. Mostly interns of the female variety, I'd say."

Wade snickered, "All those private meetings in the coffee closet, Sir?" Both men laughed and the VP indicated he was ready to see the Ambassador.

Wade got up, walked over and opened the door, "Mr. Ambassa-dor. The Vice President will see you, now."

Wade showed the Ambassador to a chair sitting opposite the VP. The Ambassador was a slight man in his fifties. He wore the conventional off-white business suit and looked quite the part of a tropical Latino. He remained standing.

R. Barry King

The VP stood up and greeted his guest, "Nice to see you again, Miguel." The two shook hands.

"I am glad you could see me on such a short notice, Jefe."

"Oh, it's El Jefe again, is it?"

"Por favor, Jefe. When I was Alcalde of Mejico City and you were a Senator, it was a title you liked very much. Now, everyone knows you are the one who runs things in this country, my friend."

"Oh, cut out the bullshit and have a seat, Miguel. You could charm the fruit off a prickly-pear cactus." The men took their seats.

"Now, what can I do for you?"

"Jefe, the military commander in Quintana Roo is Jente Jeneral Mendoza. I believe you know who he is. He is trying to make a lot of trouble for you. He has been bending the ears of our Presidente. He called me to complain as well. Now, my government threatens to lodge an official complaint against the U.S. for what he termed "an invasion.""

"Well Miguel, as you know, we were called in to help the good General out of a problem down there yesterday. We sent in some Navy jets to cover his operation. I tried to help him out of the problem he'd gotten himself into the best I could, and that's all. It was all at his request."

"Yes, I know that my government asked for your Navy to provide air cover against that band of insurgents down there. But, now the Jeneral claims the jets severely damaged the facility and there were some casualties among his men, Jefe. The raid was supposed to help the situation, but instead we have lost everything."

"Well, that's unfortunate, Miguel. The Navy tells me that it was simply a mistake. Can't always tell what'll happen in a military engagement, can you? Your people will have to take some of the responsibility for this. You can make them see that, can't you?"

"Well, I do not know, Jefe. You see, it was your Navy…….."

"I'll tell you what, Miguel. This would never have happened if you had paid attention and had that limp-brain General of yours provide the protection we're paying him for."

298

The Ambassador looked at the VP for a long moment. "Jefe, you cannot hold me responsible for this. I have done the best I could do for you."

"For me? The hell you say." The VP stood up and leaned over his desk toward his guest, "I've been paying you and the General very well for your trouble. You've been lining your pockets ever since we started this operation and I've paid you people quite a bundle. And what do I get in return? Threats! That's what I get for my trouble. And I don't need that, Miguel. So, you'd better fix things and fix 'em fast. Or I'll show you some trouble, alright."

The Ambassador had shrunk down in his chair. "Si, Jefe, if you say so." The Ambassador wore the sullen look of a child who had just been severely scolded. He got slowly to his feet, then looked at the VP.

"The Jeneral is mistaken. The pilots got confused. It was only a mistake. I will see what I can do."

"You do that, Miguel. You do that. And my best wishes to your Presidente."

The Ambassador shook hands with the VP, nodded to Wade and walked out the door.

"Wade, pull up a chair. We've got some re-thinking to do about all this. Over the past few months, we've managed to push the little guys out in the cold. We've had the market pretty much to ourselves lately. But, with that Indian getting into our business and the base down south out of commission now, we're just plain out of the picture. I don't dare to start back up using the big transports. I'm in a helluva bind already to explain the losses we've had. We're too vulnerable and we risk getting caught and exposed."

Wade sat down opposite the VP and leaned back in his chair.

"Well, Sir. I have to agree. The Jente Jeneral is running an independent operation, I'd say. He goes with the highest bidder and he'd sell us out in a New York nanosecond. I think we're at a stalemate as long as that Indian is on the loose down there. He seems to be able to strike at will."

The VP grunted, "And I'm not convinced the General is all that inept, Wade. Sometimes he just wants to appear that way in order to up the ante and get more money from us. He's a sly old fox, alright. Never did like that man. Nope, never did."

"What'll we do now, Sir?"

"Our South American competition has got no idea what has happened down there. They'll be none the wiser about the big picture. What say we sell 'em all the action and say we're getting out of the business."

"What in hell would make them believe that, Sir?"

"Well, with the election coming up, we could say we've just got to concentrate on the campaign and all. They've been out of the money for so long I think they'll jump at the chance to make a buck. Won't matter much to them about the whys and the wherefores."

"By golly, you're right, Sir. We can get a sizeable cut of the action by maintaining safe landing sites up here, and they can begin to move product right away. Let them worry about that crazy Indian."

"Wade, you're reading my mind. I'm sure glad I brought you up here to Washington with me. You're a goodun, son. And you know how to make a buck. You'll make a fine Vice President, if I say so myself."

Wade grinned, "Now, that's an offer I can't refuse."

The VP rose and walked to the window, "Now take a message for immediate press release, Wade. Say that the Indian is the man behind all the drugs coming into the U.S. and represents the highest threat to the New World Order. Say that he takes his orders from the drug cartels and that he and his guerrillas blew up that medical base in Mexico while trying to seize the airstrip for their drug operation. Say he represents everything I've fought against. We can make some points here, my boy."

"Yessir."

"And say that the Federales called upon us…., that is ME, to help them out. And that's exactly what I did. Sent in the F-14s and put that troublesome Indian clean out of business. You know what to say—made the world safe again, etcetera. We'll just rely on the Ambassador to take care of things down there on his end. And if the Indian shows himself again, we'll just put the blame on the Mexicans. He's their responsibility now."

"Yessir, I'm on it."

"I want to review that release before it goes out. And when you're done, make damn sure that WNN bunch reports this. They've gotten way out of hand lately. Then we'll want to schedule a news briefing, Wade. I can make some hay out of this after all."

The VP strode back to his desk and sat down in his chair. He took a stogy out of the walnut cigar box and lit up. He set the lighter on the desktop, then leaned back, took a long pull and began to puff a long string of perfect smoke rings into the air, one behind the other.

"Damn, I'm good!"

42

The USS Saratoga spent the morning engaged in a mock battle with two Navy submarines. Her helicopter squadron played cat and mouse with the subs while the carrier steamed a zigzag course toward the north across the Gulf of Mexico. She launched and received choppers in a steady stream. Jabe and Juanita watched the action from an upper deck relaxing in the sun.

Commander Jack McPherson stood nearby leaning out over the railing and smoking his pipe.

"War games," he muttered. "Amazing, isn't it, J.B.? Those subs can't get within a hundred nautical miles of us and remain undetected."

Jabe shifted his weight in the chaise-lounge deck chair. He rolled onto his side, cupped his chin in his palm and leaned back into the pillows Juanita rearranged for him.

"It's a different Navy from when I served, Jack. Everything's gone computerized."

It was a little past noon as the pharmacist's mate came up the ladder followed by two cook's carrying luncheon trays.

"Let's have a look at those wounds, sir. Anybody hungry up here?"

The cooks left the trays and Pills pulled up a deck chair and began inspecting Jabe's wounds. "Ummmm, that looks pretty good. The sutures are fairly dry and there's no drainage. Let me salve those for you. That still sore, Sir?"

"Nope. You done a fine job, Doc."

Juanita lifted the lids on the trays and peeked inside. "Ah, mi Amor. Beefsteak!" She dished up a plate and handed it to her patient. "Arros y calabasitas, tambien. Uh, that's rice and squash to you Gringos."

Jack laughed, "Calabasitas. The first time I heard that term I was confused. Saw it on a menu in an Albuquerque South Valley restaurant. I puzzled over that for some time. I knew the noun was feminine and the

R. Barry King

term 'calaboose' referred to a jail, so I figured it must be a little jail for women, or maybe a jail for little women."

Juanita waved her hand, "Aye, yiyae. You only know enough Español to be dangerous, señor Jack."

Jabe chuckled, "He's dangerous without even knowing any Spanish. Just ask those Federales back there in the jungle."

"Now, señor Jabe. You will eat your dinner, por favor."

The Commander grinned, "She's still pretty formal with you, isn't she, J.B.?"

"Only when others are around. She's proper that way."

Juanita lifted a chunk of beef and shoved it in Jabe's mouth.

"Oh, shut up and eat your steak," she giggled.

The pharmacist's mate re-bandaged Jabe's wounds and then handed some pills to Juanita.

"Make sure he takes these with his meals."

The mate turned to leave, "Those wounds are clean and healing fast. I think you're out of danger now, sir."

"Much obliged, Doc. You can just send the bill to the White House."

Jack McPherson sat down to his dinner and scolded, "Look out, now. You wouldn't want to impugn the integrity of our fearless leader, would you?"

Jabe snarled, "Hell, he's never even been *in* the military. Ran away from his duty as an American. That's the way it was, like it or not. And most Americans don't seem to find any problem with that. Hell, Jack, for crying out loud. Look what we've been involved in down here. What does that say for the integrity of our national leadership?"

"Okay, calm down. You get sorta testy when you're mad, don't you. I was only kidding. I'm still on your side."

"Well, don't get me started then. I damn near got killed back there. I might be shot up and hurting, but if they don't leave my people alone, they haven't seen the last of me."

Jabe rolled over and sat up on the edge of his chair. He rubbed his leg and flexed his sore arm. Then he dug into his dinner.

"You can have that cook rustle me up another one of these T-bones, Jack. This one here ain't nearly enough for a starving Indian."

The cooks kept the food coming until the trio was quite satisfied.

Jack McPherson dropped his fork on his plate and leaned back as the cooks cleaned off the dishes and retired downstairs.

"Damn fine vittles, eh J.B.?"

"Just what the patient ordered, Commander."

"At this rate, you oughta be back on your feet in just a few days."

"You bet, Jack. Now hand me those crutches over there, will you? I've got to move around and exercise this leg before I get all stove up."

Jabe strode about the deck and found he could do just fine on a single crutch.

"All I'm going to need is a good walking stick."

The Captain came up the steps and joined his guests, "And how is our patient today? Up and around I see."

Jabe grinned, "It'll take more than that puny Federale infantry to do in a Seal, Sir."

The Captain nodded, "Aye that, Lieutenant. I'm glad to see you're up and about. Have you been enjoying the amenities? The crew has orders to take good care of you folks."

Juanita spoke up, "Si, senor Capitan. The food was muy bien. Muchas gracias."

The Captain nodded, "I'm glad you approve."

Then he addressed the Commander.

"Jack, I've prepared my written report for the CNO. It's the official version of what I've already told him. I need you to come and read it—make sure it's complete before I put it on the radio. Your signature is required."

"Aye aye, Sir."

The Captain continued, "J.B., you and I need to discuss your plans. These war game maneuvers we're engaged in will take us up north a ways and I'll have a chance to put you two ashore by helicopter. Any preference on where you'd like to put in? I know you'll want to get back home as soon as possible."

"I'll need to talk with a friend back home and get something arranged, Sir."

"Very well. I can have the radio room patch through a call for you. Just ask for Ensign Johannassen in the communications center whenever you're ready."

"Thank you, Captain."

"Glad to help you out, Lieutenant. You've done this country a great service, although you won't get any official credit for what you've done. Commander, bring these folks to see me in my cabin after they've phoned home. Now, if you will excuse me, I must get back to the bridge."

The Captain bowed to Juanita, "My Lady. Gentlemen, at your pleasure."

In the radio room, the Ensign called up a secure satellite channel on the microwave transceiver and Jabe gave him the phone number. A moment later the Ensign passed the handset to Jabe, "It's ringing, Sir."

Jabe took the phone and heard Franklin Gilmer answer on the other end. "Hello, Gilmer here."

Jabe fell into the code his friend knew so very well.

"Hi there, old boy. I'll bet you're surprised to hear from me."

"Jabe? The Indian who disappears and never calls home anymore? Where in hell have you been hiding? Man, there's a whole continent looking for you down there."

"Aw, I'm safe where I am right now. I'm coming home tomorrow."

"You got a personal delivery service at your disposal or something?"

"Or something. The Navy's giving me a ride to the beach, anyway. Can you have Indian Joe drive down and meet me?"

"If you'll tell me where. Man, you've got a lot of people madder than hell up here. The VP went on TV this morning to outline the Administration's plan on how the U.S. will participate in the New World Order. Said a lot of strange things. But, he also allowed that there were some grave dangers to peace in the Northern Hemisphere, etcetera."

"Yeah, those grave dangers are real alright. He's talking about me and the guerrillas who cut down his profit machine."

Bad Medicine

"He claims he ordered F-14s from the Saratoga to intercept a scoundrel down in Mexico who had blown up a mercy mission. He's taking credit for blowing your ass away. Says he's restored peace and tranquility. Oh, he also claimed the President has blessed the action as necessary to preserve the World Order."

"Did he, now? Looks like I'm going to have to pay that fellow a visit. Thank him personally for all the trouble he's put me through. He's drawn blood down here and I'm not about to let him get away with it."

"Well, I don't know how you did it, J.B., but their whole affair down there is on hold. They're about out of the drug business as long as they think you're still out there in the jungle. It looks like you've got them in a Check-mate."

"Well, don't tell them any different and we'll see how long that lasts."

So, did you get re-acquainted with Commander Jack?"

"Yes, indeed I did. He's the reason I'm still alive. Thanks for all your help filling him in. I'll pay you a visit when I get back."

"Okay, Pal. Where do you want Joe to meet you?"

"Tell him I'm flying ashore south of Corpus Christi. He can get to the beach at the Padre Island National Seashore. Tell him to drive south about ten miles and wait for me. I should be along tomorrow about dawn. Then I'll want to head straight back to the pueblo."

Jabe said goodbye to his friend and gave the handset back to the Ensign, "Thanks, sailor."

The Ensign terminated the satellite connection and turning to Jabe, he asked in his heavy Swedish accent, "Vas dat real Indian talk der, Lieutenant?"

"Well, sorta."

Commander Jack escorted Jabe and Juanita to the Captain's quarters. The Captain was waiting, "Well, did you get through to your friend?"

"Yessir, I did. If we can hitch a ride ashore in the morning, he'll be waiting for me."

"Can do, Lieutenant. Now, I'm curious about something. I want to feel good about the damage we did back there. My superiors aren't saying much about this whole affair. But, the Commander here says you're pretty well connected upstairs. He didn't as much as say so, but I figure you know some folks at the Pentagon. Now, I certainly wouldn't ask you about that specifically. That's your business. But, I'd sure like to hear whatever you can tell me about all that trouble we left back over the stern—just so I can sleep better tonight."

"Well, Captain, I can tell you this. The operation you saw down there with your own eyes was no illusion. But, it will never make the five o'clock news, I'm sure you know. There are only a handful of reporters at the news networks who care to report the unadulterated truth. The rest just read the scripts the way they are written. If anybody tries to cover a top story on his own and report all the facts, he gets beat up real fast. They do that to anybody who wants to tell the truth without the official spin."

"Or worse. How well I know. I had a close friend from high school who became an attorney and a pretty good one. Went to work for a law office down south and found some strange doings that led straight to the White House. Must have wanted to come clean about it all, but they found him dead of 'suicide' in a parked car. Ensign Johannessen says they have a term for that kind of thing back in the old country."

"I've heard it—'da fish ist shtinken in Shveeden'?"

"Yeah, that's what he says, alright."

"Well, my contact is at Naval Intelligence. You can trace the number I just gave your man Johannassen easy enough. But, for that matter, it's a call you make yourself every day or two anyway, so it doesn't put my man at risk. He tells me I am a wanted man."

"Wanted by whom?"

"By something the VP called the New World Order."

"Oh, that. He's been ranting about that NWO since before the election."

"Well, they're for real, even though the news gurus don't report anything about them. They're really put out over the result of our actions down there. But, I'm getting the blame for everything. Frankly, I'm quite flattered about that."

The Commander interjected, "Flattered? You ought to be downright paranoid, J.B.?" Jabe laughed.

"Not at all, Jack. They're reporting I'm dead. Seems the VP has assumed credit for taking me out. Anyway, their operation is down for the count. No way can they fly any more drugs through that facility. I don't even think they'll try and rebuild it as long as they think Juan and I might still be out there in the bushes. We were able to accomplish a lot with that raid, Captain. Your Tomcats made sure they won't be using that facility any time soon. As it stands now, we've fought them to a standoff."

Juanita had listened to Jabe's every word. "Mi amor. It sounds like, how you say, a duel?"

"Not exactly, Juanita. It's just a classic Mexican standoff. Violence is optional. And each side is waiting to see what comes next. It can get real interesting sometimes, according to how it plays out. A few years ago, I was smack in the middle of another one."

The Captain was taking an interest in this. He took a seat and asked, "What happened, Lieutenant?"

"Well, it was back when I was a deputy on the tribal police force. Way back there in my youth, you understand. I don't go out tracking or cutting sign anymore, unless I'm asked. Anyway, there was a series of terrible killings at one of the pueblos. Everyone said it was Chupadera Charlie, an Indian I knew well. He was a tough Indian alright, but I didn't think he was the type to go around killing folks. He just didn't let people push him around. Anyway, he was known to have been around the scenes of some of the shootings and was supposed to have killed and robbed some people of about fifty thousand dollars."

Jabe paused and adjusted his leg bandage.

"Well, all that money might be enough to entice someone, and now I wasn't sure about Charlie anymore. They looked for him for a few days, but it was apparent he had disappeared. The tribal police thought he might still be hanging around in the woods and I was sent in there to find him. But, it just didn't make any sense. Why he would stay around in the mountains when he had all that cash was more than I was willing to believe. But, there we were with an apparent fugitive on our hands."

Jabe felt Juanita grip his good arm.

The Commander asked, "Did you run him to ground, J.B.?"

"Well, I'd been out in the mountains all week. It had been snowing off and on all day long and my two horses and I were just whipped. I was cold and hungry and disgusted, besides. I'd been trailing close onto that Indian's heels all day long and I was sure he knew I was there, but he hadn't taken a shot at me. Didn't try to ambush me or anything. And that was curious activity for such a dangerous killer."

The Captain was taken in, "Curious.... Wouldn't he want to blow you away if he could?"

"Yeah, that's just it. You expect to get shot at when you're trailing a desperado. But, for some reason, this man wasn't shooting."

Jabe adjusted his pillows.

"I had tracked him into a thicket of aspens and firs up above the snowline and the sun was already down. So, I was expecting he'd set a trap for me. The light was getting really dim, almost dark, when I thought I heard a twig snap."

Juanita was beside herself, "The Indian Charlie, he step on a stick and make a noise, no?" Juanita tightened her grip on Jabe's arm and shook it. He winced at the pain and held her hand fast.

"Oh, perdona mi, amor." Juanita withdrew her hand and folded her arms, "Go on."

Jabe shifted his weight and continued, "Indians know how to move around without making a sound. So, I thought it must be a badger or a coyote. I had already chambered a round into my Winchester and had it ready for a quick shot. I was just creeping around the edge of a huge fir when I came face-to-face with the man pointing a rifle at my eyes. We both froze instantly and I must have surprised him as much as he had startled me. It was old Charlie alright. We just stood there with our rifles cocked and aimed. He sure had a lot of grit!"

"What happened next, amor?"

"Well, nothing. Not much at all. He didn't seem all that anxious to kill me. So, I just pulled a firm pressure on my trigger and waited. If he shot me, my fist would tighten and he'd be signing his own death warrant. He knew that. I stood perfectly still expecting he might shoot me. But he didn't."

"Now, I figured that if he was guilty of all that mayhem, he'd have shot me on first sight, him being such a blood-thirsty scoundrel and all. But, if he were innocent, he'd likely wait to see what I was going to do— see if he would have to defend himself. I didn't have any real evidence that would allow me to kill another man, so I just waited too. I guess you'd say I just gave him the benefit of the doubt."

The Commander said, "What then?"

"So, there we were a few yards apart with our Winchesters cocked, just staring at each other." Jabe stopped and waited for the silence to take effect.

After a moment, the Captain blurted, "Well, get on with it, J.B. How long did the two of you just stand there and look at each other?"

"We both stood there without moving a muscle. It must have been several minutes in all, but at the time it seemed like an eternity—standing there silently in the dim afterglow of twilight in the snow. We could barely see. We watched each other without even blinking, waiting for some sign of movement. Then the snow began to fall heavy again."

Jabe waited another moment, but the wide eyes of his companions warned him he'd better get on with it.

"At last, I thought I saw him give a hint of movement and tightened my grip on the trigger. He looked at me with narrowing eyes. That was a good sign. It's wide eyes that give me the willies."

Jabe looked at his friends and saw them become aware of their appearances. They all had wide-open eyes.

"So I slowly took a tiny step backwards and stopped. After about another minute, he did the same thing. Now, I was feeling much better. We both just kept creeping slowly backwards until he was out of my sight. Then I mounted up and headed my ponies for home."

"And you catch up to him later, amor?"

"No, My Dear, I didn't. I just let him go. I was confident he wasn't the man we were after. That Indian left the country for good and I never saw him again. But a few weeks later, there was another killing and the real scoundrel was shot dead. They even found all the loot he'd buried in his hideout. Old Charlie had been presumed guilty. But, I was dealing with an innocent man and I'll never forget the lesson I learned."

Jack McPherson finally let out a long breath, "And, what was the lesson, J.B?"

"You don't have to get in a hurry when you're in the right. If you're sure he's wrong, always give the other man some room. Give him time enough to hang himself. Always let your enemy draw first blood. That's all the reason you need to go after him. And the fact that you're right and he's wrong is all the edge you need. Every one of us has a conscience that will convict us. When a man is wrong, he always knows it. All you have to do is just let him know you're after him and you're not backing off until you've got him. First, he'll get panicky and then careless. Then you've got him where you want him. It works every time."

Juanita nodded in agreement, "Si, mi amour, like that fellow Gomez. He come to our village to demand that we provide him protection and escort his drug shipments along the roads to the norte. Then we tell him we will not do this, and we wait to see what he will do. We did not have to wait very long. He shoot up and burn our village. Since then, we have been living in the jungle without a home. And he has taken to flying the drugs over our heads in aeroplanes. So we begin to fight him the only way we know how. And that is the way that you found us."

This woman of honesty and simple truth was a thing to behold. Not to mention Jabe was thoroughly in love with her.

43

The Saratoga was making twenty knots into a gentle swell. A big Sikorsky sat all fired up and ready on the flight deck. The giant chopper was dimly silhouetted against the gray pre-dawn sky.

Commander Jack McPherson escorted his friends to the open side door and wished them a fond farewell. Jabe walked with the aid of a cane and sat down in the doorway.

The Commander reached past Jabe and grabbed a step-stool for Juanita. He placed it in front of the high doorway and offered her a hand up, "Now, Juanita. You take good care of yourself."

Instead of taking Jack's hand, Juanita slipped under his arm and gave him a big bear-hug.

"Señor, I want to thank you for all your help to me and my people. If you had not come along when you did, perhaps my brother and all my friends would be dead now. Maybe señor Jabe and I would be dead as well. She kissed the Commander's cheek and held his face in her hands.

"Gracias, senor. Muchesa mas gracias."

Jabe protested, "Hey, what about me? I'm the one who needs attention!"

Jabe pushed his walking cane inside, swung his legs aboard and leaned back against the cabin bulkhead.

The Commander tried not to take notice, "What's that? Oh, J.B.! I'd forgotten all about you. Your nurse here can take care of whatever's bugging you. I've done about all I can for your worthless carcass." He was talking to Jabe, but he was smiling at Juanita.

Jabe snorted. "Well, don't you two bother about ME! I'll be alright. You just go ahead. I'll be okay."

Juanita just laughed, "Sometimes he is such a baby, señor Jack."

Jack backed away and shook Juanita's hand, "It's been a pleasure to know you, ma'am. That better, J.B.?"

"That's a lot better, Commander. You take care now, ya hear? And thanks for all your help."

They shook on it.

"Anytime, Lieutenant. Bon voyage."

The Commander backed away and saluted the pilot. The crew slid the door closed and the turbine spooled quickly up to high revs. The sixteen-ton chopper lifted off slowly and swung out toward the rising sun. Then she veered north and made for the waves to stay under the shore-based radar. They would make the trip to the beach undetected.

There was no reason to frighten the FAA controllers. In accordance with Visual Flight Rules, her pilot would maintain positive surveillance to see-and-avoid other aircraft they might encounter over the Gulf.

Jabe pondered the past few weeks as he watched the carrier grow smaller in the gathering light. He and Juanita were in safe hands now, and it was a welcome relief. Last night, he had slept soundly for the first time since he'd left the pueblo. It was the first good night's rest he'd had in quite a while. The same was true for Juanita. They'd been chased, harassed, and attacked. Juanita had been kidnapped, held hostage, and severely mistreated. They had been strafed, machine-gunned, and shot at. And Jabe had been *HIT*.

It had all started when he and his people had been molested in his own Indian home by sinister forces. Now that he knew the truth about what and who those forces represented, he wished he had somehow been able to avoid being sucked into this mess. But, here he was with a beautiful woman asleep beside him with her head against his chest and her arms around his neck. And as fortune would have it, they were now the guests of the very people who had been sent in to kill them. Fate had a strange way of showing up, just when he most needed help. It had been that way ever since Jabe was just a kid. Now, headed home again safe and sound, all of it seemed like just a bad dream.

An hour later the Texas shoreline loomed large on the horizon. White sand dunes gleamed in the morning sun as the chopper came in low over the blue waves. Jabe could see Indian Joe's white Bronco moving down the beach from the north.

The pilot raised his helmet visor and turned to look at his passengers, "That your taxi, Sir?"

Jabe nodded, "That'll be him, okay. And he's right on time."

Juanita stirred and awakened. She looked out at the blue water and the sand dunes, "We are back in the Yucatan?"

"Not likely. I know it looks like Mexico, but it'll be a while yet before I can take you back home. This is Texas, My Dear—Gateway to the American Southwest."

The pilot put the chopper down on a flat stretch of sand. The beach was deserted, except for the Bronco that came to a halt a few yards away. A sailor rolled open the door and Jabe pushed his sea bag through it and into the waiting hands of a grinning Indian. Joe threw the bag over his shoulder.

Juanita jumped to the sand, "And you are Policeman Joe?"

"Yep, that's me alright. And you'd be Juanita."

She just smiled.

Jabe was assisted to the sand by a crewman. "Joe, it's good to see you." He let himself down easily and took his cane from the sailor in the doorway, "Much obliged, gentlemen. Thanks for the ride."

"Any time, Lieutenant. Glad to be of service."

He shook the sailor's hand and the door slid shut. They moved toward the Bronco as the pilot brought the turbine back up to full revs. Jabe turned and saluted the pilot. Then the big Sikorsky lifted off and turned out over the waves.

Indian Joe shoved the sea bag through the open rear window of the Bronco as Juanita helped Jabe into the front seat. Then she jumped into the back and curled up on the sea bag. They watched the big chopper move out low over the Gulf.

Indian Joe looked at Jabe, "Man, you look like you ran into the business end of a shotgun. How in hell did you get so bunged up anyway?"

"His name was Gomez."

"Was? As in past tense?"

315

"You don't think I'm going to let someone do me this way without a fight, do you? And besides, he was holding Juanita hostage. I didn't have much of a choice."

Joe looked over at Juanita and seemed to understand. He nodded and raised his eyebrows, "Yeah, I see what you mean."

They watched the chopper fade into the horizon.

Jabe asked, "And Longrifle? How is my Grandfather, Joe?"

"Oh, things are pretty much the same as they were a few weeks ago when you had to high-tail it. I've kept him out of sight like you asked me. He's still out there with old Hahtahway......That's the biggest damned airplane I've ever been up close to. You two really travel first class, don't you?"

"Oh, yeah. We've had a regular party these past few weeks. We've just been having loads of fun. Now, let's get out of here before some curious beach patrol shows up. I know a shortcut back up to the highway."

Joe started the engine and wheeled the Bronco toward the northeast along the beach. He lost no time in leaving the area. The rising sun cast a long shadow behind the speeding Bronco.

Jabe pressed his friend, "Joe, what's the status of that airstrip up on the mesa? Has there been a lot of air traffic into there?"

"Well, they've been using it quite a lot over the past two weeks. Those big four-engine jobs have been coming and going all hours of the day and night. Then they just quit showing up. That was about a week ago."

"Yeah, I know. They've been coming up from the Yucatan. That's where I've been, since I last saw you."

"Franklin called and told me a little about what you'd gotten yourself into down there. I climbed the mesa one night to have a look, but the armed patrols up there are thick as hot-air balloons during a mass ascension."

"Those airplanes have been supplying this entire country with South American dope, Joe. They've had a complete monopoly on the U.S. and Canadian drug business for quite a while. They started out with little twins, but they had some trouble moving them over the jungle, thanks to Juanita and her friends. Then they moved up to the big transports that could move the stuff safely out over the gulf. Those Lockheeds carry huge loads, twenty tons or more at a time. They've been operating out of a secure airstrip in the Yucatan. At least they were."

"Until you put a stop to it?"

"With the help of Juanita and her friends.... and the Navy."

"Juanita, you must hang out with a pretty tough crowd."

"It is our home, señor Joe. Sometimes you have to get rough." Juanita leaned over the seat and said, "Señor Joe, the sand dunes remind me of my home in Mejico. But there are no palms trees along here. Por que no?"

Joe nodded toward Jabe, "Better ask J.B. He's the Texan."

Jabe complained, "Oh, so I'm a Texan now, eh?"

Joe laughed, "Well, you've been living in Texas for a while now. And you've certainly hung out here before, or you wouldn't know about the back roads along this stretch of beach, now would you?"

"Yeah, okay. I was here before. But that was a long time ago, Joe."

Jabe's memory took him back to the time when he ran this stretch of beach with someone else. But, this time the memory was dimmer. He looked back over his shoulder and into the eyes of the one who was with him now. He reached back and stroked Juanita's cheek. "A long, long time ago."

Juanita looked back at Jabe and grew a faint smile. Then she took Jabe's hand in hers and changed the subject. She half whispered, "No palms trees?"

Jabe came back to reality, "This part of the coast is grazing land. The natives call it Padre—Big Daddy Island. It starts way up north of here and stretches all the way south into Mexico. The cattle ranchers along here own the dunes clear to the water's edge. So, any coconuts that find their way to these beaches get eaten quickly. They ride the Gulf Stream up from Mexico and get beached by the heavy surf. A new batch of them arrives every day. When the Longhorns ran wild back in the 1800's, they got fat on 'em. Even in a drought, those Longhorns would just move to the beaches and comb them for coconuts. A coconut has got

R. Barry King

everything those cattle need. Food and water right there together inside that shell. Pretty smart, I'd say. I don't know what idiot started that myth about cows being dumb animals."

A couple of miles down the beach a small herd of shorthorn cattle moved out of the breakers and back into the dunes. They broke into a run as the Bronco neared them.

Juanita saw them, "They see us come. Then they run away. They are wild, Amor?"

"I'll say they are." Jabe indicated the opening into the Jeep trail he'd been anticipating and Joe made the turn off the beach and up through the dunes, right on the shorthorns trail.

"They're born out here on the range and never see much of anything but their own kind. They seldom see a human, except for an occasional cowboy on horseback. As long as a man is mounted, he can move among them at will. The cattle see just the horse and they are not afraid. So, they can be easily herded. But, as soon as the cowboy steps to the ground, they'll recognize the two-legged threat and scatter quickly. This whole place is still pretty wild."

Joe agreed, "It's a wild coast south of here all the way to the Yucatan, Juanita. Our pueblo people told me about Texas. In the old days, this place was covered with Comanches and it took a while to tame 'em down. Now it's all quite lonely."

Juanita leaned forward, "Comanches! I have heard a lot about them. They are the ones who came into my country many years ago. Some of my people are part Comanche."

"Yeah, I'm sure they are," Joe continued. "Those folks really got around and mixed with the other tribes. That was just good politics. Whenever they went on the warpath, they could always count on some help from their confederates in most any tribe around. Blood kin will rarely let you down. Those Comanches would raid clear over to the Rio Grande pueblos. They gave us a lot of trouble, but, they never whipped us."

Jabe reflected on that. The pueblos had never been whipped—it was true. The Pueblos and the Navajo Nation had been some of the few American Indians to retain a large part of their native lands when

318

the white man came. The Spanish Conquistadors had rounded up the Indians, killed a lot of them and forced them to give up their food and grain. They had been forced to pay tribute to the priests and the governors. Their people were captive laborers in building the missions and the Spanish towns. They saw their lands confiscated and used by the foreigners. But, they had finally thrown off that yoke and come to live in relative peace with the Spaniards.

But, now they faced a new threat. The government operation up on the mesa would gobble up a large part of their remaining lands. But, Jabe Rainwater was not about to let that happen. He needed a plan of action that could take advantage of pueblo brains and brawn.

They made the highway and Joe turned the Bronco northwest. They could make good time now. Jabe figured they'd be back in New Mexico by tomorrow morning. Then he'd have a powwow with Longrifle and the elders. He only hoped that the pueblo could survive what he knew they were facing. But, that plan of action that he needed—was the one thing about which he hadn't the vaguest notion.

44

Jabe felt good all over to be in the States again. He felt even better about going back home to New Mexico. Every mile brought him closer to his own country.

The trip up from the Padre Island beaches had been a revelation to Juanita. The orderly fields and orchards of semi-tropical Gulf Coast agriculture was quite a different kind of place than her native Yucatan where things just grew wild for the taking. Here, it was all business and organization. She asked Jabe an endless stream of questions.

"What are they growing there?"

"Where do they sell so much grain and hay?"

She seemed to find everything about Texas to be a wonder. Glued to the window watching the farms and ranches of south Texas roll by in an endless stream, once in a while she would remark about a scene that she thought was especially beautiful, "Muy verde," and "So many fat cattle." Crossing the breadth of the coastal plain, they passed through huge rice plantations and truck farms. Then the gentle rise to the hill country of central Texas took them through upland meadows of scrub oak and juniper and the coastal humidity began to abate. Coming through San Antonio and Kerrville, the scene passed from lush green to darker shades of olive and chartreuse. The land began to take on the smooth roll of a sea swell. White layers of limestone became visible on the outcrops above creek beds and the horizon was cut by buttes and low ridges. The town names were peculiar and picturesque—Comanche, Rising Star, Cross Plains. Jabe allowed as how they fairly painted their own picture of the past. Place names often do that.

Close onto mid-day now, Jabe had watched the fuel gauge drop ever closer to the "E" mark. His butt had gone plumb numb an hour before and he needed to be outside moving around. He was sure Joe was aware, but he was getting antsy for relief. "Town coming up, Joe."

"Yeah, we'll take a break and fuel this pony. You ready for a stop, señorita?"

Juanita didn't miss much, "Comanche? Los Comanches viver aqui, Amor?"

Jabe was caught by surprise, "Well, I don't know if they *live* here or not. I've never been here before."

Joe slowed to the speed limit and cruised the main street looking for a fueling stop. Juanita inspected every person on the street. "No, no Comanches aqui. They are all Gringos."

Joe pulled into a filling station with a convenient café nearby. He got out and headed for the john. "You two get us a booth over at the diner and I'll join you directly."

Jabe and Juanita stretched their legs a bit and made for the café. The smells coming from the kitchen made Jabe's mouth water for country cooking. Most times it was hard to get a good meal in a city restaurant, but country towns always had good diners and this one looked typical.

There was a package store in the back and a TV hung from the ceiling behind the café counter. The ongoing women's volleyball match featured the University of Houston Cougars. The score showed U. of H. well ahead of some southeastern team. The Cougars had a tall dark-haired girl who delivered a serve that was almost unreturnable.

Juanita selected a booth by the front windows. The waitress was a wispy blonde wearing more than her share of makeup. She spoke fluent Texan. The words tumbled out one after the other, kind of slow and deliberate.

"Hower yew? What're yew folks gonna have today? Can I gitchall a menyew?"

Jabe tried to keep track, but he wasn't sure which question deserved an answer first. "Well, yeah, we're fine. We're having lunch. Menu works for me."

"Kin I gitchall somthin' to drank?"

"Coffee, please. Three cups."

Even Juanita noticed it. "Mi amor, I have never heard this language before. Only in the movies."

"Well, yore in Texas now, little darlin. So, you'll have to pay close attention. There's only two languages spoken here—Tex-Mex and Texican. If you listen close, you might even be able to tell the difference."

Joe parked the Bronco in front and came inside.

"We're fueled and ready to roll. What's for lunch?"

Jabe was reading the menu, "I think we're out of luck, Joe. No lunch. Says here they only serve breakfast, dinner, and supper."

Joe sat down and gulped his coffee.

"Okay then, dinner it is. They got any chicken fried steak?"

"Unless you prefer liver and onions."

"I'll take a steak and well done, thank you."

After lunch, they had a last round of coffee. Someone turned up the TV volume......"This news flash just in from World News Network Campaign Central in Washington, D.C. You have just heard the Vice President commenting on the trouble down in Mexico. Our commentator in Washington is WNN Newsman Don Samuelson. Don?"

"Well Jim, the Vice President has outlined the Administration's campaign strategy for the November election in no uncertain terms. He met his opponent's charges that his party favor's the legalization of drugs in America, saying that he thinks that would be a bad decision. "Answering for the President, who refused to comment on the tense situation down in the Yucatan, the VP reiterated this country's commitment to fostering peace in that area. Although some Mexican officials have denounced the arrival of the carrier USS Saratoga in the Bay of Campeche, the VP stated that it is the aim of this administration to assist the Mexican Federal troops against aggression by any outside forces. The recent fighter sortie into the interior was merely a defensive sweep that resulted in the elimination of the guerrilla threat to the safety of mercy missions flying food and medicine to victims of recent flooding in that area. The American Indian mercenary who was the leader of the guerrillas is believed to have been killed in the raid." Jabe's military photograph was shown on the screen. "The Vice President regretted that lives had to be taken, but he sent his personal congratulations to the officers and crew of the Saratoga for a job well done."

"Thank you Don Samuelson. We return you now to the regular Saturday afternoon program in progress……." Someone turned the sound off and it grew quiet in the diner.

Jabe hadn't dared to look up since his photo was shown, but the news of it being Saturday left him a bit startled.

Joe cleared his throat, but Jabe only went to shoveling down his lunch again.

Jabe mumbled half under his breath, "It's Saturday. Just think of that. I haven't even thought about what day of the week it was since we went into the interior after that airstrip……."

He looked up from his steak and froze in mid-sentence. Every eye in the diner was looking straight at him.

Waitress walked slowly over, "Kin I gitchall anything else?"

Silence.

She continued in a kindly tone, "We don't see many Indians 'round here no more. I guess folks find it kind of interesting. Last Indians that lived around here was in about 1910. My GrandDaddy told me."

Joe eyed the patrons and forced a nervous laugh. Then he said in a tone loud enough to be heard throughout the room, "Well, we've been on the road for several weeks. The time really flies when you're on the rodeo circuit. It gets hard to keep up with what day it is."

The patrons returned to their meals and quiet conversation.

"Oh? Ya'll rodeo folks? Where ya'll from?"

Jabe took over, hoping he hadn't flushed too red, "Arizona." Then he thought a moment, "…and New Mexico. Been gone for quite a spell. Be glad to get back home."

It wouldn't do to tell a fib. That yellow license tag on the Bronco's rear bumper clearly said "Land of Enchantment." It was funny, Jabe thought, but the New Mexico license plate is the only one in the union that carries the trailer 'USA' after the state name. Some Americans apparently aren't entirely sure it's part of the United States.

"Ya'll been down to the big Roundup Rodeo in Simonton, ain't ya? Win anything?"

Joe grinned his most convincing grin, "He damn near broke his leg trying to ride a big Longhorn steer, that's all."

Someone sitting at the counter chuckled.

Joe gathered his hat and slid out of his seat.

Waitress looked straight at Jabe, "Too bad. Maybe yew'll have better luck next time." She placed the check on the table and lowered her voice, "Ya'll come back now, ya hear?"

They lost no time in paying up and getting back to the truck.

Jabe buckled his seatbelt and was surprised to find Waitress standing outside his door. He rolled down the window.

"I saw that was yer pitcher on the TV. At least it sure looks like you. Anyway, if that was you down there making all that trouble in the Yucatan, all I can say is you were probly doin' the right thing. Nobody in these parts believes politicians. If that sorry bunch says one thing, I can always do better by takin' the exact opposite side. If that Vice President of ours is upset with you, then I bet it suits me just fine. That *was* yer pitcher on the TV, wasn't it?"

Jabe only winked at her.

She smiled, turned slowly and headed back inside. "Ya'll have a nice trip now, ya hear?"

It was well past dark when Joe pulled the Bronco off the highway and took the tree-lined gravel road along the river toward the pueblo. Jabe thought back to an earlier time when he and Joe had tracked many a fugitive along these back roads and trails. They'd hitch a horse trailer to the truck and go as far as they could in the Bronco, then park it, mount their broncs and proceed on horseback.

Jabe thought the Bronco was appropriately named. It might be less than comfortable on a long trip, but what it lacked as a highway transport, it more than made up for off-road.

All in all, they had made pretty good time coming up from the coast. Now in the late evening Joe approached the pueblo cautiously, then cut the headlights and drove slowly through the village. Jabe could see a newly arrived modular building sitting on the slab where the old council office had been. All was quiet and nothing was moving. Joe pulled up to Longrifle's place. Everything was dark and still. With no moon out, the starlight shed a pale glow over the house and yard.

Joe killed the engine, "Man, I've got to get out of this truck and move around some. My legs are killing me."

Juanita awoke from a nap and asked, "Are we home yet, Mi Corazon?"

Joe opened his door and stepped down, "Just like a little kid, isn't she?"

He fetched the sea bag and Juanita's bundles out of the back seat and set them on the ground under the big cottonwood in the front yard.

Jabe was glad to be home again. He stirred and swung his door open. His legs were numb from sitting. He let himself down gingerly and steadied himself with his metal walking cane. Then he felt the tingle and sting of blood circulation returning to normal and his leg wound began to throb with the rhythm of his heartbeat.

"Ooooo, Ouch," he grumbled.

"Que?" Juanita climbed out of the back seat and stretched herself.

"Oh, nothing. I'm fine."

"You didn't take your medicine, did you?"

Juanita touched her toes several times and rolled her hips to get the kinks out. Then she looked up and froze, "Aye, yai yai, Jabe! Look at the stars." She was standing flat-footed and staring straight up.

Jabe leaned back against the Bronco, looked up and beheld a sky with which he was quite familiar. Aquila and Lyra were wheeling overhead on their way toward the west. He could see the bright stars Altair, Vega, Rigel and Deneb following along the circle of the heavens. The great galaxy in Andromeda, two million light-years distant and 180,000 light-years in diameter, lent a yardstick to the grand stretch of the firmament. Jabe could see the hazy outline of this mother of all galaxies. It covered a swath of sky five times the diameter of a full moon.

The Milky Way was ablaze from horizon to horizon. The sky was perfectly black and it seemed he could see forever. No light pollution out here!

A bright meteor shot across the sky and Jabe thought of another meteor he had seen before on a lonely beach in Mexico.

Juanita oozed a hushed, "Oooooooo…." She couldn't get enough, "I never see so many stars. Why are the stars so many here in your home, mi amor? Are the heavens brighter for your people than for mine?"

Jabe thought on that.

"No, I don't think so. Well, yeah, maybe they are."

His leg and arm wounds felt like someone was shoving hot knives into them. He winced.

"I mean, we've just got the advantage of altitude up here. We're standing more than a mile above sea level. Not as much atmosphere and haze to hinder your vision. Ouch. Yow. Hand me that medicine bag, will you Joe?"

"Juanita's got it."

She snipped back, "Oh, you want your medicine, now? Didn't you throw it away?" Juanita pulled the sack of pills out of her bundle and doled out the proper dose.

Jabe downed the medicine with his last swig of soda pop, "I don't know. Maybe I did."

Joe chuckled, "She takes pretty good care of you, J.B. But, you'd better start taking those meds."

Joe climbed back into the Bronco, "I'll see you folks sometime tomorrow. I'm going to get some sleep."

Jabe and Juanita took shelter in Longrifle's kiva. Jabe lit the fire more for the light it would give than the warmth. Juanita curled up in a blanket and was fast asleep before the kindling caught the firewood. Jabe lay back and looked around this familiar place as the flames cast a red glow. For the first time in nearly a month, he felt safe and secure once again. Beside him lay the woman he had risked his life for. And she had risked hers to stem the tide of drugs coming through her country on its way to his. There in that kiva, Jabe felt the warmth of the fire meld with the warmth in his heart. It was a culmination that signaled a new start for him. He fell asleep easily.

The smell of venison stew gently caressed Jabe's nose and he stirred into a dim consciousness. His eyelids seemed to be glued shut, so he just listened for any movement. He heard nothing.

The smell lingered. It was fresh Indian fare that he hadn't tasted since he had left the pueblo. It was the unmistakable traditional dish, huevos rancheros and Paa Quna that Isabel really had a knack for. She liked to serve it over hot flour tortillas.

His mouth began to water. Then he opened one eye and surveyed the kiva. Juanita was sitting close beside him smiling. She offered her hand and Jabe rolled over expecting to see some of that scrumptious breakfast he'd envisioned, but he and his hunger were disappointed to find the offering was a handful of pills instead.

"Take your medicine and then we can have some food. Isabel has brought your favorite breakfast."

In her other hand Juanita held a plate of his absolute favorite fare.

"What time is it?" Jabe downed the pills and reached for the steaming hot plate of Indian food.

"Medias dia, amor. You slept a good while."

It was well past noon when Juanita finished salving his stitches and changing the bandages. The pain had subsided, but his leg was stiff from lack of exercise. He would get a chance to remedy that soon enough.

After they'd eaten, Jabe and Juanita went up to the house to see Isabel. Sure enough, Longrifle's housekeeper was on the job. She met them at the door, "Señor Jabe, it is really you. You are home from your trip. It is good to see you back again." Isabel gave Jabe a hug. "And I have met your señorita. She es muy bonita."

Juanita smiled and took Isabel's hand, "Isabel, I think I should take cooking lessons from you. The Paa Quna es magnifico."

"Gracias, Juanita."

Jabe rubbed his tummy, "Isabel, you know exactly what I like for breakfast. It was delicious. Gracias."

"That was your lunch, Señor Jabe. You sleep through breakfast. Indian Joe was here early and I fix him some huevos. He say he will come back soon. So, I make you the lunch."

"What can you tell me about Grandfather?"

"Oh, Señor Jabe. Since those bad hombres came to the pueblo, he has been staying with Hahtahway. Those banditos think they keel him and do not look for him. But, I am sure he is ready to come home. The way those two argue is a peety. The banditos say that you are dead, tambien. But, your Grandfather say they lie. He will be so glad to see you."

Indian Joe wheeled the Bronco into the yard and parked in the shade of the big cottonwood. He bounced out and walked straight up licking his lips.

"Is that your famous deer stew I smell, Isabel?"

"Si, señor Joe. And there is enough for your lunch. Come and eat with us."

"Don't mind if I do, Isabel. I was hoping you'd ask." Joe sat down on the back steps and Isabel fetched him a plate. Jabe pulled up a yard chair and took the weight off his leg.

"What kind of police business got you up so early?"

Joe swallowed and stopped chewing long enough to say, "In a minute, J.B.—first things first. Isabel, this is mucho gusto."

Then he pushed another heaping spoonful into his mouth. He cleaned his plate, laid it aside and stood up. "Let's go up and see the Cacique. He'll be pleased to see you're back safe. Gracias, Isabel. Hasta la bye-bye."

They all boarded the Bronco and headed out.

Joe continued, "I didn't tell the Cacique you're back, so this will be quite a surprise for him. He thinks I'm in Santa Fe taking care of some BIA business up there."

It was a short drive up the riverbank to Hahtahway's place. Jabe and Juanita found Ten Eagles sitting in a rocking chair on the front porch. He had his blanket wrapped around his shoulders and he was mumbling. He seemed to be staring out into thin air. Jabe approached him and said hello, but the medicine man didn't respond. He just went right on mumbling.

Juanita asked, "Amor, what does he say?"

"I don't know. He's talking some kind of Indian medicine. I wanted to introduce you, but I guess it'll have to wait."

Inside they heard Longrifle and Hahtahway engrossed in a rambling argument. Jabe motioned for Joe to stop so they could have a listen.

Longrifle was saying, "I don't have to listen to you. You need to respect your elders. I am older than you."

"Only by an hour or so. And that isn't enough to count."

"I still say that Bureau man up in Santa Fe is no help to us, Hahtahway. He is controlled by those Washington men. He is controlled by the system that pays his wages. He will be of no help to us."

"Maybe you had better sit with him and talk anyway."

"It will do no good. He has allowed those bad Indians to take over the whole pueblo. He is no use to us. The only answer is for Ten Eagles and me to go into that new office and throw those toughs out in the street."

"They tried to kill you before, you know. The only reason you are alive today is that your Grandson and Indian Joe went up against them in your place. I am sorry, Cacique, but now they say they have killed Joe Bob, too."

Longrifle hung his head, "What do they know? I do not believe the white man's government. All they ever tell us is lies. My Grandson lives. If he was dead, the Great Spirit would have told me. The Creator always talks to the Cacique. That is why you never know anything, Hahtahway. That is why I have to tell you everything. I am ready for my coffee now. Aren't you going to offer your guest any coffee?"

"My guests can get their own coffee. Have you forgotten how to make coffee?"

"The Cacique never makes his own coffee. If Isabel was here, she would make it for me. And if Joe Bob was here, he would make it for me. Now, Hahtahway, you are here. So why don't you make some coffee for the Cacique?"

"This pueblo would be better off it the Cacique knew how to take care of himself."

Jabe walked around to the kitchen and called to his Grandfather, "One pot of coffee coming right up, Grandfather."

Longrifle laughed, "That is the voice of my Grandson, Hahtahway. What do you think of the word of the white man now?"

Hahtahway addressed the voice from the kitchen, "Is that the voice of a ghost?"

Longrifle answered, "A ghost doesn't arrive in a car. I saw him drive up through the window."

Joe introduced Juanita. She stepped into the room and took Longrifle's hand.

"I am so pleased to meet you, Grandfather. Jabe has told me so much about the great Cacique of this pueblo."

"Ummm." Longrifle held her hand and looked at her. Jabe came in and Longrifle took his hand, too.

"The Great Spirit has kept you safe and now he has returned you to me, just as I have asked him to do. You live, and the white-eyes are liars." He held them both by the hand.

Longrifle's gaze fell upon Juanita again. "And I can see that this Juanita is a good woman. She is exactly what you need, my son. My Grandson is a good man. For many years he has not brought any woman for me to meet. I am glad he has chosen well."

Juanita nodded, "Gracias, Grandfather. Muchesa mas gracias."

"Aha, she calls me Grandfather. That is a good sign. Now, Joe Bob, come and tell me where you have been and the reason for all the bad stories they tell about you."

Juanita fetched Longrifle's coffee and he listened in silence as Jabe related the whole story.

When he had finished, Jabe asked, "Have they been using the airstrip over the past few days, Grandfather?"

Hahtahway jumped in, "The airport up on the mesa? They have a fence ten feet high, and the guards have dogs, and......"

"No, my son," Longrifle cut him off. "The airplanes have stopped coming. Hahtahway thought that they would leave soon and that we could have the use of our land again. But, Ten Eagles has seen something in a vision."

Jabe said, "He was mumbling something about the stars when we came in. What has he been saying?"

Longrifle continued, "He says he has seen an awful thing. He says every time he looks up at the mesa, he has seen the stars falling to the ground. He says they bring fire out of the earth. Fire and brimstone come up out of the earth. Everything is on fire. He has been saying this for the past few days. He has eaten only once and sits with his blanket over his shoulders."

Hahtahway scoffed, "That old man sees more than I can see. I have seen the stars in the sky. I have seen falling stars and shooting stars. But, he says the stars he sees will fall to the ground. I have never seen one of them come to the ground."

The rattle of cooking pots came from the kitchen. Jabe could see Ten Eagles was digging around in the cupboards. The old medicine man came to the doorway, "They will fall to the ground, Hahtahway, just as I have told you they will. There is much trouble up there on the mesa. Have you got any food around here? Making medicine can drive a man to hunger."

Hahtahway shook his head, "I am surrounded by a bunch of old fools and there is no escape."

The Cacique got up from the table, "Come my son. You can take me home, now. I have got the better of Hahtahway again, but I think I have worn out my welcome at this man's house."

Hahtahway continued, "It is good that you had a house like mine, Cacique, to come and visit when you were in trouble. It gave me a chance to give you some good advice. You need all you can get."

Outside, Ten Eagles sat on the front porch eating his lunch. He rocked quietly now and addressed Jabe and Juanita, "I see the two of you are home now. I saw your troubles when you were down there in the south. Now, you think your troubles are over. But they are just beginning." Then the old medicine man laid his plate aside and went back to mumbling and rocking again.

Ten Eagle's words made Jabe feel all tired out, "Well, I didn't need to hear anything like that. I've about had it with that bunch of government trash up there on the mesa. Grandfather, it's about time we put you back into your office of Cacique. The sooner we get rid of that bunch, the better I'll like it. Then maybe I can get some rest." Juanita assisted Longrifle into the Bronco.

The Cacique took the back seat, "I will go up to my office now and throw out that impostor."

Hahtahway scolded Longrifle from the porch, "You let Indian Joe and Tsoomn Pa'a handle the hard work, Cacique. These young bucks can take care of that lawyer fellow and his friends."

Joe was about to get into the driver's seat when Jabe thought he heard something. He waved his hand and Joe stepped back out.

"What is it, J.B?"

"There it is again, Joe."

The sound was a long way off, but it was unmistakable. It was the drone of a turboprop—a Hercules. Jabe reached for the binoculars lying on the front seat and peered at the western horizon. There in the distance he could make out two of the big Lockheeds making their turn for landing on the mesa airstrip. Jabe lowered the binocs.

"Dammit. They're back in business again."

45

Back in his own home again, Longrifle sat in the kitchen talking with Juanita. Isabel was sitting in the small parlor off the back side of the kitchen watching her favorite afternoon TV programs. She always kept the volume turned down so it didn't bother the Cacique.

Jabe came into the kitchen and leaned against the door to listen as Juanita got a healthy dose of pueblo history from Longrifle. Then she got her first lesson in speaking pueblo Indian. Jabe couldn't remember ever hearing the Cacique talk this much with anyone. He was evidently enjoying himself very much and Juanita asked a steady stream of questions.

Longrifle looked up, "You are a lucky man, my son. This woman is both intelligent and good looking. I think she is part Indian. She tells me you saved her life. Now, you have someone to take care of again."

Juanita said, "And your Grandfather is a wise leader, mi Amor. He tells me much about this pueblo people and many stories about when you were a little boy." She put on her biggest grin for Jabe.

"Yeah, I'll bet he does. Be careful how much you tell her about me, Grandfather." He smiled back at her and winked.

Isabel turned up the volume on the WNN newscast. ".......and Congress has countered the President with a resolution against the legalization of hard narcotics in America. Nevertheless, the Administration has vowed to veto any legislation hindering their proposed program of free use and possession of drugs in this country. Citing the necessity for the U.S. to conform with the leadership of the European Community of nations, the President insists his move toward legalization is necessary in order to cement the U.S. position in the New World Order.

"In other breaking news, WNN has learned that the White House has just completed initial agreements with the Chinese over the relaxation of import duties on American goods entering that country. The terms of the deal are still to be worked out, but Administration officials, speaking on condition of anonymity, say the President has finally made good on his promises, vowing to open the Chinese market to American manufacturers. This is Don Samuelson reporting from Washington.....' Isabel turned off the TV with a string of mumbled epithets.

Jabe walked out to the front yard and found Indian Joe sitting under the cottonwoods. Joe was watching the approach of an beat-up old Chevy pickup. Its driver was gunning the engine between shifts, grinding the gears and generally dogging the hell out of the ancient vehicle. Jabe took a seat beside him.

Joe chuckled, "Hahtahway has been driving that old pickup since before I was born. It must have half a million miles on it by now."

Jabe watched the truck kicking up a huge cloud of dust and smoke as it turned into the yard. The driver gunned it once more for good measure and turned off the ignition. Its fenders shook as it rolled to a stop and backfired twice. Then it went quiet and just sat there smoking. Hahtahway had arrived.

"Who does he find that'll work on that old truck when it needs fixing?" Jabe wondered.

"Fixing? You've sure missed a lot being away from here for so long. Nobody's worked on that old truck in decades. All Hahtahway ever does is change the oil and put gasoline in it. Whenever it makes a funny noise or starts acting up, he just has Ten Eagles do some of his medicine and wave a few feathers over it."

"And.....?" Jabe was curious.

"Well, it straightens up and just keeps on going."

Jabe shook his head. Hahtahway and Ten Eagles climbed out of the truck and made for the house.

Joe said in a low tone, "Longrifle must have called for a council powwow."

"Yeah, he must have. I wonder what they're up to."

Then, from far up on the mesa came the whine of turboprops again. A Hercules was taking off. Jabe walked over and grabbed the binocs off the seat of the Bronco. He watched the big transport climb out and turn away to the west.

Joe walked over and watched as the airplane became a speck and disappeared over the horizon.

"That guy isn't going south. He's headed west, J.B. If you took out their refueling base down south, then what use do they have for this airstrip up here on the mesa?"

"Yeah, I wonder. That Herkybird doesn't look like it's heading for Mexico."

"Maybe they've got another refueling base somewhere."

"I doubt it. But if they're still moving drugs, my work isn't finished yet. Joe, while the old timers are occupied there in the house, what say you and I take a ride up to the council office and have a talk with that Lawyer? I'd like to see what he's up to."

They climbed into the Bronco and made the short drive into the village. They arrived about a block to the rear of the council office. They could see a black Mercedes was parked near the back door. Joe parked in the trees some distance back of the building and they went in on foot.

Arriving at a back window, Jabe peeked in and saw the Lawyer sitting at the desk talking on a cell phone. He and Joe circled around to the sides and peeked into all the windows. Nobody else was home and the Lawyer was alone.

The two friends squatted close to the ground and exchanged thoughts, "Looks like his helpers are gone now, Joe. He's all alone in there."

"Yeah, their confidence level is high right now. With Longrifle out of the picture, they've had their run of the place. They think the Cacique and you are dead."

A distant backfire diverted their attention. Joe squinted into the afternoon sun at a cloud of dust approaching from the general direction of Longrifle's place.

"Uh-oh, is that who I think it is?"

Jabe glanced up the road and watched the swift approach of the old Chevy pick-up. Longrifle was sitting astride the hood with one foot on each of its ancient headlights. His Winchester was held at the ready. The truck swerved into the front parking lot and came to a sudden stop.

Both its doors opened simultaneously. Hahtahway and Ten Eagles bounded out and faced off square to the council office. Three rifles opened fire at the same instant. Window glass flew in every direction. Hahtahway and Ten Eagles fanned out to the sides and poured lead into every window. The ploy had its desired effect. Longrifle dismounted the truck and went straight in the front door, just as the Lawyer made his getaway out the back.

The scared Indian jumped into the Mercedes and tore off keeping his head low. Ten Eagles rounded the building and kept up a steady fire. He leveled the barrel, took instant aim and squeezed the trigger—firing several rounds in quick succession. Every round found its mark and took all the glass out of the speeding sedan. Only when his Winchester's hammer fell on an empty breach did he lower the rifle and yell, "And don't you ever come back here. We are not afraid of *you* anymore."

The gunfire had announced the arrival of the tribal elders. The street quickly filled with curious townsfolk who came out to see what all the noise was about. Longrifle came out of the council office and stood on the doorstep. Jabe and Joe stood on one side of the porch, Ten Eagles and Hahtahway stood on the other.

Juanita and Isabel came running up the road as the Cacique raised his rifle over his head and greeted his people again as their leader.

One of the village men approached the Cacique, "Longrifle, we thought you were dead."

"Well, you can see that I am not yet dead. The bad Indians are gone now and I am still the Cacique of this place."

Hahtahway spoke next, "Joe Bob has returned to us as well. You can see he is not dead either. And he has brought his lady with him. It is a good day to celebrate. We will have a village feast to properly welcome them back again."

Ten Eagles volunteered to bring in a big elk and roast it himself. So the pueblo people dispersed in order to prepare for the feast and Longrifle called a meeting of the council elders.

One by one, the tribal elders arrived from the farthest parts of the pueblo. They gathered with Longrifle, Hahtahway and Ten Eagles in the council chamber. Jabe and Joe went about cleaning up all the glass shards on the floors then sat down in the business office. There on the desk was Lawyers cell phone.

Joe eyed the phone, "Imagine that. That Lawyer left here in such a hurry he forgot his telephone."

Jabe picked it up, "I can only guess the kind of people he's been talking to over this thing."

At that very moment, the cell phone rang. Jabe looked at Joe. The phone rang again. Joe said, "Maybe you'd better answer it."

"I think you're right." Jabe flipped it open and answered, "Yeah?"

There was an instant of silence on the other end, then "This is Breggard. You got your mouth full or something?"

"Yeah."

"Well, get done with it. I've got a word for you from the top man. That troublesome Indian you failed to take care of is back again—probably heading up there as we speak. And this time he'll be coming for you personally. So, you'd better take whatever precautions you can. The Man wants him taken out for good this time. You savvy that? Hello?"

"Yeah, I savvy that. But you're a little late, asshole. I'm already here."

A click was all Jabe heard on the other end.

Joe was curious, "Who was that, now?"

"Don't know him. Said his name was Breggard."

Joe reached for the cell phone and pushed some buttons, "This thing can ring up the last number that called. See who answers." He handed the phone back to Jabe.

Jabe heard the operator answer, "Eisenhower Executive Building. How may I direct your call?"

He put on his white man's voice and said slowly, "Oh, I'm sorry. I must have gotten a wrong number."

He folded the phone and laid it on the desk. Then he got up and walked over to the window. His leg still stung him where the powder burns had left their mark along the bullet track. The stitches were beginning to prickle and he felt a little queasy.

Joe asked, "Well, who was it, J.B.?"

"Somebody who has an office in the Old Executive Building."

"Where's that?"

"Just across 17ᵗʰ Street from the White House, Joe. Somebody real important, I'd say."

"Any idea who?"

"No, not really. But I know someone who will."

Just then, Juanita came into the room. "Señores, the celebration will begin in the mañana. Come and get some rest, Amor. Have you taken your medicine?"

She held out a handful of pills.

Jabe threw them into his mouth and chased them with the can of Dr. Pepper Juanita held in her other hand.

"Know what, Joe? I need an Indian cure for these stitches. This white man's medicine is getting me nowhere."

"Well, there's that hot spring we always used in the old days, amigo." Joe knew what Jabe had on his mind. He threw Jabe the keys to the Bronco.

"Exactamundo."

An hour later and well out on the west end of the pueblo land holdings, another flight of Lockheeds roared over the mountain trail as the Bronco headed up into the high country. Jabe pulled up a steep grade and parked the big Ford under a grove of aspen. He and Juanita rolled out and hefted a pack from the rear seat. They carried it between them and started up the trail.

Jabe took Juanita by the hand, "Here's where we leave this pony. She can't pull any higher than this. But, it's not far now."

They hiked the last hundred yards as the sun fell toward the western horizon. The bright yellow light began to fade into orange and red as they shed clothes and stood on the rock ledge over the hot spring. Under the darkening blue sky, Juanita presented quite a sight as the red light of sunset lit her bronzed skin. She looked absolutely golden beside the darker hue of the Indian by her side.

Jabe wondered how many years his kin had stood where they were standing. How many generations had treated themselves to the natural healing power of this very spring? Steam rose from a dozen trickling vents on the rocks above them. The water streamed down in rivulets and collected at the base in a natural hot tub. The ledge of rock surrounding the pool was testimony to the aggressiveness of these waters. They had carved a smooth bowl that resulted in this chamber surrounded by solid limestone rock.

The high sulfur content of these hot springs gave the air a pungent odor that promised good medicine.

Juanita plunged straight in and she giggled at the tickle of the bubbles. Jabe slipped into the steaming water a few inches at a time. He felt a gentle tug at his stitches as the mineral water began to constrict his skin. These waters had served his people for many generations and he had been here many times. Nothing could heal faster than the pure mineral water and the naturally heated springs of the high country. Jabe settled in and rested his body against the smooth rock. Juanita settled in beside him.

They watched the sky go from pink to indigo and then purple as the sun continued to sink. A few puffy white clouds went crimson and faded to dark gray as the light paled in the west.

The stars were out well before dark. Juanita snuggled up close as Jabe pointed out the constellations he had learned as a child. Each one had a certain significance in pueblo culture. She stroked his sore arm and leg and gently kissed his face. Jabe stopped talking and began kissing her back. He could feel the heat of the water doing its work. In fact, the dull pain he had endured for the past week had completely gone now. Jabe thought he felt the water heating up as the steam thickened and drifted with the cool night air. His head went light and his pulse rate doubled. The scent of a woman, this woman, was an intoxicating tonic. He leaned back in the water and let his ears go under. He could hear the pounding of his own heart and the sound was deafening. Juanita rolled over him and stroked his back with her fingers. Her lips met his and the passion in her kiss was infectious.

The moon was not up yet and everything was lit by dim starlight. The steam rising off the water was barely visible and Juanita's magnificent form was only a silhouette against the stars. She lifted her hands to the sky and swayed gently. All the sensations came back again that he'd had with her on the beach—all the sensations that he'd thought were long dead. He straightened his legs and arched his back. Slowly the world turned upside down and Jabe felt a swelling down deep in his soul. And then a big, bright, flaming meteor raced across the sky.

Next morning, the cackling chatter of a mountain scrub jay filtered into Jabe's consciousness as he lay wrapped in a blanket on a makeshift bed of pine needles. In the dim light of dawn he listened, but heard nothing more. He felt the warmth of an arm across his chest. His feet were cold now, but his heart was warm. Beside him lay his only reason for living. He remembered the night just passed and he smiled. This was the woman he wanted. She was the one who knew how to make him feel alive again.

He lapsed in and out of slumber and then awoke to the feel of Juanita's hand touching his, "I have brought you something to eat, Amor. Come and sit with me." Juanita held a tortilla filled with venison steak.

They sat on the rock ledge wrapped up in a blanket. They munched some of Isabel's best and Jabe dangled his feet in the hot spring water. His leg and arm wounds had faded from the angry red of the day before to a healthy pale pink. Juanita sat up Indian style on the rock bench and clipped his stitches. Jabe was glad to be free of the bandages.

"The water is very good, no?" Juanita looked up into Jabe's eyes and kissed him again.

"Yes, it is good. But not nearly as good as you are." Jabe held Juanita's face in his hands. "I want you to be....., I mean, I'd like to have you as....."

"Tu esposa?" Juanita finished his sentence for him.

Jabe hesitated a moment, but Juanita had nailed it. He shook his head, yes.

"Yes, I want you to be my wife. I know you'll need some time to think about it. But, don't take too long."

Juanita bowed her head and finished up with the stitches in silence. She bathed the wound and salved it. When she looked up at him again, her cheeks were drenched in tears. Jabe felt a tightness in his chest that was all too familiar.

There was a quiver in her voice, "I have thought about this many times since I first saw you, Amor. I can tell you what my answer is, but I think you know already. I want to be with you forever, my love."

She touched his cheek, "But, I wonder if it can ever be that way for us. I am afraid that the terrible trouble we have seen will not leave us alone. The banditos who threaten my homeland are the same ones who fight against you and your own people. They are everywhere. Where can we go and what will we do?"

Juanita was right. What kind of a future would they have?

Jabe felt the knot in his stomach relax a bit, "I'll find us a way. Don't you worry about that."

They walked hand in hand back to the Bronco. Rolling down through the foothills toward the pueblo, Jabe turned the Bronco out on a prominence and they got out to have a look at the valley. The bosque was clothed in the green fullness of early autumn and the air was crisp. At this altitude, the air was always clean and pure. His ancestors had wisely chosen their place of abode.

Down below, Jabe could see his home pueblo. The scene had a lasting quality. It probably looked the same as it had for who knows how many centuries. But for the occasional passing of an auto or a truck, his earliest ancestors would not have known the difference in time.

He loved everything about this land. He looked off to the horizon and surveyed the distant mountain range. The sky had taken on that deep blue color that signaled the approach of fall. Soon the bosque would turn bright yellow and the new snow would fall on the highest peaks.

He saw the high snow-field and thought about his loved one who lay there under the snow. But, this time his heart was not cold and lonely. In his deepest soul, he praised the Great Creator for His kindness and for the blessing of a new companion.

Then Jabe saw something in the distance. It was just a speck moving low across the sky. As it neared, he could hear the whine of its turbine and the steady rhythm of its rotors. It was a helicopter making a pass up the river.

It swung low over the pueblo and slowed on its approach. Its crew appeared to be searching for something. It hovered over the houses and then attempted to land in the council office yard. Gunshots rang out and the chopper made a hasty getaway. This time it circled out of rifle range and flew off toward the mesa. The tribal elders had had enough of the white man's "help" for a while.

Jabe watched the chopper until he felt safe in moving out in the Bronco.

"Those bastards never give up. They're back again, but I'll bet they don't get another chance at blowing up any council office. Ten Eagles and Hahtahway will see to the safety of Longrifle."

A mile short of the pueblo, he stopped and got out and motioned for Juanita to move into the driver's seat. He leaned back inside long enough to give her a goodbye kiss.

"You can do something for me. I don't dare show up at the celebration today. Get Indian Joe to pack my bag for a short trip. There's someone I've got to go and have a talk with."

"Oh, can't I go with you, Amor?"

"Not this time, sweetheart. I'll only be gone for a couple of days. Then I'll be back for you. Help Joe pack me some food and then bring my sea bag to the kiva. I'll be in to pick it up tonight. Can you do that for me?"

Juanita frowned back at him. She kissed him again and said, "And you, mi esposa. Just make sure you come back home to me safely. I am tired of playing the medical nurse. I only want to be a good wife and to have my husband back again in one piece. Is that too much to ask?"

"No ma'am, it surely isn't."

Juanita squeezed his hand. Then she drove away toward the pueblo.

Jabe wasn't looking forward to this journey. But, it was the one thing he had to do. First, he needed some answers only Franklin Gilmer could supply. Then he would take care of that last little item in person.

If he succeeded, he would be back home again safe and sound very soon. If not? Well, it had been a good life, after all.

46

Little more than two days later, Jabe shouldered his sea bag and stepped down from the slowly moving boxcar. It was just after the D.C. morning rush hour and the eastbound freight had delivered him right on schedule. He had been here along this same hedgerow only a couple weeks before. The rail yard neighborhood on the outskirts of the city was familiar to him this time. And this time he wouldn't use a rental car.

Crossing under the yard fence and rounding a street corner, he transformed his walk into a shuffle and pulled his slouch hat low over his eyes. The shuffle came easy because of the stiffness in his injured leg. The pain was gone now, but the fullness of his strength was slow to return. He blended into the street scene like a natural. He made for the nearest subway line and just ahead he could see the square post marking the entrance to the Metro Station. Two dollars and twenty minutes later he stepped onto the platform at the Smithsonian station. He took the escalator up, called Franklin from a pay phone and then began the mile walk south to the Jefferson Memorial.

Franklin had warned Jabe about the increased security at ONI. The sortie carried out by Saratoga's jets and the possible repercussions had everyone in the intelligence community under the microscope. The administration wanted no leaks. Their meeting would not be as casual as the last time.

Jabe approached from the south entrance and circled the giant steps of the memorial around to the west side and out of sight from the parking lot. He chose a seat on the top step next to the third column, just as Gilmer had instructed.

Ten minutes passed with no sign of Franklin and no other sound than the steady roar of airliners departing Reagan National Airport across the Potomac. The jet noise provided the perfect cover for a conversation. And Indians had a way of coming and going without being seen, so Jabe just waited patiently for Franklin.

Directly, Jabe heard Franklin's voice giving the native salutation, "Tsoomn Pa'a?" Gilmer was standing on the opposite side of the column out of sight. This arrangement gave them a clear view in all directions without standing together. Jabe fell into their code language and answered Franklin.

"Yeah, it's me."

"Glad to see you back again, J.B. I had a talk with McPherson about all that business down there. He said you had a peculiar way of riding a mustang."

"I do whatever's needed to get the job done."

"What brings you back to D.C., Jabe? I could have told you what I know over short-wave radio."

"Well, this time I had to be here in person. I got this telephone call that was meant for one of their folks—that Lawyer Indian at the pueblo. It came from a fellow named Breggard. When I find out who he is, I'm going to pay him a visit. Then he will know what comes of fooling with an Indian."

"Jabe, that guy Breggard is only an administration handy-man. I've been looking into the source of power behind all the Customs activity. Those drugs have provided a huge war chest for the upcoming election campaign. But, you put quite a ding in their cash flow. That business down in the Yucatan got too much media attention and they can't risk getting discovered. They're afraid of that Samuelson fellow over at WNN getting wind of their Colombian operation. So, the new tack is to let the drug business cool down and improve commerce with China."

"That's all we need, as if we don't already have more than enough Communist Chinese goods clogging the shelves of every SprawlMart. It's choking our whole economy."

"The items the Chinese are looking for aren't the sorts that end up on the shelves of your local department store. Their critical items of interest are the things we have and they don't have."

"Isn't that always their game?"

"Well, yeah. But, these are things they can't copy, can't make and can't steal."

A chatty couple walked by on the grass. They stopped under the trees long enough to light up cigarettes, then moved on.

"That would be weapons."

"They're concentrating on improving their long-range strategic materiel and delivery systems technology. And both of those can be provided right out of your back yard."

"The national lab at Los Alamos?"

"You got it."

"And that's why the pueblo airstrip is still in use?"

"Precisely. They can move anything they want through there without being seen. And the guru of this whole business is none other than the Vice President. Breggard is his personal secretary."

Jabe was silent for a moment.

"Well, that sheds a new light on things. Breggard thought he was talking with the Lawyer. Said I was a target for destruction. Said it was ordered by someone he called 'The Man'."

"Yep, that's right. He's the boss, the top man. The Federales call him 'El Jefe'."

"Well, that tears it, for sure. I'm going to arrange a little meeting with this El Jefe. If he wants me dead, I'm going to give him the chance of a lifetime. He can do me himself, if he wants to try."

"How are you going to manage that, J.B.?"

Jabe was getting mad now, *"You want to come along and find out?"*

It was an unfair question. Jabe continued, *"Better I go in alone, Franklin. It's a one-man mission from here on, but you've been a big help to me. I just want to make sure your position isn't compromised on account of my personal troubles. Where is he located?"*

"His office is in the Old Executive Office Building just across West Executive Avenue from the White House."

"I thought so. Birds of a feather......."

"I'm not so sure the President knows much about what's going on these days. All he really cares about is watching the money roll in for the campaign. As long as the VP performs that function, he isn't likely to ask many questions. Seems the VP

is running things these days. You know the security and surveillance is top drawer over there, J.B."

"As secure as a nuclear submarine base?"

"No, I doubt if it's that good."

"Seal Team 21 had a reputation when I was there. During war game maneuvers, we penetrated the electronic perimeter all the way into the sub pens. First we got into the base nuclear arsenal and crippled it. Then we slipped through and boarded the boats and reprogrammed the onboard missile targets. We could have taken out the whole eastern United States and the security forces never even knew we were there. His place will be a piece of cake."

"Yeah, well, if anyone can get to him, I suppose it'd be you."

"What time does the security watch change hands?"

"Well, nothing runs right on schedule, but it's usually around nine."

Gilmer was silent for a moment.

Then, *"I remember when you got your name, Tsoomn Pa'a——the deer who runs swift and sure'"*

"You do, huh?"

"You were on a deer hunt and you got onto the trail of a particularly fast buck. You ran that deer to ground and lead him into the pueblo on the end of a rope. That name gave you an attitude right from the day you got it."

"Well, I never asked for any of this, Franklin. These sonsabitches came into MY territory, unasked and uninvited. And they drew first blood."

"I know that. And I know you're mad as hell about it. I am too. I just don't want to see you lose your head and get caught, that's all. Don't want to see you go into that building and just disappear. If they corner you, they can't afford to make it public. You'd just end up another one of their 'suicides' or just plain disappear. I know you're determined to do this, so I anticipated it. But, if you get caught you'll buy the whole enchilada, J.B. And there won't be a damn thing I can do to save you."

"The only one who'll need saving is that rat bastard who wants me dead. Franklin, is there a way you can bait him into his office after dark? Maybe have him expect a phone call from the pueblo operation or something?"

"Yeah, I can manage that, alright. I've got his personal access codes. I'll route an email through the maze and have it delivered in-bound from the west. I

know enough to be able to fool that bastard. But, after that, all I can do is wish you good hunting, J.B."

"Just have him arrive in his office twenty minutes after the shift change. I plan to be in position to have a little heart-to-heart chat with the man."

"If you're really going in there, you'll need this. Franklin slipped a roll of paper around to the front of the column and laid it there.

"Go with the wind, Tsoomn Pa'a."

Jabe reached for it and tucked it into his shirt. *"Much obliged, Old Man. The sooner I get this done, the better,...... Franklin?"*

There was no answer. Franklin had gone.

Jabe waited an hour before he moved inside the Memorial. This early in the day he was in no hurry and he liked to read the inscriptions that were chiseled into the granite around the outer walls—Indian wisdom all. Jabe took some comfort in the fact that high principles always gravitated to the top in any decent society.

But, his heart was heavy when he thought about the future of his country. Where in the world was it heading and where would it all end? In this New Age, America had turned its back on many of the principles its founders knew were true. It had lasted barely two hundred years. He thought about his home pueblo and the fact that his forebears had taken those same truths to be self-evident. But, they had not turned their backs on high principle. And their culture was still going strong after a hundred centuries.

He killed the remainder of the daylight hours sitting around the benches on the Mall. Then he walked up to the Ellipse and surveyed his quarry. The floor-plan Franklin had given him was complete with office locations. Franklin had indicated a second floor corner office with windows overlooking State Place. A penciled note said this was a seldom used room and if the lights were on after dark, the room was occupied by the VP. He had also conveniently marked the motion detector locations and security system layout for Jabe's benefit. Franklin had anticipated all.

Jabe walked around the building and noted the possible entry points. There were dozens of them, and so obvious. This system had been designed by amateurs. Everything was out in the open. The magnolias in the yard provided a veritable aerial highway through the sensors. No sweat for even the dumbest Indian.

Then he noticed what might present a problem. A tree-trimming crew was busy in the magnolias that covered the south lawn. They had removed vegetation in some of the trees that Jabe could have counted on for cover. But, they were quitting work for the day and Jabe watched them lock up their chainsaws inside two vans parked along State Place. Then they locked up the vans and drove away in cars.

But luckily, they had not yet completed the job and enough vegetation was left in the trees to cover his entry. And these plain white vans parked along the street would come in handy. They were just what an Indian would have ordered. No logo or lettering on their sides, just plain white. And they were in full view of the VP's corner office.

Just at sunset and hungry now, he took a stroll up a side street and bought a satisfying southwestern meal at one of the street-deli juice joints—some kind of an organic burrito. Man those guys could cook!

He sat at an outside table and studied Franklin's map. When he had it memorized, he folded it and dropped it in a waste can.

His hunger satisfied, the idea Jabe had in mind for those parked vans began to take shape. He walked over and poked around in one of the planter boxes that decorated the sidewalk.

He found just what he wanted and removed some of the black plastic sheeting just under the mulch the grounds people used for weed and moisture control. He used his pocket knife to carve eight rounds about six inches in diameter and folded them into his pocket. Then he went inside the deli and pocketed several of those small plastic packs of honey. Now he was ready for his mission.

Lightning was playing in the clouds off to the northeast in the gathering dusk as Jabe arrived back at the Old Executive Office Building. If that nor'easter came ashore, it looked like Washington was in for quite a blow tonight.

He approached the vans parked along State Place in full darkness. They were lit only in the dim reflection from the exterior lighting coming from across the street. Jabe used the honey to glue the rounds to the sides of the vans. He placed them in a row about head-high and evenly spaced, four to a van they sort of resembled gunports. They were in plain view from the VP's office windows—just what Jabe wanted.

Then he walked a circuitous route that brought him around and up a side street. He stopped opposite to a corner of the building that gave him a commanding view of his objective. He looked up and saw exactly what he'd wanted to see. The entire second floor was dark including the VP's corner office.

He moved around to an entry position that he figured was the most vulnerable to covert penetration. Then he shed his coat and hat and stashed them behind a garbage can in the alley. From an alcove along the wrought iron fence, he vaulted up and over it, being careful to avoid the laser beam from the perimeter detectors. He caught a low branch and squirreled up through the tall magnolias. Then he moved all the way up to the second floor windows. He had no trouble at all in avoiding the motion detector beams.

Standing just above the second floor windows now, he felt something touch his sleeve. Jabe's adrenaline raced and he felt a cold shiver run up his backside. He jerked instinctively around and ducked, expecting to parry a blow that would be coming from some secret service type on lookout.

He faced only thin air when he felt his shirt sleeve tear away. His torn shirt-sleeve was dangling from a chainsaw, obviously left behind by the tree-trimming crew. His sleeve had brushed it in the dark and snagged its teeth. Now it was swinging there in the breeze threatening to crash to the ground.

Damn. That's all I need. I've come all this way just to be tripped up by some dingbat yard-crew idiot.

He reached out with his other hand and made a grab for the saw. If he'd been a split second sooner, he might have had it. But, no such luck— it tore away and went tumbling down, thrashing every limb as it went.

Jabe watched in horrified amazement as it tumbled. Every guard on duty would be there in an instant. The chainsaw bounced off every limb and showered the air with leaf-litter. To Jabe, it seemed to hang suspended on each bounce and descended in slow motion. The thunder seemed to go on forever. It finally hit the ground some thirty feet below with a resounding thump.

Jabe froze against the tree trunk and waited. His temples were pulsing and his jaw muscles wouldn't keep still. He listened.

Then he heard voices close by and the cold chill made another pass up his back. Muffled tones came from the sidewalk just beyond the fence as two guards approached. But, they didn't appear to be in any particular hurry. Jabe watched them stop and light up cigarettes. A breeze was kicking up and the two had to strike several matches to kindle their smokes.

The magnolias crackled in the wind and the light on their faces gave Jabe reason to relax. Incredible as it seemed, they hadn't heard a thing. Simply unbelievable! If they'd been out guarding instead of simply out walking, listening instead of talking, they'd have heard the ruckus and Jabe would have been in custody by now. The security guards passed right along and continued in conversation.

A thing like that would tend to make a tenderfoot relax and get careless and overconfident. Jabe couldn't afford that luxury. Too much was at stake here. For the first time tonight, Jabe began to take stock of his situation.

He tried to think of what lay ahead of him, what kind of pitfalls might lay there. When he felt another chill begin the trip up his backbone, he lay those thoughts aside and turned to his business. It wouldn't do to think too hard on it just now. He had a job to do, so he'd just as well get on with it. He would just have to trust his instincts.

He stepped out of the tree at the second-floor level and found a foothold on the wall atop the cornice stone in the shadow of the great magnolia. Just overhead, he found the air conditioning vent in short order. This vent was the return air from the evaporators and the air was warm. The grating came away and swung open easily. Once inside, he closed the grating door and let his eyes accommodate to the darkness, then he moved out through the ductwork on the course he had memorized from Franklin's floor plan.

Jabe felt the press of the hunt. The game was simple enough. All he had to do was to get in undetected, find the right office, meet with the VP, convince him to leave the pueblo out of his plans for international dominance, and then get out again—undetected. Simple.

One thing at a time, Jabe thought. He'd just have to take it slow and easy. Right now it was just a matter of navigating the dark vent system and finding the right office. Everything else would surely just fall into place. It was just that simple.

But, for starters the vent system went directly across the ceiling of the second floor security room. And the slightest sound would signal his presence. There were long odds against him, but it wasn't the first time he'd been in a tight situation. All he needed was to get across the security room—undetected.

Just beyond, he would have no trouble letting himself down into the VP's office. His biggest concern was the creaking noises made by the old sheet-metal ducting. Jabe checked his watch. It was eleven minutes to nine. Better take it slow and wait for the shift change. No reason to get in a hurry this close in. Timing was going to be a problem. He wished he hadn't played it this close. No room for error. He could only hope the VP was a little late.

Jabe tried to relax and lay flat against the cold metal in an attempt to distribute his weight more evenly. With his ear close to the vent register, he could hear the conversations below him. The guards were filing their shift reports and getting things ready for the change. Jabe crept up close to the air vent, rolled up on his left shoulder and peeked down.

Below him he could see the reception desk and the guard sitting on a high stool. The visitor log lay directly beneath the vent in the center of the desk and Jabe was almost close enough to read the entries. The guard signed his watch report and turned around to the filing cabinet behind him.

Jabe heard someone come into the room. He leaned out just a tad for a better look at the newcomer. It was the janitor who had come in pushing a dust mop around the waiting area. She was making her regular cleanup round just before going off duty for the night.

Just then Jabe heard a faint crack and felt a jolt just under his shoulder in the duct work. To his horror, a piece of ceiling plaster about the size of a graham cracker came away from the edge of the air register and fell away toward the reception desk below. Jabe watched it fall.

His first instinct was to duck away, but his military training held him still. The plaster hit the logbook with a dull thud and Jabe held his breath.

Gilmer's words rang in his ears, "You'll buy the whole enchilada and there won't be a damn thing I can do to save you."

It wouldn't do to get caught in a national security zone. He'd probably get the regular treatment for security risks close to the top and they'd make certain the truth of it would never make the public news reports. He had visions of turning up dead of an apparent suicide.

Several seconds passed without any reaction from the guard. The plaster shard just lay there on the open logbook. So far, so good. But, if the guard saw it, he'd react immediately.

Then the janitor parked her mop and took out her feather duster. She started at the end of the reception desk and dusted toward the logbook. She stopped and reached for the plaster. Then she hesitated a moment and looked straight up at the register above. Jabe's heart stopped and he froze instinctively. Not even his eyeballs moved.

She stared at the ceiling for a moment, right into Jabe's eyes. Only the vanes in the register hid Jabe's face. Then she lifted the plaster shard off the logbook and dusted off the pages.

"This place is falling apart, Wilson."

At that, the guard closed the file drawer and turned around to his desk again, "Huh?"

"I said it's a full-time job cleaning up around this old place."

The guard lifted the logbook and blew the dust off it, "Oh, yeah—the dust. It's horrific in here. But, you should have seen it before the renovations."

Jabe exhaled slowly and hadn't realized he had been holding his breath. He remained frozen for fear of loosening more plaster.

Then he heard voices and the approach of footsteps from down the hallway. The new shift was arriving. The commotion in the room below allowed him to move on to the VP's office just beyond.

Over the next room, he squeezed down the air shaft, removed the vent register and crawled through the narrow opening into the VP's own office. The room's sole illumination came from the blinking lights on the desk telephone. Keeping to the wall, Jabe slipped over and quietly seated himself at the VP's desk.

Feeling around the edge of the desk, he quickly found the alarm trip button under the corner ledge and had it disconnected in seconds. Seeing there was no overhead light fixture, he unscrewed the bulbs in the desk lamps, then crept over and tried the light switch by the door. No sign of a light. Now he was set.

He glanced at the luminous dial of his Navy diver's watch. It was eight fifty-eight. That was cutting it too damn close!

Jabe leaned back against the cold plastered wall. He hadn't noticed it before, but his skin was hot to the touch and he was drenched with sweat.

Now he felt the cool of the conditioned air, but it was different from the cold chill he'd had earlier. His heart was thumping his chest like a punching bag and he breathed in short puffs.

Come on now, settle down.

Now he was no longer so positive that coming here was such a great idea. Oh sure, it had seemed quite the thing to do a few hours ago. But, there were so many variables. Jabe wasn't sure he'd thought them all through.

He considered his next move, then slipped back again and took a seat in the big leather chair behind the huge executive desk. This way he'd have a full view of the room.

What if the VP came in with company? What if he didn't come at all? What if…..and that was the problem. There were too damn many what-ifs.

His thoughts trailed off as he heard the sound of approaching footsteps.

47

The lights came on in the outer office and he heard the door close. Then the footsteps came closer and a shadow broke the line of light showing under the door. This man was alone. And he was right on time.

Just how lucky can an Indian get?

Jabe's eyes had adjusted to the dark, but this man would be completely blind. Only an occasional lightning flash illuminated the room.

He heard the man punching numbers into the ID sentry keypad outside the office door. Then the door bolt popped open and Jabe watched the man come inside. Reaching for the light switch he flipped it once, then again with no result.

"Dammit."

Jabe stood up and moved around to the side of the desk, ready for whatever was coming next.

The VP made a beeline for his desk in the dark and reached for the telephone. But, Jabe's hand got there first. In an instant, he grabbed the VP by the wrist and pulled his arm up behind his back. Jabe threw his free arm around the VP's neck and caught the executive in a classic choke hold. He was just in time to cut off a yell that was welling up in the VP's throat.

The startled man gasped and began to wiggle.

"What the hell?" choked the VEEP.

Jabe tightened his clinch-hold on the man's windpipe. "Now, you just keep quiet and I won't have to kill you. I came here to have a nice quiet talk with you. But, if you don't follow directions, I'm gonna snap your neck like a pencil. Now, are you going to quiet down and be still?"

The struggling stopped and the VP shook his head in agreement.

Jabe kept a tight grip and continued.

"I came here to talk some business with you. But if you sound any kind of alarm, you'll be dead before anyone can get to you. You savvy that?"

Another shake of the VP's head and Jabe loosened his grip just a tad.

The VP rasped, "Just who in the hell *are* you?"

"You don't know me personally. We've never met. But, you know who I am. My name is J.B. Rainwater. I'm the guy you've been trying to kill."

Jabe let go a little more, but he kept a convincing pressure on the VP's throat. He felt the slight tremble of a shiver run through the VP.

There was a long silence. Then, "You came here to kill me, didn't you?"

Jabe let the silence build before he answered........

"Only if I have to. I came here for some talk, just like I said. I'm going to offer you the business opportunity of a lifetime." Jabe relaxed his hold enough for the VP to speak more easily.

"Oh yeah, I'm sure. You sneak in here and violate my office in order to offer me a business deal? How in the hell did you get in here anyway? You're nothing but a common bandit."

Jabe held the man fast and shoved him toward the windows.

"Oh, I'm sure it'd take more than a bandit of the common variety to get in here, wouldn't you say?"

"Alright, you had special training in the Navy. I read your file. But, you'll never get out of here alive."

"Oh, I think *I* will. The real question is, *will you?*

Step right over here and let me show you something."

Jabe tightened his grip on the VP's throat again and turned him face-on to the window. The wind was picking up outside and the lightning came in blinding flashes.

"Now you just look down there and tell me what you see over across the street. Can you see those two white vans down there?"

"Yeah," the VP shook his head yes.

"Good. Now see those portholes? There are four in each van. Can you guess what they're for?"

360

Jabe gave the VP a little jerk. This time the head-shake was negative.

"Well, then I'll tell you. Behind each one of those portholes is a Stinger missile pointed at this window, right at your head. The men in those vans have orders to shoot on my signal. Do you have any idea what kind of damage eight Stinger missile warheads can do?"

The VP was motionless as he stared wide-eyed at the vans.

Jabe continued, "They'll take out this whole end of the building. You won't have an office any more, mister." Jabe loosened his choke-hold and turned the VP around. He pushed his face up close and looked directly into the VP's frightened eyes.

"Are you ready to die?"

A flash of lightning illuminated the two men's faces. The VP's face was pale. The first thunderclap rolled through the capital complex and echoed out across the tidal basin.

The VP growled, "You'd be dead right along with me."

"Oh! I guess I never thought about that. You're absolutely right. But, the difference is, *I'm ready to die. Are you?*"

Jabe shook the VP by the neck.

"I've had lots of experience with cowards like you. You've got no principles, mister. I'm betting you're so egotistical you'll want to remain alive no matter what the cost. I'd also bet you'd sell your mother to the devil if there was a dollar in it."

"You think you're a tough guy, don't you?"

Jabe didn't answer.

"You're on a power trip, mister. And there isn't one damn thing you wouldn't do to preserve that. That's the difference between you and me. The fact is I'd like nothing better than to take you out permanently. I'd consider it an honor to rid this country of just one more slimball like you—even if it cost me my life. You see, I just plain don't give a damn."

"I think you just might do it."

"You're damn right I will! Just try me. You can die right here, or you can sit down and listen to a real business opportunity. Like I told you, I'm going to make you a deal you can't refuse."

"Oh, yeah? What kind of a business opportunity?"

"Now that's more like it. You just have a seat."

Jabe relaxed and let the VP stand on his own. Then he pushed the man backwards toward his desk chair. The VP flopped into it. Jabe sat down on the desk just an arms-length away in front of the man and leaned toward him.

"You've been a busy boy, haven't you? You've been in the drug business quite a while now. Several years I'd say. Moved a lot of drugs and made a pile of money. Pretty good scheme using those convict pilots. But, I think you've done enough damage to the citizens of this country and it's time you got out of that business. So I came to offer you a way out of it for good."

The VP started to get up, "The hell with you...."

Jabe pushed him back into his chair. "I'm not done yet. I came here to offer you your neck."

"My neck?"

"That's it. Your neck, dumb-ass."

Jabe leaned right down into the VP's face.

"You see, here's how it works. You get out of the drug business for good and get your gunmen out of MY pueblo. You let me and my people alone and you stop dealing drugs in this country. That way, I'll let you live. It's that simple."

The VP cocked his head and sneered, "Oh that's some kind of business opportunity!"

The VP's left hand felt for the alarm button and Jabe let him press it.

Jabe leaned back and folded his arms, "Well, I told you it was a deal you couldn't refuse. I stopped your whole operation down in the Yucatan right under the noses of those Federale friends of yours. And here I sit right in your office. Now you just think about that. I don't care where you go—I can get to you any time I want. And if you don't believe me, you can hide in the bushes and watch."

Outside the clouds opened up and the wind whipped the rain against the window panes in torrents. The lightning flashes came only seconds apart and thunder rolled continuously.

"You're crazy as hell if you think you can tell *me* what to do!"

"Crazy?"

Jabe got up and walked toward the door.

Then he turned and said, "I might be ugly, but I'm not stupid. And I'm telling you plain and simple. You get out of the drug business for good. And you get outta my pueblo. Do it now, and I'll let you live."

The VP got to his feet, "I'll see you dead within the hour."

Jabe reached the door, turned and saw the VP press the alarm button again.

"That panic-button's not going to do you any good. You just remember I can get to you at any time. Not another load of dope comes into the states, or I'll be back."

Jabe walked through the door and closed it behind him. In the entry room he flipped off the lights and ducked under the secretary's desk.

The VP came flying out and ran into the hallway looking to see which way Jabe had gone. Then he turned and ran toward the security post at full speed.

Jabe re-entered the VP's office, squeezed back inside the return air duct and pulled the register closed behind him.

Sirens and claxon horns wailed and the place was soon crawling with shouting, black-uniformed security forces combing every part of the building, inside and out.

Jabe made his way back along his entry route and crossed right over the security desk again. The thunder of the storm covered the noise he made in scrambling back along the ductwork and this time he was careful not to knock any more plaster down from the ceiling.

When he arrived at the outside vent grating, he rested and contented himself in watching the security guards pursue pedestrians along the sidewalks. They obviously figured he'd gotten out the same way he'd gotten in—undetected.

No way could he climb outside and get back to the ground tonight. He would have to wait until morning.

48

Rain lashed the magnolias outside the vent grating and the wind gusts sent an occasional spray through the grill. Jabe pulled back away from the opening and stretched out flat against the sheet metal duct-work. With all the activity in the yard below him and inside the building behind him, there wasn't a thing he could do but keep still. He could hear the guards moving from room to room checking the window locks. How long would it take them to find the loose grill on the air return duct in the VP's office? He gulped and tried not to think about it.

Down in the yard, roving security patrols called up to others on the roof and played spotlights up and down the walls of the Old Executive Office Building, so Jabe made it a point to keep his face far away from the vent grill. He was thankful the building architects had been so meticulous about the blending of lines in their design. Even this ventilation grill looked like a continuous part of the structure. The heavy metal grill was a contrast against the stone wall, sure enough. But, it appeared to any casual outside observer as if it were an integral part of the wall and coping-stones. It blended right in. They took such good care of details like that in the design of public buildings back in 1888.

Jabe watched with amused interest as the security forces made a regular military assault on the empty vans across the street. They approached from all sides with spotlights and bull-horns. Jabe could see that the rain had already dissolved the honey and washed the plastic "portholes" into the gutter. They were probably already in the Potomac.

The rain had guaranteed that any traces he might have left behind were obliterated. The armed assault that followed only netted the security forces a couple of vans full of yard gear. No Stinger missiles. No Indians. Not even a sign of the eight gun-ports they'd been expecting. At this point the VP's credibility with the security folks was probably fading fast.

Those security people know the VP well enough. They probably suspect it's yet another of his attempts at free publicity. He chuckled.

The building finally quieted down and the excitement out in the yard abated after midnight, but Jabe could see that the roving patrols were still on the move and barely a hundred feet apart. No way could he get outside under present circumstances. And his leg was beginning to cramp and turn sore again.

What he needed was a diversion. What he could really use was someone to come along like that kook who shot up the White House a few years back. Yep, that's the kind of thing he needed all right. The sudden eruption of automatic rifle fire across the street would be sure to give him the brief instant when he could vault into the magnolias and back over the wrought iron fence onto the sidewalk.

His mind raced ahead and searched for a possibility—any possibility at all. Where are all the nut-cases when you really need them?

He took stock of his situation. Here he was, stuck between floors in a hyper-secure government building. Without some stroke of pure luck, a move outside in any direction was sure to be noticed. And it simply would not do to get caught now.

The folks he'd left behind at the pueblo knew little of what was really happening on their own turf, and there was no way they could know what he had in mind. When it came to a showdown, with the odds greatly against them, they'd be almost totally ineffective. There was no way he could communicate to them the strategy he was planning that would rid them of the menace they were facing. He was trapped again and everything he held dear was in jeopardy. He'd have to figure a way out of here. And soon!

In the meantime here he sat, holed up in a damp air duct. He'd just have to stay awake and watch for his chance to move out. If he saw any chance at all, he'd make a jump for it. How long that might take, he didn't know. Besides his aching leg, all he really knew was that he was cold, wet and tired—very tired. The adrenaline rush he'd had when confronting the VP had abated and left him exhausted.

Jabe closed his eyes and rested his mind. He would just rest for a little while and get his strength back. He listened to the thrashing of the magnolias and the pelting rain. The thunder rolled away toward the southwest and the wind settled down into a breeze. Then it went dead calm and the steady drizzle set up a mesmerizing rhythm that threatened to lull Jabe to sleep.

Sleep? Hell, that would be the death of me! Gotta stay awake. Gotta keep alert so I don't miss my chance to........ get outta here.... Just....... gotta.... stay....

All was quiet there inside the ventilation duct. Jabe was half-conscious. He felt a calm and serenity he hadn't experienced for a long time. He stretched his arms and legs. His whole body felt rested and relaxed. The aching in his leg had gone now. Perhaps he had relaxed a little more than he'd intended to.

Then there came the sound of distant thunder.

At first, Jabe could only make out a low rumbling rattle echoing off the buildings across the street. Had another storm crept in, or was this the last whimper of the one that was passing?

Then the rasping growl broke into a full fury that brought Jabe around to stark reality. He opened his left eye and saw sunlight filtering in. It was dawn!

Dammit, I've been asleep....

He raised his head and banged it loudly against the ductwork— loud enough for the guards to come to their senses. Jabe wondered and just didn't care anymore. He was trapped and GOOD. And he saw little chance for escape.

He rolled onto his belly and leaned forward to have a look. It wasn't thunder. It was the sound of chainsaws. The yard crew had returned and was busy at the magnolias again.

This just might be the diversion he needed. The roaring of their saws was making a racket that would cover any sound Jabe might make. But, even if he made it to the ground, how would he blend in with the yard crew?

367

He had to look twice to believe his eyes. These guys were wearing camouflage combat fatigues, just like the ones he was wearing.

What a stroke of luck! These guys must have been in the guerrilla forces in their native country. They wore the familiar uniform of the jungle fighter. Then Jabe remembered the stacks and stacks of similar clothing he had seen on sale at the Army-Navy stores. This stuff was available coast-to-coast. A guy could get a complete outfit for a sawbuck.

Nevertheless, it looked as though these guys could have served under Capitan Juan Goyona. Their shouts in crude Spanish grated on Jabe's ears and it was a far cry from the smooth Castilian so gracefully articulated by Juanita.

Juanita!

The thought of her jolted Jabe. Would he ever see her again? No time to contemplate it now. He needed to get out of there.

He surveyed the grounds and watched for any guards that may be afoot. A two-man patrol passed by over on the sidewalk. Two other patrols were in view outside the yard around the perimeter fence. The patrols were arrayed in regular intervals in their movements. Not nearly enough room to get out between them.

But, the security people were out on the sidewalks keeping clear of the chainsaws and only the tree-trimming crew inhabited the lawn. Limbs were crashing to the ground in all directions. They were thinning the trees, and the magnolias were his only salvation. He'd have to move fast now. But, he would have to wait and make his move just after one of the patrols passed by. If he was spotted once he was outside, he would be easy meat.

Jabe pushed the grating open a half-inch or so and positioned himself to make a fast exit. The next patrol passed by and when they were hidden momentarily by the thick foliage, Jabe made his move.

He slid out of the ventilation duct and let himself down along the wall. He found a footing on the capstones and poised himself on his good leg. Then he made a leap for the nearest magnolia and landed on a stout limb where he clung tight and froze.

Jabe watched for any sign that he'd been discovered, but the yard crew was far too busy to notice. He was hidden from the security patrols at the moment and out of their sight. For an instant he felt that familiar cold chill creep up his backside.

True enough, he was outside the building now, but he was still on their turf and he was sure those security folks had orders to shoot him on sight. No way was the VP going to give him a fair chance.

The chill continued on its upward course. His very next move might be his last. He would be in plain sight of anyone caring to look in his direction. So, he pulled his slouch hat down low over his brow and hoped he blended in. Lacking any tree tools to work with, he would have to get to the ground quickly. He kept an eye out for patrols and began a slow descent, stepping from limb to limb and keeping to the shady side of the big magnolia.

Half-way down to the ground, Jabe hoped the chainsaw he'd had the fight with the night before might still be lying beneath. He looked down and saw it lying there still nestled among the tree limbs left from the previous day's cutting. Last night, high up in the magnolia, it had been an unwelcome intruder. But, this morning Jabe saw it in a much different light. It was just the tool he needed for his escape.

He made a quick reconnaissance and started down again. Then he saw something that made him freeze and hug the trunk. From behind the trunk of the mighty tree, a hand appeared and reached out for the saw.

Directly below him, a Mexican in fatigues was cleaning up the refuse from the previous day's cutting. He picked up the saw and looked at it, "Aye, Carrumba! You leetle bandit. You try to hide from your Papa? Now, you will only have to go back to work again."

Jabe gulped at the thought of losing the saw. He was so close, and yet so far away. The thought flashed through his head that he should jump this guy and take him out. But, what would he do next? He drew a blank. Besides, this guy had done him no harm.

It was only his Navy training coming back to him as instinct. Self-preservation, plain and simple. Jabe stood fast and watched.

The yardman hooked the saw on a low-hanging limb, "Now, you stay there and I will be back for you." Then he went about his work. Jabe let the man get out and away from the magnolia and then he slowly released the breath he had been holding.

When he was sure no one was looking, he scrambled lower, reached down and grabbed the saw. Getting to the ground, he walked right out into the open. He confirmed the ignition switch was off and pulled the starter rope. "Aye, Caramba!" He intoned.

Again and again, Jabe pulled the starter rope. But, the motor failed to start. Several of the yard crew glanced toward him and shook their heads, then resumed their own labor—he would have to get the damned thing started on his own.

He was thankful for that. It was just the reaction he'd counted on.

He walked straight toward the yard gate still pulling at the dead saw. Two guards were standing just outside the gate. They were smoking and passing some mumbling talk between them. They hardly looked up as Jabe approached.

He looked them right in the eye and put on his best Mexican accent, "Dees chingada. Chee no wanna start."

One of the guards glanced at him and then looked quickly away, "Tough shit, old boy." The two chuckled at this poor Mexican and his troubles. "Maybe 'chee' got drowned in the rain last night."

"Si, maybe so, senor. Gracias. I take her to the truck. Dees saw es un chingada grande!"

Jabe continued pulling on the starter rope and made straight for the two white vans. And wouldn't you just know it—nobody even offered to help!

Slipping away from the Capitol Complex and back to the railyard, Jabe caught a west-bound freight toward New Mexico.

49

It was half past eight when Wade Breggard strode into the VP's office carrying a cup of java in his boss's favorite cup. The VP was pacing the floor as Wade entered. He was not smiling. He pointed to his desk chair.

"Wade, that Rainwater guy was sitting right here last night when I came in about nine o'clock."

"WHAT?"

He threatened me personally and I'm not taking that lying down. How in the hell he slipped in and out of here completely undetected is more than I can abide. We've spent millions to secure this place. I believe we sent the Navy out to eliminate him, didn't we? And yet he shows up here in my office—*MY OFFICE*! That sonofa......, if the Navy can't take care of that guy, you get me somebody who can."

"That's quite a story, sir. You mean to tell me he got in here and then back out again completely undetected?"

"Yeah, you bet your ass he did!" The VP walked over to the window and looked out at the two vans.

"But, I can't figure how he managed it. He must have had a lot of inside help to do it, that's all."

"Oh, I'm not so sure he needed any help from people inside, Sir. After all, he was trained by our own military in the tactics he needed to ensure perfectly undetected insertion and withdrawal. His service record is full of that kind of stuff. He may have been all by himself." Wade placed the cup on the VP's desk and joined his boss at the window. "You know, I was reading his file and this one time he actually got all the way into the sub pens down at...."

"The hell you say! I'm *sure* he had to have some inside help. Either that or these people here we call our 'security force' were fast asleep, Wade. I mean shnokered—out cold! I saw what looked like portholes on those vans over there across the street. He claimed there were missiles aimed at the place. Now, there's nothing. How in hell did he pull that off? I'm damn sure I saw those portholes. Did they just wash away in the rain?"

"I know how it must have upset you, Sir. But, we've got a bigger problem than that. General Mendoza has been talking to the international press corps."

Wade handed the VP a sheaf of papers, then picked up the TV remote and turned on WNN.

The VP took the papers and sat down at his desk. He sipped Java while he read. Slowly, the VP placed the cup on the desk and stood up. Then he looked at Wade in apparent disbelief.

"That sonofabitch! What the hell is he trying to do?"

The images on the TV screen came into focus. Wade turned up the volume. Don Samuelson was reporting.

"......and our World News Network sources in Mexico City tell us they have even more convincing evidence that the United States Customs Service has been active in facilitating the drug traffic into Texas and the Southwest for months now. When I showed up at the Customs offices in Houston, the door was slammed in my face. On top of that, our calls to the White House have been ignored.

"Nobody seems to be talking, John. One can only imagine the kinds of things that have been going on here. Perhaps this is only the tip of the iceberg. The rumors about a Bolivian connection in Washington's highest office might be true after all......"

Wade turned down the sound.

"Oh, Mendoza knows what he's trying to do, Sir. He's plenty pissed off about losing his airfield and the cash you were paying him. He's lost his prestige and he's holding us up for ransom. Why else would he go to the media like that?"

The VP glanced at the papers again and came around his desk waving the report in the air.

"That crazy Mendoza bastard is saying he was duped by the U.S. into playing a role in a game he knew nothing about. Oh, he takes our money easy enough. Then, when we have a few problems, he rats us out the first chance he gets."

Wade took a seat.

"Well Sir, money is the only thing those bastards understand. That Rainwater guy put a kink in things for Mendoza and now I think the General is just trying to avoid the consequences of failing to deliver the goods. Those cartel folks you've been dealing with down in Colombia want results, not excuses. I'd say they've put the pressure on Mendoza and now he's trying to save his own skin at our expense.

"That pompous bastard. I never did like the way he referred to me as 'El Jefe' like I was gonna ease right up and eat out of his hand. Now he's got that Samuelson fellow down our throats for sure."

The VP flopped into his chair and put his head down on his desk. "That's all I need. Samuelson's not the kinda guy who'll listen to reason. Didn't you have that visit with his boss, Wade?"

Wade hesitated, "Well, Yessir, I did. But that's one of the things I wanted to tell you, Sir. WNN is backing their man Samuelson and they've been calling here since first light this morning. They want to send over a crew for an interview on the Mexican situation. That report by Samuelson on the early news gave the definite impression that General Mendoza might be telling the truth. And the President also called for you."

"What did that buffoon want?"

"He wants you to take care of the WNN interview."

"Oh, I'll just bet he does."

The VP was silent for a moment. Then he raised his head and smiled. He swiveled around and gazed out the window. After another moment he grinned, "Then, by golly, that's just what we'll do."

Wade looked up and noticed the grin on his boss's face, "Sir?"

"Yeah, you're damn right we will. We'll talk with that WNN bunch alright. We're going to have to rethink our strategy, my boy. This could be the chance I've been waiting for. You get that Samuelson fellow over here tonight, say around ten o'clock. That'll be late enough that they can't get anything on the air until tomorrow. That'll be all the time

I need. Now, get the majority leaders of both houses on the horn and have them get over here right away. Wade my boy, I think we're back in business again."

Less than an hour later, the two most powerful men in all of Congress were seated across the desk from the Vice President. Wade Breggard listened as the VP laid out his plan. He had a strategy that would distance him from the congressional firefight that he knew lay just ahead and also make him the most favored candidate in the upcoming election.

The VP leaned back, drew heavily on his freshly lit stogy and assumed his most serious facial expression, "You gentlemen know how concerned I am about the Chief Executive. I've tried to help him all I can, but most of the time he just isn't listening. I've told him personally to let those folks south of the border alone and to get out of bed with those Mexicans and that South American trash. And you know how far that got me.

"Now he's got his tail in a crack for sure and the media is going to have a field day over this thing. But, frankly, I'm at a loss. I'm not sure I can save him this time. And if he goes down, he might take a lot of us right along with him."

The VP let the silence come to bear full-on.

"So, tell me. What can you two gentlemen do for me?"

Wright Peterson, Senate Majority Leader, leaned forward and voiced his concern.

"Well, in the first place, like I've been trying to tell you, that sonofabitch has been asleep at the wheel ever since taking office. You've only tried to help him the same as we have. All of us worked damned hard to put him in there and all he can do is screw up by the numbers; wheedles around the Oval Office in the dark over there doing practically nothing besides interns. He needs to be taking care of business."

Morgan Feldman, Speaker of the House spoke up.

"Is that what you really think of our President, Wright?"

"Hell, Morg. He hasn't even got a solid foreign policy. Justice is a wreck. They go around killing just about everybody they don't agree with, and now his self-appointed Surgeon General wants to legalize drugs—kill all our children. Hell, he'll do anything for money and everybody knows the kind of cock-eyed things he's done with the military."

"Well, I don't think it's all as bad as you make it sound."

"He's completely self-centered. He's out of touch with reality and knows nothing about what the people of this country want or need. He creates nothing but problems for us on all sides. But, he can't seem to find anything to do but play golf and go on expensive vacations every time there is a new crisis. No wonder he doesn't know what's going on these days. We can't just stand around and let him ruin everything we've worked so hard for a lifetime to build, Morg."

"Aw hell, Wright. You hold on there a minute. I really believe he hasn't the slightest idea what's been going on down there. If he did, he'd have told me. I just know he would. I know he's pretty sleazy and he does some stupid things now and again, but the man would never *lie* to us."

The VP pointed to the TV and Wade turned up the volume. The President was shaking his fist at the camera. "I never knew a thing about all of that business down there…." The next image to appear was the face of Don Samuelson.

"Now there's the clip I wanted our viewers to see. The President denies knowing anything at all about this Mexican business. Claims he never knew his own federal people were involved in the transport and sale of hard narcotics on the streets of Houston. A federal grand jury is being called at this very minute to question the President and other high officials in order to give them a chance to prove their claims of innocence. And while the echoes of his denials are dying away in the halls of justice, WNN has confirmed that a Columbian Connection does indeed exist between Washington and the drug lords of Mexico and South America. We vow to bring the truth to the American people no matter how painful it may turn out to be, John."

Wade hit the kill button and the TV went dark.

Peterson continued, "Morgan. Dammit man, listen to reason. The President has lied at every turn. There's a better than even chance the man'll be indicted for his previous false testimony before this same grand jury. He's been in the drug business ever since he was a governor. Now he says if we can't cover for him…. Well, he's making sounds like he'll take some of us down with him. I can't believe you'd have any confidence in that rat-fink bastard at all. He's turned out to be the biggest mistake we've ever made."

The Speaker leaned back in his chair, "Well, I just don't want to do the wrong thing here."

The VP chimed in, "Well dammit, neither do we, Morgan. But we've gotta do something. Hell, he's making fools out of all of us. Once he destroys all the confidence the public has in the party, we're all out on the street and it'll take us years to regroup.

I've been trying to run things around here for the last three years all by myself. Hell, I've been so busy getting him out of one scrape after another, I don't know which way is up. And now this!"

Peterson jumped in again, "I'd say you've been doing a bang-up job of damage control, too. And you've gotten little enough thanks from anyone."

Wade couldn't sit still with the sentiments running this high, "You got that right, Senator. I'll testify to that. He's kept the whole damn ship of state afloat all by himself these past few years."

Wright turned to Wade, "Aye, my boy, and it hasn't gone unnoticed. Your boss ought to be up there in the Big House himself, instead of that idiot we put in there.

When that fat cat up there in the Big House goes down, my boy, we'll have to get your boss here into office as smoothly as possible. What we need in the President's Office is an upstanding man like the VP here. What do you say, Morg?"

Morgan Feldman was quiet for a moment. Then, "We're going to need a consensus on this, Wright. I can't make a decision like that on my own. If anything goes wrong…"

The senator cut him off in mid-sentence, "Oh, I think I can safely say we'll have a consensus before tomorrow sunset, Morg. My colleagues have been after me for months to do something about this problem. And now we've got a golden opportunity to get rid of him."

Morgan Feldman said, "Well, If it's gotta be that way, then let's get to it."

50

Little more than two days later, Jabe roused himself and sat up in the heaving boxcar. He had been asleep for half the morning. By this time, the freight had pulled up through Raton Pass and was heading south into New Mexico.

He sat cross-legged Indian-style just inside the open boxcar door. The haze and clouds that had obscured the sun in the Capital City were gone now, and the sky was crystal blue. He had a clear view of his home mountains and he wished never to leave them again. It would be a straight downhill ride to the Rio Grande.

Later that day the freight slowed going up a steep grade and Jabe gathered his sea bag and let himself down to the ground in a trot. It would be a ten-mile hike to the pueblo, but Jabe was glad for the chance to exercise his stiff leg. The run would refresh his spirit and his body. He would keep to the river and under the cover of the cottonwoods—no need to announce his arrival.

Coming through the scrub cedars and down toward the bosque, Jabe topped a grassy knoll. He slowed to a trot and covered the same ground he and Indian Joe had ridden just a couple weeks before. He slowed to a walk. There below him was the familiar sight of his home. The soulful cry of an eagle came to his ear as he stopped to take in the scene.

The past two days riding the freight had given him a chance to reflect on his adventures. The realization of the extreme danger he'd been in finally came home to him and it made him feel tired to the bone.

He'd covered a lot of ground over the past two weeks and the venture hadn't been without its risks. He'd had some close calls. He'd been halfway to the equator and back again. He'd been inside the VP's office and had looked that Death Angel square in the face.

Now, he stood looking at his home again. Home again! What he wouldn't give to be able to settle down with Juanita in his pueblo home and go a-roaming no more!

Down below, he could see that all was just as he'd left it. He wondered if it had ever looked otherwise. There, just across the river, was Longrifle's adobe and the kiva. There also were the homes of his neighbors. Jabe could see Hahtahway's place and there went his old Chevy pickup pulling out of the front yard. It turned up the back road leading north. Hahtahway usually avoided the heat and didn't go out until late in the afternoon. Jabe wondered where the old man was heading this time of day.

Then he noticed something that wasn't quite right. Parked at the pueblo offices were half a dozen dark blue Broncos and they didn't belong to the tribe. Another one pulled out of the parking lot and drove up the road toward the entrance. Jabe stood up and squinted against the glare of the midday sun.

Then he saw them. There must have been a hundred people lined up and standing against the perimeter fence out on the highway—Network News trucks and official-looking vans, several BIA cars and even a Border Patrol Humvee. He heard an aircraft turbine come up to full revs and a helicopter lifted off from behind the pueblo offices in a cloud of dust. It turned out toward the highway, made a low pass over the crowd and began a straight run up along the perimeter fence.

Jabe walked the last mile into the pueblo. He avoided the footbridge and waded across the river at the narrows. When he got close to Longrifle's, he ducked into the kiva to have a look around. He found it empty—Longrifle must be in the house.

Halfway up the path to the big house, Jabe stopped in his tracks. A BIA man came out of the door and walked straight toward him. Jabe froze in mid-stride. The BIA man hailed him.

"Hey, there. Do you have business with these people?"

Jabe hesitated a moment.

"Just came by to see the Cacique. Any problem with that?"

"No, I guess not. You look like you might even belong here." The BIA man nodded toward the highway, "You don't work for any of those news people out there, do you?"

"Not hardly."

The BIA man just walked off toward the pueblo offices and Jabe made for the front door of the adobe. Ten Eagles sat in his rocking chair in the shade. His gaze was toward the sky and he was mumbling to himself. He raised his hand in greeting, but Jabe knew better than to speak. So, he just patted the medicine man's shoulder as he passed by him. *Mustn't break the spell.*

Jabe dropped his bindle on the porch and opened the screen door, "Anybody home in here?" There was a shriek and Juanita ran straight into his arms. The force of her impact nearly toppled them into the yard.

Jabe barely had time to say, "Hey, take it easy on a man of the road, will ya?"

Then his mouth was covered with a kiss. Juanita wasn't in a hurry to break the kiss, and Jabe didn't resist.

Finally she pulled away, "You don't even let a girl know when you're coming home. How can I cook a decent meal for you then?"

From inside the house Longrifle let out a bellow, "Keep it quiet out there. It's more than an old man can take. All that noise. This man needs to hear what the Cacique and his grandson have to say."

Jabe looked at Juanita, "What man is that? Did he come with that bunch out on the highway?"

"He is a friend, Amor. You need to come inside and meet him."

They joined Longrifle and his visitor in the den. Jabe glanced at the Indian seated across from Longrifle. Somehow he looked familiar. Then the old Cacique rose to his feet and embraced his Grandson. "You are home again from your hunt. I see you are well."

He nodded toward Juanita, "This woman has been bothered a lot while you have been gone. She was worried that you might get hurt. But, she does not know you as well as I do."

The cacique nodded toward his visitor, "This man has come to talk with you." Longrifle took his seat again and Jabe sat down beside him.

Juanita started toward the kitchen. "And I will make your favorite dish. Isabel has been teaching me to be a good Indian cook. You might want to take a shower before you eat your dinner, Amor. I think we would all be grateful."

Jabe smiled at her as she turned and disappeared through the door.

"I apologize, Grandfather. I have had a good run through the bosque just now and I probably smell like a……"

"There is no reason to apologize for the smell of hard work, my son. That wounded leg must have recovered its strength again."

At the mention of his wound, Jabe glanced again at the visitor who was sitting quietly in the easy chair by the window. Jabe began to study this character and take notice of his appearance. The thing that struck Jabe was that Longrifle had failed to introduce this fellow. And it wasn't like the Cacique to ignore courtesy. Jabe unconsciously rubbed his thigh.

The Indian stirred in his chair and leaned forward, "You've been running with a wounded leg?"

Jabe didn't answer.

This guy sure doesn't sound Indian. No accent whatsoever.

He studied the face of the man. His look and the sound of his voice seemed very familiar. The man wore the clothing of a fellow tribesman and he was red-skinned like an Indian alright, but something was missing about the look—he was the strangest Indian Jabe had ever laid eyes on. Then Jabe thought he recognized the purple shirt. Was that one of Hahtahway's favorites?

"Where'd you get that shirt?" Jabe was feeling slightly paranoid, and he didn't even know why.

Longrifle spoke up, "That's a donation."

Jabe looked at his Grandfather, "A donation?"

"From that crazy man, Hahtahway—the one who talks too much. He has made a donation of that shirt to this poor Indian. He didn't have a decent thing to wear. And he has come a long way to talk with you."

"An Indian you say?" Jabe looked straight at the man. "Well, he doesn't even look like an Indian to me. And how did he know he'd find me here?"

The visitor smiled at Jabe.

Longrifle continued, "He seems to know a lot, Joe Bob. Maybe he can be some help to us in our problems."

The visitor leaned back in his easy chair and said, "You're right, Mr. Rainwater. I'm no Indian. But, I've got to look like I belong. Hell, I can't even wash my face while I'm here." Then he chuckled.

"I'd be recognized in a heartbeat if all this color came off. I had trouble enough getting inside here as it is. But, your Granddaddy and his friends sure know how to fool a white man. They drove me here in the bed of that rickety old pickup with a couple more real Indians. They told us to just lay there and mumble a bunch of crazy talk. He told the guards out there on the highway we were drunk."

Jabe wasn't amused, "So then, just who the hell are you?"

The man leaned forward and offered Jabe his hand.

"I'm Don Samuelson, World News Network."

51

Jabe couldn't believe his ears. He studied the man in detail. Then the newsman's familiar face unfolded in his memory like the opening of a book.

Jabe settled slowly back against the sofa. His eyes might have deceived him briefly, but he knew he was indeed looking at the most influential newsman on the planet. Jabe had to smile, "That war paint sure had me fooled. Whose work is that, anyway?"

Longrifle laughed, "Even my Grandson is fooled. That old Hahtahway might be crazy, but he sure knows his war paint. Those BIA men were fooled, too."

Jabe was amused at the event. "You sure went to a lot of trouble to get in here, Mr. Samuelson."

"Well, you know how it is, Mr. Rainwater. At WNN we go wherever we need to go, so......"

Jabe finished the jingle, "......so you'll always get the news you need to know, right? Yeah, I know all that. But, this place is plenty dangerous right now. Was it worth the risk?"

"I'd have risked practically anything to get down here to talk with you. And I think I already know where you got that sore leg of yours..."

His voice was drowned out by the roar of a Hercules coming in low overhead. Samuelson looked up toward the ceiling and yelled, "That's a military transport. And it's heading for a landing somewhere on this reservation, isn't it?"

Jabe glanced at his Grandfather as the thunder of the big Lockheed receded into the distance.

Longrifle was wearing his most authoritative expression. He held his head up high.

"We have told him nothing, Joe Bob."

Then he lowered his head again, "But, he knows a lot already."

Then the Cacique responded to the newsman's question. "My Grandson will take you up there and show you what these white-eyes have done to our pueblo. We have had no peace since they came here."

Samuelson shifted in his chair, "Yessir. I'm getting to know those people very well. I can just imagine the kind of trouble you people have been through."

Jabe wondered if he really could, "Oh, I'm sure. What would you know about our troubles?"

Samuelson rose to his feet, "Mr. Rainwater, I can't blame you for being put off by my presence. Ordinarily, I would not have succeeded in getting inside your home reservation, especially under the present circumstances. The news media out there has arrived at the same conclusion. They want to talk with you as much as I do. That's why they're here. And they've been banned from getting anywhere close to you. I wouldn't have had a ghost of a chance, but for your Grandfather and his friend......"

Longrifle burst out, "It was Hahtahway's idea. That kid of his, Charlie......"

"Okay, Grandfather. It's okay. I think we can trust Mr. Samuelson. I've seen his reports on TV. You made the first report on the Customs Department drug-smuggling, didn't you?"

"Indeed, I did. And there's been no end of the trouble that's got me into with the administration. So far, I've had to take every kind of punishment there is, just for reporting the truth."

Jabe agreed, "I think I can understand that."

Juanita called through the door, "You hombres come and take your dinner. But, one of you has to take a shower before he can come in here."

Samuelson retorted, "With that leg wound, I'm betting you've had your own introduction to these people. Looks like you've taken your share of punishment too."

Jabe half-smiled, "Let's eat, gentlemen. I'm starved. Then, Mr. Samuelson, you will see for yourself what you came here to see."

Longrifle led the procession to the dinner table while Jabe retired to the shower.

When he returned, Samuelson bibbed himself with his linen napkin and continued, "I broke the story of the Customs-drug connection some weeks ago and I've been hot on that story ever since. We know some of the people who are involved in the flying and we know they've been landing their cargo in south Texas. Until recently, that is. They almost lost a twin-engine aircraft and a whole load of dope down in Texas not long ago...."

He looked at Jabe and paused for a moment. "Their shipments just stopped all of a sudden and the trail went cold. Then I got wind of the carrier exercises in the Bay of Campeche.

"My contacts at Navy said they were holding amphibious landing practice on the Mexican beaches. But, that's something they just don't do down there. Pentagon clammed up tight. The Vice President got steamed as hell when I asked him about it, and I knew I'd hit pay-dirt again."

Jabe glanced at the newsman, "You asked the VP about the Navy exercises down there?"

"You bet I did. My sources say he's the one who ordered the carrier task group down there." Samuelson helped himself to the fry bread.

"Mr. Rainwater, were you the one kicking up all the fuss down there in the Yucatan, sir?"

Jabe winked back at him, "I've never been there, officially."

Juanita served up heaping plates of Jabe's favorite dish without any help from Isabel. She placed the first serving on the table in front of Jabe. Then she served the newsman and gave him a smile.

"He is funny looking for an Indian, no?"

"Muchas gracias, señorita. Now that's a Yucatan accent if I ever heard one."

Juanita retired to the kitchen.

"My bet, Mr. Rainwater, is that you went down to Mexico in an effort to stop the drug traffic coming up through your home reservation. And, by God, you did it. You stopped them cold. But, that C-130 that flew over just now gives a clear signal they're back in business again."

385

Jabe found it hard to shed his mistrust, "And you've come all the way out here to help the red man out of his troubles, have you?"

"I came out here to find out the truth about what's been going on. And I believe it's the truth that's going to help you folks, and the rest of the nation, in the long run."

Longrifle spoke up, "My Grandson has had a pretty rough time with the white-eyes. He has the good of this people in his heart. But, he is only one man against many."

Then Longrifle said to Jabe, "I think we will have to trust this man, my son. He seems to be the only one who is willing to report the trouble we have been having."

Jabe considered the thought, "I think we need to include the other pueblos in the decision to talk with this man, Grandfather."

Longrifle said, "Hahtahway has gone up to the Pueblo Council to see about getting their help. I figured you would be taking this man up to that place on the mesa tonight."

Jabe nodded, "Eat your dinner, Mr. Samuelson. Then we will go and have a good look at what you came to see."

Jabe wondered himself what the big transports could be carrying. Had the VP been dumb enough to ignore his warning?

Jabe took Juanita for a long walk after lunch and Longrifle entertained his guest in the best Indian fashion until late in the afternoon. Everyone gathered in the den to watch the WNN evening newscast. The number two anchorman was reporting,"........sitting in for Don Samuelson who is away on assignment. Tonight's top story comes to us from Capital Hill Correspondent John Cameron. John?"

"Charlie, I'm standing in the foyer of the House Chambers where a special session is in progress. We reported earlier that a roll-call vote is being taken tonight in a sudden and unexpected move for impeachment of the President.

"The Chief Executive is in plenty of trouble with both parties over his questionable conduct while in office, his false testimony before the federal grand jury, and now his apparent involvement in the alleged Colombian drug connection reported some weeks ago by WNN's own Don Samuelson."

"How do you think the vote for impeachment will turn out, John?"

"No one here has a clue as to the probable outcome of the session, Charlie. Everyone has had a tight lip over this one. But, the Congressmen who passed us on their way inside a couple of hours ago wore some pretty grim faces. The session is ending just about now and we'll have the answer shortly."

Jabe hit the mute button for the commercial break as Juanita refilled their iced tea glasses.

Samuelson said, "That guy is going down for sure. Everybody knows the VP has been running things around Capitol Hill for years now, and it wouldn't surprise me if he's the man behind this whole business."

Jabe just shrugged, "Could be. He's got an ego that's plenty big enough for that sort of thing."

Samuelson shot Jabe a curious glance.

John Cameron came on, "Charlie, we have the results of the voting now and the news is shattering. The vote went against the President who now finds himself impeached. He will now stand trial before the Senate. He becomes only the third U.S. President to be impeached by the House. The last impeachment trial held in the United States saw Bill Clinton just squeak by during his trial in the Senate and barely gain an acquittal. But, nobody I've spoken with agrees that would be the result this time around, if the President actually stands trial and refuses to resign. Back to you now, Charlie…"

"So there you have it. Straight from the WNN newsroom and our correspondent on Capitol Hill……."

Jabe pushed the kill button and the TV went dark.

Samuelson shook his head, "Now that scenario explains a lot. I'm not a bit surprised by it, but it sure explains a lot."

Longrifle asked, "Explains what?"

Jabe replied, "It explains a lot about the politicians that are involved and why BIA and Customs has closed this pueblo up tight as a drum, that's what."

Samuelson agreed, "There's going to be a funeral and a wedding held on the same day. Congress is going to bury that goof-ball Chief Executive who's been hiding out in the White House and marry-up with a brand new one."

Longrifle started to get the concept, "They'll be trading bad for worse and they don't want anything to spoil the ceremony?"

"Exactly. The VP is going to want a smooth ride into the White House and they don't want Joe Bob here discovered. They simply can't afford to have any new problems cropping up now. So, they've bottled him up here away from the cameras and reporters. If it gets out what really happened to Joe Bob……"

"Just call me Jabe, will ya?"

Samuelson never missed a beat, "……They're going to need quite a war chest for the upcoming election and they need time to cement their relationship with the nation. You know—fire-side chats and all."

Longrifle got to his feet and made for the kitchen. "Well, it's more than an old man can figure out. These white-eyes are as crazy as that man Hahtahway. Somebody forgot my coffee."

Jabe rubbed the dull ache in his leg again.

The newsman continued, "So, the last thing they want is for the truth about all that Yucatan action to get out to the people."

Samuelson saw the rub, "That wound still bothering you?"

Jabe moved his hand away from his leg and looked out the window, "It's just an old football injury."

"Yeah, uh huh." Samuelson hardly broke his cadence, "There's already been a rumbling of a showdown. Ever since you shut down the shipments into the states, there's been a drug shortage on the streets. The cost of a buy has tripled and availability is getting real iffy. The users are getting out of control and crime in the cities is going ballistic. The President is getting incredibly unpopular these days."

Jabe took up the line of reasoning, "And the VP will propose that he is the one man who can straighten things up for the nation?"

"That's the way I figure it."

Jabe was hardly optimistic, "How real is the chance you'd be able to get the truth out?"

"My contacts in Bogotá say the cartels are sensing the tight spot they've got the VP in and they're demanding all they can get in the way of foreign aid. But at this point, I don't believe the new President could afford to show favor to those drug-selling thugs. Things are heating up all around."

Jabe wondered aloud, "And that's why you showed up here?"

"I'd say my best chance to get to the bottom of this is right here in your pueblo. I'd like very much to help put a stop to the free and open drug trade into this country. It's the one thing that can bring the nation down. Will you let me join forces with you?"

Jabe rose and walked toward the front porch. He paused by the door, lifted his gun belt off its peg and strapped it on.

"So, you came way out here expecting to get a story?" He turned and looked back at Samuelson. "You think those guys up on the mesa will grant you an interview, do you?"

The newsman just grinned, "More likely they'd take a shot at me. My bet is they'll try and keep the money and the drugs flowing at all costs. They need close on to a couple billion to fund a winning campaign if the impeachment fails. But, I won't need to talk with any of them to get what I came for, Jabe. All I need is for you to get me close enough to get their operation on film." Samuelson reached inside a bag at his feet and produced a video camera.

Ten Eagles had been ready for them out on the porch, and less than an hour later, the little band had circled past the BIA guards, skirted the news crews out on the highway and quietly made their way up the deer trail toward the west mesa.

On the way up the slope, they had to hide behind a boulder to escape being seen by a patrolling helicopter. Jabe was first to reach the lava flow up on the rim. He made the short leap up to the top of the mesa.

Juanita ascended close behind him and he pulled her up. Then Ten Eagles scrambled up followed by the newsman.

Samuelson found a seat on a rock. He was winded. "What say we take breather, okay?"

Ten Eagles was unfazed. He stood with his Winchester slung over his shoulder, "We better get a move on. Hahtahway said he would meet us about dark." The old man had barely broken a sweat.

Samuelson groaned, "Whatever. Say, Ten Eagles, do you ever go anywhere without that rifle?"

"Whenever I go among the white-eyes, I feel plumb naked without it."

"Are you any good with that thing?"

Ten Eagles turned and led off on the march at a blistering pace, "I hit where I aim, young man."

They arrived at a sage thicket outside the perimeter fence, just as the sun slid behind the western mountains. Jabe could see a sentry patrol making its rounds inside the fence a hundred yards away, so they lay quiet until it had moved on.

Then another patrolling helicopter began a pass that would bring it close overhead. The entire party hit the deck. A warrior can curl up and practically disappear if he has as much as a bare branch to hide behind. Jabe watched Samuelson who seemed to have a knack for it as well.

He must be part Indian.

The chopper curved in toward them, swooped by and arced out low over the canyon. When it looked safe, Ten Eagles cut the fence wire and the four ducked under it and advanced through the tall grass. They got to the cover of another thicket and held up there.

Jabe surveyed the scene through his Navy binocs. One of the C-130s was being unloaded. But, two more appeared to be ready for loading out on the gravel ramp. What would they carry?

Jabe could see fuel drums stacked three-high nearby. A column of deuce-and-a-half trucks came trundling up and halted under the high tails of the airplanes.

The early dusk lit the blue-and-gold Customs logo painted on the tails of the big transports and "US Customs" was emblazoned on the dark blue jackets worn by the ground crew. That part was familiar to Jabe. Then he saw something he'd never seen before.

Several aircrew personnel descended from one of the aircraft and set about unloading the trucks. They were assisted by the truck drivers who were dressed in U.S. Army fatigues. But, the aircrew personnel were wearing light green uniforms.

Just who the hell are these guys?

Jabe handed the binocs to Samuelson, "You recognize those green uniforms, Mr. Samuelson?"

The newsman took a long look and then handed the field glasses back to Jabe.

"Yep, I'm afraid I do. They're Chinese."

Jabe lifted the glasses to his eyes again, "The hell you say."

Then old Gilmer was right about that after all.

Jabe was intent on the loading activities. The Customs men were hefting metal casks and long cylindrical cases off the trucks and stacking them on the ground. The men in green were transferring them into the Herky Birds.

Samuelson put his camera to his eye, "Can't see enough from here. I'll have to get closer for this lens to be effective. And the light is fading fast."

Jabe signaled for Ten Eagles to stay behind with Juanita. Then he led out crawling slowly and carefully through the brush on his belly with Samuelson close behind. When they were about fifty feet from the runway, they found the prairie grass had been clipped short, and they had to hold up there.

Jabe put his binocs to his eyes just as Samuelson began filming the activity. The twilight was fading as he adjusted the focus and could barely make out the wording on the casks.

They read WARHEAD MATERIEL.

Then on another of the cylindrical casks, INERTIAL GUID-ANCE HEAD, and on another, TARGET ACQUISITION MODULE.

But what bothered him the most was when he read, ALPHA RA-DIATION HAZARD—PLUTONIUM 239.

Jabe looked at Samuelson who was busy panning his camera back and forth over the entire scene, getting it all on videotape. Neither of them said a single word. They didn't have to.

Gilmer had been right on everything. Here was the very deed that Gilmer had predicted—the sale of weapons technology to the Communist Chinese for campaign funding. And this time what was changing hands was not just plans and formulas. It wasn't a couple of loose computer discs, or lost hard-drives, or just a sheaf of printouts. This was the Real McCoy—the actual weapon components being shipped right out of the Los Alamos Weapons Laboratory.

The gall of these guys!

It made Jabe's blood run hot.

He looked toward where he had left Juanita and the medicine man and was shocked to see them standing bolt upright with their hands in the air. A foot patrol had found them and was moving them toward the airfield.

Then Jabe saw a helicopter rise from the canyon beyond them and swoop in low overhead. It made a beeline straight for him and Samuelson. He turned his face toward the ground hoping for the best, but the chopper slowed and hovered right over them. The door gunner leveled a mini-gun right at them and motioned for the two of them to stand.

The jig was up and there was no way out.

52

Samuelson was quickly up on his feet and held his hands high as he moved toward the approaching Customs men. Jabe noticed he no longer held his camera. What had he done with it?

Jabe took the cue and stood up just as the two gunners jumped from the hovering helicopter and grabbed him. They jerked open his shirt, made a pat search and disarmed him. The next instant, helicopters swooped in and landed from all directions.

Juanita and Ten Eagles were marched up and the guards shoved the lot of them toward the nearest Hercules.

Samuelson hurried and went up the ramp first. Then he slipped and fell down. Jabe took the cue and made a violent struggle to get loose, but the Customs men were on him at once. In the turmoil he saw Samuelson reach up for a handhold and slip his video cassette behind the first-aid kit bolted to the bulkhead. Samuelson winked at Jabe and let out a howl of mock pain as one of the Customs men grabbed him and shoved him inside the aircraft.

They were lined up against the cabin wall and made to sit down while the leader was summoned.

Several of the Chinese troops came closer and peered down at them. It made Jabe feel like a caged animal in a zoo. They pointed and jabbered and generally had a fine time making fun of these odd-looking comic book caricatures. Jabe figured they'd only ever seen pictures of Indians.

But, this kind of treatment was absurd. He'd had about all he wanted from these knotheads when, just then, an American Army Colonel stomped up the ramp followed by a Chinese Major.

The Colonel shouted, "What the hell are you people doing on my airfield?"

Samuelson kept quiet and looked at Jabe. Ten Eagles half chuckled, "You've only been here for a few weeks and you think this is your mesa now?"

The Colonel whipped around to face the old man, "Just who in the hell are you?"

"I am a Native American. My people have farmed and hunted this territory for over a hundred centuries and it belongs to Native Americans—not only by possession, but by treaty as well."

The Colonel scowled, "We've got a lease on this mesa from the BIA. You people are trespassing on government property."

Then he turned and walked back down the ramp. He waved an arm and yelled, "Get these people the hell off my airplane."

The guards jerked them to their feet and marched them back outside. One of the Customs men handed the Winchester and Jabe's Colt automatic to the Colonel.

"This your rifle, grandpa?"

Ten Eagles straightened his back, "That is my rifle, sure enough."

The Colonel levered the rounds through until the rifle was empty, "What's the rifle for, old man?"

The medicine man turned around slowly as he surveyed the lot of them, "Pests and varmints."

The Colonel studied the medicine man for a moment.

"Well, you can't come in here with a loaded rifle." He handed the empty rifle back to the Customs man, "If it happened to go off while you were stumbling around out there in the dark, you might have hurt somebody."

"Whenever it goes off, it does just that."

The Colonel looked over at Juanita and fixed his gaze there.

Ten Eagles continued, "I'm just out here in the country teaching my granddaughter how to hunt."

The Chinese officer surveyed the likes of Jabe and Samuelson and asked, "And who are these men, please?"

"An old man does not see and hear too well. They are my eyes and my ears. They are my grand-nephews. I always bring my guides and trackers when I come to this mesa to hunt."

The Major hefted the Colt, "And they come hunting with military weapons? This is no rabbit gun, please."

The Colonel broke in, "I don't think these people are up here on any rabbit hunt, Major. We'd better keep them on ice until I can get to the bottom of this. I don't want any mishaps tonight with The Man coming up here. Get this shipment ready to depart. Your people and mine want no delays tonight."

The Major walked up and studied Jabe's face. Then he turned to the Colonel.

"These are only a few of your American Indians. Didn't your Army whip them into submission back a hundred years ago?"

"Well, we thought we did."

The Major turned back and looked Jabe right in the face. Jabe could see nothing but hate in the eyes of this barbarian.

The Major squinted slightly, "And yet, after all this time, here they are giving you trouble again. You should have done a better job of it, please. You should learn from the Chinese how to handle dissidents. You should have killed them all. Never let any of your enemies live to fight another day. You see, it is just Chinese wisdom."

Jabe winked at the man and waited for a reaction. The Major made ever so slight a move as he stiffened at the unexpected jibe. This satisfied Jabe no end.

The Major turned and walked slowly away, "Yes, Colonel. You should have slaughtered them all."

Ten Eagles warned, "If I am not back at the pueblo soon, they will come out to look for me. Then you will have many more than just a few Indians on your hands."

Jabe looked around the horizon and thought, 'Now where is that Hahtahway when you really need him?'

The Major said, "I do not think that will be a problem, old Indian man. What will they bring with them? Some of these old rifles, please?"

Jabe winked at Ten Eagles.

We should be so lucky.

The Colonel conferred with a junior officer, "Go over to the reservation office and fetch me one of those BIA agents who is familiar with the residents and bring him back here pronto. I'm gunna need some answers as soon as......" He was turning to his aide when the faint sound of another helicopter filtered through the night air. The Colonel stopped to listen to the heavy rotor beat that was unlike the sound his own support choppers made. This one was BIG.

The Colonel raised his voice and his manner was less than confident, "Son-of-a-bitch, he's here already. Get these Indians out of sight. The Chief's coming in. Not a word about this from anybody. I'll do all the talking."

Everybody jumped at his command. Jabe and Company were herded back up inside the Hercules and the ramp was winched shut. The Customs men assembled close by and the Army formed up in rank and file behind their leader as the huge Army Sikorsky settled onto the ground.

The side door slid open and the Vice President of the United States emerged as a crew member jumped down and gave him the usual assist.

Now, ain't this sweet! The Jackal's in the henhouse, now. Where's that Hahtahway and the help he went after?

The military men saluted their VP as he hurried past. He replaced the cigar in his mouth and brought both his hands to his forehead several times simultaneously in mock salute.

The Colonel held his own salute and mumbled to the Major, "I hate when that asshole does that. Shows us no respect at all and here we are busting our butts for him."

The VP marched right up to the Colonel, took his hand and pumped it like a good politician, "Good to see you, Colonel. It's real good to see you again. Yessir, it is."

Then he turned and took the Major in hand, "Major Chin, how good to see you again. I wanted to be on hand for this historic event. I believe this marks the beginning of a new era for the New World Order. I trust everything we agreed upon is satisfactory?"

The Major bowed, then glanced carelessly at the Colonel, "Well, yes please. It seems as though everything I have seen here meets with your assurances."

The VP smiled and turned, "Then is everything ready to go as planned, Colonel?"

"Yessir, we're about half-way loaded. We'll be ready to launch these birds in about half an hour."

A Customs man came running up, "Colonel! We've got some more trouble out here, sir. You'd better come and take a look at this."

At that news, Jabe peered out through a cabin window. The dim light of dusk was fading and the full moon was rising low in the east. Jabe thought about the last time he'd seen the full moon. Had it been only a month ago? It seemed like a hundred years.

The prairie was lit by the rare combination of blue twilight and moonlight. Now it somehow made every object crystal clear.

The Customs man was pointing out toward the west. Jabe could see a lone campfire that blazed just beyond the perimeter fence a couple hundred yards away.

The Colonel said, "Now who in the hell is that out there lighting fires?"

One of the helicopter pilots walked up, "Damned if I know, sir. It wasn't there a minute ago."

The Colonel barked at him, "Well, get one of your choppers over there and see."

"Ain't got any airborne, Colonel. You called them all back in here when we saw these fellas in the grass and...."

"Colonel!" The Customs man interrupted. He was pointing in another direction.

A second fire burst into flames out on the perimeter fence over on the north, then another came to life out toward the south. The Colonel and his men swept the horizon in wide-eyed amazement.

The VP's eyes narrowed and he blurted, "Colonel, what the hell's going on here?"

Jabe scanned the perimeter fence and saw one signal fire after another come to life. Hahtahway was back from the pueblo council and he had brought reinforcements. A line of fires came to life one after another out along the perimeter.

The chopper pilot held a pair of binoculars to his eyes and slowly swept the scene in a full circle, "Colonel, there's a hell of a bunch of wild Indians out there with Winchesters. We're surrounded!"

Even at this distance, Jabe could plainly make out the shadows of the men Hahtahway had brought with him and they encircled the entire facility. They were arranged in line abreast and three deep. The gunners on the front line were lying prone and a line of kneeling riflemen backed them up. Behind these was a line of Indians standing erect with their Winchesters to their shoulders.

Jabe smiled and muttered, "Native American Homeland Security—ever since 1492!"

The Colonel grabbed the binocs and took a long look for himself. His mouth gaped open and he gasped.....

"Dammit, this is my airfield!" Then much louder, "And they're all trespassing on *my airfield*."

The fires came to light one by one until they completely encircled the perimeter.

The chopper pilot pointed toward the line of Indians, "Hell, those old repeaters are no match for our fire-power, Colonel."

The VP had gotten no answer, "Colonel?"

The Colonel paid him no attention. He had been busy counting.

"Yeah, but there's about a thousand of 'em."

The VP was getting edgy, "Colonel, please! What's going on here? I thought you said we'd be safe way out here." But, nobody was paying him any attention at all.

The Customs man offered, "We can take 'em, Colonel."

The Colonel shook his head, "I don't know about that. They're all spread out and we're all in a bunch."

The Major was for taking the risk. He stepped up close beside the commander, "Your modern American mini-guns can take them down, Colonel. Your Gatlings can fire at 4000 rounds per minute, please, and they've only got a few old lever actions. Those rifles were made a hundred years ago."

The VP looked around him, "Will somebody please tell me what in hell's going on?"

The Colonel said, "Patent of 1894, I'd say. Old reliable .30-.30s and they can hit hard at this range. With all those rifles they can fire maybe 60,000 rounds a minute, Major. And that's enough to wipe us the hell out in about three seconds. You really think our gunners could kill all thousand of them in under three seconds?"

Then he looked at the Major dead-on, "If you think so, then you're a damned fool."

Chinese wisdom had failed the Major. He took another look at the opposition and gritted his teeth, "Well, I don't know."

Jabe had that tight sensation in his stomach again. It was another classic standoff. He wondered who would be the first to flinch. The pueblo men were pitting their ancient Winchesters against the terror of modern mini-guns aboard the choppers and deuce-and-a-half trucks. If it came to it, the Indians were capable of inflicting major damage. But there would be no winners here. Each side was sure to blow the other clear to hell. Here was Mutually Assured Destruction in all its glory— and everybody knew it.

The VP was even louder now, "Dammit all to hell, Colonel. What are we going to do now?"

"I'm thinking. I'm thinking."

Then from out on the perimeter, a single rifle shot brought everyone to attention. The bullet was well-placed and ripped through several of the fuel drums stacked close by the aircraft. Jabe watched as the fuel spray showered the other drums and ran down the slope under the trucks. It quickly gathered in pools around the aircraft landing gear and streamed past the standing soldiers.

Suddenly the men in one of the trucks threw the tailgate open and rolled out a mini-gun.

The Colonel reacted fast, "What the hell?" Then he shouted, "Get that gun back inside."

The gun crew held fast. Jabe glanced back out to the line of signal fires where Hahtahway stood ready. Everybody in the military crowd seemed to be watching Hahtahway.

Hahtahway leaned down toward the fire and lit an arrow tip. He raised the flaming arrow and laid it into his bow. One quick pull and the fire-arrow would fly. Even a blind Indian could hardly miss his mark at this distance.

Ten Eagles saw it all. He slipped the hold of his guard and bolted out of the aircraft. Helpless to stop him, the guards ran out behind him.

The VP said, "And just who the hell is this, Colonel?"

Ten Eagles addressed the Colonel, "Now here is what an old Indian medicine man thinks. I think you should all leave this place. You can take your BIA lease and leave here and go away on your own, or you can go up in smoke. On my signal, another old Indian out there will light fire to this whole operation."

"COLONEL?" The VP was incredulous.

Jabe joined Ten Eagles outside, "What's it going to be, Colonel?"

The V.P. shouted, "Isn't anybody listening to me?" Then his gaze fell upon Jabe........., "YOU!"

Jabe stared straight at the VP and let the fact of his presence take full effect.

The Colonel asked the VP, "You know this man, Sir?"

Jabe spoke next. Having fixed the VP with an icy stare, "You should have taken my advice. Now it's payday."

The Major waved frantically toward the fire-arrow ready for launch out on the perimeter fence and stammered, "Kill that man, Colonel, or he'll set fire to us."

The Colonel looked around slowly at the Major, "And you're crazy as hell if you think they have only one man who can do the deed. They'll light this place up in a nanosecond."

The Major hesitated only a split second. Then he grabbed his side-arm and leveled it toward the perimeter fence.

The Colonel made one quick lunge and knocked the pistol out of his hand, "Major, you're a damned idiot. You haven't got sense enough to see when you're whipped and outsmarted. God knows what your leaders plan to do with all this weapons materiel. And I don't care if the Vice President himself is standing here. I don't believe your government's promises of peace for a minute. If they're all as stupid as you're acting, the world would be a lot better off if you went back home to your country empty-handed and we kept our missile technology here at home. The Chinese people are lovely folks, but their government stinks." He looked directly at the VP, "And I'll go on record with that."

The VP seemed to wilt under the load, "Now see here, Colonel. The U.S. military won't be held hostage by anyone. I've said so in a speech I made. Can't we find some way to work something out with these heathens? Maybe if I talked with them...."

The Colonel retorted, "Aw, shut up. This is my command and I'll give the orders here. What the hell do you civilian sonsabitches know about the military anyway?"

He looked in the direction of the fire arrow and then turned to address Jabe and Ten Eagles, "I didn't join the military to get my people killed for no good reason, and you folks sure have us dead to rights."

Ten Eagles lifted both his arms and waved to Hahtahway and the flaming arrow was extinguished. Then he turned to the Vice President who seemed to be looking for something he'd lost in the dirt, "My people only want to live here in peace."

The VP still looked at the ground.

Ten Eagles raised his voice, "I'm talking to you, white-eyes."

When he had the man's attention Ten Eagles continued, "We have lived here for ten thousand years. Before the white man came, we roamed this land from the far western mountains in the high Jemez to the Chisos range in the Big Bend. This good land along the river is all we have ever known. We have had a good life here. We only want to live here in peace."

The VP only shrugged his shoulders, but his rage was evident as he glanced repeatedly toward J.B. and mumbled a string of epithets.

The Colonel nodded, "Sir, you are right as rain. It is the same thing most Americans want as well. Why in the hell we're selling this stuff to the Communists is more than I can understand. It's a dirty business. Damned dirty."

The Colonel left the VP standing and pushed the Major ahead of him as he started toward the trucks.

Then he barked, "Load 'em up, Captain. We're taking this materiel back to the Weapons Lab. It's all going back to Los Alamos and hopefully it will stay in the U.S. where it belongs!" He was looking straight at the VP. "And if anyone wants to make a federal case outta this,…I'd be glad to testify as to what was going down here for the Congressional Record."

He turned and faced Jabe and Ten Eagles, "We're out of here, gentlemen. Let the politicians make the excuses. I'm not getting any of my men killed over this sorry business."

The VP stomped off briskly toward his chopper. He turned and yelled over his shoulder, "Well, I'm not through with you, Colonel! No sir, not by a long shot. I made a deal here and I won't back out now. The Order doesn't stand for mistakes or public exposure and I stand by my word."

The Major stopped and hesitated. He seemed torn between going with the Colonel or the VP. He waited to see what would happen next.

The VP neared his chopper and the pilot engaged the starter. He stepped up into the open door and yelled after the Colonel, "When I get back to Washington, we'll see what kind of charges the government can bring against you and these fool redskins…….."

At that instant rifle fire drowned out the VP. Everyone on the airstrip hit the deck and those inside the chopper poured out of the doorways as bullets ripped into the aluminum. Fire broke out in the big chopper as the VP and his crew crawled toward safety.

The Colonel yelled out, "Okay, now what was that you were saying, Sir? And did you need us to give you a ride into town?"

The VP came trotting up sheepishly and climbed into a truck.

The Colonel personally supervised the loading of weapon components, the Chinese personnel, and all of his men into the waiting trucks. Then he got aboard the last truck as it pulled out for the highway.

Ten Eagles took Juanita's arm and led off toward the perimeter fence, "Let's give them some light to help them find their way home."

Samuelson ran back up inside the transport, "I've got to get something." He fetched his videotape and then hustled to catch up.

Hahtahway and Longrifle were waiting for them at the fence. The Cacique hailed Ten Eagles, "And what kind of medicine was that? What did you think you would do, going in there like that? Did you think they would listen to reason? Just like on the Little Big Horn, the only thing they have ever understood is force in numbers."

No one could argue with that analysis.

Jabe looked around at his countrymen. All of them were painted up in their war gear. They looked magnificent in the firelight of the VPs burning helicopter. Charlie was standing beside his grandfather Hahtahway, who still had his bow loaded with the smoldering fire-arrow.

Jabe chided, "You're a long way from Tucson, Charlie."

"Oh, we got word there was going to be trouble up here. I wouldn't have missed this shindig for all the elk in Catron County." He held up the smoking arrow, "My grandfather really wanted to light that place up."

Hahtahway took up the reasoning, "Well, why don't I go right ahead, Joe Bob? Those truck-driver white-eyes could use some help finding their way home in the dark."

"Sounds like a plan, Hahtahway."

Hahtahway offered Jabe the honor, "It would be more fitting if you would make the shot, J.B. The Cacique thinks you have earned the right. And the whole tribe welcomes you back to your rightful place as War Captain of this pueblo. After tonight, you will come and join the tribal council as a new War Chief."

Jabe grinned at the prospect of renewing his place in his old tribal home. He took the bow and arrow, "Whose shot was it that opened those fuel drums?"

Longrifle took a step forward, "Well, I had to put in my two cents. I came up to have some say in what went on up here. I can't let this man Hahtahway run around loose without someone to keep him under control."

Hahtahway grunted, "It's a wonder you found your way up here at all. And you were late."

Longrifle was getting Hahtahway riled up and he was enjoying himself, "You are wrong again, Hahtahway, as usual. Maybe you just got here a little too early."

Hahtahway's voice rose in irritation, "I am never wrong, Cacique. I might not always be right, but I am never wrong."

Longrifle looked at Juanita, "This good woman showed me my old amulet that you gave her. It has brought us good luck once more again."

Jabe answered, "It's in the family to stay, Grandfather. You'd never know the trouble she's had keeping that thing."

Charlie produced another fire-arrow. He lit the missile and handed it to Jabe who loaded the arrow and raised his bow. All the Indians out around the perimeter stood up and took up the war cry.

The last of the trucks was heading toward the perimeter fence on its way back up the road toward the highway. A news-service chopper was circling in for a low pass.

Samuelson said, "Now isn't that just like a pesky news service? Always around when the administration has something to hide."

Jabe drew back and let fly. The flaming arrow arced up and traced a fiery line through the night sky like a meteor.

Juanita squeezed Jabe's arm and whispered, "Just like our night on the beach, Amor."

Jabe remembered the night only too well. He looked at her and smiled. He waved a hand through the air, "Pssssssttt."

The arrow arced over and began to fall. She smiled back, "I only wish my brother Juan was here tonight to see this."

The arrow fell straight in and landed square between the two transports. For a moment, all was still and dark. Then a puff of flame appeared where the arrow had landed and fire began to spread in all directions. Flames leapt into the night air, ran out under the aircraft and engulfed the landing gear tires. The heat of the inferno soon turned the metal skins of the big transports red-hot and then yellow.

The Lockheed nearest the fuel dump went first. A terrific explosion ripped it apart and shrapnel showered the entire scene. Flames quickly consumed the other aircraft and the fuel dump.

At that, the warriors who had come from a dozen pueblos felt the need to be involved. The deafening roar of a thousand Winchester's came from out along the perimeter fence. The .30 caliber fire poured in from all directions at once and ripped into the Customs Service choppers that were lone targets standing in the fire-light. The impact of steel on aluminum took a terrible effect. One by one, the choppers flew into pieces and exploded. The spreading inferno completely engulfed the camp.

No one said a word as the clandestine airstrip dissolved into a funeral pyre. The flames reached for the sky and soared a thousand feet into the air. Jabe reckoned the light could be seen all the way to Albuquerque. He said aloud, "I wonder if this will even make the evening news tomorrow."

Samuelson tapped him on the shoulder with the videotape, "I can practical guarantee it. It might well be the last report of a brilliant career, but it's *my* story and I'm going to make damn sure the American people know what's been happening to their nation. If you folks hadn't had the guts to take on these infernal yayhoos and stick to your Winchesters, I would never have had a chance to break this story. It's the most blatant scandal in the nation's history and it's sure to rock the whole country for decades. Then maybe the citizens can get back to electing decent people again. My gratitude to you all."

Jabe reflected a moment, "And our gratitude to you, Mr. Samuelson. You are a friend of freedom." They shook on it.

Juanita pulled herself up and gave Jabe a long kiss on the mouth. Everybody cheered for them and Jabe knew he had a good life ahead of him. And with Juanita, he'd learned he could love again.

R. Barry King

Then he looked at the newsman standing there in the glow of the inferno and was impressed at how much Samuelson now really did look like a genuine Indian after all.

THE END